# INVICTUS

By *Simon Scarrow*

**The *Roman Empire* Series**
*The Britannia Campaign*
Under the Eagle (AD 42–43, Britannia)
The Eagle's Conquest (AD 43, Britannia)
When the Eagle Hunts (AD 44, Britannia)
The Eagle and the Wolves (AD 44, Britannia)
The Eagle's Prey (AD 44, Britannia)

*Rome and the Eastern Provinces*
The Eagle's Prophecy (AD 45, Rome)
The Eagle in the Sand (AD 46, Judaea)
Centurion (AD 46, Syria)

*The Mediterranean*
The Gladiator (AD 48–49, Crete)
The Legion (AD 49, Egypt)
Praetorian (AD 51, Rome)

*The Return to Britannia*
The Blood Crows (AD 51, Britannia)
Brothers in Blood (AD 51, Britannia)
Britannia (AD 52, Britannia)

*Hispania*
Invictus (AD 54, Hispania)

**The *Wellington and Napoleon* Quartet**
Young Bloods
The Generals
Fire and Sword
The Fields of Death

Sword and Scimitar (Great Siege of Malta)

Hearts of Stone (Second World War)

**The *Gladiator* Series**
Gladiator: Fight for Freedom
Gladiator: Street Fighter
Gladiator: Son of Spartacus

*Writing with T.J. Andrews*
Arena (AD 41, Rome)
Invader (AD 44, Britannia)

# SIMON
# SCARROW
## EAGLES·OF·THE·EMPIRE
# INVICTUS

HEADLINE

First published in Great Britain in 2016
by HEADLINE PUBLISHING GROUP

1

Cataloguing in Publication Data is available from the British Library

ISBN 978 1 4722 1336 5 (Hardback)
ISBN 978 1 4722 1335 8 (Trade paperback)

Typeset in Bembo by Avon DataSet Ltd, Bidford-on-Avon, Warwickshire

Printed and bound in Great Britain by Clays Ltd, St Ives plc

Headline's policy is to use papers that are natural, renewable and recyclable
products and made from wood grown in well-managed forests and other controlled
sources. The logging and manufacturing processes are expected to conform to the
environmental regulations of the country of origin.

HEADLINE PUBLISHING GROUP
An Hachette UK Company
Carmelite House
50 Victoria Embankment
London EC4Y 0DZ

www.headline.co.uk
www.hachette.co.uk

For Louise
LMLX

# CONTENTS

# HISPANIA
## AD 54

Mine
Asturica Augusta
Clunia
Cæsar Augusta
Barcino
Tarraco
Rome
HISPANIA TERRACONENSIS
LUSITANIA
BAETICA

# THE IMPERIAL MINE
# AT ARGENTIUM

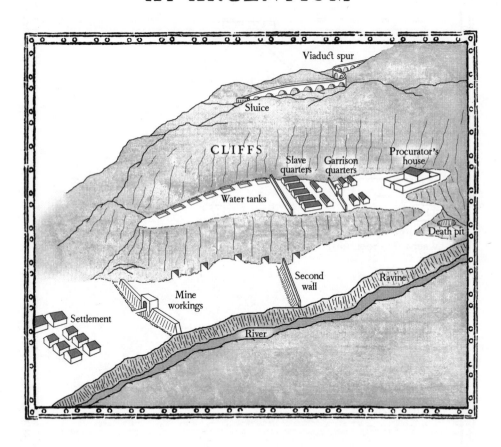

# PRAETORIAN GUARD
# CHAIN OF COMMAND

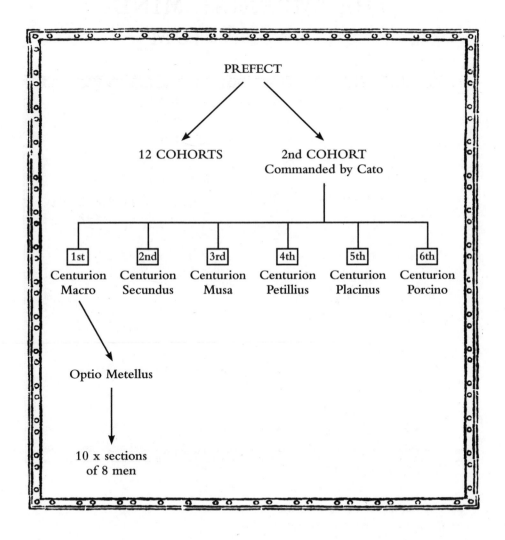

# CAST LIST

**In Rome**
Quintus Licinius Cato, Prefect
Lucius Cornelius Macro, Centurion
Emperor Tiberius Claudius Augustus Germanicus
Agrippina, Claudius' fourth wife
Nero, Agrippina's son and Claudius' great nephew
Britannicus, Claudius' son by his third wife, Messalina
Narcissus, Greek imperial freedman, supporter of Britannicus
Pallas, Greek imperial freedman, Agrippina's lover and supporter of Nero
Legate Aulus Vitellius, part of Nero's faction
Senator Lucius Annaeus Seneca, a wealthy landowner
Lucius Scabarus, inn-keeper
Gaius Gannicus, guardsman
Polidorus, master of ceremonies at the Imperial Palace

**At the mine**
Procurator Gaius Nepo, responsible for the Emperor's gold supply

***Second Praetorian Cohort***
Tribune Aulus Valerius Cristus
Centurions Placinus, Secundus, Porcino, Petillius, Musa, Pulcher
Gaius Getellus Cimber, town magistrate of Lancia
Metellus, optio to Pulcher
Sentiacus, optio to Petillius
Pastericus, optio to Nepo

Collenus, optio of the Fourth Praetorian Cohort

**Others**

Iskerbeles, rebel leader
Caratacus, captured British king of the Catuvellauni tribe
Julia, Cato's deceased wife
Lucius, Julia and Cato's son
Senator Sempronius, Julia's father
Petronella, Lucius' nurse
Amatapus, housekeeper at Julia's house
Titus Pelonius Aufidius, magistrate of Asturia Augusta
Callaecus, rebel
Publius Ballinus, governor of Hispania Terraconensis
Caius Glaecus, chief of the olive traders' guild
Micus Aeschleus, slave dealer
Gaius Hettius Gordo, senior magistrate of Antium Barca

In the fell clutch of circumstance
　　I have not winced nor cried aloud.
Under the bludgeonings of chance
　　My head is bloody, but unbowed.

Beyond this place of wrath and tears
　　Looms but the Horror of the shade,
And yet the menace of the years
　　Finds, and shall find me, unafraid.

William Ernest Henley, 'Invictus'

# PROLOGUE

*The Province of Hispania Terraconensis,*
*early summer AD 54*

There were cries of anger from the large crowd as the prisoner was dragged, blinking, into the bright sunlight bathing the forum in the heart of Asturica Augusta. He had been held in chains in one of the dank cells beneath the senate house for over a month while he waited for the Roman magistrate to return from his farming estate to pronounce sentence. Now, the magistrate stood on the steps of the senate house, surrounded by the other worthies of the town dressed in their finery of togas and embroidered tunics, ready to deliver his judgement. But there was little doubt in the minds of the crowd, and that of the prisoner, over his fate.

Iskerbeles had struck down and killed the official who had come to his village to demand slaves in lieu of the repayment of the debt owed to a fabulously wealthy senator back in Rome. He had killed the man in front of hundreds of witnesses and the auxiliary soldiers who were escorting the hapless freedman sent to collect the debt. It did not matter that the official had just given orders to seize ten of the village's children and that the blow had been struck in a moment of anger. Iskerbeles was a powerfully built man with dark, fierce eyes beneath a sturdy brow. He had punched the freedman in the face, causing the man to tumble back and split his skull open on the corner of a stone water trough. It had been a cruel twist of fate, made crueller still when the officer in charge of the auxiliaries ordered his men to take the village chief prisoner, along with the children. But while the children were to be taken away to be sold into slavery, Iskerbeles was fated to be tried for murder and condemned to public execution.

The last he had seen of his wife had been her despair as she embraced their two young daughters, sobbing into the folds of her tunic. A day's march had brought the captives to Asturica Augusta and here Iskerbeles had been chained into the cell while the children were shackled to a column of those condemned to be sold in the great slave market at the provincial capital of Tarraco. He had been half starved in the time since, and the heavy iron manacles had worn painful sores about his wrists. His hair was matted and he was so smeared with his own filth that the ten guards escorting him kept their distance and prodded him with the tips of their spears to make him stumble through the crowd towards the foot of the steps.

The angry cries of the townspeople, and those who had come from the surrounding countryside, began to fade as they saw his pitiful condition and by the time he was brought to a halt at the foot of the steps there was a grim silence in the forum. Even those at the market stalls on the far side paused to turn and look across towards the senate house, caught up in the tense atmosphere.

'Stand up straight, you!' one of the guards hissed, digging the butt of his spear into the small of the prisoner's back. Iskerbeles stumbled forward half a pace and then drew himself up defiantly and glared up at the magistrate. The centurion in charge of the escort cleared his throat and bellowed in a parade ground voice so that all in the forum might hear him. 'Most honourable Titus Pelonius Aufidius, magistrate of Asturica Augusta, I present Iskerbeles, the village headman of Guapacina, for your judgement on the charge of murdering Gaius Democles, the agent of Senator Lucius Annaeus in Rome. The murder took place on the Ides of the previous month, witnessed by myself and the men of the escort charged with protecting Democles. He now waits your judgement.'

The centurion smartly snapped his chin down in a swift bow of the head and stepped to one side as the magistrate descended a few steps so that he stood out from the other local senators and town officials, but still stood above the crowd gathered before him. Aufidius fixed his features in a disdainful expression as he surveyed their faces. There was no mistaking the broad spread of hostility there. From the crude attire and unkempt hair of many he deduced that the prisoner's people were amongst the townsfolk,

2

and they would not welcome what was to come. There might be trouble, the magistrate decided, and he was relieved that he had taken the precaution of having the rest of the auxiliary soldiers standing ready in the street to the side of the town's senate house. Even though the first emperor, Augustus, had declared the pacification of Hispania nearly a hundred years earlier, that was only after two centuries of conflict. There were still some northern tribes who refused to genuflect to Rome, and many more who were recalcitrant at best, and would like nothing better than to throw off the Roman yoke that had proved such a burden. Indeed, Aufidius reflected, it was surprising that such a proud, warlike people had ever accepted the pax Romana. Peace was simply not in their nature.

Which was why they must be ruled with an iron rod. His brow creased sternly.

'That you committed the crime is not in doubt. There were ample witnesses to the act. Therefore, I am obliged to pronounce a capital sentence. However, before I do so, in the name of Roman justice I give the condemned man one last chance to beg forgiveness for his actions and make his peace with the world before he passes into the shadows. Iskerbeles, have you any final words?'

The village chief's jaw jutted out and he took a deep breath before he responded in a loud, clear voice. 'Roman justice? I spit on Roman justice!'

The centurion raised his fist and made to strike but the magistrate waved him back. 'No! Let him speak. Let him condemn himself even further in the eyes of the law and before these people!'

The soldier reluctantly resumed his position and Iskerbeles curled his lips in contempt before he continued. 'The death of that accursed son of a whore freedman was natural justice. He came to our village to take our grain, our oil and everything of any value that we had. When we refused his demands, he threatened to take our children. He laid his hands on a son of our village, and so I slew him. By accident, not design.'

Aufidius shook his head. 'It is of no consequence. The victim was acting in the course of his lawful duty. Calling in a debt on behalf of his master.'

'The same master who made a loan to our village when the

harvest failed three years ago, and then raised the interest rate on every anniversary of the loan so that we could never repay him.'

The magistrate shrugged. 'That may be so, but it is legal. You had an agreement with Senator Annaeus, through his agent. You knew the terms before you set your seal on the document on behalf of your people. Therefore the senator is acting within his rights to demand repayment in full.'

'In full, plus interest. As much as half again of the original loan! How can we repay him? And nor are we alone in being the victims of this vile dog.' Iskerbeles half-turned to address the crowd. 'You all know the man I killed. The vile Democles, who cheated not just the people of my village, but almost every village in this region. His men had already seized hundreds of people from our tribe when they could not repay his master. Most are condemned to the mines in the hills. There they will labour until they die from exhaustion, or are buried alive in the deathtrap tunnels dug into the cliffs. No one here needs to be reminded of the horrors of those mines!'

Aufidius smiled. 'And yet you seek to remind us. The fate of those condemned to the mines is well known, Iskerbeles. But that is the well-deserved punishment of all those who break the law.'

'Hah! You speak of the law. The law thrust on us by our Roman masters. The law which is little more than a tool to justify the theft of our gold, our silver, our land, our homes and our liberty. Roman law is an affront to nature, a scourge on every last fibre of our dignity.' He paused to glare at the crowd. 'Who here is so low a creature that he will endure this shame? Are you all mangy dogs sunk to the depths of begging for scraps and licking the boots of those who whip and starve you into utter submission? Are there none who will stand against the tyranny of Rome . . . ? None?'

'Down with Rome!' a voice cried from the heart of the throng. Faces turned and looked round. Another voice took up the cry, and more added to the swelling anger. Then a man close to the front of the crowd shook his fist and shouted, 'Death to Aufidius!' He was a powerfully built man with a bald crown. He had a rolled shepherd's cloak tied around his body and he punched his hand into the air and began to chant and those around him joined in.

The magistrate recoiled half a step at the protest and quickly

4

rounded on the centurion. 'Carry out the sentence. Get him out of here! Now!'

The centurion nodded and cleared his throat. 'Escort! Close up around the prisoner!'

Hefting their shields and spears the auxiliaries formed a tight screen around Iskerbeles while the centurion took up the loose end of the chain hanging from the prisoner's neck and gave it a jerk as he led him away. 'Let's go.'

They started out along the steps at the foot of the senate house and began to work their way around the edge of the forum to the street leading to the town's eastern gate. Beyond, there was a low hill with gentle slopes, upon the crest of which the town executed its criminals. Looking up, over the tiled roofs of the town, Iskerbeles could see the tiny figures of the execution party who had been sent ahead to dig the post hole and construct the timber frame on which he was to be crucified. Then, with a painful jerk of the chain, the centurion drew him into the narrow street. Like most established Roman settlements, Asturica Augusta's main thoroughfares were lined with small shops while above them additional storeys had been constructed to accommodate the town's burgeoning population.

The centurion barked out a command for those in the street to clear the way and the townspeople did their best to hurry aside, women grabbing their young children and older folk climbing stiffly out of the road onto the pavement. Behind the prisoner and his escort the crowd surged into the street and their angry cries were trapped between the walls rising on either side and filled the stifling air with their din. The centurion glanced back over his shoulder at the prisoner and sneered.

'Your lot won't be so mouthy when they see you nailed down and hoisted into place.'

Iskerbeles did not reply to the taunt, but concentrated on staying on his feet as he was dragged along over the cobbled street. Around him the auxiliaries jostled past onlookers crowding the pavement.

'What's his story?' a wizened old man demanded of the centurion.

'None of your damned business,' the officer snapped. 'Clear the way ahead!'

'That's Iskerbeles,' a fat woman responded to the old man.

'Iskerbeles? Chief Iskerbeles?'

'Aye, poor soul's to be executed. For killing a money lender.'

'Executed?' The old man spat into the gutter at the feet of the nearest auxiliary. 'That's no crime. Or shouldn't be.'

The woman raised her fists. 'Let 'im go! You Roman dogs. Set 'im free!'

Those on either side quickly echoed her cry and it spread up and down the length of the street and into the mouths of the mob following the small party of soldiers. Soon the deafening sound of his name rang in the ears of Iskerbeles and his escort and the chieftain could not help a thin smile of satisfaction, even though he was being marched to an agonising death. The people of his tribe, and many of those native people who had come to live in the towns, continued to harbour a spirit of resistance towards the invader that they had fought for so many generations. The peace that the Romans had proclaimed came at the price of being ground under their heel and Iskerbeles prayed to the goddess Ataecina that she would unleash her full fury against Rome and inspire her followers to slaughter and burn the invaders and drive them back into the sea.

A short distance ahead, several young men had emerged from an inn to see what the disturbance was about. As Iskerbeles looked up he noted their neat tunics and clean-shaven cheeks and saw them for what they were: the offspring of the wealthier families of the town who had long since thrown in their lot with the invader and enthusiastically adopted Roman airs and graces. A few of the young men still carried glazed flagons in their hands and the nearest raised his in a toast as he called out loudly.

'Death to murderers! I say death to Iskerbeles!'

Some of his companions shot him an anxious look, but the rest repeated the toast and jeered the oncoming prisoner. The fat woman turned on them in an instant and, hitching up the hem of her ragged stola, she charged along the pavement and slapped the ringleader hard across the face with a meaty hand. 'You drunken fool.'

He may have been inebriated, but he rode the blow well and shook his head briefly to clear it before he balled his right hand into a fist and smashed it into the woman's face, breaking her nose and causing a bright crimson stream to pour from her nostrils.

'Keep your mouth shut, you hag. Unless you want to join your friend there, when they crucify him.'

The woman clutched a hand to her nose, then looked down at the blood on her palm, and let out a shrill screech as she hurled herself on the youth, fists flailing.

'You bastards! Bastards! Sucking us dry!'

Her screams were so loud that the nearest elements of the mob stilled their tongues and turned to look in her direction. They divined the nature of the clash in an instant and there was a surge towards the inn as they rushed to join her attack on the youths who had instantly become symbols for all the causes of their misery. Fists flew, hair was grabbed, insults screamed and feet lashed out in a frenzied outburst of rage. At once the mêlée spilled out into the street ahead of the prisoner and his escort. The centurion drew up and let out an explosive sigh.

'Fucking great . . . That's all I need.' He handed the chain to one of his men and hefted his stout vine cane. 'Keep closed up as we get through this lot. And I don't want to see anyone getting stuck in. Clobber them if they get in the way, but no more. They're pissed off enough as it is, without one of you bastards giving them any further excuse. Clear? Then stay together and let's move.'

He gestured along the street with his vine cane and set off at a slow, steady pace. As the squad approached the fringes of the violent struggle, the centurion raised his cane and barked, 'Clear the way!'

A one-armed man glanced round nervously and scurried to the side of the street, but the rest continued fighting heedlessly.

'Fair enough,' muttered the centurion. He raised his cane and smashed it down across the shoulders of the nearest man. His victim lurched into the crowd with a pained grunt as the officer swung again, this time punching the gnarled head of the cane into the small of a woman's back. She collapsed onto her knees and he thrust her aside with his spare hand and stepped into the gap. It only took a few more blows before the townsfolk became aware of the danger and made efforts to get out of his way. The soldiers followed on, using their shields to force their way through the fighting, Iskerbeles doing his best to remain on his feet as he was jostled by

7

the men on either side. As they broke free of the mêlée they came to a crossroads and a flash of movement to one side drew the attention of Iskerbeles. Glancing down the intersecting street he saw a small party of men in dark brown cloaks dashing across a parallel junction. Then they were gone.

A sharp yank of the chain brought him back as the auxiliary charged with leading him growled, 'Shift your arse.'

The soldier spoke the local dialect with only a slight accent and Iskerbeles stared hard at him. 'You're no Roman. From the east of the province, am I right?'

The auxiliary shrugged. 'Barcino.'

'Then you are one of us. Why serve those Roman dogs? Don't you want to be free?'

'Free to be what?' The soldier laughed harshly. 'A hairy-arsed peasant scratching a living on some shitty scrap of land? If that's freedom, then you can bloody keep it.'

Iskerbeles' eyes narrowed. 'Have you no heart? No pride? No shame?'

'The only shame I'm feeling is that it's a shame I have to listen to your bellyaching.' The soldier gave the chain a quick wrench. 'So keep your trap shut, friend, and spare me the lecture.'

Free of the crowd, the centurion increased his pace, and as the street bent to the left around a small temple, the town gate came into view. The sentries on either side stirred into life at the sight of an officer and shuffled to attention as he approached. Unlike the auxiliaries, they were not proper soldiers, just men recruited by the town senate to extract the tolls for entering the city. They were equipped with weapons and whatever armour could be acquired cheaply to make them look the part. The centurion barely acknowledged them as he led his squad through the shadow of the gate and out into the bright sunlight of the open countryside beyond the town's wall. The road was paved for a few miles before it became a dusty track picking its way through the hills of the region. A line of merchants' carts, and heavily laden mules led by peasants, waited to enter the town and they barely spared a glance as the prisoner was marched past them. A horse trader and his companions with a long string of mounts passed at the rear of the line and the centurion cast an envious eye over the horseflesh as he compared them to the poor-quality mounts that his cohort had to make best use of.

A short distance from the gate a path stretched from the road up to the crest of the hill used for executions and the centurion and his men climbed towards the waiting work party. A small cluster of townsfolk stood to one side, waiting to witness the spectacle, and those who had been sitting rose to their feet as the condemned man and his escort approached. Iskerbeles felt his stomach tighten into a painful knot as he saw the crossed timber lying beside the small pile of loose soil and stone dug out of the ground for the post hole. He had managed to hide his feelings so far, and now gritted his teeth, determined not to betray himself to his enemies. It would be good to hide the fear and pain and show disdain and contempt for Rome until his last breath. Let the townsfolk witness that and let those who continued the struggle against the invader draw strength from his example.

'Off your arses!' the centurion called out and half turned to indicate Iskerbeles. 'Here's your customer. Get him nailed up nice and quick and we can be on our way.'

The decurion in charge of the work party waved a hand in acknowledgement and turned to mutter an order to his men, who were squatting around the crossed timbers and tools used to prepare the execution. They sat with their backs to the approaching auxiliaries and did not bother to stir at the sound of nailed boots crunching over the sun-baked ground.

'On your feet I said!' bellowed the centurion as he strode forward, cane raised to strike at the nearest of the men who had defied his initial order. Then he caught sight of the dark patch of dried blood beside the shaft of the crucifix. There were more stains on the ground. He abruptly halted, a chilly tingle raising the hairs at the base of his skull. Then he saw the bare foot protruding beyond a nearby outcrop of rock, and instantly switched his cane into his left hand as he wrenched out his sword.

'Ambush! To arms!'

Before his startled men could respond, the decurion shouted an order in the native tongue and the men of the work party leaped to their feet, swords and spears in hand, and charged towards the soldiers of the escort. The onlookers who had been waiting to one side also cast off their cloaks to reveal more weapons. They rushed towards the auxiliaries and their prisoner without uttering a word. Iskerbeles, who had been trying to harden his resolve against the dread prospect of having his wrists and ankles pierced by iron nails, felt a surge of exhilaration at the sudden prospect of salvation. The man who had been masquerading as the decurion in charge of the execution party surged ahead of his men, swinging his sword at the centurion in a savage arc. The latter was a thorough professional and had trained many years for such a moment. He went into a crouch and parried the blow, then used his vine cane to strike his foe a glancing blow to the head, sending the man reeling back. The auxiliary officer glanced round at his men.

'Close up!'

The shock of the ambush swiftly faded as the soldiers raised their shields and lowered the points of their spears, facing out to meet the charge from two directions. The man who had been tasked with holding the prisoner's chain hesitated, unsure whether to drop it and join the others, or continue to guard the prisoner. Iskerbeles swung his manacled hands up, snatched the chain from the auxiliary's grasp and swung the short length against the man's helmet. Metal clattered on metal and the soldier staggered back with a dazed expression, barging into the back of one of his comrades and nearly sending both men crashing to the ground. A gap opened between two of the auxiliaries and Iskerbeles bunched his raised hands into fists and rushed for the opening as fast as the length of chain between his leg manacles would permit. Leading with his right shoulder, he barged one of his escort aside and then tried to sprint a few paces, but the chain tripped him up and he fell headlong no more than ten feet from the Roman soldiers.

The centurion thrust his cane out. 'Don't let the bastard escape!'

One of his men rushed forward and drew his spear arm back, ready to strike. Iskerbeles rolled onto his side, raising his hands in a futile bid to ward off the blow. He squinted as he stared up at the soldier, black against the dazzling backdrop of the blazing sun. Then another shape slammed into the side of the auxiliary and sent him tumbling to one side with a loud clatter as the soldier's shield struck the stony ground. Out of the corner of his eye Iskerbeles saw a blade rise and strike down three times and then a hand grabbed his arm and hauled him to his feet and he saw the grinning face of the man from the crowd who had called for the death of Aufidius.

'Well met, Callaecus, my friend.'

'Greetings later,' the man panted. 'Kill Romans first.'

He helped Iskerbeles to a safe distance and then sprinted back towards the knot of combatants near the crest of the hillock. Several men were already down in the swirling dust, three of them soldiers. Their comrades now fought back to back, with their centurion. But they were outnumbered and the fearless savagery of their attackers ensured the outcome. One by one they were dragged down and finished with frenzied blows from blades and thrusts of spears, until only the centurion and two of his men still lived, half crouched and eyes flickering at the men around them as they held their weapons out, ready to ward off any attack. As if by some unspoken agreement both sides drew away from each other and the remaining twenty or so ambushers stood two sword lengths back in a ring around the trio of auxiliaries. All were breathing hard as they braced themselves to continue the fight.

'Throw down your weapons!' Iskerbeles called out.

The centurion's lips curled in contempt, but before he could reply one of his men dropped his sword and released the grip of his shield so it fell beside his blade. His comrade glanced at the centurion before he followed suit.

The centurion sniffed. 'You cowards . . .'

'Surrender!' Iskerbeles ordered. 'Do it now, or die!'

The officer gritted his teeth, slowly turning to cover all angles, as the two survivors of the escort party edged away from him. Then he sighed with frustration as he straightened up and tossed his sword and cane at Iskerbeles' feet.

'You may escape now, but we'll be on your trail soon enough, and you'll be hunted down like dogs.'

'Really?' Iskerbeles smiled. 'We'll have to see about that. Callaecus, get these chains off me.'

The tribesman came over and pulled the pin from the neck ring and then the manacles on each hand before bending to remove

11

those around his chief's ankles. Iskerbeles tenderly rubbed the red welts that had formed on his skin as he regarded the other men from his village. 'You're fools, the lot of you. The Romans would have been satisfied with my blood alone for the murder of the money lender. Now they'll kill us all.'

'Only if they get the chance!' Callaecus chuckled. He jabbed a thumb at the three auxiliaries. 'And if they fight like these milk-livered cowards, then we've nothing to worry about.'

Iskerbeles frowned. 'They have far better men than these to send against us. Make no mistake about that. If we start a fight against Rome now, then it will be a fight to the finish. We can only win if we survive long enough to inspire the other tribes and unite them behind us.' He paused to let his next words have their full effect. 'The odds are against us. Us, and all our people. The Romans will not content themselves with pursuing us alone. They will come after all of us. Our women and children too. Are you prepared to risk that, my friends? Think carefully on it.'

Callaecus threw back his head and laughed before he responded. 'Do you think that we have not talked this through? Every one of us. We have sworn an oath to rescue you, Chief Iskerbeles. You will lead us to victory, or death.'

Iskerbeles sucked in a breath as he regarded the expectant faces watching for his reaction. Then he shook his head. 'You fools . . . So be it. Until victory, or death.'

Callaecus punched his sword arm into the air and a cheer ripped from his lips. The others followed suit as Iskerbeles rolled his head and flexed his muscles. Then he stooped to pick up the centurion's sword and examined the weapon. It was finely balanced and the ivory handle was worn smooth with use. The blade was well looked after and had a keen edge and he nodded approvingly at the centurion. 'You know your business.'

'I do. And I know that I'll be having that back before long. I swear it, by Mithras.'

'He won't come to your aid, Roman. Not if our Gods can help it. And failing that, not if my friends and I can help it.'

The centurion snorted with derision. 'You? You're nothing but a bunch of peasants who stink of goat shit and sweat. You surprised us this time, I'll admit. But next time, we'll be ready, and then you'll see what Roman soldiers can really do.'

'Perhaps.' Iskerbeles looked towards the town gate and saw the sentries there shading their eyes as they looked towards the crest of the hill. Already one of them had turned to rush through the gate and raise the alarm.

'We had better leave. Get into the hills before they send someone after us.'

'I've already thought of that.' Callaecus turned towards the road and waved his hand from side to side. At once the men who had been posing as horse-traders vaulted onto their saddles and led strings of mounts up the slope. 'We'll be miles away before they get off their fat Roman arses and start any pursuit.'

'Good man.' Iskerbeles grinned with approval. Then his expression hardened. 'But then what becomes of us? They will be sure to burn our village to the ground. We'll have to take the women and children and hide in the mountains.'

His comrade shrugged. 'It won't be easy, but we know the ground. We'll survive.'

'Survive?' Iskerbeles' brow creased in thought. 'No. Survival is not enough. I'll not let our people live to be hunted down like starving dogs. That is not worthy of them. We must give them a cause to fight for, my friend. We must raise the standard of our tribe and call on all our people to rise up and fight Rome. Unless we can drive them out of our land then we will only ever be their slaves.'

'You think we can fight Rome?' Callaecus' eyebrows rose in surprise at the hubris of his chief. He lowered his voice so as not to be overheard by the other men. 'Have you lost your mind? We cannot defeat Rome.'

'Why not? We would not be the first people in Hispania to try. Nor the last should we fail, I'll warrant. Viriathus and Sertorius came very close to victory. They only failed because they were betrayed. I'll not make the same mistake.' The chieftain's eyes blazed. 'Besides, the province is ripe for revolt. Our people are not alone in being ground under the enemy's boots. There's a hunger for rebellion, and we will feed that appetite, my friend. Our example will give heart to all those who hate Rome . . . But now is not the time to talk about this. Later, when we have led our people to safety.'

Callaecus nodded and was about to turn towards the approaching horses when he paused and gestured towards the three survivors of the prisoner escort. 'What about them?'

Iskerbeles considered the centurion and his comrades for an instant before he decided. 'Kill the soldiers. As for the centurion, it would be a shame not to make use of the crucifix and these nails . . .'

# CHAPTER ONE

*The Port of Ostia, a day's march from Rome*

'What's all the fuss about, friend?' Macro asked the inn-keeper as he nodded at the drunken crowd at the far end of the bar called 'Neptune's Bounty'. Several men were talking in excited tones as they shared a large jug of wine. A pair of the inn's prostitutes had joined the party and were sitting on the men's laps as they angled for a share of the wine, and subsequent business if they were lucky.

Without answering the question, the inn-keeper, a weathered-looking individual with a patch over one eye, fixed his diminished gaze on his customer and took a guess. 'Just come off a ship, eh?'

Macro nodded at his gruff question and indicated his tall, rangy companion who was using the hem of his cloak to wipe down the surface of a bench near the entrance. Cato removed the worst of the sticky mess with a quick wince and then sat down, silhouetted against the bright light outside. The street was busy and the cries of scavenging gulls swirling in the clear blue sky cut across the hubbub of voices and the shouts of street-sellers. Even though it was mid-morning the heat was oppressive and the shade of the inn provided a welcome respite from the blistering sunshine.

'That's right. Needed a drink before taking a boat up the Tiber to Rome.'

'Boat? Fat chance of that. Won't be space on any boat now. There's a public holiday in the capital coming up. So every boat is piled high with wine, treats and tourists. You'll have to go by road, my friend. You on your own?'

'No. It's me and the prefect there.'

'Prefect?' The inn-keeper's one eye widened, and then shrewdly narrowed as he reassessed his latest customers. There was not much outward sign of rank or wealth. Both men were dressed in military cloaks and plain tunics. The shorter man at the bar was wearing sturdy soldier's boots, but his companion, the prefect, had expensive-looking calf-skin boots, dyed red. Both had small haversacks slung over the shoulder, and the pendulous bulge of each betokened a heavy purse. The inn-keeper cracked a gap-toothed smile. 'Always a pleasure to serve gentlemen of quality. So he's a prefect and how about you? Same rank?'

'Not me.' Macro smiled back. 'I work for a living.' He patted his chest. 'Centurion Macro. Late of the Fourteenth Legion, serving in Britannia, and before that the Second Augusta, best legion in the entire army. So, like I said, what's the fuss? The whole town seems to be in high spirits.'

'And why not, sir? You should know the reason as well as any, given that you've come back from Britannia. It's over that King Caratacus, the one who's been giving our generals the runaround.'

Macro sighed. 'No need to tell me about it. That bastard was as slippery as an eel and as fierce as a lion. Good thing we finally ran him to ground. What about him? Last I heard of Caratacus was that he was being sent to Rome under lock and key.'

'And so he was, sir. Him and his kin have been held in the Mamertine prison for the last six months while the Emperor decided what to do with him. Now we know. Claudius has decided to have the lot of 'em paraded through Rome and taken up to the Temple of Jupiter for strangling. Going to be quite a celebration. His nibs is going to feast the city and put on five days of gladiator fights and chariot races at the Circus Maximus.' The inn-keeper paused and shrugged. 'Of course, Ostia is going to be quiet as the grave when all that happens. Bad for business. So I might as well sell as much now as I can. What'll you have, sir?'

'What's your best? We deserve something good to celebrate our home-coming. None of that watered-down piss that you sell to the usual customers just off the boat, eh?'

The inn-keeper looked offended and took a deep breath before he stiffened his neck with indignation. 'I do not run that kind of establishment, sir. I'll have you know that Lucius Scabarus serves some of the finest wines to be found in all the inns of Ostia.'

That's not saying much, thought Macro. This inn, like all the others crowding the streets close to the wharf, enjoyed a roaring trade with recent arrivals desperate for a drink, as well as those needing one before setting off on a voyage. Such customers were inclined to be more mindful of the effects rather than the taste of the inn-keepers' wares.

'So,' he tried again. 'Your best?'

The inn-keeper nodded towards a small row of jugs on the top shelf behind the counter. 'Had some nice stuff come in from Barcino last month.'

'Good vintage?'

'Well, it is now, sir.'

Macro nodded. 'A jar then, and two cups. Make 'em clean. The prefect has standards.'

The inn-keeper frowned. 'As do I, sir. Anything to eat with that?'

'Maybe later. When the wine's settled our guts after that passage from Massilia. Quite a storm.'

'Very well, sir. I'll have one of the girls rustle up something good, if you need food. And speaking of girls; they're clean, eager and know plenty of tricks. For a fair price.'

'I'm sure. At least as far as the last two qualities go. I didn't survive three campaigns in Britannia to be taken down by a dose of the clap. So, I'll pass on your tarts this time, thanks. Bring the drink to our table.'

Macro turned away and made his way to the table where Cato had settled, his back leaning against the cracked and stained plaster. His expression was sombre and Macro felt a stab of pity for his friend. A few months earlier, while in Britannia, Cato had received news of his wife's death. The return to his home in the capital would renew the terrible grief he had suffered. Julia had been a lovely girl, Macro reflected, and he grieved for her. But all was not lost. She had given birth to a boy who might yet offer Cato some comfort, when he met his son for the first time. He had that at least, and something of her lived on in young Lucius. He forced a smile as he sat down opposite Cato.

'Wine's coming. The best this flea-pit can offer. Be good to wash the taste of salt out of my mouth. Never been a big fan of taking a sea voyage. Especially after that time we were shipwrecked off Creta. Remember?'

'How could I forget?'

Macro silently cursed himself. That had been the time when Cato was in the first flush of love for Julia. He hurriedly changed the subject. 'Some interesting news. Just got it from the inn-keeper. He says that Claudius has decided to put an end to Caratacus and his family. That's why that lot over there are in their cups. The Emperor's throwing a huge shindig to celebrate the event.'

Cato took a deep breath. 'Execution? That isn't right. He deserves better, even if he was our enemy. He fought honourably. It does Rome no credit to put him to death like a criminal. When word of that gets back to the tribes he led in Britannia, they're not going to be happy. We'll be lucky if it doesn't provoke them into open revolt.'

'Maybe,' Macro responded. 'But it's just possible that they might be smart enough to learn that it doesn't pay to defy the will of Rome. Caratacus' death will prove that well enough. Once they hear about his fate, then they'll be only too willing to keep their heads down and do as they are told.'

Both were silent for a moment before Cato cleared his throat. 'I'm not surprised, though. What with recent events in Britannia. Emperor Claudius and his advisers will want to gloss over that as much as possible for a while. Defeats never go down well with the mob.'

'That's true.' Macro nodded emphatically. 'The hill tribes gave us a right good kicking. Praise be to Fortuna that we managed to get out with as many men as we did.'

The inn-keeper came over with a modest jug of wine and two glazed goblets and set them down on the table with a sharp rap. 'Best in the house. Reserve them only for gentlemen of quality, such as yourselves, who frequent my establishment.'

Macro picked up the nearest goblet and gave it a cursory inspection. 'Don't get much use then.'

The inn-keeper made to reply, then thought better of it, and held out his hand. 'Ten sestertii, sir.'

'Ten?' Macro shot him a look. 'Daylight robbery.'

'No, sir. Supply and demand. What with the big do coming up in Rome, the palace is buying up every last drop of wine it can lay its hands on.'

Cato cleared his throat. 'Just pay the man.'

'Now, wait a minute. He's trying to pull a fast one.'

'Here.' Cato reached down into his purse for some coins and placed them in the man's open palm. 'Now go.'

The inn-keeper's fingers closed quickly over the silver and he bowed his thanks and retreated to the bar before Macro could continue to protest. The centurion puffed his cheeks but passed no comment on his friend's action. Instead he reached for the jug and plucked out the cork plug with a dull pop and sniffed at the contents.

'Surprisingly good.'

He filled the goblets, gently pushed one towards Cato and raised his own. 'To absent comrades.'

Cato lifted his goblet. 'Absent comrades.'

They each took a sip and there was a brief silence as they recalled the most recent campaign through the mountains of the Decangli tribe. They had been part of the column attempting to take the Druids' island of Mona. Instead they had fallen into a trap and been forced into a retreat through bitter snowstorms. The legate in command, and thousands of his men, had perished in the desperate struggle to reach the safety of their base. Cato and Macro's units had formed the rearguard and only a handful of their men had survived. The new governor of the province, Didius Gallus, had ordered them to return to Rome to make a full report on the disaster while he attempted to secure the frontier. Ten years after the invasion of Britannia, many of the native tribes were still very far from being conquered. Now this latest setback threatened to undermine the Emperor who had awarded himself a triumph for his victory over the Britons within only a few months of the first troops landing on the island, a decade earlier.

What a hollow triumph it had proved, Cato mused as he took another sip. No wonder the Emperor and his advisers had chosen this moment to celebrate the defeat and capture of Caratacus. That was the way of politics: smother bad news with good and hope that the mob was too hungover to notice the sleight of hand. Or even care. Bread, wine, circuses and deception – the tried and tested recipe for keeping the people of Rome distracted enough to remain docile. No doubt they would enjoy the opening spectacle of their enemies being put to death. But it was an unfitting and unworthy end for Caratacus and his family and the prospect made Cato's heart heavy.

He sensed someone approaching the table and looked up to see one of the drinkers from the far end of the bar. A man in his early forties, Cato guessed. He wore an old military tunic and a leather thong held back a thick mass of grey-streaked hair. His left hand held a Samian-ware cup and his right was missing, the stump at the end of his forearm covered with a leather cap from which an iron hook extended in place of his fingers.

Cato swallowed the wine in his mouth. 'Yes?'

'Pardon me, sir. But old Scabarus says that you two have just returned from Britannia. That right?'

'Yes. What of it?'

'I was wondering if I could trouble you for some news of what's happening there. I was with the Ninth Legion, back in the first year of the invasion. I lost my hand in the battle outside Camulodunum.'

Cato nodded. 'I remember the battle. Close-run thing. Caratacus nearly had us beaten that day.'

'Yes he did, sir.'

'What's your name?'

'Marcus Salinus, sir.' The man automatically stiffened as he addressed a superior. 'Optio, Sixth Century, First Cohort, Ninth Legion . . . Or at least I was.'

'At ease, Optio.' Cato smiled. 'The centurion and I would be honoured to share a cup of wine with an old comrade of the Ninth. Sit down.'

Macro shuffled over to make room and Salinus hesitated a moment before accepting the offer. His companions hung back a small distance as Macro poured their friend some wine. Salinus nodded his thanks and a fleeting look of caution crossed his face as he glanced round the inn. He lowered his voice as he spoke. 'The rumour is that we've suffered a bad defeat. Is it true?'

20

Cato was silent for a moment, wondering if he should be discreet. But it hardly seemed likely that there would be a palace informer in such a nondescript drinking house unless things had changed since he was last in Ostia. Besides, he and Macro were already likely to face the ire of the Emperor when they came to make their report about the situation in Britannia. He doubted if answering the veteran's question would make things worse.

'It is true. We lost the equivalent of a legion, five thousand men, and half as many auxiliaries, along with the legate of the Fourteenth. The enemy have pushed us right back out of the mountains and may already be launching strikes deep into the province.'

Salinus could not hide his shock, and nor could his companions. The old soldier shook his head. 'How is that possible?'

'It should never have happened,' said Macro. 'It was late in the season, we had little information about the enemy or the ground we were advancing over. It began to snow and then the enemy cut our supply lines. Fucking disaster from start to finish.'

'So why did the campaign even go ahead, sir?'

'Same old reason as always. Some broad-striper decides to put posterity above what's possible and leads the rest of us deep into the shit. In this case, Legate Quintatus. When the previous governor died, Quintatus thought he would grab all the glory before a new governor could be appointed.'

'Them bastards always do for us,' growled Salinus. 'Someone should pay for that with their head.'

'They did. Quintatus went down fighting. Came good in the end, like a proper soldier. Shame he took so many of our mates with him. Worst defeat we've suffered since setting foot in Britannia.'

'Hang about,' one of the other men from the inn cut in. 'How come this happened, now that we've got our hands on Caratacus? Thought he was supposed to be their commander? They've been telling us that with him in chains it was as good as over.'

Macro smiled. 'Come on, friend. Do you believe everything that appears in the gazetteer?'

'It could have been worse, if Caratacus was still on the scene,' said Cato. 'Far worse. We have that to be thankful for. He kept us on the hop for nigh on ten years before we ran him to ground.

There's one enemy of Rome I've plenty of good reason to respect.'

Salinus' eyes brightened. 'You came up against him then, sir? In battle?'

Macro laughed heartily as he reached for the jug and topped up his goblet. 'We're the lads who finally captured him, brother. The prefect and I. Took him in battle, together with his family.'

The veteran's eyes widened and then he grinned. 'Bloody heroes then, the pair of you. D'you hear that, lads? We're in the company of the men who only went and took down Rome's greatest enemy! Here's to you, Centurion, and you, sir.' The man slapped his head with his iron hook and winced. 'And I don't even know your names. Sir?'

'Centurion Lucius Cornelius Macro, and Prefect Quintus Licinius Cato, at your service.'

The veteran raised his cup. 'Lads, let's hear it for Centurion Macro and Prefect Cato!'

There was a deafening raucous cheer from his comrades as their cups went up, sloshing liquid, before they shouted their newfound heroes' names and drained their wine. Macro toasted them back while Cato forced a smile, mindful of the fact that while they had indeed captured the enemy commander, Caratacus had escaped from his custody and had to be hunted down again. A matter he would rather not admit to. He nodded his gratitude to Salinus and the others. Then the veteran turned his attention to Cato and leaned forward.

'So what's he like then, Caratacus? I've heard he's a giant of a man, covered in those bloody tattoos the natives go for, and he carries the heads of the men he's defeated from his saddle horns. And he's supposed to have filed his teeth. That and taken part in the human sacrifices those druid bastards go in for. Is it true?'

Cato could not help a brief laugh. 'What do you think? Does that sound like any man we ever fought in Britannia? Or anywhere else in the empire, for that matter? Caratacus is just a man, a soldier, like you and me. Not a giant, not a wild man, nor even much of a barbarian. Just a man, leading his people against invaders who came to take their land and enslave them. In his place, we'd have done the same . . . That's all I have to say about that,' Cato concluded and drained his cup before gazing contemplatively at the dregs.

Salinus stared back, mouth slightly agape, and then glanced at Macro who scratched his chin before he offered an excuse. 'Been a long voyage. I'd love to stay and talk shop with an old comrade but we've got business waiting for us in Rome. So we'd better drink up and be on our way.'

The veteran took the hint, emptied his cup and rose from the bench. 'It's been an honour. I hope the Emperor gives you the reward you deserve.'

'That would be a pleasant change,' Macro answered ruefully. 'But that's another story for another time, brother Salinus.'

'Then, if you come back through Ostia, look me up here at the inn. I'll stand you a jar of wine, of your choice, sir.'

Macro grinned. 'Then you can be sure I will.'

He held out his hand and he and the veteran clasped forearms before the latter bowed his head towards Cato. 'Hope to see you again, sir.'

'What?' Cato looked up, hurriedly took stock and nodded. 'Indeed.'

As Salinus led his comrades back to their spot at the far end of the bar, in a somewhat subdued mood, Macro let out a sigh. 'Nice work. You killed the moment stone dead. I thought we were about to be in for free drinks all night.'

Cato shook his head slowly. 'I'm sorry. I was miles away.'

Macro sighed gently. 'It's only natural to miss her, lad. I understand.'

'Yes . . .' Cato cleared his throat and continued. 'And then, there's Lucius. I am a father who has never seen his son before. I am not sure how to react. Not sure how I will feel about him.' He looked up. 'Macro, my friend, I am not sure how to cope with this. When we were in Britannia, I longed to return to Rome. But now we are here, it no longer feels like home. I have nothing to do but grieve and the world seems very dark . . . I'm sorry.' He smiled guiltily. 'It must remind you of the pathetic, shivering recruit you first met on that cold winter evening on the Rhenus frontier.'

Macro cocked an eyebrow. 'Well, I wasn't going to say so, but . . . Anyway, let me top you up.'

Cato sighed. 'You think that's going to help?'

'Who knows? But it ain't going to make things any worse. Is it?'

Cato managed a light chuckle and they drank some more before Macro continued. 'Lad, I've known you for over ten years now. There's not much you haven't coped with in that time. No challenge you haven't taken on and beaten. I know this is different, and that it feels like some bastard has ripped the stuffing out of you, but life goes on. Always. Julia was a lovely girl. And you loved her as dearly as life itself. I could see that. And, as your friend, I share your grief. But you have a son who needs you. And there will be other campaigns, where me and the men you command will need you too. You understand what I'm trying to say?' Macro rubbed his lined brow. 'Fuck, I'm no good with words. No good at all.'

Cato smiled. 'You say what you need to. And I think I understand. Not so sure that you do though.'

His friend frowned, made to reply and then growled, 'I'll just stick with soldiering, then. That's something I do understand, at least.'

'Oh yes. No doubt about that.'

There was a brief pause, then Macro raised the jug and gave it a gentle shake and there was the lightest of sloshing noises from within. He poured it into his goblet and drained it with one swift action and set it down with a smack of his lips.

'Right then. Time for moping around is over. Let's get on the road.'

# CHAPTER TWO

The excitement in the capital was evident some miles before Cato and Macro were even in sight of the walls of Rome. The road from Ostia was filled with carts, mule trains and people on foot, all keenly anticipating the celebrations to mark the defeat and capture of King Caratacus. Even though the event was not for three days there would be plenty of entertainment in the Forum and the surrounding streets. The markets would swell with extra stalls trading in snacks and delicacies, luxuries, such as scents and spices from the east, and souvenirs of the main event, with the usual range of forged militaria purporting to be captured Celtic weapons and druidic curios. Those families and individuals making the trip to the capital would seek out friends and relations to accommodate them, or simply find a place to sleep in the streets until the celebration was over.

Rome was overcrowded and malodorous at the best of times and Cato could imagine how much worse it would be with the influx of visitors, especially in the current weather. It had been many days since any rain had fallen. The two soldiers had been baked most of the time at sea and were again now on land. The road to the capital was shrouded in a fine light dust that left a patina on every surface and irritated the eyes and throats of the travellers. But even the sapping heat and the dust did not quell the high spirits of all those trudging along the paved route. Cato and Macro had left instructions with an agent in Ostia to send their baggage on to the prefect's house, and set out on foot. Long years of marching in armour laden with kit meant that they were easily able to overtake the civilians trudging along the road. They stopped once at a crowded roadside inn and shared a bench in the shade of some pine trees with an optio from the Praetorian Guard returning from leave.

'Britannia, eh?' The guardsman puffed his cheeks. 'Tough posting, that.'

'Tough as it gets.' Macro nodded with feeling, as he rubbed the puckered white scar tissue above his knee, the result of an arrow wound he had suffered in the most recent campaign. It still itched from time to time, a hot tingling sensation. The guardsman noticed the action and gestured.

'You got that over there?'

'Some little prick with a hunting bow took a pop. Nearly finished me for good. Not quite the glorious end that a centurion of more than twenty years of service might wish for.' Macro laughed. 'But then, most of us never get the chance to go into the shadows in a blaze of glory. Ten to one, it'll be some foolish injury, sickness or the clap that'll finish a man off. Plenty of time for any of that yet. But I'll settle for the clap if I have the choice.'

'Not wrong there,' the guardsman laughed and offered his hand. 'Gaius Gannicus, sir.'

Macro made the introductions and took a swig of water to clear the dust from his mouth before spitting it to one side. 'Of course, for you Praetorian layabouts the greatest danger to life and limb is the clap. Believe me, I have personal experience of how easy you have it.'

Gannicus cocked an eyebrow. 'You served in the Guard?'

Macro sensed Cato stiffening uneasily at his side. They had both served as Praetorians in an undercover operation a few years earlier. The kind of work that is best forgotten when its purpose is over. He decided to bluster over the slip-up.

'Oh, come on! Every soldier in the empire knows what a cushy number your lot have. Swanning around Rome in your white togas and tunics, best seats at the games and first in line for any handouts of silver the Emperor decides to distribute to the army. Am I right?'

Gannicus had the good grace to nod.

'The nearest thing you lot get to regular action is quietly disposing of those who have fallen foul of the Emperor, or his wife, or even those freedmen of his.'

26

'Too true, sir,' Gannicus responded ruefully. 'There's been a lot of that in recent months, I can tell you.'

'Oh?' Cato leaned forward, looking round Macro. 'What's been happening, then?'

'It's those two Greek freedmen of his. Pallas and Narcissus. They've been fighting to be top dog for as many years as I can remember. It used to be fairly bloodless. But with the Emperor getting on, there's the question of who comes next. Pallas wants his boy Nero on the throne, while Narcissus is pinning his hopes on young Britannicus. They know Claudius is not long for the world. Especially if he is given a helping hand by that wife of his, Agrippina.' He glanced round warily before lowering his voice. 'The grapevine says she and Pallas are more than a little cosy. Truth is she's angling on using his influence behind the scenes and he needs her to make sure he's the last man standing amongst Claudius' advisers if, more likely when, Nero takes the purple. But you didn't hear that from me, sir.'

'I understand,' said Cato. 'So things are coming to a head?'

'You bet. Narcissus has been using his agents to stitch up his rival's supporters, and those senators close to Agrippina. Meanwhile, she and Pallas have been leaning on the old man to favour Nero over Britannicus, and at the same time getting rid of as many of Britannicus' followers as possible.' The Praetorian shook his head. 'Been a right old bloodbath, I can tell you. So, as you can imagine, everyone is on edge in Rome these days. You could have picked a better time to return home, sir. At least you're soldiers, so you should be safer than most. If you want my advice, steer clear of any senators, and their scheming. Most important of all, stay well away from those two bastards, Pallas and Narcissus.'

Cato and Macro exchanged a quick look. It was Narcissus who had compelled them to serve his purposes on a number of occasions in the past. Cato had good reason to loathe the imperial freedman but still more reason to hate and fear Pallas who had plotted to murder the Emperor, and Cato and Macro along with him.

Gannicus flipped open his haversack and took out a loaf of bread and a hunk of cold pork. 'Care to share this with me, sirs? It ain't much, but I'd be honoured.'

'Thanks.' Cato held out a hand and Gannicus cut him a generous wedge of bread and then tore him a strip of meat. He did the same for Macro and all three chewed in silence for a moment as they watched the people and mule-hauled carts and wagons passing by. Then Gannicus cleared his throat and took a swig from his canteen.

'If you don't mind my asking, sir, are you two home on leave?'

'That's right,' Cato replied, keen not to be an unnecessary topic of conversation amongst Gannicus' comrades. 'Some rest and relaxation, while we await a new posting.'

'I imagine there's family looking forward to seeing both of you?'

Cato nodded. 'I have a son. Ironically, Macro's mother is in Britannia.'

'Really?' The guardsman turned his attention to Macro. 'What would a decent Roman woman be doing in a barbaric dump like that?'

'Long story,' Macro answered with his mouth half full. He swallowed and continued. 'But the short of it is that she's running a drinking hole in Londinium. I own a half share. So, no family for me in Rome, but I dare say I'll find ways of making myself at home.'

They finished eating and while Gannicus went to find a shady spot to sleep off his meal Cato and Macro got back on the road. The afternoon heat was oppressive and soon sweat was coursing down their faces as they strode mile after mile through the neatly tended farms on either side of the route. At length, as the sun began to dip towards the horizon, the road curved round a gentle hill and a few miles ahead of them they caught sight of the sprawling environs of Rome, lying over the landscape in a vast mantle of red tiled roofs with the lofty structures of temples and palaces rising above it all. It was a sight both men had seen many times before but it still caused a quickening of Cato's pulse as he gazed on the capital of the greatest empire in the known world. From the grand palace overlooking the Forum, the Emperor and his staff had dominion over lands that stretched from the endless expanse of Oceanus to the parched deserts of the east. Peoples of every hue, of every degree of civilisation, or barbarity, sent tribute to Rome and lived under her laws. It was the responsibility of men like Macro and himself to defend the frontiers of that vast empire from those tribes and kingdoms without who looked on with envy and hostility.

Cato led his friend a short distance off the road to take in the view while he mopped his brow and they drank from Macro's canteen. The awe of a moment earlier had passed and Cato now felt a twinge of apprehension. Somewhere amid that densely populated city was the home he had looked forward to sharing with Julia, where they would raise a family. Now she was dead, and no doubt her remains lay in a small urn, placed in a niche in the cold family tomb by her father, Senator Sempronius. All that remained of the lively, intelligent and courageous woman who had won Cato's heart now lived on in their only child. It was the birth of Lucius that had fatally weakened his mother, and ultimately led to her death. For that reason Cato feared that there would be a bitter struggle between resentment and paternal love in his heart when he first beheld his son, already more than two years old.

'Come on, brother,' Macro urged him gently. 'Not far to go now.'

Cato made no reply.

'Are you sure you want to offer me a billet at your house? If you want some time alone, then I'll understand. Time for you to get to know the boy, and time to grieve for Julia.'

Cato shook his head and tried to put on a brave face. 'No. I've done grieving. You are welcome to stay with me. I dare say I could use the company.'

'All right then. But I warn you. I've worked up a pretty big appetite. I'm liable to eat you out of house and home. I'm still hungry. Bloody hungry. Sooner we down packs and pitch up for the night, the better.'

They rejoined the road and even as dusk closed in over the landscape and the last of the light washed the hills and city in a warm glow, the vehicles and those on foot did not pause, but wound on, drawn towards the great city that demanded to be fed in exchange for the entertainment and other delights with which it lured visitors by the tens of thousands. The bright flicker of torches appeared along the city wall as darkness fell, and there were more lights further into the city, as well as the sprawl of campfires outside the gates where some of the travellers had stopped for the night. They gathered in circles about the blazes and there was singing and laughter as families enjoyed the cool air of the evening.

Cato and Macro pressed on and the blast of a horn announced the passing of the first hour of the night as they reached the towering Raudusculan gate leading into the city. They presented their military seals to the optio of the watch to avoid having to pay the toll, and passed beneath the arched gateway. It had been nearly three years since they had last been in Rome and the stench of sewage, rotting vegetables and sour mustiness was overpowering for a moment. The line of the Ostian Way continued through the densely populated Aventine quarter where the ramshackle tenement blocks, rising even higher than those of Ostia, loomed over the street. There were only occasional lamps and the thin light spilling from doors and windows to light the way as the two soldiers marched along the raised pavement beside the street. There were still plenty of people abroad, dodging round the carts that rattled over the rutted cobblestones, and though Cato could not help feeling conspicuous in his army tunic no one appeared to pay him or Macro any attention.

That gave rise to a slight, familiar, sense of resentment. Back in Britannia he and Macro had commanded hundreds of men who respected them and their rank. Comrades who had shed blood and given their lives so that the people of Rome could sleep free of the fear of any enemy, and live off the fruits of their soldiers' conquests. Yet the hard-won victories of Cato and Macro and the army in Britannia were almost unknown here in Rome, and merely a detail on the capital's gazetteer which itself was rarely read by the people going about their daily routine. They might as well be invisible. The deflating thought added to the ache in his heart as they passed the towering end of the Great Circus and started down the hill towards the Forum.

The centre of the city was ablaze with the light of torches and braziers, and the streets and open spaces were filled with carousers, hawkers, prostitutes and pickpockets, their din echoing off the walls of the temples and civic buildings. Cato kept a hand firmly on the

30

flap of his haversack and proceeded warily as they picked their way across the Forum. At his side Macro did the same, even as his hungry eyes roved over the women leaning against the entrances of brothels. Some called out their services as the two soldiers passed by, but most stood with dull, powdered expressions, drunk, or utterly bored by the endless bump and grind of their trade.

'Hello you!' A tall, blonde woman with a small chin and an easy smile stepped into their path. 'Soldiers, right? I do special rates for soldiers. Special rates and special services.' She winked at Cato, who made to step round her and continue on his way. So she turned her attention to Macro and took his hand before he could react. He had enjoyed the company of a few women along the route back from Britannia, but still felt the familiar tingle stirring in his loins and paused to look her over.

'Like what you see, do you?' She smiled knowingly and held his hand tightly as she pulled it down and pressed it against the hairy mound between her legs. 'And do you like what you feel?'

'Very much,' Macro chuckled, sorely tempted. Then he saw Cato stop and look back with a frown and he withdrew his hand. 'Another time.'

'That's a pity.' She gave his arm a squeeze. 'You look like you could please a girl. If you come back this way, ask for Columnella. I'll keep it warm for you. And what I said about special rates still holds true.'

Macro cocked an eyebrow. 'And special services?'

'That too.' She gave him a quick kiss on the lips and Macro tasted wine on her breath.

'See you again soon then.' Macro increased his pace to catch up with his friend as they made for the long, straight street that led to the Quirinal district.

As they left the Forum behind Cato paused under a lamp hanging from a bracket outside a pie shop and took out the letter Julia had sent him over a year before, in which she gave directions to the house she had purchased. The home where she had awaited his return. While on campaign he had often imagined his homecoming and the wondrous prospect of holding her in his arms again. The dream seemed to mock him now. Cruelly. He felt his heart lurch as he stared at the words written in her neat script, then hurriedly folded the letter and tucked it back in his haversack.

'Not far. It's this way.'

Without waiting for a response he strode off and Macro cast a quick backward glance at Columnella, who was accosting a skinny grey-haired man with baggy eyes. He let out a deep sigh and caught up with his friend. Even though the Quirinal was one of the better quarters of Rome, the street was still narrow, with sinister-looking alleys leading off it on both sides. The kind of place where footpads liked to hide in the shadows to pick off unwary individuals. At the top of the hill, where the air was less fetid, the tenement blocks were replaced by the first of the town houses that belonged to well-off merchants, members of the equestrian class like Cato, and the least affluent of the senatorial families. There were many shops here, on either side of the imposing doorways, some trading their upmarket wares: spices, cloth and fine wine and bread.

They passed over two crossroads and then Cato turned right at the third. He counted the doors they passed and stopped outside a neat studded door, fifty paces along the street. Three worn steps led up from the street and a single oil lamp burned from an iron bracket set far enough above the door that it would escape the clutches of any light-fingered passer-by. He stared at the door, gently pinching his chin between his thumb and forefinger.

'Are you all right, Cato?'

'No . . . Not really.'

Macro reached out and rested his hand on Cato's shoulder. He had been present when his friend had met Julia and knew her well enough to mourn her death in his own right, and not just because it affected Cato. A fine woman, who would have been a fine mother, and more importantly the person who would have made Cato happy and less melancholic. Macro had known his friend since Cato first joined the legions and had watched him fight his way up through the ranks, to centurion, and then surpass Macro and become his superior. It was an odd thing, he reflected once in a while, to be comrade, friend and subordinate. But it was more than that. Cato might well be a brother-in-arms but he was also more like a kid brother, or a son, and, like any father, Macro shared his joy and his pain in equal measure.

32

'Julia is gone, but your child is in there. He needs you now he has no mother.'

Cato shot him a bleak look. 'What do I know of being a father, Macro? There has been hardly a moment that I have not been a soldier for the last ten years. I am steeped in the blood of men I have killed, and seen killed before me. What do I know of nurture and child-raising?'

'I wasn't suggesting you suckle him at your tit, lad. Just saying that he'll need a man to look up to and teach him what's what. That sort of thing. You're as good as anyone for the job. Do it right and I'm certain young Lucius will turn out every bit as fine a man as his dad, eh? Now, I'm tired. My feet ache and I need food. So, are we going to stand around much longer like a pair of vagrants, or are we going inside?'

Cato smiled weakly. 'All right. Here goes.'

He took a deep breath, climbed the steps and rapped the knocker twice, loudly. All was quiet for a moment, and he was about to try again, when they both heard a cough and a moment later the sound of a small bolt scraping. A small viewing slot opened behind an iron grille and a pair of eyes regarded them suspiciously.

'Who are you?' a gruff voice demanded. 'We're not expecting anyone. Well?'

Cato met the man's gaze. 'I am Prefect Quintus Licinius Cato, returned from campaigning in Britannia, and this is my house. My home. So let me in.'

# CHAPTER THREE

'Prefect Cato?' The man behind the door sounded shocked. Then his eyes narrowed. 'The master is in Britannia. Be on your way!'

He made to shut the flap and Cato thrust his hand in between the small iron bars to stop him. 'Wait. I am who I say. Look here.'

He fumbled for his military seal and held it out, angling it towards the dull gleam of the lamp so that the man could make out the inscription. There was a brief pause as the doorkeeper appeared to scrutinise the seal, and Cato wondered if he could even read. Then he looked at Cato once again. 'If you are who you say you are, then how do you come to be here in Rome, when you should be fighting them barbarians in Britannia?'

'My comrade and I were sent back to Rome by the new governor.' Cato was tired and his patience was wearing thin. 'Now open the door, and let me in.'

'And who is he, then? Your comrade.'

'Centurion Macro. I am sure my wife has mentioned him.'

'The lady did speak of him . . . Fair enough, sir. I believe you.' The doorkeeper stepped back from the door and the viewing flap dropped back into place. A moment later there was the muffled sound of a heavy bolt being drawn and the door opened easily on oiled hinges to reveal a solid individual with dark features. He wore a plain brown tunic and bowed deeply as he stood aside to admit Cato and Macro.

'Welcome home, sir.'

He closed the door and locked it before continuing in an apologetic tone. 'Forgive me, Master Cato. I had to be sure who you were. There's only me and the nurse in the house at the moment. And young Master Lucius of course. So I have to be careful, what with things on the streets being as they are these last months.'

'There's been trouble even round here?'

'Yes, Master. The followers of the Emperor's heirs have been stirring things up. Trying to get the mob behind their man, and using the street gangs to ram the point home.'

'That's too bad,' Cato responded as he looked round the modest entrance hall, curious to know more about the house Julia had chosen for their home. A candle in a holder on a small side table provided just enough illumination to make out the details. To the left was an alcove with a small shrine and a handful of figures depicting the household spirits. On the opposite wall was another alcove within which a pale face gleamed. Cato felt the hairs on the back of his neck stiffen as he recognised the features. He swallowed and slowly approached. The wax death mask was illuminated from behind by the small wavering flame of an oil lamp. Close up he could see the lines of her face more clearly and he felt a sharp pang of longing for his dead wife. Tentatively, he reached out and touched the mask, and any illusion that it resembled her face shattered as he sensed the smooth hardness of the wax. All the same, he stroked the curve of the cheek for a moment before he turned back to the others.

'I am so sorry for your loss, Master.'

'Thank you.' Cato nodded. 'What's your name, fellow?'

'Amatapus, Master.'

'How long have you been living here?'

'All my life, Master. I was born in the slave quarters. My previous master included me in the price when Lady Julia bought the house. She appointed me the major-domo.'

'I see. And the nurse?'

'Petronella? She was hired as a wet-nurse. After the lady died, she was kept on by your father-in-law to look after Master Lucius.'

'Very well. I would like to see the rest of the house. But first I'd like to see my son.'

'Of course, Master.' Amatapus held out his hands. 'Your cloaks, please?'

Cato handed over his cloak and haversack and Macro followed

suit. Once he had hung them on the pegs in the corner of the hall, Amatapus gestured to them to follow him down a short passageway. There were barred doors on each side, and Cato guessed that they led through to the rooms fronting the street either side of the entrance.

'Are there shops attached to the house?'

'There's a basket weaver to the left and a baker to the right, Master.'

'And what rent do they make?'

The slave shook his head. 'I do not know, Master. Such matters were never in my purview. Lady Julia's father took responsibility for such matters until you returned.'

'I see.'

At the end of the passage they emerged into an atrium. A small square pond with tessellated representations of fish lay under the open sky. The faint light of the stars provided just enough illumination to make out their surroundings and Cato saw that a handful of doors opened onto the atrium, with a narrow staircase in one corner leading up to the next floor.

'Very nice,' Macro commented, as he looked round. 'Very nice indeed. You've landed on your feet, lad, and no mistake.'

'There's four rooms upstairs, Master. All empty at the moment. The mistress never had the chance to decorate them, or furnish them. That's her sleeping chamber over there. There's the study she had prepared for you, a dining room next to it, and the last door is Master Lucius' room. Do you wish to see him? He'll be asleep.'

Cato nodded. 'I'll see him now.'

'Excuse me then, Master. I'll fetch a lamp from the kitchen.'

He left the atrium by a further passage and they heard a muted exchange with a woman. Macro turned to his friend.

'How do you feel?'

'Feel?' Cato thought for a moment. 'Like a trespasser if I am honest. I've never had a home before. This is all new to me. I'm not sure how to cope with it all.'

'We get what fate deals out to us, lad. And we have no choice about how we handle it.'

Cato smiled. 'What's this? Philosophy?'

'Experience, lad. Much better.'

A faint glow and the sound of shuffling footsteps announced the return of Amatapus. He was accompanied by a large woman in a loose-fitting tunic that hung on her like a tent. The major-domo waved her forward and she bowed to Cato and Macro.

'This is Petronella, Master.'

By the light of the lamp Cato could see that she had a pretty, plump face with fierce dark eyes, a high forehead and fine dark hair cut short. She appeared to be in her early thirties, though it was hard to be certain in the dim light.

'I assume you've been told who I am.'

She nodded.

'I'd like to see my son.'

'Yes, Master.' She took the lamp from Amatapus, led them to the door of Lucius' chamber but paused as she took the latch. 'Master, it might be best if it was just the two of us. No point in scaring the poor child if he wakes to find himself surrounded by grown-ups.'

'All right.' Cato turned to his friend. 'Do you mind?'

'Not at all. He's your son. I'll get to know him well enough in due course.'

'Thank you.' Cato turned and nodded to the nurse who lifted the latch and gently pushed the door open. Raising the lamp, the nurse led the way into the chamber, a modestly proportioned room with simple furnishings. Besides the bed, against the far wall there was a stool and a chest at the foot of the bed.

'Careful, Master,' Petronella whispered and gestured towards his feet. Cato glanced down and saw that he had been about to step on some small wooden figurines. He stooped and picked one up and saw that it was crudely carved into the shape of a legionary.

'He loves those,' the nurse commented. 'Has them out all the time, Master. The trouble is getting him to help put them away when he goes to bed.'

Cato put the figurine down and softly paced over to the side of the bed. As Petronella held the lamp up he saw the boy lying on his front with his head to one side and arms splayed out on his mattress. He had kicked off his thin cover and a pair of chubby legs stretched down. His nose wrinkled and he murmured something incoherent and then sighed before his breathing became light and regular again. Easing himself down on the edge of the bed, Cato gently touched the soft, dark curls and felt his heart lurch.

This was his son. Lucius. His flesh and blood, as well as that of Julia. Already he fancied that he could see that the boy had inherited her snub nose and petite chin. The thought pained his heart and once again he ached for her, Julia. He silently cursed the Gods for taking her from him.

Easing himself up, he nodded back towards the atrium. They left the boy to continue sleeping and silently closed the door behind them.

Macro tilted his head. 'Well?'

'He's spark out and sleeping like a veteran.'

Macro chuckled. 'A chip off the old block then. Good for him.' Then his face wrinkled up and his mouth stretched open in an involuntary yawn. 'Fuck me, I'm shattered.'

'So I can see. Amatapus, find the centurion a comfortable bed.'

'Yes, Master. And for yourself?'

'I'll sleep in the main bedchamber.'

'Yes, Master.'

'Good, then you can wake us both at the second hour tomorrow. I take it there's enough food.'

Petronella nodded. 'Plenty, Master.'

'Then we'll get some sleep.'

Amatapus' brow creased. 'Do you not want to see the rest of the house, Master?'

Cato glanced round the atrium. 'There's more?'

'Oh, yes, Master. The kitchens, slave quarters, but most of all the garden and outside dining area. That was the mistress' favourite part of the house. You can't see much now, of course.'

'Then we can see it in the morning,' Cato cut in. 'For now, we both need sleep. Please see to Centurion Macro. Better get him another lamp and let me have that one. I'll find my own way.'

With the lamp in hand, Cato turned to his friend. 'Sleep well.'

'I'm sure I will.' Macro gestured at his surroundings. 'A billet doesn't come much better than this!'

They exchanged a weary smile, and then Cato made his way

around the colonnaded pond to the room that Amatapus had indicated earlier. He lifted the latch and the door hinges gave a light squeak as the door swung inwards. Stepping across the threshold Cato caught a sweet scent lingering in the air, something Julia must have placed in the room to make it more pleasing. The sleeping chamber was a large space with chests against one wall, a table, chair and shelves with pots and jars against the opposite wall, and in between a large bed with a thick mattress with fine linen coverings and two well-padded bolsters. Some small sandals lay at the foot of the bed.

He crossed to the table and saw that there were brushes and a mirror there, as well as small pots of face colours, some scents and a wooden frame upon which hung some necklaces and bracelets. To one side lay a thick silver amulet and Cato smiled at the thought that she had bought this to give him on his return. Then he turned towards the bed.

He put the lamp down on the small table beside the bed and undressed, leaving his folded clothes on the chair. Then he pulled back the coverings and climbed into the bed and lay on his side, nose pressed into the bolster covering and inhaling the faint odour of yet another scent. More subtle this time, more human. The un-mistakable odour of hair. Julia's hair. He closed his eyes and reached out across the empty bed and ran his fingers over the mattress, tracing the small indents where she had once lain. Sleep would not come, and he lay restless, his mind seething with memories and a terrible aching sense of loss, and the far more raw sense of facing life without Julia, without love.

But there was his son. And there was Macro. He tried to console himself with that, and yet he felt more alone than he had ever felt before in his life.

# CHAPTER FOUR

Cato heard the sound of laughter as he emerged from the sleeping chamber the next morning. He had barely slept. Rubbing his eyes, he stretched his shoulders before turning towards the sound that echoed down the corridor leading towards the rear of the house and the garden. He passed the three small doors of the slave quarters before reaching the open door of the kitchen. Breathing in a rich aroma of frying he realised how hungry he was and paused to look into the kitchen.

Petronella was feeding charcoal to a fire under a grill. On top was a large pan in which onions and sausages were sizzling and spitting. She straightened up, rubbing her hands on a stained apron, and caught sight of him.

'Oh, Master! You surprised me.'

'Sorry.'

'We aren't used to company in the house. Not since the mistress passed away.' She smiled sympathetically at him. 'Some breakfast, Master? The other officer ordered this, after he had finished our last cuts of pork and bread. There's heated wine too.'

'That'll do fine.'

Cato paced out of the corridor and into bright sunshine and blinked for a moment before he could take in the view. The garden at the rear of the house was not very wide, but stretched a full forty paces to the wall at the back where another street ran parallel to that on which the entrance opened. There were tall walls on either side, giving privacy from the neighbours, and on the far side of the street only tiled roofs were visible for some distance, meaning that the garden was not overlooked. He heard the laughter again and saw a covered area a short distance along the garden wall. There was a simple stone table, with cushioned eating couches on three sides. On the largest, Macro was lying on his back and holding Lucius up above his face. The child was giggling and then let out a shrill peal of laughter as Macro lowered him and blew a raspberry into his stomach.

'That's what we say to the primus pilus!'

Cato could not help laughing as he strode over to join them.

Macro looked up and grinned. 'And here's your daddy!'

He lowered the boy into his lap and then onto the floor and gave him a gentle shove. 'Go and say hello.'

Lucius hesitated, staring uncertainly at his father, sticking the middle fingers of his right hand in his mouth. Cato smiled warmly at him and hunkered down so that they were on more even terms. He held out his hands.

'Lucius, come here, my boy.'

The child did not approach but lowered his head and continued watching Cato from under his brow, as if that might hide him from sight.

Cato awkwardly shuffled forward a step and tried again. 'Come, Lucius . . . Here, I won't eat you.' He forced a smile as his son abruptly turned and hugged Macro's knee.

'Oh, come on now!' Macro frowned. 'He may scare the shit out of some hairy-arsed barbarian warrior but you're better than that, little soldier. Here.' Macro lifted him up, flipped him round and looked at Cato over the boy's shoulder. 'That there is Prefect Cato, one of the bravest men and brightest officers in the whole bloody army. You're lucky to have him as your daddy. Now say hello properly, lad.'

Lucius could not help looking up to his father and smiled shyly. ''Lo.'

Cato felt a pang of jealous hurt that Macro had taken the opportunity to introduce himself first. He should have held back and given Cato that chance. The unworthy thought was hurriedly dismissed as Cato realised his friend would never have done such a thing deliberately. It was just a shame that Cato had slept longer. Now he had some ground to make up because of it. And perhaps the scar that crossed his face made him a somewhat frightening prospect. He sat down in front of his son and slowly reached out and took Lucius in his hands. Then, inspired by Macro's example, he lifted Lucius up, pursed his lips and blew into the soft skin of the boy's stomach.

Lucius let out a shrill cry of fright and began to bawl as he waved his tiny fists and kicked his legs. Cato lowered him and looked at him in alarm. 'What did I do? Are you all right? Macro, what's wrong with him?'

Macro gave an amused click of his tongue. 'Beats me. He loved that a moment ago. You saw.'

Lucius shrieked inconsolably and tears ran down his plump cheeks as his mouth gaped to expose two tiny pearl-like teeth.

'What's all this nonsense?' demanded Petronella as she emerged from the house. She was carrying the pan of sausages and onion and hurriedly set it down before she took Lucius and hugged him close. 'What's the matter, little master? Were the great big men scaring you? Shame on them, eh? Poor lamb.'

'But I didn't do anything,' Cato protested, his hands held out innocently. 'I was just saying hello to him.'

'Soldiers. What are they like?' Petronella muttered. 'Here's your breakfast, Master. Enjoy it while I calm the boy and give him his porridge.'

'Then you can feed him out here,' Cato ordered. 'With us. He might as well start getting used to being with his father.'

'And his uncle Macro!' Macro grinned.

Cato turned to his friend and raised an eyebrow. 'Uncle Macro?'

'Why not? I'm the nearest thing he's ever going to have to an uncle. Now then, let's obey the good lady, and do some damage to these fine-smelling sausages!'

As the nurse and her charge retreated to the kitchen Macro picked up his dagger, impaled a sausage, tore off the end with his teeth and chewed heartily. 'Delicious! Tuck in, Cato.'

There was no denying his hunger so Cato slipped onto the couch next to Macro and helped himself to a platter of sausages and onions. A short time later, Petronella returned with Lucius on one arm and a steaming bowl in her other hand. She took the remaining couch with the boy settled onto her ample lap. Moments later Macro slapped his belly and belched. 'Delicious!'

Lucius' eyes widened at the sound and he pointed and laughed. 'Mac, Mac!'

Macro smiled with delight and tapped his chest. 'That's it! Uncle Macmac.'

Cato sighed. 'For the Gods' sake . . . If the men you commanded could see you now.'

'Well they can't. Even those that survived the campaign.'

There was a brief silence following the remark as both men recalled the terrible cold and gnawing hunger of the retreat from the island of Mona that had cost the lives of so many of their comrades. Then Macro coughed and reached out with his blade to impale another sausage, and saw that it was the last. He glanced at Cato and withdrew his dagger.

'It's yours.'

Cato finished his meal as he watched his son eat the porridge. Towards the end, Lucius clamped his lips shut and turned his head to one side defiantly.

Petronella tutted. 'Come now, Master Lucius. Just a few more.'

The boy turned his head away every time the spoon approached.

'Let me have a go,' said Macro, shifting from his couch. 'I seem to have a way with the lad.'

'If you wish, Master.' Petronella passed the bowl to him. Macro scooped up a spoonful and directed it towards Lucius' mouth. The latter drew his chin back and kept his mouth closed as his eyes twinkled.

'There's always one recruit who tries to defy his drill instructor,' Macro smiled. 'And if you think you'll succeed where hundreds of others haven't, then you are in for a great big fucking surprise, my little friend.'

Cato swallowed and cleared his throat loudly. 'I'll thank you to tone down the parade-ground vocabulary in front of my infant son, if you please.'

'Yes, sir.' Macro paused and then his lips gave a crafty twitch. 'Very well then, let's try something else. He made a clicking noise with his tongue against the roof of his mouth. 'Here comes the chariot, heading back to the stable. Open the gate.' He dropped his jaw and a moment later Lucius' mouth opened and in went the porridge.

Cato watched with a mixture of amusement and niggling jealousy at the easy manner between his best friend and his son, then he heard a distant rap on the door. Shortly after, he heard the bolt rattle back and a muted exchange between Amatapus and another man, then footsteps in the hall. The shuffle of the major-domo's light sandals and the harsher sound of the nailed boots of a soldier. Then Amatapus entered the garden, closely followed by a Praetorian guardsman in a white tunic, the polished leather of his sword belt gleaming like glass.

'Excuse me, Master, but this man has come from the palace to see you.'

Cato nodded. He had half expected an early summons to make his report. But not first thing in the morning. He beckoned to the guardsman who stepped round Amatapus and approached the dining area, halting two paces from Cato's couch.

'You are Quintus Licinius Cato?'

'Yes.'

'And you, sir?' The guardsman turned to Macro who was attempting to coax Lucius into taking the next spoonful of porridge. 'Lucius Cornelius Macro?'

Macro looked round at the Praetorian. 'That is Centurion Macro to you, soldier. And Prefect Cato. Stand to attention when you address us.'

The guardsman abruptly stiffened and stared straight ahead.

'Better. Now what do you want?'

'I have been sent to notify you that you are both summoned to the palace to present yourselves to Emperor Claudius and his council of advisers. You are to report to the office of the imperial freedman Narcissus at once. He will escort you to the Emperor.'

Cato and Macro exchanged a look before Cato responded. 'Narcissus?'

'Yes, sir.'

Macro's shoulders lifted in a resigned sigh. 'Here comes trouble.'

'Did he say why he wants us to report to him first?'

'No, sir. That was all I was told. That and to insist that you accompany me at once.'

'We're hardly dressed for the occasion.'

The guardsman hesitated for an instant. 'That is not covered by my orders, sir. I was just told to take you to Narcissus at once.'

Macro folded his arms. 'And if we don't decide to come until we're ready?'

The guardsman jerked a thumb over his shoulder. 'That's why I brought my squad with me, sir. Seven of the lads are waiting out in the street. It would be best if I didn't have to call them in, not in front of your wife and boy there.'

Macro glared. 'She's not my wife. She's a bloody slave.'

Petronella raised her eyes and muttered irritably. 'Thank you, Master.'

Cato rose from his couch. 'And the boy is *my* son. Understood?'

'Yes, sir . . . Sorry, sir.'

'Very well then, we'll come. Wait in the hall.'

The guardsman looked embarrassed.

'Problem?'

'I was instructed not to let you out of my sight, sir. It seems the imperial freedman is not convinced you will be willing to see him.'

'Fancy that,' said Macro. 'I wonder why on earth he might think such a thing? Being such a great friend to us over the years and all.'

Cato did not react to his comrade's sarcasm. 'We'll get our boots then. Petronella?'

'Master?'

'Send word to Senator Sempronius and let him know where we have gone. If there are any, uh, consequences, then Lucius is to be taken to the senator. He'll be safer there.'

'Yes, Master.'

'Macro, let's go and see our old friend Narcissus.'

# CHAPTER FIVE

The imperial freedman had visibly aged since the last time Cato had set eyes on him. It hardly seemed possible but he was even thinner and more gaunt and his tunic hung on him as if he was a wooden frame. The quick dark eyes had shrunk in their sockets and his hair was almost all grey and receding across his mottled scalp. He was hunched forward across his desk as his two visitors entered his office and sat down on the stools opposite without waiting to be invited.

'Make yourselves at home, why don't you?'

'It's only fair, since you abducted us from my house,' Cato replied. 'I'd ask for refreshments, if I could be sure they would be safe to eat.'

Narcissus offered a thin grin. 'It's good to have two such trusting allies back at my side. Especially at this testing time.'

'Allies?' Macro pretended to choke.

'Call it as you will, but all three of us have sworn to serve the Emperor and at least that is one thing we agree on: keeping true to our vow. Which is more than can be said for some. Especially that cold viper, Pallas.' Narcissus folded his hands together and cracked his bony knuckles. 'You two took a chance last night. Entering the city and making for your home before reporting directly to the palace.'

'I wanted to see my son,' Cato responded flatly. 'I thought that reporting to the palace could wait until this morning.'

'Your paternal devotion is admirable, Prefect Cato, but it is more politic to tend to your duty first. It's lucky for you that the optio on the gate answers to one of my men so I got to hear of your presence first. The squad I sent to fetch you were as much for your protection as your coercion.'

'And for that we should be grateful? Ordered here without a chance to wash or change?'

'What good would it do you to be a neat corpse?' Narcissus stared back coldly. 'Yes, Cato, you should be grateful. Now you have a chance to represent yourself directly to the Emperor, rather than falling to the blade of one of Pallas' agents the moment he realised you are here in Rome.'

'And why would he go to such an effort to kill us?' asked Macro. 'We've been keeping our noses clean while we were campaigning in Britannia. Surely we are of no interest to him any more?'

Narcissus could not help a brief snort of amusement. 'Firstly, it really would be no effort at all for him to have you killed. A mere word in the ear of one of his henchmen and you'd be found face down in the sewer with your throat cut. Secondly, the pair of you have rather more knowledge of what we might call the affairs of state than is good for you. At least while Claudius is still living. When he's gone then it will all be different. Old secrets will die with the Emperor and things that were dangerous to know will have lost their significance. Of course, there will still be grudges and I'm afraid that Pallas is precisely the kind of man for whom revenge is a dish that is best served cold. Cold as the grave. I strongly advise you to be on your guard, the pair of you.'

'We are, of course, touched by your solicitude,' Cato responded with a faint bow of his head. 'However, I am curious to know why you have brought us here at such an early hour and in such haste.'

'For your own good, like I said.' Narcissus gave him a long look and Cato felt a slight tremor of surprise as he recognised the pity in the imperial secretary's expression.

'What's the matter, Narcissus? What dirty work do you have in mind for us this time?'

Narcissus recoiled, as if he had been slapped. He was still for a moment before he eased himself out of his chair and turned to gaze out of the arched window that overlooked the Forum, bustling with the inhabitants of the city. 'I know that the pair of you despise me. You are by no means alone in that respect.'

Macro coughed. 'Who could possibly have imagined?'

Narcissus did not deign to react to the barbed comment and folded his bony arms as he reflected briefly before he continued. 'Despite what you may think of me, I do what I must in order to protect Rome. The empire is not perfect, but it is a force for order in a barbarous and cruel world. The people who live within its frontiers, whether they like it or not, are spared the endless cycle of conquest and savagery visited upon them by one despot after another. Rome spares them that, at least, so that they may go about their lives, raise families, grow crops, and survive without having to keep looking over their shoulders for the first sign of some savage warband determined to kill, rape and pillage. And at the same time, all that we have here in Rome depends upon the peace and prosperity of the wider empire. It is like some intricate device those Alexandrians are so keen on. A complex arrangement of components all working together. It is my job, my duty, to ensure that it all functions as smoothly as possible, and for that I must occasionally remove and replace certain pieces of the whole.'

'That's an interesting way of describing murder.'

Narcissus spared Macro a brief frown before his gaze returned to the view over the capital. 'Do you think I am insensitive to the injustices I must mete out for the greater good? I have been forced to live a life without friends, for I can trust no one. I have given my all in the service of Rome, and it has been a lonely life.'

'Your choice,' Macro pointed out. 'You did not have to devote your life to knifing people in the back.'

Narcissus arched an eyebrow. 'I knife them in the back, you knife them in the front. At the end of the day they're dead either way. The difference is you think there's some kind of moral distinction that arises from where the blade lands.'

Macro stirred as he thought about this. 'There's a world of difference between what you do and what I do. I take my chances man to man in a fair fight, whereas your kind stabs your enemy in the back, like the cowards you are.'

'There are different forms of courage and cowardice, my friend.'

'*Never* call me that again.'

Narcissus pulled a face. 'As you wish. But the point I am making is that we serve Rome according to our talents. I could never take my place beside you in battle, Macro. I wouldn't last a moment. How is that a fair fight? My body is of little use to Rome. But as for my mind, it is as potent a weapon as any number of swords. We both serve Rome as best we can, in our own way. That is our duty.'

'Duty?' Macro's lips curled into a sneer. 'A very lucrative duty as far as I can see. It's no secret that you are one of the wealthiest men in Rome. You and Pallas both. Spare me the bollocks about duty. You're in this for yourself as much as anything else. Like all those who meddle in politics. You wrap yourself up in fine words and fine sentiments, while peddling your influence, taking bribes and scheming to steal the wealth of others.' Macro jabbed his thumb at his chest and then at Cato. 'And men like us pay the price for the games you play. We pay with our blood, Narcissus.'

'He's right,' Cato added in a more measured tone. 'We've seen enough blood shed across the fields, forests and mountains of Britannia to know the truth of it. Ten years we've been fighting there, and the island is still barely more than a province in name only. And why did we invade in the first place? Just so that Claudius could have a military triumph to dangle in front of the mob. Yet there was no great victory, just one more bloody campaign after another. We only stayed the distance because it would shame the Emperor if Rome pulled out of Britannia.' Cato felt his anger building and paused to calm down. 'From what I hear, there's plenty of men in the Senate who would be happy for us to quit Britannia. And Nero himself is of similar mind. And he's first in line to succeed Claudius. Any hope of your lad taking the purple is fast fading.'

Narcissus winced. 'Britannicus is the natural son of the Emperor. Claudius may yet favour him. But it really doesn't matter who wins out. Rome will remain in Britannia. If Britannicus takes the throne then he will be obliged to honour the policy of the father who named him after the conquest of the island.'

'Some conquest,' Macro sniffed derisively.

'And if Nero takes the throne then he is surrounded by men who have made huge investments in Britannia. Pallas and Seneca alone have tens of millions of sestertii on loan to the rulers of native tribes.

I doubt they will be prepared to write off such sums in the event of the legions pulling out of the island.' Narcissus let his words sink in for a moment. 'So, we're in Britannia for the long haul . . . Not that it will concern me for much longer.'

Cato saw the haunted look in the imperial freedman's eyes. 'And why is that?'

'Because my days are numbered. While Claudius lives, I live. But when he dies, then I can expect no mercy from Pallas, or that bitch Agrippina. The first thing they will do if Nero takes the purple is indulge in a little score-settling. I will be one of the first to get a visit from the Praetorian death squads.'

'What goes round, comes round,' said Macro. 'You've sent enough men to their deaths in your time, Narcissus. Don't expect any sympathy from me.'

The freedman glared back. 'I don't ask, or expect, sympathy. The Gods know I have enough blood on my hands. And it's not just men who have been sent to their deaths on my orders, but women and children too. I considered it necessary at the time, and that's good enough for me. Now my death is going to be the price I pay for the part I played in keeping Rome safe from those who would harm her.'

Macro laughed. 'By the Gods, you are full of yourself, aren't you?'

'Think what you like about me, Macro, but at least Cato here has the intelligence to see that what I do is for the good of Rome.' Narcissus turned his watery eyes to Cato. 'Is that not so?'

Cato sat still and silent, conscious that he was being closely watched by the other men. At length Narcissus sighed and ran his bony fingers through his thinning hair. 'The question is, what will happen after I have been disposed of? There is little doubt that Pallas will fill my shoes and be the real power behind Nero. My fear is that his ultimate motives are somewhat less altruistic than mine, and the interests of Rome will suffer as a consequence. I readily admit that Nero has the makings of a decent ruler. He is intelligent, charming and has the common touch. But he is also vain and too willing to accept flattery at face value. Pallas will be able to control him like a puppet, or use his hold over Agrippina to pull the strings for him.' Narcissus stared out of his window again, his face etched with worry. 'I fear for Rome . . .'

Then he turned away abruptly and resumed his place behind the desk. 'Which is why it is important that I do what I can to protect you two.'

'Us?' Macro chuckled. 'Don't worry about us. We can look after ourselves. We've survived more danger than most.'

'Undoubtedly. But it is the danger you don't see that will kill you. Look here, Macro, Cato, I know you have both served Rome well, and me unwillingly. I know that you understand what your duty is. There are many other good men like you. Good men are going to be needed more than ever in the days to come. That is why it is important that you survive when they come for me, and all those closely associated with me. That's the reason I saw to it that you were posted to Britannia. Now you are back here, in this nest of vipers, and you are in danger again. So listen to what I have to say.'

He leaned forward across the desk and lowered his voice, as if there was some danger they might be overheard. Force of habit in the world in which the imperial secretary lived, Cato reasoned.

'I have persuaded the Emperor to decorate you both for your services in Britannia. Specifically for the part you played in the defeat and capture of Caratacus. We are shortly due to have an audience with the Emperor, where you will give an account of the recent campaign and conditions in the new province. I would suggest that you don't paint too bleak a picture. Say that conditions are hard, but the legions are meeting the challenges. The outcome is never in doubt – that kind of thing. Then play up your role in crushing Caratacus. After that, Claudius will announce your rewards and assign you a prominent place in the public celebration of our victory over the enemy. Rome loves its heroes and that should provide you with one line of defence against Pallas. But there's something more you need to do.'

Cato felt a familiar weariness at the imperial secretary's words as they heralded the coercion of Macro and himself into yet another of Narcissus' schemes.

'As soon as the celebrations are over, it would be wise of you to deny any connection to me.'

Macro nodded. 'Done!'

Cato shot his friend a frown and then turned back to Narcissus. 'Why?'

'It's obvious. You need to save your skins. It has to be clear that you no longer serve my needs. That relations are hostile between us and that you would be happy to see an end to me and my scheming. Pallas will need to think that you have turned your backs on me. Better still, if he offers you his patronage, then take it. Work with him. Earn his confidence and trust and you will be better placed to learn his weaknesses and be ready to do him down when the time comes for him to fall from grace. And it will come for him, as it has come for me. But hopefully before he does too much damage to Rome,' Narcissus concluded. He scrutinised them closely. 'But you can only do that if you survive. Do you understand?'

Cato nodded, while Macro sighed wearily.

'Do you have a problem with living, Centurion?'

'No. I like life well enough. It's all this cloak and dagger bollocks that I have a problem with. I always have.'

'Which is precisely why you would do well to hide your feelings and let Prefect Cato make the decisions. You are a brave man, with an admirable capacity for dishing out violence. But I'd advise you to know, and accept, your limits.'

They were interrupted by the notes of a trumpet sounding the hour and Narcissus sat erect and adopted a more formal tone. 'It's time for us to attend the Emperor's morning council. There's some business about an uprising in Hispania that needs attention first, but after that you will have the chance to report on the campaign in Britannia. Stick to the line I suggested, and everything will be fine. We need to go soon. But first, I need a word with Cato. Alone.'

Cato's brow creased. 'Alone?'

'Yes.'

'I will not have anything hidden from Macro. What is it?'

'Something of a personal nature. It does not concern Macro. Trust me.'

Cato shook his head. 'Trust is not a commodity we have had reason to trade in as far as you go.'

'Nevertheless, I think it would be best if what I have to say is for your ears only.'

Macro slapped his hand on his thigh. 'No skin off my nose, lad. Frankly I've heard all I want to hear from him. I'll wait outside.'

Before Cato could respond, Macro rose to his feet and strode towards the door. When he had shut it behind him, Cato stared back at the imperial secretary, hurt on his friend's behalf. 'What is it? What can be so personal that my best friend cannot hear of it?'

Narcissus closed his eyes for a moment. 'It concerns your wife.'

'Julia?' Cato felt his heart lurch. 'What about her?'

Narcissus made a sympathetic expression and reached to touch the younger man's shoulder but hesitated a moment and withdrew his hand. 'There's no painless way to say what I need to, but please trust that what I am about to tell you is for your own good.'

Cato felt a surge of anger. 'Just spit it out and be done with it. What about my wife?'

Narcissus retreated to his desk and sat down behind it, so that there would at least be some kind of obstacle between him and Cato. 'In the days to come you will start to discover something of your wife's . . . activities during your absence. I know that you and she were very close and that you were only married for the briefest of periods before you were ordered to take up your command in Britannia. I am certain that she loved you until the end. Her death was a tragedy of course, and—'

Cato leaned forward, his eyes wide and his expression intense. 'What are you saying about Julia?'

'She is – was – human. All of us have our needs, Cato. I am sure that you don't need me to draw you a picture. You had gone off to war, and there was a good chance that you would be away for many years, possibly never to return. Julia was flesh and blood. No doubt she felt alone from time to time. Who knows? But can you blame her for seeking solace in someone else's arms?'

The words struck Cato like a hammer blow to his heart and mind, and a wave of nausea rushed up from the very pit of his stomach.

'No . . . It's a lie.'

'I know that's what you want to believe. I wish that it wasn't true, with all my heart.'

'You haven't got a heart, you bloody bastard! I don't believe you.' Cato slapped his hands down on the desk and Narcissus recoiled instinctively, but kept a composed expression.

'I didn't expect you to believe me. But nonetheless it is true.'

'No.'

Narcissus began to speak, then eased himself back into his chair and folded his hands patiently. Cato's mind was in turmoil, refusing to believe, but needing to hear more, to understand.

'How do you know this?' Cato demanded. 'How?'

'It is my business to know. I had her watched.'

Cato shook his head. 'How could she possibly have been of any interest to you? She was never a threat to anyone. So why spy on her?'

'I wasn't spying on her. It was her father I had under observation. Senator Sempronius may not be a very wealthy man, but he has influence in the Senate. He is the kind of man others listen to, and therefore precisely the kind of man I would be a fool to ignore.'

'What has that got to do with my wife?'

'Nothing. Except that she was seen leaving the senator's house in the company of another man who is of interest to me. They were followed back to the house on the Quirinal where the man was seen to enter the house and emerge the following morning.'

Cato flinched away from the only conclusion he could draw from the freedman's account. He felt anger twisted with despair and hate constrict his chest and his breath came in shallow gasps. How could she? How could this be true? How could she do this to him? How could she betray him? He placed a palm against his forehead and closed his eyes to try and shut it out. But there, in his mind's eye, he saw Julia and this stranger entering the same hall he had entered for the first time the previous night. He imagined them entering the bedchamber. Julia turning to the man, then embracing him, kissing him and then . . . He thrust the image from his mind and snapped his eyes open.

'Who is he?'

'It doesn't concern you, Cato.'

'Doesn't concern me? A man fucks my wife and you say it doesn't concern me? I say it does. Now tell me his name, before I have to make you cough it up, you oily little bastard.'

Cato made to move round the table and Narcissus held out his hand. 'Stop! If I told you his name then you'd only try something foolish. Even if you were able to get close enough to strike at him, then the retribution would not only fall on you, but on your son and associates too. Lucius, Macro and Senator Sempronius. Would you have their blood on your hands as well, Cato?'

'It's not true,' he muttered. 'It's a lie. All of it.'

'Believe me, I wish it was not so, Cato. It is not an easy thing for a man to hear.'

Cato looked up with a bleak expression. 'Then why tell me?'

'You would have discovered the truth sooner or later. Better you hear it all from me than from scraps you pick up from others. I would imagine that you would rather not have men laugh at you behind your back.'

Cato had to bite back on his anger even as he clenched his teeth. He wanted to lash out, strike at something, but he knew it would serve no purpose. It would not take away the hurt and the sudden shocking stab of hatred he felt for Julia.

'Cato,' said Narcissus, 'you must pull yourself together. You have an audience with the Emperor soon. You must be composed, no matter what has happened. Do you understand? You must put this out of your mind. For your sake, and Macro's too. We must go now.' Narcissus rose from behind the desk and made for the door.

Cato stood still, dazed by what he had heard. What remained of his world after he had heard of Julia's death was now reduced to ruin. Yet he knew that he must go on. For the sake of his son and his best friend, whatever had happened. He could think about Julia later, when he was on his own.

'Ready?' Narcissus cocked an eyebrow, but did not wait for a reply as he lifted the latch and opened the door. Macro was leaning against the wall of the corridor a short distance away and he now strode towards them with a rueful grin.

'Time to go and face the Emperor then?'

Narcissus nodded.

The centurion turned to Cato. 'Ready for this, sir?'

Cato took a deep breath, conscious that he was being scrutinised by the others, and nodded. 'Ready as I'll ever be.'

# CHAPTER SIX

The high-ceilinged audience chamber was crowded by the time they were searched by one of the German mercenaries who served as the Emperor's bodyguard. Like many of his kind, the mercenary was tall and broad and wore his hair and beard long. His command of Latin was rudimentary and heavily accented and Macro instantly took a dislike to him.

'Look, mate, I've sent more than a few of you bastards into the afterlife. So keep your bloody paws to yourself, eh?'

'Ha,' the German grunted. 'And I kill many Romans before I do this.'

'Really? Fancy trying your hand against me, once you get off duty?'

'Macro,' Cato intervened softly. 'Enough.'

They followed Narcissus down the side of the chamber, behind the ranks of senators, officials and petitioners, and took their place a short distance from the dais where Emperor Claudius presided from the comfort of his purple-cushioned throne. Like Narcissus, the Emperor had aged considerably since the last time Cato had seen him, and sat head stooped forward and cocked slightly as he struggled to hear what was being said. On either side of him, in smaller chairs, sat the Empress, Agrippina, her son, Nero, and the younger Britannicus. Behind them stood Pallas and several other imperial freedmen, some making notes on waxed slates as they made a record of the event. Four more German mercenaries stood at ease on each corner of the dais, hands resting on the pommels of their long swords as they scrutinised those in the chamber, watching for any sign of danger.

There was an open space in front of the imperial party and a young tribune was addressing the Emperor. He was clearly nervous and Cato saw the gleam of sweat on his brow, beneath the neatly oiled ringlets of his fringe. 'His excellency, the Governor of Hispania Terraconensis, instructed me to assure you that the uprising is being contained and that the rebel leader, Iskerbeles, and his followers will be caught and crushed before the year is out. While he has adequate forces at Asturica Augusta to contain the problem he requests reinforcements to ensure the earliest resolution of the situation.'

Claudius nodded vacantly as Pallas took a step forward to respond to the tribune. 'How many men does the governor request?'

The tribune took a sharp breath and tried to reply calmly. 'He says an extra legion should suffice . . . If you could make the Third Legion available.'

There was a brief muttering from the crowd before Claudius beckoned to Pallas and they conducted a short exchange as the muttering died away, save for the distant hubbub from the Forum that carried through the windows set close to the ceiling. Pallas stood up and turned his attention to the tribune.

'An entire legion, you say?'

'Yes.'

'To put down a handful of villagers?'

The tribune's expression flickered for an instant. 'The rebels are ranging over a wide area of difficult terrain. We cannot guard every town, every villa and every mine and at the same time send forces out to corner them and bring them to battle. That is why the governor needs reinforcements. He is confident that with enough men he can bring the uprising to an end.'

Pallas sneered. 'Given enough men, I should think anything is possible, Tribune.'

The Emperor stirred, as if from a nap, and blinked. 'Can't we give him the l–legion, if he needs it, P–P–Pallas?'

The freedman bent to his master's ear. 'Sire, the Third Legion is needed elsewhere in Spain. If we send it to Asturica Augusta then we will have to thin out the garrisons across the rest of Hispania. It's too much of a risk.'

'Oh . . .' Claudius nodded vaguely. 'Very well, I s–suppose.'

Cato saw a figure emerge from the crowd, corpulent with fleshy jowls and a fringe of grey hair around his bald head. The man bowed deeply towards the Emperor before he spoke.

'Sire, if I may interject a few words?'

Claudius flipped his hand in assent. 'As you will, Senator Lucius Annaeus S–S–Seneca.'

Seneca turned his dark eyes towards Pallas. 'I think we should heed the advice of the governor of the province. After all, he is there, dealing with the threat, while we are far away and have no knowledge of the precise circumstances of the situation. If he deems it necessary to request the assistance of the Third Legion, then we should respect his judgement.'

Pallas took a step forward to ensure that all would have an unobstructed view of him and hear his words. 'Your point of view would have something to do with the fact that you have extensive landholdings in the region, not to mention shares in many of the silver mines, I take it.'

'That is true, freedman,' Seneca replied, lacing the final word with contempt. 'But then so do many other senators, and even the Emperor himself. It is for the sake of his interests that I intervene on the side of the governor in this matter. If we lose control of the mines then the rebels will have access to enough silver to recruit many more tribes to their cause. And let us not forget, it is the same silver that pays the legionaries and auxiliaries who garrison Hispania. I need not remind you, nor his imperial majesty, that the loyalty of our brave legions is bought, not freely given. We only have to look back a few years to Legate Scribonianus' attempt to overthrow the Emperor to see the proof of that. It was only because his legions were bribed from under him that his coup failed. I do not think we can afford to be too sanguine about the governor's chances of crushing the uprising with the limited troops he has presently at his disposal.' Seneca paused to let his words sink in. Then he took a half step towards the dais and lowered his voice and continued in a more pleading tone. 'Sire, I beseech you, do not take any risks. Send the Third Legion in to decide the issue. The sooner order is restored, the sooner the flow of silver can resume.'

Cato saw the indecision in Claudius' expression and before the Emperor could respond, Pallas intervened once again.

'Your advice is noted, Senator. But I repeat: there is a real danger that we are too thinly spread across Hispania to risk concentrating our forces to suppress the uprising.'

'Then we need to find reinforcements from elsewhere,' Seneca persisted.

'And where, precisely, do we find these men?' Pallas demanded. 'The campaign in Britannia has drained our reserves from Gaul and the Rhenus frontier. We can't just make soldiers.'

'Then draw them from further afield.'

'The nearest available legions are stationed along the Danuvius. It would take several months to transfer them to Hispania.' Pallas folded his arms. 'The governor will have to make do with the men that he has. Is that not so, sire?' Pallas deferred to the Emperor.

But Seneca was not done yet. 'There are other forces readily available, sire. There are nearly ten thousand men in the Praetorian Guard cohorts who have little to keep themselves occupied at present. And I am given to understand that two auxiliary cohorts landed at Ostia a few days ago, en route to join the army in Britannia. There are more than enough men readily available to send to the aid of the hard-pressed Governor of Hispania Terraconensis. All it would take is a word from you, sire . . .'

'I think that the good senator, thanks to the paucity of his military experience, fails to grasp the wider strategic situation,' Pallas countered. 'The auxiliary cohorts are desperately needed in Britannia. We cannot afford to send them to Hispania Terraconensis.'

Cato could not help a smile, despite his heavy heart. Seneca was one of the many of his rank who had chosen not to serve in the army early on in their senatorial careers. The imperial freedman had struck a neat point, judging from the amused expressions of many in the audience chamber. There would be some who would feel a measure of vindication for their contempt for the dandified politician.

Seneca affected to ignore the slight as he continued. 'The re-direction of the cohorts would not amount to more than a brief diversion from their transfer to Britannia. And it is not as if Rome could not afford to spare the services of several Praetorian cohorts. Besides, it would be a fine opportunity to prove themselves in action again and demonstrate that they serve more than a ceremonial purpose. Sire, I can see no good reason not to send the forces I speak of to Hispania to put an end to this fellow Iskerbeles and his followers. A swift victory and some ruthless punitive measures will serve as a good lesson to any others who might contemplate defying the will of Rome. And not just the will of Rome, sire. They present a challenge to your authority. It is you they are defying . . . It is your name they mock by their deeds. I can only imagine how that might wound your pride and inspire you to decisive action.'

It was taking a risk to address the Emperor so personally, Cato realised, and he turned his attention to Claudius and saw at once that the words had struck home. The old man stiffened his back, straightened up and assumed as imperious a posture as his age and spindly physique permitted. At his side, Pallas shot a withering glance at Seneca, but before he could argue back the Emperor coughed loudly and cleared his throat.

'These upstarts in H–Hi–Hispania will be dealt with. How dare they de–defy me? Seneca is right. We have the men for the job. It's about t–time the Praetorians earned the gifts I have lavished on them. We'll send eight cohorts to Hispania. And the two c–c–cohorts at Ostia. See that their orders are drafted at once, P–Pallas.'

The freedman glanced towards the empress imploringly but she gave the slightest shake of the head and Pallas bit back on his protest and bowed his head. 'As your imperial majesty commands.'

Seneca made no effort to stifle his satisfied expression, while beside him the tribune sighed with relief.

'That leaves the question of who should c–command this force,' Claudius continued, reaching a hand up to his chin to stroke it contemplatively as he gazed round the faces of those assembled before him. At once, Pallas' expression was calculating and he interposed himself between Claudius and Seneca.

'Might I suggest Senator Vitellius, sire? He has experience of smaller independent commands such as this.'

Macro let out a soft hiss, then muttered, 'That lard arse is the last one I'd trust to give the command to.'

Cato nodded and nudged Narcissus. 'Why Vitellius? What is Pallas playing at?'

'Vitellius is part of the Nero faction,' Narcissus whispered. 'I imagine that it would be a useful thing to have Vitellius win over the loyalty of a large section of the Praetorian Guard when the time comes to see who succeeds Claudius.'

The Emperor reflected a moment and nodded. 'Is Vitellius in attendance this m–morning?'

Cato scanned the chamber and then saw movement as several men stood aside and a figure emerged from those standing opposite the dais. A tall, well-built man with neatly oiled dark hair. He strode up to the side of Seneca and bowed.

'Fuck me,' said Macro. 'He's in better shape than I've ever seen him.'

Cato nodded. It was true. They had served with Vitellius before and the aristocrat's fondness for fine food and wine had made him as corpulent as he was corrupt. He was worse than corrupt, as Cato had discovered. The man had insatiable ambition and cared little for those he manipulated to achieve his ends. As Macro had observed, Vitellius had worked to improve his physique and had lost much weight and toned his body so that he now cut quite a commanding figure, Cato conceded.

Claudius squinted at him. 'Senator Vitellius, do you accept the command?'

Vitellius smiled easily. 'It would be an honour, sire. As would any opportunity to serve you.'

Macro snorted softly. 'Bloody arse-licker.'

'Might I prevail upon you, sire?' Vitellius continued. 'If I am to carry out this mission effectively, then I ask that I may select the officers to serve under me.'

'Of course. Then you may have eight cohorts of my P–P–Praetorians, and the pick of the officers to accompany you on this mission. I am certain you will do great honour to me, Rome and your family name.'

Vitellius bowed graciously.

'You will also have the t–t–two cohorts in camp outside Ostia. They will be sent on to join the army in B–Br–Br–Britannia the moment this rascal, Iskerbeles, is put down.'

'Yes, sire.'

Claudius raised a trembling hand and lightly clicked his fingers. 'Britannia . . . That brings us on to the next m–matter. Narcissus!'

The imperial secretary gestured to Cato and Macro to accompany him and eased his way through those ahead of him to emerge into the open space in front of the dais. Vitellius glanced in their direction and Cato saw his eyebrows rise in surprise before he smiled coolly at them.

'Centurions Cato and Macro, it has been a while. You've done well for yourself, Cato. I hear you are a prefect these days.'

Cato nodded in acknowledgement. 'And you remain what you always were, sir.'

He turned away as he and Macro joined Narcissus in bowing to the Emperor. Claudius gestured towards the two officers. 'These are the men?'

'Yes, sire. May I present Prefect Quintus Licinius Cato and Centurion Lucius Cornelius Macro, just arrived from the campaign in Britannia.'

'Good, good!' Claudius' brow creased. 'We have met before, haven't we?'

'Yes, sire,' Narcissus replied before either of the officers could speak. 'They have performed valuable services for you in the past. But most recently, these were the two heroes who were responsible for the capture of Caratacus, the leader of the tribes who opposed us in Britannia.'

Cato was conscious of the extra scrutiny accorded them as all eyes in the audience chamber fixed on them where they stood to attention in front of the Emperor. Claudius beamed at them and clapped his hands together.

'A fine ef–effort! Narcissus read me the first account of his capture in the heat of battle! Is it true that the p–pair of you had to f–f–fight your way through his bodyguards before he was taken?'

Cato paused and forced himself to think quickly. Now was not the time to go into any more detail than was necessary to accept the accolade and get this over with as soon as possible. He still desperately needed to be alone to consider all that Narcissus had told him about Julia. Besides, too much detail might mean admitting that Caratacus had escaped from them after the battle and had to be run to ground in the land of the Brigantes. He took a breath.

'It was a hard fight, sire. As hard as any battle Centurion Macro and I have ever fought. The enemy had chosen to defend a steep hill behind a river. Heavy rain meant we had to struggle against the mud as well as the native warriors and for a while the struggle hung in the balance, until the centurion and I led our men in a flank attack. We caught them unawares, and went in hard and fast and they broke. That's when we captured Caratacus, sire. Him, and most of his family.'

'And now, they are languishing in ch–cha–chains, beneath our very feet!' Claudius let out a shrill laugh and, as Pallas followed suit, others joined in sycophantically until the Emperor stopped in order to continue addressing the two officers. 'And in two days' time they will be led through R–Rome for all to see, before they are put to death on the steps of the T–T–Temple of Jupiter, Best and Greatest. And you, my dear Prefect, and you, Cen–Cen–Centurion, will be rewarded by leading the guard of honour in the pr–procession.'

Cato bowed his head in a display of deference.

'You have earned our gratitude, gentlemen. As long as Rome has soldiers like you, our frontiers are safe, our enemies will f–f–fear us and the Gods will surely favour us.' Claudius rose awkwardly and raised his hand in salute. 'All hail Prefect Cato and Centurion M–Macro!'

The audience repeated the Emperor's words and cheered. The din filled the chamber and echoed off its high walls. Macro could not help grinning in delight at the acclaim. But Cato's expression crumpled as the moment when he should have been most happy, most proud of himself, was soured by the loss of his wife, and the poison of her betrayal of his trust. The chamber, the noise and the attention of everyone was suddenly stifling and he wanted to escape. But there was no escape from the cheering and stamping of feet. Not until the Emperor raised his hands to command silence. As the sound faded Claudius made to speak, then winced and clutched a hand to his stomach. He grimaced in agony and slumped back onto his throne as Narcissus hurried up the steps of the dais and beckoned to the body slaves standing behind.

'His imperial majesty is tired. Take him back to his quarters.'

The cheers of a moment before were replaced by anxious muttering and Cato saw Agrippina sitting motionless in her chair, not even stirring to come to the aide of her ailing husband. Beside her, her son looked on, and the corners of his mouth lifted in a slight smile of satisfaction before he became aware of his surroundings and tried to look concerned. As the slaves lifted the Emperor from his throne and carried him carefully towards a small door at the back of the chamber, Narcissus and Pallas exchanged a few words before Pallas nodded and strode to the front of the dais to address the audience.

'The session has concluded. Any petitions are to be lodged with my clerks. Thank you . . . Thank you.' He nodded to the German mercenaries at the rear of the audience chamber and they opened the doors leading out onto the wide corridor beyond. The audience began to filter out, then Vitellius turned towards Narcissus and his companions.

'That worked out well for all concerned. You're war heroes and I'm about to become one.'

Macro glowered. 'That anyone should live to see the day.'

Vitellius chuckled. 'You've not changed then, Centurion. Caustic to the last. But, I'm forgetting myself. My dear Cato . . .' He faced the prefect and steered him a short distance away from Macro as he affected a sorrowful expression. 'I wish to offer my condolences on your sad loss. I know it was some months ago, but having returned home for the first time I am sure that your grief is very raw. Your wife was a fine woman. Very intelligent, charming and quite beautiful. It is a sad loss for all those who knew her.'

There was an added emphasis to the last words and Cato felt his anger rise at once. 'What are you saying?'

Narcissus hurried across, took his arm and tried to steer him away from Vitellius. 'Come, Cato. This is not the time or place.'

Cato shook his hand off and squared up to Vitellius. 'What are you saying about Julia?'

'With you away, and given how attractive she was, it is only understandable that some men might want to take the opportunity to win her affections. I imagine it was all quite harmless . . . in most cases. After all, she was an honourable woman.'

'He's goading you,' said Narcissus. 'Let's go. We can deal with this later.'

'No. We can deal with it now,' Cato replied fiercely. He stepped up to Vitellius, face to face. 'Say it. I dare you, you sleazy, arrogant bastard. Say it.'

'Say what? That your wife was attractive? That she had a certain following amongst the men in Rome?'

Cato raised his fist, but before he could strike, Narcissus grabbed his wrist.

'Not in here, Cato. Not in front of witnesses. That's what he wants. You attack him here, in the palace, and you're as good as banished. From Rome. Maybe sent to the farthest corner of the empire. You're no good to anyone there. And far from your son. So get control of yourself, Cato. Do it now!'

His blood was pounding in his ears, and hate and anger tore at his heart and for a moment Cato was consumed with a thoughtless urge to destroy Vitellius. To tear at him with his bare hands. To tear him apart. There was no self-control. No control at all. And that was what brought him back from the edge of the abyss. The horror of the prospect of an appetite and a capability within him that was as dangerous and inchoate as a rabid animal. He breathed deeply, his chest heaving, as he forced his feelings under control, made himself loosen his fists and let them drop at his sides. Cato shut his eyes and bowed his head.

'All right . . . I'm all right.'

# CHAPTER SEVEN

After they returned to the house on the Quirinal Cato explained to Macro that he was feeling tired and needed a rest. He took a deep breath and entered the sleeping chamber. It was shadowy and felt gloomy, so he opened the shuttered window that overlooked the atrium. A small bird had just alighted on the edge of the shallow pool that caught the rain falling from the roof tiles. Cato watched as it jumped in with a tiny flash of spray and began to clean itself with flicks of the head and wings. The bird's obvious delight and obliviousness to the burdens of the world moved him unbearably and he had to turn away quickly. Before him he saw the bed. Last night he had slept there and taken some comfort from feeling closer to his wife. Now, as he looked, he felt the first ripple of anger at the scene of his betrayal. That bed had been shared by Julia and her lover. It felt sullied now.

The dull gleam of the amulet he had seen the night before caught his eye and he felt a slight twist in his guts. He picked it up and examined it closely. The workmanship was fine and an intricate pattern of vine leaves wound their way around it. Was this a present for him after all? he wondered bitterly. Or had it been left here by Julia's lover? Then he noticed two letters etched in amongst the leaf design, a C overlapped by a J. His heart sank into the very pit of his stomach. He threw the amulet down and it tumbled under the bed.

Bending down, he looked underneath and saw the amulet lying beside a small box tucked away where it would not easily be seen by a casual visitor to the room. Getting down onto his belly Cato stretched out an arm and managed to get a finger grip on the catch.

He pulled the box out and sat cross-legged on the tiled floor as he eased open the catch and tilted the lid back.

Inside was a bundle of flattened papyrus scrolls, weighted down by a portrait of a fair-haired man painted on a thin piece of wood. Cato winced. He swallowed and cleared his throat harshly. He picked the portrait up and saw the fine features of a man roughly the same age as himself. The eyes were brown and a slight knowing smile played on his lips. Unlike Cato's face, this one was completely unscarred and smoothly featured. Handsome . . . The thought struck at him as he imagined Julia looking at the same image with affection, and lust. Rage coursed through his veins and he shoved the image to the bottom of the box, face down, and took out the scrolls.

It was instantly clear what they were. Love letters, all written in the same hand and signed 'Cristus', sometimes with the shortened form, 'Cris'. Cato read through them steadily, with a growing sense of agony and fury. They told of a passionate love affair that had grown across the seasons, of the gifts that Julia had showered on her lover, of the exquisite physical pleasure they had shared and then, most painful of all, how they might remove the inconvenient obstacle to their happiness presented by Julia's husband. It was possible, Cristus hoped, that he might do the decent thing and die while away on campaign . . . Failing that, he must be confronted on his return from Britannia. Julia must tell her husband as soon as possible and demand a divorce.

At length, Cato finished reading and replaced the letters in the box and closed the lid, pressing the catch firmly into place.

'Why have you done this to me? Why, Julia? I've done nothing wrong . . . Nothing to deserve this.'

At length he climbed onto the bed and curled up in a ball as he drowned in a dark tide of misery. He lay still, eyes shut but unsleeping, and time crept past like a cat careful not to wake its master. Then, he heard a sharp rapping from the front door. A pause and then it came again. And again. At last he heard the footsteps of Amatapus as he unhurriedly made his way to answer the brusque impatience of the visitor at the door. Cato heard the rattle of the bolt and the scrape of the latch and the muffled swell of the noise from the street, before a sharp exchange of voices. They grew louder as Amatapus and the caller entered the atrium.

'I can assure you that the master is not here, sir,' said Amatapus. 'Now leave, before I send for the vigiles.'

'Go ahead. Send for 'em,' a voice countered. 'I'd be happy to put this matter in front of the authorities. Let's see what the city magistrates have to say about it, eh?'

'Sir, I respectfully ask that you go,' Amatapus responded patiently. 'Leave me a message to convey to the master and I am sure he will respond as soon as he can.'

'Bollocks. I'm staying put until the prefect returns.'

'You can't, sir.'

'No? What are you going to do about it then?'

Cato sighed and eased himself off the bed and onto his feet. Opening the door to the sleeping chamber, he emerged into the atrium and saw a stocky man with a shaved head facing Amatapus as the latter implored him to leave. The visitor was wearing an ochre tunic and a thick gold chain hung around his thick neck. His arms were like hams as he folded them across his barrel chest, and short sturdy legs showed beneath the hem of his tunic. Army boots completed his threatening appearance. Cato frowned as he approached them.

'Who in Hades are you, and what do you mean by coming into my home uninvited?'

The visitor turned abruptly and scrutinised Cato swiftly. 'You're Quintus Licinius Cato?'

'Prefect Quintus Licinius Cato, yes.'

The man shrugged. 'We're not in the army here, are we? So we'll dispense with that bullshit for a start.'

Cato stopped a sword's length away and eyed the man coldly. 'Very well. But you're ex-army. I can tell that easily enough. Not old enough to have served out your enlistment, and clearly not discharged as unfit. I'd say you were an optio, or maybe even a centurion.'

The man's lips pursed for an instant, then he nodded. 'Tenth Legion. I made centurion.'

'Not for long I'll warrant. I'd wager that you were given a dishonourable discharge.'

The pride faded from the man's face and he glared at Cato.

'So, I'll have your name, soldier,' Cato demanded. 'Right now.'

'All right. The name's Marcus Tortius Taurus.'

'And what can I do for you, Taurus?'

'You can pay what's owed to me, is what you can do.'

Cato frowned. 'Owed to you? I don't even know you. What's this about?'

Taurus reached into his side-bag and brought out a bound set of waxed slates. He flipped it open and read out loud. 'Outstanding debt on the account of Prefect Quintus Licinius Cato, eighty-five thousand, nine hundred and five denarii, not including interest due on the open month.'

Cato's eyes widened. 'You are mistaken. I haven't borrowed any money from you. I don't even know you.'

'The money was borrowed by your late wife, sir. She took out the loans in your name, against the value of your estate.'

'Julia? I don't believe it.'

'I have the complete record of accounts at my office in the Forum. All signed by her and sealed with her ring. I have summaries in these tablets, if you want to see them. But I can assure you, it is all verifiable, and – more importantly – legally binding.'

Cato held out his hand. 'Let me see.'

Taurus hesitated and then stepped closer, holding the tablets up for Cato to see, but not letting them out of his hands. Cato read down the long columns of figures and dates with a sinking feeling. Just what had Julia been up to in his absence? What kind of life had she been living? He knew some of the answer already, but surely, she could not have spent such a fortune on high living? It was unthinkable. Then his gaze was arrested by a particularly large figure towards the end of the listing. Thirty thousand denarii.

'What's this?'

Taurus glanced at the tablets. 'That was for a small villa she wanted. Just outside Ostia. I know the place. Small, but right on the sea.'

'She bought another house?' Cato felt bewildered. 'She never said anything about that.'

'I should think not, sir,' Taurus shrugged. 'Given that I heard she made a gift of it to someone else.'

'A gift?' Cato felt his anger stirring anew. 'A gift to whom?'

'That would be Tribune Cristus, sir. No secret that. He was bragging about it round the Forum soon as the papers were signed. But that don't change nothing, as far as you are concerned. Your wife borrowed money from me, against the value of this place. She never got the chance to repay the debt, may she rest in peace, and the interest has been building up in your absence. All quite legal. So, I've come to collect.'

Cato shook his head. 'But I don't have it. I don't have a fraction of it. Nearly all my pay was signed over to my wife in my absence.'

'I can't help that, sir. That was between you and your wife. She signed for the loan in your name and thus the debt is yours. So, I'd like to know how you intend to repay me, and right now would do nicely, if you please.'

The demand hit Cato like a blow. 'How the fuck can I repay that amount? I can't just make money. This is preposterous.' He paused and sniffed. 'This has to be a mistake, or a trick. There's no way Julia could have run up such a debt.'

'That's the effect of compound interest, Prefect. And the profligate tastes of your former wife, no doubt.'

Cato felt an urge to hit him in the face there and then, but for the fact that it would serve no useful purpose. All the same, he wanted him gone.

'I have your name,' he said calmly. 'I will look into this matter as soon as it is convenient and, if what you say is true, then I will come to see you to negotiate a solution.'

'Negotiate?' Taurus laughed. 'The only thing you'll be negotiating, my friend, is whether you settle up in cash, or give me this house instead.'

'Get out,' Cato ordered. 'Get out now. While you still can, you money-grabbing piece of shit.'

His expression must have been intent indeed, as Cato saw the first glint of fear in the man's eyes and Taurus backed off a step. 'Very well then, Prefect. If that's how it is. I'll leave the matter with you. If I do not see you at my offices, or hear from you, within the next three days, then I will place the matter before the court. War hero or no, the magistrate of the debtors' court takes a very dim view of those who default on their debts.'

'OUT!' Cato thrust his hand towards the front door.

'As you wish, Prefect. Just don't forget: three days. That's all you have.'

Taurus turned and strode away down the corridor leading to the front door, with Amatapus struggling to keep up with him. The money lender pulled the door open and stepped out into the street and was gone, leaving the door ajar for Amatapus to deal with. Cato slumped back against the wall beside the open window of the bedchamber and tilted his head back.

'Oh, Julia . . . What have you done to me? What have you done to poor Lucius?'

# CHAPTER EIGHT

Two days later, on the morning of the triumph, Cato rose just before dawn. He ate a quick breakfast of cold pork and bread, washed down with watered wine, before taking up his cloak and waking Amatapus to lock the door after him. As they passed through the atrium the sounds of Macro's snoring rumbled in the still air. Cato had considered taking Macro with him on his errand but had decided that he would prefer to have the time it took to walk across the city to the Mamertine prison to himself in order to think about his circumstances.

The first hint of the coming dawn provided just enough light to see his way down the street outside the house. Despite the law forbidding the carrying of swords within the walls of Rome, Cato had strapped on his scabbard and the weight of the sword beneath his cloak was comforting. Especially given the violent nature of some districts of the capital, where small street gangs lurked in dark alleys waiting to pounce on lone passers-by or those revellers too drunk to defend themselves. There were many people already abroad: traders hurriedly driving small carts of goods to their shops before the daytime restriction on wheeled traffic came into force, urine porters laden down by the yokes from which dangled foul-smelling pots – their sloshing contents on the way to the fullers where the laundry of the more affluent inhabitants of Rome was cleaned and pressed. And those with families eager to get a good vantage point from which to enjoy the imperial procession, parents laden down with food and drink driving their yawning children along the streets.

Cato kept his wits about him, watching for any signs of danger, warily observing any men he saw lingering at the entrances to narrow alleys. He kept to the middle of the streets as he headed down to the Forum and kept a hand close to the handle of his sword. At the same time, his mind was still deeply troubled by the debt that Julia had bequeathed him. He had not told Macro the details yet. He could be told in good time, when Cato himself had recovered enough from the shock to cope with a degree of equanimity. But he had spoken with his father-in-law. Senator Sempronius had been embarrassed at first, not quite sure how much Cato had discovered about what his wife had been up to in his absence. While he sympathised with Cato's plight he claimed not to have sufficient funds available to help him with the debt, but did offer to take Lucius into his home and bring him up there once Cato was given a new command.

All the same, the prospect of losing the house Cato had only just come home to weighed heavily on his heart. Thanks to Julia he would have only the meagre savings he had brought back with him from Britannia. With any luck he might expect some kind of gift from the Emperor after the triumph was over, but after that he would have to build his fortune again if he was to have a comfortable retirement when he left the army, and if he was to leave his son a decent inheritance. Lucius would have the benefit of Cato's elevation to equestrian rank and with the help of Julia's father he might be fortunate enough to enter the Senate one day. The prospect filled Cato with pride. His own father had been a freedman and the rise from that humble rank to the floor of the Senate of Rome in three generations was a notable achievement.

He entered the Forum where gangs of slaves were clearing the streets of the ordure and accumulated rubbish, while others were busy garlanding the statues and temple columns with flowers and bright strips of cloth. Cato made his way around the base of the Capitoline Hill, where the imperial palace dominated the heart of the city, and approached the entrance to the Mamertine prison where the most important enemies of Rome were held at the pleasure of the Emperor. Most of them were destined for execution, as were Caratacus and his family. Several Praetorians stood guard at the studded gateway as Cato approached. The duty optio stepped into his path and held up a hand.

'Your name, and business?'

'Prefect Quintus Licinius Cato. I've come to see the prisoner Caratacus.'

At the mention of Cato's rank the optio stood to attention and saluted. 'Sorry, sir. But I have no orders concerning any visit.'

'I came on my own initiative, Optio. I wish to speak with Caratacus. Briefly.'

The optio shook his head. 'Not without the proper authority.'

Cato had anticipated this response. 'Do you know who I am?'

'Of course, sir. Word's been going round the barracks about you and Centurion Macro. Bloody fine work, if I may say so. It's an honour to meet you in the flesh, sir.'

'I'm sure.' Cato smiled. 'So, you will know that I am in the Emperor's good books. And that means he would not be best pleased if I had occasion to mention that you and your lads here turned me away when I merely wanted a last chance to stare Caratacus in the eye and bid him farewell before he is given the chop. One soldier to another.' Cato leaned forward and prodded the optio in the chest. 'Do you want your name to be mentioned when I tell the Emperor I was denied that last opportunity to speak with the prisoner? From what I hear, Claudius is always on the lookout for some fresh meat to throw into the arena to keep the mob happy.'

The optio winced. 'There's no need for that, sir. Of course I'll let you in. After all, I'm not going to deny a request from a hero of Rome, am I?'

'That's better.'

The optio stood aside and waved Cato through the gate. 'Paulinus, escort the prefect to the prisoners.'

One of the Praetorians saluted and hurried to open a low studded door for their visitor. Cato had to duck through and then saw a flight of steps leading down a short distance. A brazier glowed at the bottom of the stairs and several unlit torches were stacked beside it. Within the first few steps the air became noticeably more cold and dank and Cato was grateful for his cloak. He reached the bottom of the steps and waited by the brazier until the Praetorian had lit one of the torches and held it aloft to illuminate the narrow passage stretching before them. Cato could see that there were doors on either side, opening onto the cells where the Emperor's prisoners were thrown while they awaited their fate. The air was thick with the stench of human waste and a muffled coughing came from a cell at the far end.

After twenty or so paces, the guardsman stopped outside one of the doors and slid back the bolt. He pushed the door open and there was a grating squeak as it swung on its hinges. Cato lowered his head and entered. The cell was some ten feet wide and twenty in length and illuminated by a grated opening high above in the wall opposite the door. The floor was covered with straw and several iron brackets were fixed into the stone for prisoners to be hung from their manacles, should it be deemed that their incarceration be even more uncomfortable. It took a moment for Cato's eyes to adjust to the gloom and he heard a rustling sound before he could make out a figure rising to his feet at the far end of the cell.

'Want me to stay with you, sir?'

'No. Wait outside. I'll call when I need you.'

'Yes, sir.'

The guardsman pulled the door closed after him and the flames of the torch left a wavering glimmer around the rim. Cato did not move at first, squinting into the shadows as the prisoner shuffled closer.

'Who's that?' The accented voice was dry and there was a brief fit of coughing before Caratacus spoke again, more easily this time. 'Who are you?'

The light from above cast a weak beam down towards the door and Cato stepped into it so that he might be seen more clearly. 'My name is Prefect Quintus Licinius Cato.'

There was silence, and then the prisoner edged forward until he was on the fringe of the pool of light illuminating Cato. 'I know you. You're the bastard who put paid to me in Brigantia.'

'I have that honour.'

'And no doubt you will be amply rewarded because of it. I know how much Rome needs its heroes, particularly if the news from Britannia is true.'

'What news would that be?'

'That you have suffered a crushing defeat at the hands of my allies.'

Cato hesitated before he could offer a reply and the prisoner laughed drily. 'Then it's true. And there's hope yet for those still resisting your attempt to steal our lands.'

'How did you come by this news?'

'Did you think that you were the first visitor to my cell? The first Roman to come and gloat over the defeated king of the most powerful tribe in all Britannia?'

Caratacus stepped into the light and now Cato could see him clearly. The transformation in the formidable warrior he had faced less than a year before was shocking. Months of confinement in the filthy conditions of the prison had left Caratacus with long matted hair, soiled skin and just the tattered remains of the finely woven garb of a king of the Celts. Lack of exercise and a poor diet had reduced his impressive physique so that he now looked like one of the half-starved beggars struggling to survive in the gutters of Rome. His hands were manacled and had worn the skin about his wrists, leaving crusty scabs and open sores. Cato could not help a surge of pity for his former foe. And there was a small stab of shame there too. Shame for his part in reducing Caratacus to this grim condition. He had been defending his people, as Cato would have done with the same resolution had their positions been reversed.

The king smiled grimly. 'How are the mighty fallen, eh? Woe to the vanquished.'

'I am sorry to see you like this, truly.'

The British king scrutinised his visitor briefly and nodded. 'I believe you . . . It is a shame that we have met as enemies, Prefect Cato. I would have valued you as a friend if things had been different.'

'I'll take that as a compliment.'

'You should. I do not respect many men in this world.' Caratacus indicated some empty slop buckets by the door to the cell. 'Take a seat, Prefect. These are the best furnishings I can offer, I'm afraid.'

They exchanged rueful smiles and Cato upended two of the buckets to serve as stools and they sat down, facing each other. The length of chain between his wrists meant that Caratacus had to rest them on his knees and he stroked his sores gently to try and relieve the itching. 'At least I won't have to put up with this for much longer. A few more hours, then they'll take me out of here, with my kin, and we'll be dragged through the streets to the place of execution. I'm told that we are to be garrotted.'

Cato nodded. 'That's the tradition.'

'I hope it's over quickly. Not for my sake. But for my wife and children . . . I wish that we had been allowed to remain together in this place. But even that was denied to me. Still, we will have a chance to say our farewells.'

'There is that, my lord.'

'My lord?' Caratacus raised an eyebrow beneath his shaggy fringe. 'It's a long time since anyone treated me with such deference. Thank you . . . Do you know if they will execute me first, or last?'

'They will save you to the end.'

Caratacus sighed. 'A pity. I had hoped to be spared the spectacle of watching my family put to death. But I imagine that your Emperor intends to make the most of my pain and humiliation. In that, he is no better than those black-hearted bastards, the druids of the Dark Moon sect.'

Cato was surprised. 'I thought they were your allies?'

'Allies? No. More a case of my enemy's enemy. If you had not invaded when you did, I would have had to deal with them in my own time. They were not having a healthy influence on some of the tribes. Bloodthirsty fanatics is what they are. It's small consolation to know that Rome will send them to the grave after me.'

'I hope so, my lord,' Cato replied with feeling. He had encountered the sect himself and well knew of the horrors they had inflicted on their Roman enemies, and any others who chose to defy their will. It was good to know that Caratacus shared his feelings towards the druids. And there it was again, the pity. He leaned closer to the British king and lowered his voice. 'There is an alternative to being executed, my lord. You might spare your family and yourself from execution.'

'Really?' And how would that happen?' Caratacus raised his hands and the iron chain rattled harshly. 'I think escape is out of the question. Even if we could get out of our chains and get out of these cells, I think we might find it something of a challenge to pass unnoticed through the streets of Rome.'

'I was not thinking of escape.'

'Oh? Then what were you thinking, Prefect?'

'When the procession is over, and before the execution is carried out, you and your family will be presented to the Emperor who will pronounce your fate. That will be your chance to throw yourself on his mercy, my lord.'

'I will not beg my enemy for my life,' Caratacus sniffed. 'Never. I would not dishonour myself before your Emperor and your people. I'd rather die.'

'Then you will die. And so will your brothers, your wife and your children.'

Caratacus glowered. 'So be it.'

'But it need not be that way. You could all live.'

'*If* I beg for our lives.'

'That's right.'

'And what if Claudius orders that we be executed in any case? Then we die like cowards. Would you deny me and my kin an honourable death?'

Cato shook his head. 'There is no honour in the death you will be given. Just death. For you. For your family. But there might still be the chance of life, if you request it.'

'Beg for it, you mean.'

Cato bit back on his frustration. 'It is only words, my lord. A form of words. It is not beyond the wit of a man like yourself to find a way to speak to my Emperor that plays on his vanity and sense of mercy. Make him respect you. Make him realise that you do more honour to him alive than dead. It is possible. I would rather see you live out your life in peace than end it put to death like a dog for the pleasure of the mob.'

The intensity of Cato's words struck home and Caratacus stared at the Roman officer fiercely. Then he breathed deeply and his shoulders sagged. 'I am weary of life, Prefect. Death is merely a release from this dark hole I have been thrown down. I welcome death.'

'I am sorry to hear it.'

'I'd be grateful if you leave me now. I wish to prepare myself for the end. I will be composed and set the example for my family. Please go.'

Cato considered making one last appeal to his enemy, but then relented. Caratacus was right. It was his choice to decide on the manner of his death. So Cato stood up and bowed his head in farewell and turned to rap on the cell door. 'I'm done here.'

As the bolt on the outside scraped back, Caratacus cleared his throat. 'Prefect Cato.'

Cato glanced back.

'I thank you for coming to see me,' said Caratacus. 'I will consider what you have said. You are a good man, and a worthy enemy, and I regret that we could not have been friends. But fate decided otherwise.'

'Yes, my lord. Fate is a hard master indeed . . .' Cato had a passing memory of Julia, and he thrust it from his thoughts. 'Goodbye.'

The door opened and the glare of the flaming torch in the Praetorian's hand cast a ruddy hue on Cato and the British king. Caratacus lifted his chin proudly. 'Goodbye. I hope to see you one day in the afterlife, Prefect Cato. I shall feast you, and your friend Centurion Macro, in the halls of the heroes of my people.'

Cato forced himself to smile. 'Until then, my lord. Until then . . .'

He bent his head to the low doorway and stepped out into the dank corridor. The door closed behind him, the bolt slammed back into place, and Cato gratefully followed the Praetorian out of the dank depths of the prison and back into the warmth of the early-morning sun that promised a fine day for the coming celebrations. But his thoughts were still with the prisoner, and his family, languishing in the clammy, stinking cells beneath the imperial palace.

# CHAPTER NINE

'Not bad, eh?' Macro leaned closer to Cato to make sure that he could be heard above the din of the cheering crowd. 'At least they can still put on a good show in Rome, even if things are going tits up back in Britannia.'

Cato grunted and nodded in acknowledgement. It was strange to think that they had been sent back from Britannia to answer for the crushing defeat of Legate Quintatus and his column, and instead he and Macro were being fêted as the heroes responsible for the capture of King Caratacus and his family. The fates will play their games, Cato reflected. In all kinds of ways, as the revelations about Julia had painfully demonstrated. He pushed the thought from his mind and concentrated instead on the spectacle surrounding him.

The clear sky of dawn had remained unblemished by any clouds and was a deep cerulean within which the sun blazed bright and hot. On both sides of the thoroughfare the crowds pressed in, waving and shouting acclaim as two lines of Praetorians faced out to keep the processional route open. Far ahead, Cato could just make out the priests leading the imperial party. They wore bright, unblemished togas and led a string of white sacrificial goats that would be offered to Jupiter in thanks for Rome's good fortune. Behind the priests came the magistrates and senators, with the two consuls and their escorts at the rear. Then the standards of the Praetorian guards at the head of the First Cohort in full armour, red horsehair crests rising above their polished helmets and white tunics. They were followed in turn by fifty of the German bodyguards, impressing the mob with their thick beards and barbarian appearance. And then came the first of the chariots bearing members of the imperial family. Britannicus rode in the first, one hand on the rail and one occasionally rising to respond to the greeting of the crowd. He was followed by Nero, smiling broadly and waving all the time and winning an even bigger cheer than his younger step-brother. His mother, Agrippina, came next, hair intricately arranged into a fan shape. Then ten more of the German bodyguards, selected for their enormous physique, before the dazzling white horses drawing the gilded chariot of the Emperor himself.

Claudius did his best not to stoop as he held onto the rail and attempted to look as dignified as possible. The gold wreath encircling his white-haired head lay at a slight angle and every so often the body slave standing behind him would discreetly attempt to straighten it. Behind the imperial chariot paced the imperial retinue; senatorial advisers and freedmen, including Pallas and Narcissus, in modest tunics as befitted their social rank, even if they wielded almost as much influence as any other person in the procession. And then came Cato and Macro, at the head of a small column of other soldiers due to be honoured by the Emperor. Despite the heat of the day, they wore full armour, but were allowed to carry their helmets under their arms so that they could be clearly seen by the people on either side. Many people were already drunk and some of the women made lewd offers to the soldiers as they passed by. Macro had prepared plenty of small slivers of wood with the name of the nearest bar to Cato's house written on them. Every so often he handed one out to the more promising candidates offering him sexual favours.

He caught Cato giving him a disapproving look and shrugged. 'No point in not milking this for all it's worth. After all, I've served Rome well enough over the years. Now she can serve me.'

Behind the small group of soldiers came the line of carts laden with bread and sweet cakes, from which slaves hurled the snacks into the crowds. The rearmost carts carried arrangements of weapons and armour captured in Britannia, and the very last of all carried Caratacus and his family, cleaned up and in fresh tunics, as they stood in haughty silence, affecting contempt for the mob who jeered as they passed by.

'Centurion! Centurion Macro!'

81

They turned to see a tall thin woman with dark hair lifting the hem of her tunic to reveal the top of her thighs and the triangle of pubic hair between them.

'I'm yours, Centurion! My name's Persilla, best lay in the Suburra. Special price for you!'

Macro reached for his haversack and Cato shook his head. 'I thought you were spoiled for choice? So why pay for it?'

'No harm in seeing if she's willing to haggle. She might even have a friend for you.' Macro caught the warning look his friend shot him. 'Or . . . I can manage a double helping.'

Macro stepped aside to hand the slip of wood to the woman and rejoined the procession with a cheerful grin at the prospect of more fleshy pleasures. 'I think I could get used to this hero lark.'

They proceeded slowly through the heart of the Forum, past the steps leading up to the senate house and then began the steep climb up the Capitoline Hill towards the precinct of the Temple of Jupiter that vied with the imperial palace to dominate the centre of the city. The road zig-zagged up the slope and only the carts carrying the displays of enemy weaponry and the prisoners continued with the procession. The food carts turned aside and those on board threw the last of their contents to the mob. Meanwhile, a fresh team of slaves, who had been waiting in a side street, rushed forward to help the remaining wagons up the hill. They put their hands to the spokes of the wagons and strained to keep the vehicles moving up the steep incline. The head of the procession passed through the entrance to the precinct and out of sight of the crowd in the Forum. They moved into position on either side of the entrance to welcome the imperial family following them and lustily cheered the final chariot as it clattered to a halt. Claudius descended and limped across to the platform that looked out over the heart of Rome. As the mob caught sight of him again a fresh bout of cheering echoed back off the tall buildings rising up either side of the Forum. He took his seat on a throne and his family and closest advisers took position on either side, and behind him, followed by the senators.

When those who were to be honoured entered the precinct a palace freedman with an anxious expression hurried over to address them.

82

'Sirs! It is a great pleasure to meet you all.' He bowed deeply before snapping erect. 'I'm Polidorus, master of ceremonies at the palace. Just a few words on protocol before the final part of the triumph begins. The running order is that the priests will perform the sacrifice, consult to read the omens and present their findings to the Emperor. Then you're up. You'll be waiting over there, by the temple pediment. Once your name is called, there will be a brief citation, during which you come forward and kneel before the Emperor to await your reward. As soon as you have it, I'd be grateful if you left the platform as soon as possible. I'm afraid we're already running late and there's a banquet to follow and we don't want the food to be past its best by the time the guests start tucking into it.' Polidorus laughed nervously. 'No sense in poisoning adding to the existing body count of the festivities. Once you've all been in front of the Emperor we'll move on to the presentation of the prisoners. There'll be a few words spoken before they're handed over to the executioner.'

He half turned and nodded to a figure at the far end of the precinct. Cato looked up and saw a man in a black tunic examining a large wooden device. A stout post rose up from a supporting framework. A hole had been cut through the post and a loop of rope hung from one side, while the ends had been tied round a shaft of wood on the other side. As they watched, two of his assistants manhandled a skeletal wretch in a loincloth up to the frame. While the prisoner struggled feebly, his hands were tied behind the post and the loop of rope passed over his head to rest on his collarbone. At once the executioner began to rotate the shaft of wood, winding the rope round and tightening the loop about his victim's neck. The man began to struggle in earnest now that the rope was biting into his flesh and his shoulders and legs bucked wildly. But with his neck tight against the post there was nothing he could do to save himself as the executioner wound the shaft tighter and tighter, muscles bulging with the effort. The prisoner suddenly arched his chest, trembled violently, and then slumped in death.

'What was that about?' Cato demanded. 'I thought the prisoners were all to be executed publicly.'

'Just those who are a featured part of the triumph,' Polidorus explained. 'That was just to test the device.'

'Test?'

'Surely. We can't afford to have the real executions botched if there's a fault with the garrotte, can we? So we use a condemned prisoner for a dry run, to make sure there aren't any cock-ups to spoil the show.'

Macro clicked his tongue. 'Well, we can't be having that, can we?'

His dry tone was lost on the master of ceremonies who shook his head. 'Absolutely not . . . Ah! Here come the priests.'

The soldiers turned to watch as a procession of white-garbed figures emerged from the Temple of Jupiter and approached the Emperor. Some had blood spattered on their togas and smeared over their hands from where they had cut the throats of the goats. The head of their order led them onto the platform and bowed before Claudius before quietly announcing the result of his examination of the entrails of the goat selected for the purpose of divining the will of the Gods. The Emperor listened attentively before nodding his assent, then the priest backed away a few paces before turning near the edge of the platform and slowly raising his arms as he commanded the attention of the multitude gathered below. A quiet fell over the mob as upturned faces gazed back expectantly. The priest milked the moment for as long as he could to add gravitas to the proceedings and then drew a deep breath.

'Rome has beseeched Almighty Jupiter, Best and Greatest, for his blessing on the sacred ceremonies we share this day. In accordance with the rituals laid down by the college of priests of the Temple of Jupiter, we have slain a beast on the temple altar and opened its entrails for examination.' He paused in order to build on his audience's anticipation. 'By the will of Almighty Jupiter, the omens are good!'

At once the mob erupted in wild cheers of celebration, and the Emperor offered them a graceful wave of his hand. Cato watched the reaction of the crowd with disdain before he muttered to his friend, 'Have you ever known an occasion when the omens weren't favourable?'

Macro sniffed. 'Rome is the darling of the Gods, clearly. That, or the Gods are happy to bend the rules just so that they get to enjoy the sight of a few more barbarians being throttled.'

Claudius allowed the cheering to continue for a while before he gave the nod to Polidorus. The latter hurried over to the waiting soldiers.

'Right, we're up. Keep in order and be ready to move smartly when your name is called. Once you've had your turn, move to the rear of the platform and remain there until the last of the prisoners is executed and the Emperor and his retinue have left the platform. After that, please make your way to the palace as expeditiously as possible to take your places for the feast. One of my men will show you to the right table. Any questions? Good. Let's begin.' He consulted his wax tablet. 'Prefect Cato and Centurion Macro.'

Cato set his shoulders back and stiffened his neck before giving the nod to Macro and they marched out across the platform and halted directly before the dais on which the Emperor sat. Polidorus advanced to the edge of the platform and held up a hand to silence the crowd. At the same time a shrill blast of trumpets pierced the air above the capital. The mob gradually became quiet and still. A handful of children, overcome by the excitement, continued to wave strips of coloured cloth to and fro from their vantage point sitting on the shoulders of their fathers.

Polidorus lowered his hand and cleared his throat before taking a deep breath. 'His imperial majesty, Tiberius Claudius Caesar Augustus Germanicus, supreme commander of the legions of Rome and conqueror of Britannia, bids you to join him in honouring those heroes who have served the Senate and People of Rome with unswerving courage and devotion to duty . . . He presents to you Prefect Quintus Licinius Cato and Centurion Lucius Cornelius Macro, recently returned from campaigning in Britannia, where our forces have been hunting down and destroying the last desperate bands of druids and their followers who are resisting the Roman peace . . .'

Cato sensed Macro stirring a little uneasily, and shared his friend's discomfiture at the way Rome's struggle to control the British tribes was being presented in such optimistic terms. After ten years of hard fighting the legions had been dealt a humiliating blow and Rome was hanging onto what territory she controlled by her fingertips.

One more push by the tribes who still fought on against Rome might well destroy the thinly dispersed forces garrisoning the island and force a humbling retreat from Britannia. If Caratacus had managed to evade capture and continued to lead the tribes fighting Rome then Cato had little doubt that the fate of the new province would already have been decided.

'We are here today to celebrate the victory over King Caratacus, our greatest enemy in Britannia. A victory only made possible by the gallantry of Prefect Cato and Centurion Macro whose boldness in battle has struck fear into the hearts of our foes while offering an inspiring example to their comrades. It was through their direct action that Caratacus was defeated and captured, and for this signal achievement they are honoured with the gratitude of Rome and his imperial majesty!'

Polidorus stepped aside with a sweep of his arm, and the two officers approached the dais and bowed to the Emperor. Claudius rose unsteadily from his throne and approached the edge of the dais, while two slaves stepped out from behind the throne carrying red cushions upon which rested two silver spears. The slaves knelt down to each side of the Emperor and proffered their burdens as they bowed their heads, not daring to meet his gaze. Cato could see the nervous tremor in the Emperor's hands as his gnarled fingers closed around the shaft of the first spear. He lifted it up and held it in both hands.

'Rome is g–gr–grateful, Prefect.'

He offered the spear and Cato stepped forward and raised his arms, palms up. The weapon was heavier than he anticipated and close to he could see that the ornamental head was made of gold. It would be worth a small fortune, he calculated.

'Thank you, Imperial Majesty.'

Claudius was already reaching for the other spear and Cato caught sight of Polidorus gesturing to him to move back. Keeping his front towards the Emperor, Cato retreated a few paces as Macro moved forward to take his turn.

'Rome is grateful, Centurion,' Claudius repeated flatly as he handed over the prize and Macro mumbled some thanks and fell back to his position at Cato's side. They both saluted the Emperor and a fresh cheer rose up from the crowd in the Forum. Then they turned to march back to their places on the fringe of the imperial party as the next recipient came forward to collect the sword that was brought to the Emperor to dispense. As the ceremony continued Cato and Macro examined their awards more closely.

'Very nice, indeed,' Macro said quietly. 'Going to look good on the wall of the villa I buy when I retire.'

'Thought you were going to buy a tavern, or a vineyard if funds allow, and spend the rest of your days in a drunken stupor?'

'Still got to have a home to go to, haven't I?' Macro winked. 'Yours will look very fine in your house. Something for young Lucius to admire as he grows up. Maybe it'll even inspire the lad to follow in your footsteps. That'll be something you can be proud of.'

Cato had not given the matter any thought and the idea caught him by surprise. Was that the life he wanted for his son? All the hardships and dangers of serving on the frontiers of the empire? Never knowing when the barbarians might strike, and facing the hunger and cold of the northern provinces, or the heat and thirst of the eastern deserts? Lucius was only a small boy and it was hard to imagine him facing such a life at the moment. Nor was Cato too pleased at the prospect of placing his son in danger.

Even so, there were aspects of the army life that Cato valued. The comradeship, facing perils and surviving them, and testing the limits of his endurance, mental as well as physical. It was the army that had made him what he was today. Before then he had been a bookish youth with disdain for the brute realities of life. If his father had not sent him to join the legions then he feared he would have ended up as some minor functionary in the service of the Emperor, or worse in the service of the likes of Narcissus or Pallas. One of those shady individuals who spied on the enemies of their masters and stuck a knife into their backs when they were deemed to be a threat to the security of the Emperor or the wider Roman state. The kind of men whom Cato and Macro had rightly come to despise. The army had indeed been the making of him, Cato reflected. The army, and his friend Macro. He glanced sidelong and saw Macro admiring his prize. Yes, if Lucius turned out like Macro, then Cato would be very proud indeed.

'You're a lucky man, Cato,' said Macro, breaking into his thoughts. 'I wish I had a son. Truly. To have a lad like Lucius would be a fine thing indeed.'

'It's not too late, brother. Just find yourself a woman and marry her.'

'Easier said than done. Good women are hard to come by.'

Thinking of Julia, Cato felt a twist of the knife in his guts. 'Yes . . .'

Macro picked up on the strained tone in his friend's voice and looked at Cato with concern for a moment. Before he could ask anything there was a loud rumble of wheels and both turned to see the arrival of the prisoners' cart into the temple precinct. As the last of the soldiers to be honoured by the Emperor received a gold torc, a section of Praetorians began to drag the prisoners down from their cart and herd them towards the rear of the platform where Polidorus was waiting for his cue. The last soldier was cheered by the mob as he waited until he had retreated a respectful distance from the Emperor and then faced the spectators and punched his fist in the air.

The cheering continued in a deafening roar. Polidorus waited for the soldier to clear the front of the platform and then turned his attention to the Emperor. Claudius allowed the din to continue for a while before he nodded to the master of ceremonies. Polidorus called out an order to the prisoners' escort and the Praetorians thrust Caratacus and his family forward. The noise from the crowd increased to an even higher pitch at the sight of the humbled enemy.

'Not sure that I want to witness this part of the proceedings,' Cato muttered to his friend.

'Why? He had it coming to him the moment he chose to take up arms against us and try his hand against the legions. It was him or us, Cato. Besides, you know damn well that if the positions were reversed then we'd be given a far nastier end. You remember those giant wicker men they used to burn prisoners alive? Right?'

'I remember.' Cato shuddered at the image. 'But that was the druids, not Caratacus.'

'Sure, he and his warriors were content to just take the heads of our lads as trophies. So you'll forgive me if I shed no tears for him. If he'd given in several years ago and spared us all a lot of bloodshed then I might feel differently.'

Cato did not respond to his friend's cold-hearted comment. He wondered if he was being sentimental. Perhaps Macro was right to feel no remorse over the death of this enemy of Rome, he reflected. There was no place for sentimentality in war, and those who waged it and lost had no right to expect any mercy at the hands of their victors.

With the prisoners gathered in full view of those packed into the Forum, Polidorus signalled the executioner and his party to take their places. At the sight of the garrotte frame the cheers and jeering became more frenzied and bloodthirsty just as when the mob bayed for the blood of the gladiators and those condemned to death in the arena. It was the same savage appetite for suffering and death, and it made Cato feel a twinge of contempt for those who demanded the blood of their victims most vociferously. When the garotte was set up and the executioner stood ready, Claudius rose to his feet and surveyed his people with imperious disdain as they fell silent and watched him expectantly. Claudius opened his arms in an embracing gesture as he filled his lungs and began to address the people, his voice thin and shrill with the effort of trying to make himself heard.

'It is time to b–b–bear witness to the final destruction of our greatest enemy, Caratacus, king of the barbarians of Britannia. Long has he defied our legions, and inflicted m–many a reverse upon them, but in the end nothing can resist the might of Rome, and the favour of Jupiter, best and g–g–gr–greatest!' He soaked up the cheers that greeted his words. 'But b–before I pass judgement on this man, Caratacus, and his family, does the prisoner have any last words to offer his conquerors – the Se–Se–Senate and People of Rome?'

The words echoed off the towering basilicas, temples and the imperial palace that surrounded the Forum as the crowd turned their gaze to the solitary figure of Caratacus, standing apart from his family. The Briton did little to hide his disdain for the frail Emperor and those who surrounded him. Then his gaze fell on Cato and they exchanged a brief stare before he turned aside so that he could address Claudius and the crowd as equally as possible.

'I am your prisoner, as is my family. Our fate is yours to determine, by right of conquest.' He paused a moment before addressing the crowd more directly. 'Let this be my testament, then, before I go to join the spirits of my forefathers, the great kings and princes of my people. I am Caratacus, King of the Catuvellauni – the most powerful tribe in all Britannia . . . until Caesar's legions landed on our shores. We were a proud people, a warlike people, who knew no equal in battle. We humbled the Trinovantes, the Cantii and the Atrebatii and made them our vassals. When Rome invaded, it was I to whom all looked when a leader was needed . . .' He raised his manacled fists and shook his chains.

Macro chuckled. 'Fuck me, but he's a modest fellow, ain't he?'

A flicker of impatience showed in Cato's expression. 'He's about to die, Macro. Let him make a decent end of it.'

'Fair enough. As long as he doesn't try to bore us to death in revenge.' Macro was already thinking about the fleshy delights he would be seeking out when the ceremony and feasting were over.

Caratacus lowered his fist and his tone was markedly less strident as he continued. 'Three times we faced you in battle – three defeats – before our capital at Camulodunum fell. Even though we had the greater numbers, still we were defeated by your legions. Truly, the Roman soldier has no equal in this world. He is better armed, better trained, better disciplined than any other. The legionary is incomparable on the battlefield.'

'He's right on that score,' said Macro.

'True,' Cato agreed quietly. 'But Roman generals are a different matter, on occasion.'

Macro grunted his assent with feeling.

Caratacus took a deep breath. 'Defeated on the battlefield, we continued the struggle as best we could in the years that followed, with some success. But always with the honour of our people in our hearts, and the desire to live free. Long before your legions set foot on my lands I had heard of Rome's greatness. I had read of her fine cities and fabulous wealth. Why, when you have so much, do you covet our poor huts? Before you chose to make war on Britannia, I would have come to this city as an ally rather than a prisoner. But

90

now I stand before you, defeated and humbled. I once had many horses, thousands of followers at my back and great wealth. Do you wonder that I was unwilling to lose such things? If it is your desire to rule everyone, does it surely follow that everyone should accept becoming your slaves? If I had chosen to surrender immediately then neither my long defiance of Rome, nor your glory in defeating me would be worthy of this great triumph you celebrate today. It is also true that if my family, and I, are put to death here today then all of that dies with us and will fade from memory.' Caratacus now turned to speak to the Emperor directly. 'On the other hand, if you show mercy and let us live, then we shall be an eternal example of the clemency, the greatness and the civilisation of Rome. Great Caesar, I, Caratacus, the last of the kings of the Catuvellauni, beg you to spare us.'

Caratacus slowly lowered himself onto his knees, stretched out his arms towards the Emperor and bowed his head.

Claudius regarded him sternly as those around the Emperor and the crowd in the Forum awaited his response, still and quiet. Only the distant hubbub of far-off streets and the chirping of swifts darting through the air broke the silence. Cato saw the Emperor's right hand twitching as it rested on the cushioned arm of his throne, and then the thumb slowly began to ease away from the rest of the hand and Cato felt a sick feeling in the pit of his stomach as he realised that the plea was not going to succeed. There was only the briefest moment, but in that time Cato reflected that he had little to lose. His wife was lost, his home was lost, and because of that it was likely that Lucius would have to be cared for and raised by his grandfather. He took a step forward and raised his silver spear to attract the crowd's attention as he shouted, 'Live!'

Polidorus instantly turned towards the cry with a look of alarm and most of those around the Emperor turned in surprise to see the insane individual with the hubris to speak out against the imminent execution.

'Live!' Cato called out again, straining his lungs. 'Live!'

He turned to Macro with an imploring look and his friend's broad shoulders heaved in a sigh as he also raised his spear and echoed the shout.

Then, from below in the crowd, another voice joined in. There was a brief flurry of jeers and booing, but more voices rose in response to Cato and quickly competed with, and then overwhelmed, the protests of those whose bloodlust demanded satisfaction.

'Live! Live! Live!' The chant spread through the crowd and fists punched up to emphasise their wish.

Polidorus hurried round behind the back of the throne and rushed up to Cato. 'What do you think you are doing? Stop it!'

Cato ignored him and used his spare hand to add urgency to his appeal. The palace official grabbed at his arm and pulled it down.

'Enough, you fool! Stop it at once! Before it's too late. Stop!'

Cato shook his hand away and then struck Polidorus hard in the midriff, driving the air from his lungs as he bent double and staggered back, gasping.

'Not so full of yourself now, eh?' Macro laughed.

Around them the other soldiers who had also been decorated grinned at Polidorus and then took up the cry. With the raucous sound coming from the side, Claudius glanced round, frowning, and Cato feared that he might order the German bodyguards to silence him and the others. But instead he saw that the Emperor's thumb had folded back into his hand, tucking under the fingers against the palm and out of sight. Gradually the Emperor leaned forward and then rose stiffly to his feet and raised his hands to the crowd. But the cheering continued in a deafening roar like the beating of a great drum. 'Live! Live! Live!'

Cato saw the Emperor's jaw working in frustration as his subjects ignored his gestures to call for calm. At length Claudius waved Pallas over and spoke into his ear. The freedman nodded and rushed over to the party of soldiers carrying long brass trumpets. The optio in charge beckoned to them to raise their instruments and they made ready to blow at his signal. The harsh notes cut through the chant and broke it up as some in the crowd stilled their tongues while others fell out of rhythm. Slowly the Forum fell quiet again and Pallas ordered the trumpeters to cease.

Claudius took a step forward and looked down at Caratacus, who had not moved or shown any reaction to the plea for his life.

'Rise, Caratacus, King of the Ca–Cat–Catuvellauni.'

The Briton stood up and the Emperor took his hand and limped closer to the edge of the platform.

'By my will, I declare that K–King Caratacus, and his family, be spared! That they live will be testament to the gracious m–mercy of Rome. Let no one say that your Emperor, the Se–Senate and P–P–People of Rome do not recognise an honourable man when they see him . . . Caratacus shall live! Live!'

The crowd roared their approval and took up the cry again. Macro slapped Cato on the shoulder. 'You did it!'

Cato nodded ruefully. 'What worries me is what happens next.'

He saw Polidorus gasping for breath, and the freedman's expression was filled with anger. And there was little doubt that the Emperor, who had been on the verge of condemning Caratacus and his family to death, would not be so well disposed towards the man who had frustrated his intention.

'Might be an idea if you kept your distance from me, Macro. Until this blows over.'

'Fuck that,' the centurion grinned. 'Where you go, I go, my friend. It will be as it has always been as long as I have known you.'

Cato clicked his tongue. 'I hope you don't have cause to regret that.'

He looked over to see that Claudius had raised the Briton's hand, as if he had just won a boxing bout in the arena. The Emperor was smiling broadly enough, and Cato could only hope that the expression was not only skin deep. At least the mood of the mob was behind Cato and his cause. That at least might soften the ire of the Emperor and his advisers. Or so Cato fervently hoped. If not for his sake, then for Macro's.

# CHAPTER TEN

The feasting hall of the imperial palace was festooned with garlands of bright flowers and tapestries depicting the victories and conquests that had occurred under the reign of Claudius. Cato was amused to see the sequence representing the Emperor's short-lived visit to Britannia. There was Claudius in full armour leading the troops ashore against the hostile forces ranged on the cliffs above them, and again exhorting his troops as they fought their way across the River Tamesis, and finally accepting the surrender of the kings of twelve tribes outside the smoking ruins of Caratacus' capital at Camulodunum. They were fine illustrations, Cato conceded. Full of colour and action and very detailed. The only reservation he had was that the Emperor had been at neither of the first two actions and, thanks to his interference, had nearly caused a catastrophic defeat outside Camulodunum. But the perpetual struggle between the claims of truth and those of posterity tended to favour the latter in Cato's experience.

By the time Cato and his party arrived most of the other guests were already seated at the long tables stretching the length of the hall. At the far end, in a huge curved niche, was the raised area reserved for the Emperor and his immediate retinue who would attend at their leisure. Immediately in front of the dais were the tables and couches reserved for the senators and their wives. Beyond that a larger seating area for those of equestrian rank and other influential figures who had been included in the guest list. There was seating for over a thousand in all, Cato estimated as he set his son down and stretched his back. Also with him were Macro and Cato's father-in-law, Senator Sempronius, a short, stocky, serious-faced individual with lined features beneath the thinning white hair he did his best to cover his pate with. Cato and Macro had returned to the house on the Quirinal after the triumph to change out of their armour and military tunics, before donning neat plain tunics and comfortable soft leather boots. Sempronius, being something of a traditionalist, wore his toga with the narrow red stripe that denoted his aristocratic status. Lucius wore one of the tunics his mother had bought before his birth. It was slightly over-sized, which made him seem even younger than his two years. As he shrugged his shoulders to try and get the linen to settle comfortably on his small frame he looked up at Cato and smiled shyly.

At once the clear grey eyes and the shape of the hairline re-minded Cato of Julia and his heart was pained again with an aching longing for his wife, even though she had betrayed and hurt him so terribly.

'Looks like we're going to be able to fill our boots tonight!' Macro grinned as he clapped his hairy hands together and rubbed them vigorously.

Sure enough, the centres of the tables were covered with baskets of small loaves of bread and platters of pastries and other fine delicacies, as well as bowls of fruit, some of which Cato did not even recognise. Silver jugs held wine and many guests already seemed to be well in their cups as they conversed and laughed on each side of the tables.

'Try and leave some for the others, Macro.'

'I'll do my best but heroes come first. And right now we're the two biggest heroes in Rome. I aim to make the most of that before these people forget the fact.'

Sempronius smiled. 'You're right, Centurion. A month from now the mob will have forgotten all of this and they'll be back to arguing and fighting over which chariot team is the best.'

'The Yellows,' Macro replied at once. 'No question about it.'

'Up Yellows!' Lucius piped up, punching his tiny fists into the air. 'Up Yellows!'

'That's the spirit!' Macro laughed with delight and ruffled the boy's hair. 'Your uncle Macro'll take you to the races the moment you're big enough. That's if your daddy says so.'

95

'Why not?' Cato responded. 'Might as well get some bad habits out of the way first.'

Macro shook his head and sighed. 'Killjoy.'

'Kill?' Lucius' eyes widened in shock. 'Joy?'

The adults shared a chuckle before the senator's expression grew serious again. 'Are you sure about your decision, Cato?'

'Yes, sir. I know that you'll raise him well. If I live long enough and the Gods are generous with the spoils of war, then I can afford another home. Somewhere for me and Lucius. For now, I have no choice in the matter. I can't take him on campaign with me.'

'But you aren't on campaign.' Sempronius touched his arm. 'Cato, I've come to regard you as my son. Why don't you both come and live with me?'

Cato smiled sadly. 'I wish I could. But I am already haunted enough by the memory of Julia. I need to get away from Rome.'

'But you have only just returned.'

'True, but it was not the homecoming I expected, and the pain is still too raw.'

Sempronius thought a moment and nodded. 'I think I understand. When do you have to leave your house?'

'By the end of the month. Taurus already has the deeds. I have instructed Amatapus to auction the contents and hand the proceeds to you for Lucius' future. The same goes for the silver spear once it has been sold.'

'You don't have to do that. I have money enough.'

'It is your money, sir,' Cato said stiffly. 'I'll take no charity from any man, for me or my son.'

'Lucius is also my grandson,' Sempronius responded gently. 'My flesh and blood.'

Cato saw the hurt in his eyes and wished he had not been so blunt. In truth, he wanted to cut any ties with Julia that he could afford to. Not that the senator was to blame for his daughter's behaviour, but he was, and would always be, a link to her memory. As would Lucius, he admitted to himself.

'You are already doing enough for Lucius,' Cato concluded. 'And you have my gratitude.'

Macro had been standing a short distance apart and now his stomach rumbled audibly. Sempronius cocked his head towards the centurion. 'Someone needs feeding. I'll see you later?'

'Perhaps tomorrow, sir.'

Their eyes met for a moment before the senator nodded. 'All right then. Enjoy the feast. And you, Lucius, behave yourself. Or they'll never let you into the Senate.'

The boy's eyes twinkled mischievously and he pressed himself against Cato's leg as if for protection. Cato felt a thrill of pleasure at the gesture and stroked his fine hair affectionately as Sempronius turned away and strode off towards the senatorial tables.

Cato reached down for his son's hand and gave it a gentle tug. 'Come on then, Lucius.'

The boy looked up at Macro quickly and wrapped the fingers of his spare hand around the centurion's thumb. Macro grinned in delight.

'There we are! Three lads ready for a night out in the greatest city in the world! What could be better?'

'One of the lads at least will be getting an early night. And it might be an idea to spare him the delights of drink and whoring until he's a little older, don't you think?'

'Fair enough. For now we can start him on fruit tarts. He can try his hand at the other kind when he's good and ready. Right, lad?' Macro winked at him.

Lucius tried to return the gesture, but only managed to close and open his eyes a few times, before he nodded. 'Tarts!'

His father groaned and raised his eyes beseechingly. 'By the Gods! Jupiter, Best and Greatest, please spare my son from the vices of old sweats like Centurion Macro here.'

They made their way to one of the tables that was closest to the Emperor's end of the hall and found space on the couches there, with Lucius sitting cross-legged between them as they reclined in comfort. They were not kept waiting long for the Emperor. The sound of trumpets announced the arrival of the imperial party and the guests stood at once and waited until Claudius and his family were seated. A smaller procession of figures filed past the dais to take their place alongside the senators and Cato recognised Caratacus and his family, downcast, but playing their part as they got used to the prospect of being forever exiled from their homeland and spending the remainder of their days in the gilded cage of Rome. The trumpets sounded again as the Emperor helped himself to a dish from the table in front of him, and then the guests resumed their places and began to eat.

At once Macro reached for some of the pastries in front of him. He scooped several onto a bronze platter and set it before them. Lucius nibbled an end suspiciously before making a face and dropping his snack onto the platter. While Macro tucked in with gusto, and poured himself a generous goblet of wine, Cato chewed more thoughtfully on the salted and spiced pork delicacy. Looking around, he noted that many of the others on the table were taking sidelong glances at him and Macro and muttering quietly. It seemed that they had won themselves a considerable portion of fame, as Sempronius had said. Enough to make Cato feel vaguely uneasy. After all, he and Macro had only been performing their duty. There had been no thought of reward or fame at the time, just the cold thrill of danger and the dryness in his throat, and the aching fear of pain and a crippling wound that would leave him an object of pity. Fortune had spared Cato and his friend. She had not been so generous to the comrades they had left behind on the battlefields of Britannia, torn and twisted on the frozen ground. And the fact was that they had been honoured to help cover up the defeat that the legions had been dealt at the hands of those allies of Caratacus who had not yet bowed to Rome, nor showed the slightest sign of ever being willing to do so. It was a sham, and both he and Macro were party to the deception being played on the people of Rome. A sham, just as his marriage had been. Just as Julia's claims to love him had been. She had been lying when she had written to him in Britannia, telling him of her love, of her fervent wish to have him return to her . . .

So much deceit. Cato closed his eyes and wished that he was far away from Rome and back with the army in Britannia. There at least life was straightforward and honest. Do your duty, look after your men and defeat the enemy. That was all that had really mattered to him for the ten years he had been serving under the eagles. And he missed it dreadfully already.

'Cato . . . Cato, lad.'

He blinked and turned to Macro. 'What?'

'You were miles away. I was going to ask you, what are your plans?'

'Plans?'

'You know. Now that the house is fucked.' Cato had told Macro about the debt collector's visit, but had said nothing about Julia's more devastating betrayal.

'Macro, do you mind? The boy . . .'

'Oh, right. Sorry. So what you going to do now? Apply for another command?'

Cato sighed. 'Looks that way. What else can I do? Hopefully our part in today's triumph will open a few doors. Frankly, I'd take anything I was offered. Just to get back to what I know. And how about you? Still determined to drink and, er, the other, until you drop?'

'Oh yes!' Macro raised his cup. 'I'll toast that.'

He took a deep draught and set the cup down on the table in front of him with a happy smack of his lips. Then he sighed heavily and became more serious. 'It will do for now at any rate. But I'm only ever going to be a soldier. There's nothing else for me. So, if you get that command, keep a space open for me. You could always use a decent centurion at your side. And not one of those fuck-ups that they are appointing directly these days. Oh! Sorry, Lucius. Just shut your ears to what your uncle Macro says at times, all right?'

'I'd be honoured if you served with me, Macro.' Cato poured himself a cup and raised it. 'To friendship.'

'Ah, what's this?' a voice interrupted from the other side of the table. 'What's the cause of this little celebration, my old comrades from years past?'

Cato and Macro turned and saw Vitellius regarding them. He had eschewed his senator's toga in favour of a red silk tunic embroidered with gold leaves. His hair was oiled and artfully arranged in ringlets. He might have passed for handsome, but for the cold, calculating expression on his face. 'If you don't mind, I'll join you.'

He smiled thinly as he lowered himself into a space between two diners reclining opposite.

'Actually, sir, we do mind,' said Macro.

Vitellius showed no reaction to the remark, and refused to meet the centurion's gaze. Instead, he focused on the boy and offered him a friendly wave and a wink. 'And who might this fine young man be?'

Cato gritted his teeth. 'My son.'

'Your son?' There was the faintest emphasis on the first word and Cato tried not to flinch or show any sign of a reaction.

'That's right. Lucius Licinius.'

'No cognomen?'

'I have yet to get to know him well enough to decide on one. As I said, he is my son, and therefore no concern of yours.'

Cato shifted slightly and turned away from the interloper, as if to continue a conversation with Macro.

'And a fine lad he is. I'm sure he will turn out to be an equally impressive young man, regardless of who his father is.'

This time Cato could not help turning back to face the senator. 'Meaning?'

'Meaning that his father is a famous warrior and his grandfather a respected senator, but even allowing for that, I am sure he will be able to make his own mark on Roman society. Like his father before him.'

Vitellius continued to smile as he watched for any response to his provocative implications. It took all Cato's force of will to maintain an even tone as he responded.

'I have no doubt about Lucius' potential, under my guiding hand. And that of my friend, Centurion Macro.'

Vitellius acknowledged Macro with a brief nod. 'So, he'll have the manner of a street brawler, with the brains and sensitivity of a philosopher. I wish him luck. He'll need it.'

Cato had had enough. He turned fully towards the senator. 'You've had your fun. Now, if you have something to say to either of us, then say it. Otherwise, we'd be grateful if you fucked off back to whatever sewer you emerged from.'

Macro coughed. 'Cato, the lad . . . Watch your language.'

100

Lucius glanced at both men curiously. Cato picked up a sweet pastry and pressed it into his son's hands. 'Here. Try this, Lucius.'

The boy tucked in eagerly, licking the honey glaze before sinking his tiny pearl-white teeth in. While he was preoccupied Cato continued to address Vitellius. 'Say your piece. Then go.'

'That's better. No need to adopt the language of the Subura when you deal with me, my dear Prefect. I fear you have spent too long in the company of the common soldiery and lost whatever refinement you once had as a result of being raised in the imperial palace.' Vitellius leaned forward and reached for an empty goblet and held it out. 'Pour me some wine, if you please, Centurion Macro.'

Macro clamped his jaw shut, and did as he was told, filling the cup to the brim before moving the spout just enough to continue pouring the watery red liquid over the senator's hand and onto the long sleeve of his tunic.

'What the bloody hell do you think you're doing, you clumsy bastard?' Vitellius drew his hand back sharply, spilling some of the contents of his goblet. He glared angrily at Macro.

The latter affected shock. 'Sir, if you please, we are not in the Subura now.'

Cato could not help laughing, and Macro joined in, then Lucius giggled uncomprehendingly.

Vitellius pressed his lips tightly together for a moment before he recovered his veneer of equanimity and he raised the goblet. 'Well played, Centurion. I trust that you will retain such presence of mind during the tough days to come. I was about to make a toast, and I would be pleased if you shared it with me. So then, my friends, let's drink to the coming campaign. Death to the enemy and victory and honour to the soldiers of Rome.'

Cato and Macro exchanged a puzzled look before Macro cocked his grizzled head slightly. 'Come again?'

'Ah, it appears you have not been informed yet. Then allow me to be the bearer of glad tidings. News that will surely please the hearts of true soldiers like yourselves.' Vitellius lifted the goblet to his lips and took a casual sip before he set it down. 'I'll wager that by the time you return to your house, you will find your orders waiting for you.'

'Orders?' Cato's brow arched. 'What orders?'

'Both you and Centurion Macro have been assigned to the column that is being sent to Hispania Terraconensis to suppress the revolt there. The convoy carrying the advance party has already set sail. The balance of the force will arrive before the end of the month. Most of my senior officers will be sailing with me to catch up with the first units to arrive. That includes you two.'

'Bollocks to that,' said Macro. 'We've only just returned from Britannia. This must be some kind of a joke. A piss-poor one at that.'

Vitellius' expression became serious. 'It's no joke, I assure you.'

There was a moment's silence before Cato spoke again. 'Why us?'

'I was told I had the pick of the available officers. Naturally I chose the best. After all, you have proved your worth to Rome admirably on many occasions. Not least with the signal achievement of capturing Caratacus. It was easy to persuade the Emperor that it would be a good thing having you serve with my new command. You have fine service records and I am sure it will help boost the morale of the men to know that two such highly decorated officers will be fighting at their side.'

'I see.' The scar on Cato's face itched and he gave it a light scratch. 'And the real reason you picked us?'

'Real reason? Why so suspicious, Cato? Do you think I still bear you a grudge?'

'You might not. But I still do, for all the times you have tried to have Macro and me killed.'

'That was years ago. The situation is different now. I have different priorities.'

'No doubt. But old habits die hard.'

'I am not some scorpion from Aesop's fables, Cato. I am a senator, and one lesson I have learned from politics is that grudges are a luxury. I have no need to do you harm. Not for now at least.' He raised his goblet again. 'It will be just like old times, and an honour to serve with you again. So let's toast "comrades in arms", eh?'

The two officers on the other side of the table stared back, unmoving.

Vitellius shrugged, set his cup down and sat upright. 'Please yourselves. I must leave you now. I still have a few people I need to speak with before I make my final preparations for the campaign. The first of the Praetorian cohorts has already sailed. The rest of my force is making ready to join them. Make sure you are at Ostia tomorrow. We sail at first light the following day.' Vitellius turned to smile at Cato's son. 'Goodbye, young Lucius. I hope that we meet again some day. I look forward to getting to know you a little better.'

Lucius gave a little wave in response. Then Vitellius eased himself from the couch and stood up. 'Until tomorrow. Enjoy the feast.'

# CHAPTER ELEVEN

*Tarraco – capital of the Province of*
*Hispania Terraconensis*

The city of Tarraco was basking in bright sunshine as the warship passed the mole and entered the harbour. The slower merchant ships carrying the rest of Vitellius' command would not arrive for a few days yet. Cato stood with Macro in the bow turret and took in the view. It was the first time that either of them had been to Hispania and Cato's innate curiosity was thrilled by the prospect of discovering this new corner of the empire. The harbour was full of shipping: the rounded sides of cargo ships lined most of the quay, and more vessels were moored alongside, three or four deep, linked by gangways to the land. Gangs of labourers toiled across the vessels, loading and unloading, many bent under the burden of the heavy jars filled with fine olive oil that would be shipped to Italia and the eastern provinces. Meanwhile, fruits, cloth, jewellery and scents were imported from Egypt and Syria. At the far end of the quay was the modest harbour and boatsheds used by the small navy squadron that operated out of Tarraco. The handful of ageing biremes had been crowded to one side by the larger warships and troop transports that had recently arrived from Ostia.

Beyond the warehouses, inns and crowded slums of the harbour a wall encircled the original city, and beyond rose the grey mass of hills stretching into the interior of the province. Tarraco, the largest city in all Hispania, was divided into the lower and upper districts. The latter housed the temple of the imperial cult, which dominated the heart of the city, the huge columns rising above the jumble of tiled roofs to support the pediment on which a relief depicted Roma crowning a figure in a toga, standing in for Claudius, and before

104

him Caligula and Tiberius. Other large buildings were clustered around the temple, including the main forum and the palace of the provincial governor.

A short distance outside the city rose a low earth rampart and palisade containing the neat ranks of goatskin tents erected by the Praetorian cohort that had arrived a few days earlier. Cato and Macro gazed towards the camp with a professional interest, quietly gauging the quality of the men they would be fighting with in the coming campaign.

'Not bad,' Macro conceded. 'But then you'd expect the Praetorians to put on a good show of it. They do bugger-all else but train and show themselves off to the mob.'

Cato nodded as he recalled the time he and Macro had served with the guard on an undercover operation organised by Narcissus. The Praetorians believed themselves to be the elite corps of the Roman army, entrusted with the protection of the Emperor and his family. A former commander of the Praetorians had played a leading role in the assassination of the previous Emperor and Claudius had taken good care to pamper the men of the twelve cohorts ever since. A little silver went a long way towards buying their loyalty, Cato reflected. And a lot of silver bought their fanatical loyalty.

'They can fight well enough. We saw that early on in Britannia.'

'True,' Macro said grudgingly. 'But I dare say they've grown soft in the years since then. Too much good living and not nearly enough hard marching and fighting will ruin even the best soldiers.' He turned and rested his elbows on the wooden rail of the tower as he looked aft to where Vitellius and several of his companions were sharing a wineskin and talking in a good-natured manner. As men will after safely concluding a voyage across the sea. Fortunately the weather had been kind enough to the passengers aboard the trireme and there had only been one light squall in the eight days it had taken to reach Tarraco. The pitching of the vessel had brought on Cato's seasickness and he had spent several hours clutching the ship's siderail, along with some of the other landsmen, vomiting over the side until there was nothing left in their stomachs but bile. Macro, by contrast, had lifted his head to the strong breeze and salty tang and been refreshed by the experience. He had not been heedless of his friend's suffering, but knew that there was nothing that could be done about it and he left Cato alone to deal with his nausea until the seas were calm again.

Cato's misery had been compounded by having been confined with Vitellius aboard the ship. He had no trust in the man's assertion that he had chosen Cato and Macro to serve with him out of regard for their fighting qualities. A man like Vitellius was always scheming the next step of his path to power.

Cato turned his eyes away from the city and followed the direction of Macro's gaze. 'Can't say I am at all comfortable about the prospect of serving with our friend Vitellius again.'

'Nor me.' Macro sucked his teeth. 'He's a slippery bastard, and he's got it in for us. We'd best watch our step around him. At least we won't have to worry too much about the enemy this time out. Bunch of bandits roaming the hills aren't going to get very far when we pitch up with our Praetorian chums. Strikes me that we're using a bloody great hammer to crack a walnut.'

'I hope you're right . . .' Cato mused. Then he smiled at himself. He was always thinking the worst of a situation, despite considering himself as more of an epicurean than a stoic. Cato determined to put on a more optimistic face. 'No, I'm sure you're right. Hispania has been at peace for the best part of a hundred years. Once we reach Asturica Augusta and put on a show of force, Iskerbeles and his followers will see that the game is up. I dare say that Vitellius will be happy to burn enough villages to the ground to persuade the locals to hand over the ringleaders. It'll be over before winter.' Cato scratched his throat. 'The question is, what do we do next? I don't fancy being a fixture in the Praetorian Guard. Even with the handouts from the palace, it'll take many years before I can get enough together to buy another decent house. Thanks to Julia.'

Macro glanced at him in concern. 'Rough deal, that. I would have thought she was too sensible to get into debt like that. But there's nothing to be done about it. That Taurus is just like any other bastard money-lender. Bunch of sharks, living off the backs of the rest of us. But you're right about serving in the Guard. We need to get out of Rome. Find a posting where the enemy's up for a fight, and loaded with gold, silver and anything else that's worth looting. That's my kind of enemy,' he concluded, fondly.

With a last few strokes of the oars the trireme approached the other warships. The captain shouted the order to ship the blades and the long dripping shafts rose from the sea and rattled inboard. The helmsman carefully gauged the distance to the nearest cluster of warships rafted together and as the trireme lost way he eased the steering oar over and brought the vessel gently round a short distance from a trireme. A handful of sailors was ready to take the ropes cast across the gap and soon the vessel was secured and a gangway lashed into place.

A marine climbed into the tower and saluted Cato. 'Legate's compliments, sir. Officers are to join him at once and make for the governor's palace.'

'Very well.' Cato nodded and the man climbed back down the ladder.

'Wasting no time, then,' Macro mused. 'Good. Sooner this is over the better.'

Despite the familiar pace of life in the streets of the provincial capital, the mood in the governor's palace was markedly strained, from the instant that Vitellius and his party strode into the main hall. No wonder, thought Cato. Nearly three months had passed since the outbreak of the uprising. A large crowd of merchants and local dignitaries was demanding an audience with Publius Ballinus and a handful of clerks were busy holding them back while others took note of their names and the matter they wished to address with the governor. The shouting echoed off the walls and ceiling and Vitellius had to yell over the din to make himself known to the nearest of the clerks.

'Legate Aulus Vitellius. Just arrived from Rome. I must see the governor at once.'

The clerk looked relieved and nodded. 'If you'd follow me, sir.'

Those nearest to Vitellius turned towards him and one pressed forward to block his path. 'From Rome, sir? You've come to deal with the rebels?'

More flocked forward, some looking hopeful, some demanding immediate action, and Vitellius cleared his throat and raised his hands.

'Gentlemen! Gentlemen, a moment's calm, if you please.' He waited as the crowd quietened down and gazed at him expectantly. 'Rome has heard of your troubles and the Emperor has resolved to do everything in his power to crush the revolt and restore peace. Which is why he sent me, Aulus Vitellius, to do his bidding. I can assure you all that I have the necessary experience, and sufficient men, to hunt down and destroy Iskerbeles and his rabble. You can rest easy on that account, I give you my word. Now, if you please, clear the way and let me through.'

As the crowd began to assail the legate with further questions and demands Macro turned to Cato and cocked an eyebrow. 'Glad to hear that the Emperor's finest is on the case. I feel so much safer already.'

Cato was scanning the anxious expressions of the people around them. 'If this is how things are here in Tarraco, far from the uprising, then I think the situation might be somewhat worse than we've been led to believe.'

'Bollocks. You know what civvies are like. One whiff of a crisis and they could give a headless chicken a run for its money in the flapping stakes.'

Vitellius steadily worked his way through the crowd as he followed the clerk towards a corridor leading off the side of the hall. Two auxiliaries guarded the entrance to the corridor and hefted their spears and shields as the crowd spilled towards them. The clerk and the Roman officers passed into the corridor and the soldiers closed ranks behind them, shoving the locals back. As he followed the others Cato glanced from side to side through the doors of offices and saw that most of the clerks seemed unconcerned as they toiled at their desks. Some, it was true, looked anxious, and others rushed from room to room with waxed slates clutched in their hands. At the end of the corridor was an imposing arch with a large pair of studded oak doors. The clerk gestured to a slave and the latter hurriedly admitted Vitellius and his party and stood to one side with a bowed head as the party of Roman officers in their gleaming breastplates and helmets swept by.

Inside there was an anteroom where two more clerks bent over their desks, piled high with waxed slates and scrolls of various sizes. They jumped up and bowed as soon as they saw the officers.

'Legate Aulus Vitellius from Rome,' announced the officers' escort. 'Requesting an audience with the governor.'

The older of the two clerks bowed his bald head and rapped sharply on the door between the two desks. A muffled voice responded from the room beyond. 'Come!'

The clerk opened the door and announced those standing outside as Vitellius puffed his shoulders up impatiently.

'Send 'em in.'

The clerk stood aside and respectfully gestured towards the entrance to the governor's office. Vitellius led his officers through, ten men in armour with military boots that made a harsh clatter as they tramped over the tiled floor and across a sizeable chamber towards Publius Ballinus and his advisers. The governor was seated on a large cushioned chair and his closest companions sat on cushioned stools in a loose arc before him. All had discarded their togas in favour of more comfortable tunics, a sign of the seriousness of the discussion taking place before the arrival of the legate and his men. The civilians stood and Ballinus advanced and clasped forearms with Vitellius.

'Greetings. I cannot tell you how pleased I am – we all are – to see you.'

Vitellius smiled politely. 'As are we, to make landfall safely. Thanks be to Neptune.'

'Indeed. Come, be seated, Legate. You and all your officers.' Ballinus pointed out the spare stools lining the walls on each side and the governor's advisers shuffled up to make room for them. The governor resumed his seat before it occurred to him to offer some hospitality.

'I am sorry, would you and your men care for refreshment?'

'I thank you, but no. We've had experience of more than enough liquid over the previous few days.'

The comment lightened the mood and most present smiled. Cato saw the governor's eyes darting round his guests and then he smiled along with them. A man who went along with the common mood rather than stand above it, Cato reflected.

'Your arrival is most timely, Legate. We were just discussing how best to deploy the reinforcements.'

'Oh?' Vitellius raised an eyebrow. 'Were you now? And what exactly did you have in mind for me and the men under my command?'

'It's obvious, you must march to Asturica at once and crush the heart of the uprising. Crucify every rebel you take alive so no one forgets the terrible price to be paid for defying Rome.'

His advisers nodded emphatically.

'I see. At once, you say. Me, my comrades here, and the cohort of Praetorians, the one unit I presently have to hand. Against how many men? Do you know how many men Iskerbeles has at his back?'

Ballinus stared back blankly for a moment before he blustered, 'A few thousand, maybe more, but surely no match for trained soldiers.'

Vitellius scratched his nose. 'The last report I had, before leaving Rome, was that Iskerbeles has over five thousand spears behind him, and that the number is growing all the time. I dare say he will be even stronger by the time we march to Asturica Augusta. My dear governor, you are inviting me to disaster. Besides, I will make no direct move against the enemy until all my forces have landed, we are adequately provisioned and equipped and ready for the campaign.'

'And when will that be?' demanded one of the advisers, a swarthy rotund man with thick curly hair. 'We're suffering enough as things are. It's your duty to get out there and put those rebel bastards down. That's what we pay our taxes for.'

Vitellius turned to him easily. 'I'm sorry, but we haven't been introduced.'

The man glowered and then puffed his cheeks impatiently. 'Caius Glaecus, chief of the olive traders' guild.'

'Well then, Glaecus, as you may be aware, an imperial legate has the authority to requisition all necessary supplies in his theatre of operation. Moreover, he is empowered to compel all citizens to serve under him for the duration of his emergency powers. Now, if

110

you ever speak to me in that manner again I will commandeer every last thing you own, and then I will impress you into the ranks of one of my cohorts and ensure that you get placed in the very front rank of the battle line when we face the enemy. In order to satisfy your enthusiasm to see that the enemy is defeated. How does that sound?'

Glaecus paled, shrank back into himself and looked down at his sandals. Macro could not help a slight smile at the civilian's discomfort, and a grudging admiration for the smooth manner in which Vitellius had squashed the man's hubris.

'In answer to friend Glaecus' query, I am expecting the rest of my men to join me within the next five days. We should be ready to march in ten days' time.'

The governor eased himself forward to address the legate. 'That may be a little too late. Given our most recent report from the area.' He nodded towards a slender man sitting at the end of his row of advisers and Cato saw that he was covered in dust and grime. He stirred wearily and rose to his feet. Ballinus gestured towards him. 'This is Gaius Getellus Cimber. One of the town magistrates of Lancia, a provincial town not thirty miles from Asturica Augusta. He escaped from Lancia ten days ago.'

'Escaped?' one of the officers muttered.

'Speak up, Cimber. Tell the legate and these officers what you told us earlier today.'

Cimber drew a deep breath as he collected his thoughts and turned towards Vitellius and his officers. He spoke with a pronounced accent which betrayed his origins at once. He was one of those born into the local tribes who had worked his way into the Roman administration. 'The rebels took Asturica two days before I left. The survivors of the garrison arrived shortly before the first of the tribesmen pursuing them. They told the story of what happened. The leader of the local senate had boasted that he would lead the militia into the mountains himself and bring Iskerbeles back in chains, or bring his head back at any rate. The senate assumed that the rebels were of no account and no extra precautions were taken to protect Asturica. The survivors claimed that the night watch on the main gate were drunk and they were overwhelmed in an instant. With the gates open, the rebels poured in, began to slaughter the

111

garrison and any Roman citizens or officials associated with the running of the town.'

Vitellius cleared his throat. 'Asturica is in their hands? Are you certain?'

'I am only repeating what I was told, sir. Whether the rebels are still there or not is anyone's guess. But the town has fallen to Iskerbeles.'

'I see. So what has that to do with the escape that you mentioned?'

Cimber scratched his cheek anxiously. 'The morning after Asturica's survivors reached us, the rebels surrounded Lancia. I was sent to raise the alarm and request that forces were sent to relieve the town. I had an escort of six men, on horseback. We left under cover of night, but ran into one of their patrols and had to cut our way through. I, and one other, were the only ones to get away.'

'And now Lancia is under siege?'

'I believe so, sir. The rebels were setting up camp outside the walls that evening.'

Cato leaned forward so that Cimber would see him clearly. 'Can Lancia hold out against a siege? Are the defences sufficient?'

Cimber considered briefly before replying. 'Lancia has good walls, and we won't be taken by surprise, as Asturica was.'

'How about the garrison? How many fighting men can the town muster?'

'There's only the militia, sir. And a hundred or so boys in the young cadets. Five hundred in all, I would guess.'

'You see?' Ballinus intervened. 'We have lost one town, and now a second is in danger, or may have already fallen. We must act. At once. You must lead your men against the rebels immediately, Legate.'

Vitellius could not conceal his concern over the news and frowned. 'I need time to think. To make plans.'

'We haven't got any time,' Ballinus shot back. 'You don't know the worst of it yet.'

'There's more bad news?' Macro muttered. 'This is not looking like the pushover we were told it would be.'

The governor clasped his chubby hands together. 'There's an imperial mine – Argentium – twenty miles from Lancia, in the hills.

112

The largest in the region. It's the collection point for all the silver from the surrounding mines. It's this time of year that the bullion convoy is put together and sets off for Tarraco. If the rebels take the mine, and the convoy, then there will be nothing for the provincial treasury, and nothing to be remitted to Rome. The province, and the Emperor, depend on the silver to pay the troops, here and at Rome. If it's lost . . .'

He did not need to finish the train of thought. The danger was clear enough. Soldiers deprived of pay were inclined to complain. Worse still, they were inclined to look for new paymasters. Especially in the capital where the loyalty of the Praetorian Guard cohorts could be bought by any man with sufficient funds to bribe them. There were other threats too, Cato realised. With such a fortune in his hands, Iskerbeles could raise even more men to support his cause. The uprising would spread rapidly, across Terraconensis into the neighbouring provinces of Baetica and Lusitania. If that happened then Vitellius and his force would be overwhelmed, and nothing short of a vast army would be required to defeat the rebels and restore order. The trouble was, the Roman army was thinly stretched along the empire's frontiers. To amass enough troops to pacify Hispania would mean stripping them from the frontier. Rome's enemies would be sure to take advantage of the moment of weakness. Large though the Roman army was, and deadly in action, in truth its control over the empire depended upon a delicate balance of resources. Especially with the ongoing conflict in Britannia constantly draining the empire's reserves. All this Cato grasped in a moment.

'We can't let the mine, and its treasure, fall into the rebels' hands,' Ballinus continued. 'If it does, then we'll answer for it with our heads.'

Vitellius stared at him. 'We?'

'Of course. This is my province. That I will be held responsible is a given. But you can be sure that the commander of the force sent to suppress the revolt will be held equally accountable, if I have anything to do with it.'

'Ah, I understand. This is blackmail, Ballinus. A very ugly attempt at blackmail, I may say.'

'Not at all, Legate. I am simply underscoring the political realities of the situation.' The governor sat back in his chair and folded his hands. 'I think it would be wise if we co-operated to destroy Iskerbeles. It is in both our interests to do so.'

Vitellius' lips pressed tightly together as he controlled his anger and collected his thoughts. 'What would you have me do? Send my men in to be destroyed piecemeal? I can do nothing until *all* my men are here.'

'Strategy is your remit, my dear Vitellius. I am simply a politician.'

Vitellius sneered and shook his head. 'Coward.'

There was a strained silence in the audience chamber, and then Cato coughed lightly. Vitellius turned to look at him.

'You have something to offer, Prefect Cato?'

'Yes, sir.'

'Why am I not surprised?' Vitellius sighed. 'Spit it out, then.'

Cato held his irritation in check and ordered his thoughts. 'If Iskerbeles takes the mine then the consequences will be felt across the empire. So we cannot delay any attempt to prevent that. Whatever forces we have must be sent to secure the bullion.' He turned to Cimber. 'Do you know the mine?'

The man nodded. 'Yes, I have been there a few times. I have the grain contract, to feed the slaves.'

'Good, then tell me, is it fortified in any way? I assume that there must be some walls to keep the slaves in.'

'There is a slave compound, on the ledge above the mine, and then the mine itself is at the foot of the cliffs, with a river at its back, and a wall at one end.'

'How many slaves are there?'

Cimber made a quick estimate. 'Around three thousand.'

'And how many guards?'

'Two hundred, maybe. There's a century of auxiliary troops, and the rest are overseers. If the escort for the convoy has arrived, then that means another century will be there.'

Cato nodded. 'Enough men to defend the place for now. At least enough to discourage any rebel patrol that turns up. But not enough to withstand a determined attack.'

'Which they will be sure to attempt,' Vitellius cut in. 'As soon as it occurs to them to go after the silver. If they haven't taken the mine already.'

'That's if they know about the bullion, sir.' Cato turned to the governor. 'I take it that the existence of the bullion convoy isn't advertised?'

Ballinus sniffed. 'Hardly. One whiff of it getting out and you can be sure that every band of brigands in the mountains would be breathing down their necks the moment they left the mine. The ingots are placed in the bottom of wagons and concealed beneath sacks of grain and olive oil amphorae. That way it looks like an ordinary military detachment on the march and doesn't attract any unwanted local attention along the way.'

'Right, so then it's likely that Iskerbeles isn't yet aware of the bullion.' Cato paused as a thought occurred to him. 'The slaves at the mine. I assume there's a constant need for replacements. Where do they come from?'

Cimber shrugged. 'Most are brought in by slave contractors from Gigia, prisoners taken from the campaign in Britannia. Then there are those from the Astures tribe, sold into slavery as debt defaulters. Plenty of them lately. They're Iskerbeles' people. That's one of the reasons why the area was ripe for revolt. Thanks to those bloodsucking money-lenders acting for their master in the Roman senate . . .' Cimber's eyes widened and he looked at the governor anxiously. 'I meant no offence, sir. It's just that Senator Annaeus' men have been calling in debts for the last few months and they've foreclosed on several villages. That's what sparked the uprising.'

'That's no excuse,' Ballinus snapped. 'The locals should have known what they were getting into when they took on the loans.'

Cato knew better. The money-lenders were glib salesmen, keen to entrap their customers with promises of cheap loans that ultimately tied them into paying off the interest for the rest of their lives. That, or being forced to settle the debt by losing their chattels, their land, and even their liberty. He had seen enough money-lenders follow in the wake of the legions in Britannia to know how they worked. And the misery and trouble they could cause.

115

'Then we can assume that Iskerbeles is going to move against the mines in the area, to free the people from his tribe that have been sold into slavery,' said Cato. 'He's going to get round to taking Argentium at some point. If we're lucky, he'll go for the smaller mines first, building his strength from the slaves he liberates.'

Vitellius gave a dry laugh. 'And if we're not lucky?'

'Then we're all in the shit, sir. But let's assume we're lucky since we have no choice in doing whatever we can to secure the bullion.'

'What do you mean, Cato?'

'You have to send the cohort camped outside Tarraco to the mine at once, sir. You can't afford to waste a moment. The rest of your command can follow on when they land.'

'One cohort of Praetorians against thousands of rebels? Are you mad? They'd be slaughtered.'

Cato shook his head. 'They don't have to take on Iskerbeles, sir. They just have to secure the mine and hold out there until the rest of the column reaches Argentium.'

'And if the rebels happen upon the cohort before the column reaches them?'

'Then they defend the mine for as long as they can, and if it looks like the rebels are going to break in, the silver can be buried, or tipped into the river. Anything to keep it out of their hands. It can always be recovered later.'

Vitellius looked down at the floor, deep in thought, until the governor broke the silence.

'Your officer is right, Legate. You must lead your men to the mine at once. The rest can follow the instant they reach Tarraco. We have no choice but to do as he says.'

All eyes turned to Vitellius expectantly and when he looked up Cato saw that there was a cold gleam in his expression.

'Very well, the Praetorian cohort will march to Argentium at first light.'

Ballinus looked relieved, and nodded. 'Very good. I shall make sure that you and your men have all the provisions they need.'

'I thank you. But I shall not be marching with the cohort. I will remain here to plan the campaign while I await the arrival of the rest of my forces. The cohort will need to be led by someone with the nerve and quick wits to cope with the unexpected, should anything go wrong.'

Macro sucked in a breath and muttered. 'Fuck, even I can see where this is going . . .'

The legate half turned on his stool and faced Cato. 'Prefect Cato. You are the best man for the job, in my opinion. I can think of no man I would prefer to see take on such a vital, and dangerous, mission. Due to the risks entailed, I insist that you are accompanied by the redoubtable Centurion Macro. Your orders are straight-forward. Take command of the Second Cohort of the Guard. Proceed directly to the mine at Argentium as swiftly as possible. I suggest that Cimber, here, goes with you. He knows the people and the area. He'll be useful.'

Cimber shook his head. 'But I'm not a soldier.'

'Fear not, my good fellow. You'll come to no harm with Prefect Cato and his men protecting you.'

'All the same, sir, I'd rather stay here in Tarraco.'

'I am sure you would, but I require your service in assisting me to defeat the rebels. You will go with the cohort willingly, or in chains.' Vitellius folded his hands and tapped his forefingers together. 'If I were you, I'd choose to go willingly.'

Cimber stared back and then nodded meekly.

'Good man. Like the saying goes – one volunteer is worth ten pressed men.' Vitellius turned his attention back to Cato. 'Now then, Prefect, once you reach the mine you are to safeguard the bullion, and conceal it in the event that there is any danger of it falling into enemy hands. You are to remain there until I arrive with the rest of the column. Do you have any questions?'

Cato shook his head, and then Macro raised a hand.

'Well, Centurion?'

'And what if this Iskerbeles gets to the mine before us, sir?'

Vitellius smiled faintly. 'If that happens, Centurion Macro, then I expect you to attack at once and retake the mine, whatever the odds against you.'

Macro frowned. 'That could be suicide, sir.'

'In that event, I would be sure to commend your sacrifice when

I report back to Rome. Perhaps there might be another decoration to add to your fine spear, albeit posthumously.'

Macro nodded. 'Fuck you very much, sir.'

There was a sharp intake of breath as some of the other officers glanced at the centurion but Macro remained deadpan and Vitellius' eyes narrowed briefly before he took a long breath.

'You have your orders, Prefect Cato. You can assume command of the cohort at once.'

'Yes, sir.'

'May the Gods be with you, Prefect. For if you fail then no one will have mercy on you. Not Iskerbeles, and if by some miracle you escape the enemy, you can expect no mercy from me, nor the Emperor, nor the people of Rome. So, do this well, or die in the attempt.'

# CHAPTER TWELVE

'The bastard's stitched us up like a pair of kippers,' Macro growled as they marched through the tent lines of the Second Praetorian Cohort, in their camp outside the walls of Tarraco. The soldiers immediately around them stood and exchanged salutes with the officers as they strode past. There was noticeably more formality than was the case with the legionaries that Cato and Macro had served with in previous campaigns. The goatskin tents were not stained and patched like those of the legions and appeared to have been taken directly from the Guards' stores, unused. Their armour and shields had the same look, gleaming, with not a spot of rust in evidence.

'Orders are orders, Macro. Ours is not to reason why.'

'Oh, come on. You know full well why Vitellius picked us for the job. Chances are we'll march slap bang into the rebel army and be cut to pieces. Even if we reach the mine first, Iskerbeles will hear of it soon enough and come to find us. Same result. We're for the chop, and all these lads along with us. Fuck . . .' They walked on in silence a few paces before Macro glanced at his friend. 'You don't seem duly pissed off with our lot.'

'Like I said, orders.'

As they approached the headquarters area in the heart of the camp the two Praetorians on duty at the entrance to the largest tent presented their spears and stood aside to let them pass. They ducked under the flap and several clerks instantly rose from around the large campaign table where they had been working.

'At ease.' Cato looked round. 'Who is the senior officer in the cohort?'

'Centurion Gnaeus Lucullus Pulcher, sir,' one of the clerks replied. 'There's a tribune attached to us as well.'

'And who are you?' Cato demanded.

The clerk snapped to attention. 'Optio Metellus, First Century, Second Cohort, sir.'

'Right then, Metellus, I am Prefect Quintus Licinius Cato. The legate has just appointed me to command the cohort. This is Centurion Macro, my second in command. I want Pulcher, the tribune and all the other centurions and optios to come to head-quarters at once.'

The optio quickly recovered from his surprise at this turn of events. 'Fetch the officers, yes, sir.'

He hurried out of the tent and Cato turned to one of the other clerks. 'You, take two men and go down to the port. There's a trireme just arrived from Ostia. Have my kit, and that of the centurion, brought here. The rest of you, outside.'

Once the tent was empty Macro sat on one of the stools and set his helmet down on the table. 'The lads in the camp look tidy enough. I wonder how they're going to cope with several days of forced marching. Especially since they've done bugger all but lounge around in Rome for the last few years.'

Cato folded his arms. 'Not all of 'em. Some will have transferred from the legions. They'll set the standard for the rest. And despite what you think, even the Praetorians have stiff selection standards. They'll do well enough . . . They'd better.'

'I hope you're right.' Macro thought a moment. 'This is every-thing that Vitellius could wish for. He's got us out here with him, and now he can send us right into the heart of danger and if we survive then he'll claim the credit for a prompt decision to save the bullion. If we find ourselves in the thick of it, then we'll do our best to hide the bullion and he'll take the credit for that too. Of course, our heads will be decorating the gateposts of some tribesman's settlement, but hey ho. Bloody bollocks. If the Emperor awards us another silver spear for giving our lives for Rome, I'll tell you where I'd stick it.'

Cato cocked his head. 'Posthumously? Good luck with that. But you're right. We're at his mercy while we're here. I can't help wondering why he insisted on having us assigned to his command.'

'Oh, come on, Cato. It's clear as day. The bastard hates our guts. We've crossed swords with him on many occasions in the past. Too many occasions. And now he's taking his revenge. He picked us for this little excursion so he could drag us off to some dusty corner of the empire and have one of his men do us in. As things stand, it could be the rebels who get to do the deed for him and he returns home with his hands clean.'

'I don't think that's it,' Cato responded. 'It's a lot of effort to go to to get rid of us when he really has no need to. When he has tried to kill us, it's because we stood in the way of his plans. There's no point in doing that now.'

Macro shrugged. 'Maybe he's clearing the decks for the future, in case we stand in his way again.'

'But we might just as easily be of use to him alive.' Cato frowned. 'In any case, there's something odd about some of the other officers he has picked to serve under him.'

'What d'you mean?'

'When I spoke with them on the voyage over from Ostia, they were puzzled by their selection. They're not part of Vitellius' circle. Indeed, they've even opposed him in the past.'

Macro scratched his jaw. 'That don't make sense. Why surround yourself with men you can't trust? What's his game?'

Cato closed his eyes and lowered his head for a moment. He was still weary from the restless state in which he had endured the sea journey and had to struggle to concentrate. 'I'm not sure. Maybe it isn't about Vitellius at all.'

'What do you mean?'

Cato tried to force his weary mind to concentrate. 'What if picking us and the other officers has more to do with getting us away from Rome for some reason?'

'What reason? Come on, Cato, you're not making much sense.'

Cato blinked his tired eyes open and looked at Macro. 'I don't know exactly. But I'm sure Vitellius is up to something. Or if not him, then he's acting for someone else.'

Macro was silent for a moment before he spoke again. 'Vitellius was standing with Pallas at the triumph. They looked very chummy to me. You think it's him, Pallas?'

'Could be. But then, what is Pallas scheming at?' Cato rubbed his forehead. 'Something is wrong about all this. Very wrong. But there's nothing we can do about it here. We should warn Narcissus. Send him a message before we march tomorrow.'

'What would you warn him about? All you have are suspicions.' Macro chuckled drily. 'Just for a change. Seriously, lad, what can you tell him? That we suspect Vitellius has some underhand reason for picking officers he's not in the habit of inviting round to dinner? What if he really has picked us all because we happen to be the best men available for the job? Even if you are right, then what does it have to do with Pallas?' Macro shook his head dismissively. 'All a bloody storm in a thimble if you ask me.'

Cato thought hard for a moment. Macro could be right. Maybe there was less to it all than met the eye. But then again, Vitellius was as cunning as any snake, and whatever reason he gave for an action in public, there was surely another, deeper and more devious reason gliding beneath the surface of the cool charm of his persona. If he did want to do them harm, then it would have been easy enough to hire some gang members from the Subura to knife them in the streets. True, that might attract unwanted attention, and a deal of suspicion. And what if all the officers chosen for the mission had been disposed of in the same way? That would surely set the capital on edge. Everyone who feared their political enemies would be suspicious and watchful and it would make any deeper plot far more difficult to conceal.

The flap rustled as Metellus entered and offered a salute. 'The officers you requested will be here directly, sir.'

Cato nodded and was about to dismiss the man but then turned his gaze back. 'You're the senior clerk at headquarters?'

'Yes, sir.'

'Then you'll know if the cohort is ready to march. Has all the men's kit been landed?'

'Yes, sir. And I've set up a stores tent. Just waiting for some spare leather and armour segments when the rest of the ships arrive.'

'No time for that. We'll have to make do with whatever the men are carrying with them. What I need now is mules and carts. Take fifty men into Tarraco. Requisition a dozen decent-sized carts and enough mules to draw them, plus some animals for the reserve. Then I want them filled with grain, cured meat, cheese and wine and water. You can authorise it in the name of the governor and tell the suppliers to go to him for payment. I want the carts loaded and ready to leave at first light. I also want twenty mounts for scouting. Good mounts, mind you. Don't accept any broken-down nags, or any bribes offered to take them. Pick the best. Got all that?'

Metellus mentally ticked off the list and nodded. 'Yes, sir.'

The clerk hesitated. 'Are you sure about this, sir? It's going to push the noses of the locals out of joint.'

'That'll be the least of their worries if we don't get what we need. Go now.' A thought struck Cato. 'Wait. While you are in the city, I want you to go to the governor's palace and find a man called Cimber, from Asturica. He's been assigned to act as our guide. Make sure he accompanies you back to the camp and accept no excuses.'

Metellus grinned. 'I understand, sir.'

Cato saw the malevolent glint in the optio's eyes at the prospect of impressing Cimber and spared the man a little sympathy for his plight. 'Don't be too heavy-handed with Cimber. I'd rather he helped us as willingly as possible. Dismissed. '

Metellus saluted and left the tent.

Macro looked at Cato with an amused expression. 'He's right, you know. I appreciate the need to act fast, but it's going to cause a stink. Even if the governor lets it past you can be bloody sure that someone will send a petition to the Emperor in Rome to complain about it.'

'We can't worry about that now. Besides, given the odds, we may not be around to face the music even if they do complain. So it's not my problem.'

'Spoken like a true leader!' Macro laughed.

An officer appeared on the threshold of the tent and bowed his head. 'Centurion Publius Placinus, Fifth Century, sir. You sent for me?'

'Come in, Placinus. Where are the other officers?'

'Just coming, sir.'

The remaining centurions filed into the tent in their off-white tunics and Cato told them to take a seat at the table, along with Macro. Cato glanced over them, and his gaze rested on the last of them to enter the tent. A heavily built veteran with a boxer's features: flattened nose, heavy brow and thick lips and ears. The man's face was familiar, yet Cato could not quite place him in any context that would have made him recognisable. Then he realised that there was someone missing.

'Where's the tribune?'

'He's gone into Tarraco, sir,' said Placinus. 'I sent a man to fetch him.'

'I see.' Cato frowned in frustration. 'Does he have permission to be out of camp?'

'Permission? Sir, he's technically the ranking officer in the cohort.'

'Technically. But let me guess, he's a junior tribune attached to the unit to serve out his military service in Rome. Spends more time drinking with his friends than attending to the few duties he has. No doubt he knows more about the latest fashions than he does about soldiering.' Cato paused and noted the amused expressions of the centurions. Clearly they shared the same view of most professional soldiers towards the young gentlemen who completed their military service before devoting their lives to political advancement. 'We all know the type. Technically, they hold a high rank, but the reality is they are raw recruits who we are obliged to treat civilly and keep from interfering in the work that we do. Of course, I hope that the young man in question is the exception to the rule. I will give him the same chance to prove himself that I give all men under my command. But they will abide by the rules, without exception. No man leaves camp without permission from now on.' Cato added in a more steely tone, 'By the authority of Legate Vitellius, this cohort is now under my command.'

He tapped his chest. 'I am Prefect Quintus Licinius Cato. I commanded an auxiliary cohort in Britannia, and before that I served in Egypt, Palmyra, Syria, Judaea and Germania, along with my grim-looking comrade here, Centurion Macro.'

Macro nodded his head in acknowledgement.

'Some of you will know that the centurion and I were recently decorated for the capture of King Caratacus. You should also know that was not a one-off piece of good fortune. We've seen plenty of action. Don't be fooled by the scar on my face: the other man came off worse. Centurion Macro and I do our duty, we fight hard and we lead from the front. I want you to know that, because we are ordered to take the fight to the rebels at first light tomorrow.'

The centurions stirred at the news. Some had a gleam of excitement in their eyes, but two could not hide their anxiety, Cato noted.

'The cohort will force march to Argentium to secure the imperial mine there. It is located in the heart of the territory controlled by the rebels we have been sent to defeat. So you will appreciate the risks involved. Defending the mine is vital to the fortunes of the campaign and the wider empire. Which is why the legate cannot afford to wait for the remaining units to reach Tarraco. Once the other cohorts have landed, Vitellius will advance towards Asturica and we will join the main column when it reaches the mine. Gentlemen, I make no secret of the danger we may face, but it is up to us to do the job.' He let his words sink in before resuming. 'We will need to march as swiftly as possible. Therefore, the men will carry their picks, canteens, mess tins, armour and weapons only. All spare clothing, kit and personal effects will remain behind to go into the stores of the Tarraco garrison. I'd also suggest that the men lodge their wills here at the same time. We'll also be leaving our siege kit and artillery here. The only vehicles we'll be taking are carts, for the carriage of provisions and any injured . . . Any questions?'

Placinus raised a hand. 'How long before the other cohorts reach Tarraco?'

'They're expected any day. The legate will advance as soon as he has collected siege trains and provisions for the column. They will take somewhat longer to reach Asturica than we do. Maybe seven to ten days behind us.'

There were no more comments and Cato took his seat at the head of the table. 'Then it only remains for you to introduce yourselves, gentlemen. Centurion Placinus I already know. If you have legionary service before joining the Praetorians then say so.'

He indicated the man to his left, tall, thin, creased features and grey-haired. 'You first.'

'Centurion Arrius Vorenus Secundus, Second Century, sir. Been a guardsman for ten years, centurion for the last four years. Transferred from the Sixth Ferrata Legion when I was an optio.'

'The "Ironclads",' Macro commented. 'Good men.'

Centurion Secundus inclined his head in appreciation of the comment as the next man cleared his throat. He was far younger, smooth-faced and overweight.

'Centurion Gaius Metricus Porcino, Sixth Century, sir. Commissioned into the Praetorians two years ago.'

'No previous experience?' asked Cato.

'None, sir.' Porcino's gaze wavered and then he looked down at his folded hands.

'Then count yourself lucky to have this chance to prove your mettle, Centurion. Do your duty and remember your training and I am confident you will do well.'

'Yes, sir. I will.'

Cato moved directly on to the next officer, a slender man in his early thirties with finely sculpted features, thick dark hair and dark eyes. He had a neatly trimmed beard and sensitive lips that were raised slightly, as if he was finding the occasion faintly amusing. A smile flickered before he introduced himself. 'Centurion Junius Petillius, Fourth Century. I'm afraid I was also directly commissioned, some eight years ago. No prior military experience. Just some useful connections.'

Macro's eyes flashed angrily. 'You'll address the prefect as "sir". Do it now.'

Petillius' amused expression did not falter for a moment as he bowed his head. 'Yes, of course. Sir it is.'

Cato quickly weighed the officer up. A socialite, then. His family was from a junior branch of the aristocracy, not wealthy enough to enter him into the Senate, but with sufficient ancestral reputation to trade on to gain him a commission in the Praetorian Guard. No doubt he cut a fine figure in his polished ceremonial armour, and used his fine looks and easy charm to good effect at the parties and in the bedchambers of Rome. Cato felt an instant dislike for the

126

man and shifted his gaze to the other side of the table where the last two officers were seated. The first could have been Macro's younger brother. The same stocky stature, tightly curled hair and broad face.

'Centurion Marcus Horatius Musa, Third Century, sir. Been with the Guard six months. Before that, Centurion of the First Cohort, Twenty-First Rapax Legion.'

'Why were you transferred?'

'Not my choice, sir. The legate mentioned me in despatches, after action with some of the mountain tribes. Next thing I know, I'm appointed to the Praetorian Guard. Not complaining though.'

'I should think not!' Macro grinned. 'Double the pay, and all the comforts and cheap cunny of Rome.'

Musa had the grace to nod. 'I'd sooner die from the clap than have some stinking barbarian cleave my chops with an axe any day.'

Cato turned to the last man, the one he was now quite certain he had encountered before, some years earlier.

'Centurion Gnaeus Lucullus Pulcher, First Century, sir. Been a guardsman from the start. Though I've seen action on the frontier with Germania, and in Britannia. Made centurion nine years ago, after the Guard returned from Britannia.'

'You were in the battle outside Camulodunum then,' Macro queried.

'Yes, sir. A tough fight, that. Thought those Celt bastards were never going to give up.'

Macro nodded, with feeling, and turned to give a nod of approval to Cato. But the prefect was staring coldly at Pulcher. Cato now recalled where he knew the man from, and a flood of bitter memories filled his mind as he mentally stripped away the traces of the years from the man's face and recalled Pulcher, the fellow recruit who had made his life such a misery when Cato had first joined the Second Augustan Legion. Pulcher had bullied him, sneered at his educated ways and would have crushed his spirit had it not been for Macro's intervention. But that was not the only source of the cold anger rising in Cato's heart. For Pulcher had been sent to the legion to spy on some officers suspected of conspiring against the newly installed Emperor Claudius. Later, on the evening of the invasion of Britannia, Pulcher had interrogated, tortured and executed the ringleaders of an abortive mutiny, which was no doubt the cause of his promotion once he had completed his assignment and returned to the ranks of the Praetorian Guard.

Cato swallowed and took a deep calming breath. 'I believe we have met before, Centurion.'

Pulcher's brow tightened. 'I don't think so, sir.'

'I can assure you we have. I didn't have this scar then. Back in the Second Legion, when I was a fresh-faced recruit.'

The centurion looked confused for a moment before his jaw sagged a fraction and his eyes widened in shock. 'Fuck me . . . The brat from the palace.'

'I am delighted to see that you remember me. And I haven't forgotten you, Pulcher.'

Macro leaned forward and stared hard at the other centurion before he shook his head in wonder. 'It is. It is him. Bloody hell. So this is what happened to the bastard after he disappeared.' Macro rounded on him. 'You've got a lot to answer for, my friend. You killed some good men. Comrades of ours.'

Pulcher leaned back quickly in alarm. 'They were mutineers. Traitors! I was doing my duty.'

'Sure you were,' Macro sneered. 'Cutting the throats of men tied up like dogs. Instead of facing men in battle, like a real soldier.'

'But I did fight! At Camulodunum, like I said.'

'That's what you say,' Macro said mockingly. 'And we should trust the word of a back-stabbing spy?'

Pulcher's eyes darted from Macro towards Cato, pleadingly. 'That was ten years ago, sir. Like I said, I was doing my duty, and I've had a spotless record ever since.'

Cato paused to wonder if a man like Pulcher could change, and then decided that he could not take the risk in finding out. The stakes were too high for that. Besides, his treatment of Pulcher might serve as a valuable lesson to the others not to cross their new commander.

'Centurion Pulcher, you are relieved of your command of the First Century. You will take command of the baggage train. Centurion Macro?'

'Sir?'

'You will replace Pulcher as commander of the First Century.'

'Yes, sir.'

'No!' Pulcher protested, before he saw the warning in Cato's expression. 'Wait, sir. You can't replace me. I was appointed by the Emperor, back in Rome. You can't override his decision.' He gave a crafty smile. 'You wouldn't dare . . . sir.'

'As you say, "back in Rome". We're far away from Rome, and about to march to war, Pulcher. So you can make your complaint when the campaign is over. And good luck to you. Meanwhile, my orders stand and I will hear no more of it.'

'But—'

'One more word, and I'll charge you with insubordination. And then break you back to the ranks. If you treat your men like you used to treat me then I dare say they might enjoy serving with you on an equal footing.'

Cato well knew how difficult and dangerous it was to be a centurion reduced to the ranks. The harsh discipline they meted out when protected by their rank was returned to them in kind by their former victims. Pulcher opened his mouth to speak again, and caught himself just in time. He clenched his jaw and sat in brooding silence.

'That's better.' Cato looked round at the other officers. 'You know our orders, and you know what to do. Get your men ready to march at dawn. Dismissed.'

The centurions rose sharply to their feet, saluted and then left the tent. All save Macro who waited until he and his friend were alone before he spoke.

'Well, well. I always wondered what became of that vile piece of shit.'

'Now you know. He got promoted. Fair reward for foul deed would seem to be the ordure of the day.'

There was a beat before Macro smiled at the quip. Then he glanced towards the tent flap before lowering his voice. 'You didn't tell them about the bullion convoy, I notice.'

'Not yet. Last thing I want is rumours of silver doing the rounds of the rankers. I need these men to concentrate on the fight, not be distracted by treasure. We keep that quiet for as long as necessary.'

'Yes, sir.'

'Hello.'

They both turned quickly to see that another man had entered the tent. He was wearing a plain soldier's tunic, unbelted. He looked to be the same age as Cato, with a high forehead fringed with fair hair. He smiled uncertainly.

'I was told to report to the new prefect.'

'That's me,' Cato responded. 'Prefect Quintus Licinius Cato. And you are?'

The new arrival made to reply, then stared at Cato, his mouth half open as his words died in his throat.

Cato was exhausted and in no mood for any nonsense. 'Jupiter's balls! What's wrong with you? Just tell me your damn name.'

'My name? I—I . . .' he stammered, swallowed nervously, his Adam's apple bobbing. Then he forced himself to stand to attention and gave as clear an answer as he could. 'Tribune Aulus Valerius Cristus, assigned to the Second Cohort, reporting as requested, sir.'

# CHAPTER THIRTEEN

Cato felt his chest tighten, as if there was an iron band around his ribs, as he stared expressionlessly at the man who had been his wife's lover. For an instant he allowed himself a sliver of doubt. There could be two men of the same name. But the new arrival's unsettled behaviour betrayed him. His gaze could only bear to meet Cato's for an instant before shifting away and his fingers twitched until he could stand it no longer and clasped his hands behind his back and made himself stand erect, shoulders back.

Macro could not help looking bemused by the man's reaction upon entering the tent. He tried to catch Cato's eye. But the latter's stare was unwavering.

'Tribune Cristus . . .' Cato began as calmly as he could. His heart was beating fast, and the rage that had come and gone in waves since he had discovered Julia's infidelity rushed back like a violent storm. The urge to draw his sword and cut the tribune to pieces tormented him. Yet the long years of army service had taught him to master his outward appearance and to tame his inner turmoil. Even so, he had to clear his throat and begin again.

'Tribune Cristus, you look perturbed. What is the matter with you?'

Cristus chewed his bottom lip and tried to master his surprise and fear. 'I, I, er, wasn't expecting to find the cohort placed under a new commander, sir. That's all.'

'Not quite all.' Cato slowly paced across the tent towards the tribune and stopped a sword's length away, looking him over closely. Cristus' agitation increased as Cato let him suffer in silence for a moment, and then resumed. 'I was informed that you were not in camp when I arrived to take command. Why was that?'

'I was in Tarraco, sir.'

'Doing what, exactly?'

'Buying illustrating materials, sir. From the forum.'

'Illustrating materials?' Macro leaned forward and rested his hairy forearms on the table. 'What the fuck for?'

Cristus glanced at the centurion, but made no comment about being interrogated by an officer of inferior rank. 'I was interested in designing things before I became a tribune. I've always had something of a flair for that, but I could never get enough commissions to make a decent living out of it. My father was a friend of a friend of one of the Emperor's advisers who pulled a few strings to land me the post of staff tribune. It gave me independent means to live. But I still pursued my original interest. Or did until the cohort was sent to Tarraco.'

Macro stared at him and then shook his head slowly. 'Just what we need as we march to battle . . .'

Cristus stiffened his back. 'I've done my training, along with the rest of the cohort.'

'Maybe, but when we go into battle against Iskerbeles and his mob, I'd feel more comfortable knowing that the man at my side wasn't thinking about painting a portrait of the enemy, rather than sticking a sword in his guts.'

'I'm not an artist. I told you, I like to design things.'

'Things?'

Cristus squirmed a little. 'Carriages actually. It's a passion of mine. I sketch them, and design my own.'

'Carriages . . . Give me strength.' Macro puffed intolerantly. 'Sir, I think we'd be better off leaving this one here in Tarraco when we march. He's going to be bugger-all use to us.'

The curt dismissal finally drew a response from the tribune. 'Just a moment, Centurion. I am a tribune and you will accord me the respect my superior rank deserves.'

'I will respect those superiors who earn my respect, sir. The rest I will simply obey.' Macro turned back to Cato. 'Sir, what do you intend to do with this one?'

Cato had only been half-listening to the exchange. He was

more concerned with trying to understand how Julia's affections could have been transferred to the unprepossessing individual standing before him. Then he noticed that the tribune's jaw hung open slightly when he was not speaking, and the effect was to make him look simple-minded. How could Julia have loved this man? How could she have been prepared to give Cato up for this fool? She had occasionally said that she did not feel Cato's intellectual equal and that he did not need her. Cato had always said that was not true, even if he thought it. Perhaps Julia had come to decide that she wanted a man who needed her more than she needed him . . .

Cato quickly reflected on what Macro had just said and shook his head.

'He comes with us. We'll need every man who can carry a weapon. Creative types included. Since you are so adept with stylus and slate, Tribune Cristus, you will take charge of the headquarters staff. They answer to you, and you answer to me with responsibility for stores, strength returns and anything else that falls within that remit. Is that clear?'

Cristus gave Cato a calculating look, as if to see if there was any clear sign that his new commander was aware of the affair with his wife. Cato returned the scrutiny flatly and it was the tribune who looked away first.

'Yes, sir. That's clear.'

'Good.' Cato indicated the entrance to the tent. 'You can wait outside for Optio Metellus to return from Tarraco. I have sent him to requisition transport carts and supplies. When he returns you are to draft an inventory. On the march route, it will be your job to ensure that the supplies are replenished at every opportunity. I don't want us running low when we enter territory controlled by the enemy and foraging becomes difficult. You do your job and I will do my best to overlook the fact that you are no more a soldier than my dead wife ever was.'

Cristus started slightly at the mention of Julia, but saluted and withdrew from the tent. Cato stared at the tent flaps swinging a moment before they were still. He took a deep, calming breath, and let it go in a long, drawn-out sigh.

'You really don't like that one,' Macro observed. 'Beyond the fact that he's a useless deadweight. That was pretty clear. The reason?'

Cato shot him a cold look. 'The man is a fop. He has no place in the army. But I'll give him a chance to prove his mettle. And if he has to die, then let him do it like a man at least.'

His words were delivered more harshly than intended, laden with all the hurt and hate that Cato felt for Cristus and his unfaithful wife as they were, and Macro's brows rose slightly in surprise.

'Fair enough. Whatever your reasons for taking him with us, that's up to you. I won't ask.'

'Please don't.' Cato yawned and stretched his arms out and clenched his fists to relieve the tension. When he had recomposed himself, he continued. 'The tribune aside, what do you make of our comrades?'

Macro thought briefly. 'A mixed lot. Secundus, Placinus and Musa seem solid and reliable. Porcino shows some willing, but he's woefully lacking in experience and confidence. He'll need watching. As for Petillius . . . The man's in love with himself, that's clear. And he'll indulge that love when he has no woman nearby to indulge it for him. I've seen the type before.' Macro hesitated. 'I could be wrong. We'll know soon enough. And that leaves that shit, Pulcher. Frankly, I'd rather we took him for the kind of stroll where he doesn't come back. But now that the others have seen that there's unfinished business between us it wouldn't take a Socrates to work out that his disappearance would be down to foul play. Justice more like, but I doubt that Vitellius would see it that way. And if Vitellius really is out to do us in one way or another it would make no sense to gift him an excuse.'

Cato could not help a wry laugh. 'By the Gods, Macro, you have it in one! I couldn't have put it any better. I wish that we had a better selection of officers to rely on, but they'll have a chance to prove themselves worthy of the rank before this is all over, or die in the attempt.' Cato sat down again. 'I'm tired. Best that we get some rest before we set off. Have a word with the clerks and get them to bring us some bedrolls and blankets. Food and wine too.'

'Yes, sir.' Macro eased himself onto his feet and left Cato alone in the tent.

Cato folded his arms and leaned forward to rest his head. For a brief moment he closed his eyes and at once felt an overwhelming temptation to let go and slip into a deep sleep. Before that was possible an image of Cristus embracing Julia ripped through his thoughts. Why had she betrayed him? And why choose Cristus? What did he give Julia that Cato had not been able to? All he had ever wanted was to care for Julia, make certain that she wanted for nothing and grow old with her. And he had been sure that she felt the same. Only now it was all revealed to be a lie. And he was torn between hatred of her, and love for her, and grief at her death.

For Cristus he felt only rage, twisting like a blade deep in his guts. As yet he had no idea why he had not gone along with Macro's suggestion to leave Cristus behind. The man was useless. Soft and foolish-looking. He had no place in an army marching to war. Well, he would suffer, along with Cato and the rest of the men, as they marched across the heated plains of the province. And if it came to a fight, then he would shed his blood with theirs. Why should he live if Cato, Macro and the other men were to die? He deserved to die above all men, for the crime of loving Julia, and being loved by her. That was the truth of it, Cato realised. He had determined to keep Cristus close in order to punish the man.

This was the agony of jealousy, he realised. Zeno would not be proud of him, he mused. It seemed that he was neither much of an epicurean nor a stoic after all. He was as human as the rest of them, for all his learning and professed adherence to philosophical tradition. He was weak, and he despised himself for it.

His head was aching and once again Cato closed his eyes and this time tried not to think about anything. And so he was fast asleep, and snoring, when Macro entered the tent with the bedrolls and blankets bundled in his arms. He stopped to smile fondly at the prefect, then set his burdens down on the ground to one side of the tent. Spreading out the bedrolls, he put one of the blankets down for himself and gently arranged the other across Cato before he patted his friend lightly on the shoulder.

'Sleep, lad. You'll need it in the days to come. And we'll all need you to be at your best . . . So sleep.'

Optio Metellus had done a good job, Cato decided as he inspected the carts in the thin light of the pre-dawn. The sun was still below the just discernible curve of the horizon out to sea and a thin band of pink separated the dark grey of the sea and the sky. The mules were well-fed, tough-looking beasts and the carts were sturdily constructed and carefully packed with large jars, sacks of grain and cured legs of pork. There was enough to feed the men for ten days, Cato calculated. As long as the carts were replenished they should be able to hold out at the mine until Vitellius and the main column arrived. Assuming it was possible to defend the mine, Cato reflected. That could only be determined when they reached Argentium.

He nodded with satisfaction and strode to the front of the small convoy where Metellus and the men assigned as drovers waited. A short distance to one side stood Centurion Pulcher, with Tribune Cristus, both watching him warily.

'Well done, Optio. I trust you did not have to cause too much trouble in getting this together.'

Metellus grinned. 'Oh, not much trouble at all, sir. Not after I knocked a few heads together to encourage the rest. Then they were as meek as lambs and only too willing to do their patriotic duty, bless 'em.'

'Ha!' Cato returned the grin before his expression became serious and he lowered his voice. 'Centurion Pulcher is in command of the baggage train, but if he gives you or your men cause to complain, then speak to me or Centurion Macro. Understood?'

'Yes, sir. And, er, what about the tribune?'

'Him?' Cato turned to look at the man sourly. 'See that he keeps out of the way and tends to his record keeping.'

'Yes, sir.'

Cato returned the optio's salute and made his way down the column of Praetorians standing at ease along the full length of the camp's main thoroughfare. Each man carried only a rolled cloak in addition to his oval shield and spear. Canteens, worn over the

136

shoulder, completed their marching rig. On either side their tents lay empty and their meagre piles of personal effects and spare kit lay outside each tent, ready to be collected and placed in the storerooms of the Tarraco garrison. There had been some grumbling about that, Macro had informed him. The Praetorians had little faith in the honesty of the auxiliary troops of the garrison. And probably with good cause, Cato conceded. Some of their property was bound to be filched between the camp and the city.

The tents, and the camp, were left, as they were to be occupied by one of the cohorts sailing to reach the province. Normally, the tents would be struck and loaded onto carts, and the camp demolished before the cohort set off. But there was no time to spare for that. And not much point, given that it would spare the next cohort several hours of back-breaking labour. That too would be something the men grumbled about, Cato smiled to himself. No soldier liked the idea of sweating over hard work when others would reap the benefits.

At the head of the column rose the six standards of the colour party. Each carried only one battle honour, for the victory they had shared with the legions in Britannia, and Cato wondered if they would live to see another decoration for the part they played in defeating the rebels around Asturica. The small mounted contingent, under the command of Optio Metellus, waited to one side, the men holding the bridles while their mounts lifted their soft muzzles and twitched their ears expectantly. One of the riders held a spare horse for the prefect. Macro and the other five centurions were talking quietly between the standards and the open gate of the camp. Cimber stood alone to one side, looking utterly miserable. As they saw the prefect approaching they stood stiffly and saluted.

'All ready then, sir?' asked Macro.

'Yes. Gentlemen, you may join your units.'

The five centurions strode off, vine canes in hand, while Cato swung up into his saddle. Macro nodded to the optio in charge of the men selected for their riding skills.

'Scouting contingent!' barked Metellus. 'Mount!'

There was a deal of whinnying and jostling of horseflesh before the Praetorians were comfortably in the saddles, reins in hand. As the sounds died away Cato turned to look back down the length of the column. Five hundred men. All that could be spared to secure the mine at Argentium, save the bullion convoy, and prevent the uprising spilling over into a bloody widespread rebellion. Beyond the far rampart of the marching camp, far out to sea, the rising sun flared into sight, with a gleam like distant fire. Cato raised his arm.

'Second Praetorian Cohort . . . Advance!'

He swept his arm down towards the gate and tapped in his heels. His horse walked on, with Macro beside him, and behind tramped the guardsmen, out of the camp and up the road that led through the rose-tipped hills into the heart of the province.

# CHAPTER FOURTEEN

The small column of Praetorians kept up a steady pace as they followed the road through the hills and up onto the rolling plateau four days' march from Tarraco. They passed sprawling farming estates boasting olive trees, cereal crops and vineyards and marched through forests of oak and pine and at first the men thrilled to the sight of plentiful wild boar and deer amid the trees. But there was no time to stop and hunt as the centurions and optios kept them moving, the rumble of boots and wagon wheels filling their ears and stirring dust into the air so that it swirled about the main body of the column and the carts at the rear. At first the cohort marched in good spirits, the men talking, joking and occasionally joining in a song, especially if it was ribald. Macro was happy to indulge their cheeriness as he strode at the head of the leading century. As senior centurion of the cohort he was expected to set the example for the men to follow, and sang along lustily, if not altogether tunefully.

A short distance ahead of the infantry Cato rode in front of the mounted contingent, swaying easily from side to side in his saddle as he gazed at the surrounding landscape and let his thoughts wander from time to time. He was mostly preoccupied by the prospect of what was awaiting them in the mountainous mining region around Asturica. It was imperative that they reached the mine as soon as possible, but the corollary of that was that they would need to hold out for longer before Vitellius and the main column arrived. Cato imagined himself in Iskerbeles' place. The moment the enemy was alerted to the presence of the Praetorian cohort they would be sure to close with the Romans and attempt to destroy them. It would be too good an opportunity to miss. The annihilation of an elite unit of the Roman army would win Iskerbeles considerable acclaim. Men would flock to join his standard and fight against the empire, whose rule many in the region regarded as harsh and ruthless.

Cato could hardly blame them. Rome imposed one burden after another on the shoulders of the people they conquered. Even if they escaped the appropriation of their land to add to the extensive portfolio of the imperial estate, they might well have a veterans' colony founded close by. The discharged legionaries were in the habit of showing scant regard for the land, property or women of their native neighbours. Worse still, they knew full well that the Emperor would overlook all but the gravest of their transgressions. So, in effect, they were licensed to outrage the locals with impunity. Nor were these the only troubles besetting those living under the Roman yoke. They also had to deal with rapacious tax-collectors, and the money-lenders who often followed in their wake, ready to loan them the gold and silver they needed to pay their taxes at crippling rates of interest. For those that could not repay the loans the outcome was even greater poverty, then ruin and slavery. This was often the price paid by those who lived outside the thriving towns and cities of the empire.

As many lost out as benefited from the imposition of Roman rule, Cato reflected, and at times he was tempted to question the morality of serving in an army dedicated to the defence of such an empire. But, on balance, Rome represented order, prosperity and peace. He had seen the alternative at first hand and his mind turned to the savagery of the druids and their fanatical followers, and the endless tribal conflicts and vendettas of the Celtic people of Britannia. That was no way to live. No way to create the conditions under which philosophy, literature, sculpture and fine art might thrive, and those things were important to Cato, if not to the vast majority of the soldiers he served alongside. For them soldiering was an end in itself. A way of life they did not question and could not see beyond.

Every so often his thoughts also turned to Julia and Cristus. He still grieved for her, but the sentiment was coldly tempered by the pain of her betrayal. A pain that was pricked on every occasion he set eyes on Tribune Cristus, or even thought about him. So what then was the purpose of deciding to bring him along? The prospect of Cristus being killed by the enemy and thereby relieving Cato of the responsibility for taking revenge at first hand? Perhaps it was arrogance. Perhaps he needed to reassure himself that he was the better man and that Julia had made a mistake. But she would never be able to admit that to him now.

'Pride . . .' he muttered and shook his head bitterly. 'Fucking pride.'

Each day, the column marched for twenty-five miles before Cato let the men halt for the night. The heat of the summer beat down on them, forcing them to squint in the bright light and sweat so much that the beads of perspiration cut tracks through the dust that settled on them during the day. The officers imposed a strict water ration regime and the Praetorians were allowed no more than a mouthful of water from their canteens every other mile. As far as possible Cato stopped at dusk in sight of a town or village where food and water might be obtained. Each century fell out of line and the Praetorians set down their weapons and slumped into the sparse grass on each side of the road. The carts rumbled on into the middle of the cohort before the drovers reined the mules in and the evening's rations were distributed to the exhausted soldiers. Cristus then took the mounted contingent and continued along the road to the nearest settlement where supplies could be bought and set beside the road to be picked up by the carts the following morning. If it was not too far, then he took the carts with him instead. The area affected by the uprising was still far off and Cato judged it safe enough to post a picket line instead of having the men construct a marching camp. As night fell over the rolling hills the air filled with the hiss of cicadas, rising to a shrill crescendo before stopping abruptly, only to begin again.

For Cato and Macro, who had become used to the cooler, wetter climate of Britannia, the heat was galling to start with, but the evenings were pleasant and cool and lighting a fire was barely necessary.

On the fifth night, Macro joined his friend as Cato sat, legs folded, with his back to a rock in the glow of the embers of a small fire. The centurion laid his vine cane down and undid the ties under his chin before removing his helmet and padded skullcap.

'Ah, that's better!' Macro rolled his head and then eased himself down opposite Cato. 'The first watch is posted and the rest of the lads are bedded down for the night.'

Cato nodded, and glanced at the dark shapes curled up on the ground amid the scattered trees growing either side of the road. A few men were still sitting, talking, but the usual camp banter was absent, thanks to the gruelling pace of the march. 'How many stragglers today?'

Macro took out a tablet from his sidebag and leaned towards the embers so that he could make out the marks scratched into the wax. His lips moved as he added up the numbers. 'Eight dropped out. Literally dropped out, I mean. The heat did for them. They had to be picked up and loaded onto the carts. It was twelve yesterday, and only five the day before. Given that we're forcing the pace, that's not too bad. But the numbers will drop as they settle into their stride.'

That was true, Cato knew. Men who were unused to marching tended to find the first days hardest, before they got used to the hardship. 'It seems that our Praetorian friends are in need of some proper soldiering.'

'Then they've come to the right men to make it happen.' Macro closed his tablet and put it away before taking out a chunk of dried beef from his sidebag, tearing off a small strip with his teeth and chewing hard. Cato waited for him to swallow before he spoke again.

'What do you make of them?'

Macro reached up to scratch his matted scalp as he collected his thoughts. 'The training and discipline's good. So is their morale. They firmly believe they are the best soldiers in the whole army. They've good reason to believe that, of course, since most of them have been cherry-picked from the legions as a reward for courage in action and good service. Even those who enlisted directly into the Guard were picked because they were big enough and tough enough to stand alongside the rest. So they should be good.'

'But . . .'

Macro smiled. 'But, I'd pick the boys from the Second Augustan Legion over them any day. Without regular action, and getting one over tough conditions, like we had on the frontier, even the best soldiers lose their edge.'

'True.'

'Anyway, they'll have their chance to prove themselves before too long.' Macro tore off another strip of salted beef and worked his jaws furiously to soften the leathery meat before swallowing. 'Can't say that our friend Cimber is looking forward to facing the rebels. Every time I clap eyes on him he looks like he's just licked piss off a stinging nettle.'

'Can you blame him? His home town has been sacked by the rebels and just when he thought he was safely out of danger, he's been forced to march to battle.'

'If I was in his place, I'd want to go back and reclaim my home, and give the rebels a bloody good kicking.'

'Well, yes, quite.' Cato smiled, then continued. 'What about the officers? I've been keeping an eye on them, but what do you make of them?'

'The veterans are good, as you'd expect. Especially Secundus. As tough an old sweat as you could find. Most of the others are also hard men, and know their trade, and how to get the best out of their men. Hardly any of the stragglers come from their centuries. Most of those belong to Porcino.' Macro clicked his tongue. 'That one's struggling badly. Lacks fitness and can barely keep up with his men. I'd be surprised if we didn't find him on the carts with the rest of the laggards tomorrow.'

'I feared as much.' Cato considered the situation a moment. 'If he doesn't shape up quickly then I'll have to move him to the baggage carts and have Pulcher take on the Fifth Century.'

Macro puffed his cheeks. 'Think that's wise? He can't do us much harm in charge of the carts, but if he wants to get up to any mischief there's a lot he can do in command of eighty Praetorians.'

'He's in the same boat as us. If we all hold together we might come out of this alive. Even Pulcher must realise that. But for now he stays where he is. We'll keep our eyes on Porcino. If there's no improvement he gets demoted to the carts.'

'Fair enough.'

Cato reached for his canteen and took a swig. The water was warm and offered little refreshment. He patted the stopper in. 'What about Petillius?'

'Ah, now he's a bit of a puzzle, that one. He ponces around like an afternoon theatre idol. Keeps his beard neatly trimmed, hair carefully arranged and if I didn't know better I'd swear the bastard was using a dab of kohl around his eyes to make them stand out more.'

'Really?' Cato was shocked. 'No, that can't be right. No soldier would follow a man like that.'

'No proper soldier perhaps, but a Praetorian maybe. After all, they've seen enough strange shit around the imperial palace to last a normal soldier a lifetime. Guess they get used to it. In any case, he seems popular enough with his lads. They like him.'

'Jupiter did not create centurions to be liked, Macro. He created them to be surly, aggressive disciplinarians ready to put the stick about. Respect them, yes. But like them? When it comes to a desperate fix, being liked might be a dangerous thing.'

Macro's brow creased. 'What kind of a fix?'

'Oh, I don't know. Who can tell what games the Gods want to play with us? I'm just saying, as a matter of principle, it isn't necessarily healthy for a centurion to be liked by his men.' Cato picked up a pebble and tossed it into the heart of the embers where it landed with a tiny explosion of sparks.

'Anyway,' Macro continued. 'Petillius is as tough as his men. Insists on carrying his own kit too. I just hope he knows how to use a sword when the time comes and doesn't get too concerned with protecting his fine features. There's no telling what a nasty scar on that face of his will do to his chances with the ladies of Rome.'

The words were spoken with no thought of offence, Cato knew, but he still could not help reaching up to touch the raised line of scar tissue that crossed his own brow and cheek. Was it that which had turned Julia away? He had not thought it disfiguring before now. Perhaps it was, and Julia had preferred the unblemished face of Cristus. He cleared his throat with a soft growl.

'And what about the tribune?'

Macro hawked up some phlegm to clear the last shreds of beef from his teeth and spat to one side. 'He's no soldier. Certainly no officer. He's far too quiet and while he can just about cope with buying a few supplies from the locals I'd never entrust him with the command of men in battle. It would have been better if he'd stayed in Rome, drawing pictures of his fancy travel carts. Beats me why Vitellius included him in this little venture.'

'Yes, I wondered about that too.' For Cato, the only reason for Cristus' presence that made much sense was if Vitellius was aware of his affair with Julia, and thought that might provide the means of tormenting Cato. He would not put it past the legate. He looked up and caught Macro looking at him with a curious expression. 'What?'

'Is there something I should know about Cristus?'

'What do you mean?'

'Is there some reason why he had to come with us? Otherwise I can see no purpose for it, given that we could have left him behind in Tarraco.'

Cato paused, then replied tonelessly, 'Cristus is attached to the cohort. I decided that he should have the chance to go into action with the men.'

Macro looked doubtful. 'That's all there is to it?'

'Yes.'

The centurion stared back for a moment and then shrugged. 'If you say so.'

There was an uncomfortable silence before Macro spoke again. 'Are you all right, lad? You've been very distant for the last few days. Lost in yourself.'

'I'm fine. Thank you, Centurion Macro.' Cato reached for his cloak and pulled it over his body as he stretched out on the ground. 'Now, if you don't mind, I must sleep. You'd be wise to get as much as you can too. Good night.'

Macro stared at him, momentarily surprised at his friend's bluffness. But he had come to know Cato's moods well enough to know when to let him be. 'Fair enough. Good night, sir.'

★ ★ ★

As the cohort emerged from the hills beyond the military colony of Caesar Augusta the Praetorians entered the parched plains that stretched across the lands of the Celtiberi tribe. The off-white tunics of the soldiers became stained with the dust from the red soil and their exposed skin was covered in grime. Only when they camped by a river were the men able to get themselves and their kit clean, but it was filthy again by the end of the following day. As Cato and Macro had hoped, the men became increasingly inured to the hardship of the march and the stragglers had reduced to a handful. Some of the older men, and the less fit, had made it as far as the military colony but could go no further and were left behind to rest and join the main column when it arrived. Even Centurion Porcino stuck with the column, showing his grit as he led his century while blisters formed on his feet, burst and then rubbed raw.

There were far more limited signs of habitation, with only occasional farms, whose inhabitants scratched a living in a challenging landscape that baked in summer and was cold in winter. The settlements they passed through were quiet at most hours of the day as the locals kept to the shade, or the cool of the dark spaces inside their houses. Goats clustered in the shelter of whatever trees they could find and mules, tethered to posts, endured the heat and flies stoically.

Close to noon on the fifteenth day after leaving Tarraco, Cato was riding a short distance ahead of the column as usual. The sun blazed down from a clear sky and the horizon shimmered as if a thin layer of silvery water was flowing between the sky and the earth. Behind him the cohort tramped in a steady rumble of nailed boots, iron-bound wheels and the squeal of axles as the carts negotiated the uneven surface of the road. Then, ahead, Cato saw a dark blot above the heat haze. As he watched, shielding his eyes to see better in the bright light, the blot resolved into a line of figures, accompanied by several riders on each side. Four large wagons followed behind the figures. He felt a tingle of anxiety at the possibility that these men might have news of the rebels. There was still over a hundred miles to go before the cohort reached the mining region around Asturica, but it was possible that the rebels were ranging much farther afield.

Cato reined in, dropping back to join the mounted contingent, and sent word for Cimber to be brought to him before continuing along the road. As the gap between the two bodies of men closed he began to make out more detail. The rider at the front of the party had a small shelter rigged up on his saddle, but there was no shelter for the long line of ragged men who trudged behind him in chains. The riders on either side, guarding the slaves, wore straw hats and occasionally swiped at their charges with long canes to keep them moving forward. At the rear trundled the wagons. As the commander of a military column Cato had right of way and stuck to the middle of the road. When no more than a hundred paces separated the two parties, the slave trader raised a hand and waved his men to the side. The guards halted the slaves and drove them to the side of the road.

Reassured that his earlier fears were baseless, Cato urged his horse into a trot and approached the rider sitting under his shelter.

'Good day, citizen,' Cato greeted him.

The slave trader raised a fly whisk in response and nodded as Cato reined in close by. He was a large man with humourless features and such heavily pockmarked skin that his face looked like a large orange, well past its prime.

'I was wondering when I'd finally see some soldiers.' The man spoke with the unmistakable accent of the Subura in Rome. 'I was beginning to wonder if the governor had abandoned the whole province to those fucking rebels. You on the way to deal with 'em?'

'My orders are not your concern. What is your name?'

'Micus Aeschleus, of Sportimus, where I'm heading directly. To get my inventory as far from those rebel scum as possible.'

'Inventory?'

Aeschleus gestured towards the line of slaves. 'Those were destined for the mines, but as soon as I heard about the revolt I turned east. Once you lot have done your job, then I'll take 'em back and flog 'em to whichever mines have survived the fracas.' He looked past Cato towards Macro and the lead century approaching along the road. 'Praetorians?'

Cato nodded, glanced round, and saw Cimber trotting towards him. He turned back to the trader. 'The Emperor has sent his finest to deal with the uprising. There's my cohort, and another seven following up, with auxiliary troops.'

There was no harm in giving that information to the slave trader, in the hope that it might demonstrate Rome's desire to send strong forces to deal with the uprising. Merchants like Aeschleus were the carriers of gossip, news and panic. It would be best if he helped spread the word about the soldiers being sent to destroy Iskerbeles and his followers. Cato was pleased to see the reassurance in the man's expression.

'Good. Glad to hear it.'

Cimber came up, panting and running with sweat in the searing heat. Cato made the introductions and then nodded in the direction Aeschleus and his desultory procession of humanity had come from. 'I've not heard any recent reports from Asturica. Any idea how far the rebellion has spread?'

The slave trader looked surprised. 'Asturica? You're joking. Last I heard, only two days back, was that the rebels were raiding villas and small towns as far east as Pallantia. They're now being joined by men from the Vaccaei and Arenaci tribes.'

Cato glanced at Cimber and saw that the man was horrified. 'How far are we from these tribes?'

'A day's march,' the guide replied. 'Two at the most. They could be watching us even now.'

Cimber craned his neck and glanced anxiously around the landscape, but there was no sign of any movement for miles on either side of the road. He looked up at Cato. 'If the uprising has spread this far, then it'd be madness for us to continue, sir. The road goes right through the middle of Arenaci land. The rebels would know we were coming days before we got anywhere near the mine. We'd be marching right into a trap. Best we return to Tarraco,' he concluded pleadingly.

'Nothing doing,' Cato replied. 'I have my orders. We continue.'

Aeschleus swatted his shoulder lightly. 'He's got a point. Anyone making for Asturica along this road is going to be in clear view of any rebels keeping watch. If you had any plans to surprise Iskerbeles and his lads then you'd better think again, Prefect. As things stand, you run the risk of them setting a trap for you. And no disrespect to the Emperor's finest, but you're outnumbered at least ten to one, and you'll be fighting on their turf. I don't fancy your chances.'

Cato was hot, tired and his patience was wearing thin. 'That's my problem. I'll deal with it. Given what you say, there's no time to waste. Good fortune go with you, Micus Aeschleus.'

Cato pulled on his reins and edged his mount back onto the road, gesturing to the mounted Praetorians to continue the advance. Cimber scurried alongside, his face still flushed with anxiety.

'Prefect, surely you can't be serious? We can't go any further. They'll be waiting for us. We'll be cut to pieces.'

'That's enough, Cimber. I do not require your opinion on the matter. You are here to advise, and that's all. Now get back to the baggage train, before I have you flogged.'

The guide opened his mouth to protest, but saw the dangerous glint in Cato's eyes and wisely kept quiet, dropping back to the side of the road to let the column pass by. Cato rode on, casting his eyes over the line of slaves. They were perhaps the most wretched examples he had ever seen. Thin, bedraggled, barely clothed, with grimy, soiled skin. Most stared vacantly before them, others returned his gaze with undisguised hatred. If these were the kind of men toiling in the mines around Asturica then they would have everything to fight for should they be liberated by Iskerbeles and join the uprising. They would be burning with desire for revenge against their former masters and would make formidable foes. Cato shuddered at the thought, and urged his horse into a gentle trot until he had passed the last of the slaves and the heavy wagons following them. Ahead, the baking landscape no longer seemed empty. Out there, the enemy waited, and maybe they were already watching Cato and his men, their hearts filled with cruel determination to annihilate the Praetorian cohort down to the last man.

# CHAPTER FIFTEEN

There had still been no sign of the enemy by the time the column halted two days' march from Pallantia amid rolling hills and scattered clumps of stunted oak trees. There had been several more encounters with those fleeing the region affected by the uprising. Cattle drovers, merchants and more slave traders, all desperate to take what portable wealth they had and escape the danger of the spreading influence of Iskerbeles. Some told of the breakdown in Roman authority in the hinterland of the towns that once controlled the lands around them. Many tax collectors had been murdered and farming estates had been sacked, with their owners or stewards cut down. Some told lurid tales of the rebels' victims being horribly tortured before finally being granted death.

Cato had conversed with such refugees out of earshot of his men, using Cimber only when the travellers did not speak Latin or Greek. Even so, word of what lay ahead reached the ears of the Praetorians and their mood became markedly more sombre and wary. They had set out from Rome with a view to teaching the Asturian rebels a quick, sharp lesson, but now they were beginning to appreciate the scale of the danger facing them.

As the sun hung low in the sky, the fading light burnished the trees and cast long dark shadows over the dry grass. A mile off, a small village crowned a hill with good views over the surrounding landscape. As soon as the Praetorians reached the campsite chosen by Cato each century was given permission to fall out and the men set down their shields, spears and helmets and slumped to the ground to rest while the optios marked out the sleeping lines and the centurions assigned men to the forage party. A short distance away the mounted contingent was removing saddles and tackle and roping off an area for the horses to graze.

Cato untied his neck-cloth and mopped the sweat from his brow before turning his attention to the routine tasks of the evening. To begin with, there was Tribune Cristus, proffering the ledger for Cato to approve the drawing of five hundred sestertii from the cohort's strongbox to purchase stores from the nearby village. The rations for the evening meal were unloaded. As the carts rumbled off down a side track leading to the village, Macro approached, with rosy sunburned cheeks, waxed tablet in hand, ready to report the number of stragglers and the sick and the number of men fit for duty in each section.

'Not a bad day,' he commented as he handed the tablet to Cato for inspection. 'Five down from heat exhaustion, two still on the carts from yesterday and – you'll love this – one of the men in the baggage train kicked senseless by a mule. Centurion Pulcher, to be precise.'

Cato looked up hopefully. 'Badly?'

'He'll live, more's the pity. But he's come round with a blinding headache and a bump the size of an avocado to show for it. Nothing that won't improve his already cheerful disposition.'

They shared a smile and then Cato indicated the nearest copse of oak trees, half a mile off. 'The forage party can take firewood from there. Fifty men should do it.'

Macro nodded and then scanned the peaceful-looking surroundings. 'Time for a proper marching camp perhaps? I'd sleep more happily with a ditch and rampart around me.'

Cato had already considered it, weighing up the exhaustion of the men, and the need for them to conserve their energy for yet another day's march on the morrow, against the possible threat of enemy action. The mounted scouts he had sent out well ahead of the column, and on each flank, had reported no sign of the rebels.

'Tomorrow. We'll be safe enough for the night.'

'All the same—'

'The decision's made.' Cato stamped his boot on the parched ground. 'And the men would not thank you for having them break this up to make a ditch and rampart.'

Macro frowned and gave his friend a disapproving look. 'Since when were we in the business of seeking their thanks, sir? You give the order, and I'll have them back on their feet, trench tools in hand, quick as boiled asparagus.'

'I'm sure. But I need them in good shape for when we meet the rebels. So let 'em rest tonight. They'll need all their strength soon enough.'

Macro sighed. 'As you wish, sir. I'll see to the watch setting, then.'

He strode off leaving Cato feeling a little guilty over his curt attitude towards the centurion. Macro deserved better; Cato's weariness and the growing tension as they drew closer to Asturica was not an acceptable excuse. He could not directly apologise to Macro as the latter would see that as weakness, so there would have to be some other way to make it up. Few officers of his rank would be concerned by such thoughts, he knew, but then he refused to be like them, even as he wanted to be a success and win their respect. On his terms.

The rumble of the cart wheels distracted his train of thought and he looked up to see Cristus waving them on. On the rearmost sat Pulcher, legs swaying, one hand nursing his head while the other clasped the side of the wagon. Cato could not resist a delighted smile at the reversal of positions. How things had changed over the ten years since he had joined the army. The man who had made his life a living hell was now a matter of such small consequence, a monster rendered harmless and pathetic. He watched the carts trundle away for a moment and then called Metellus to bring some food and watered wine for himself and Macro.

As the sun began to set behind a line of distant hills the camp settled into a quiet, peaceful state. Conversation was muted, the air was still and the shrilling of cicadas began. The men had gathered light brush and scrub to make a bed for the night, and some had begun to clear ground for the campfires, due to the dryness of the grass. Any fire that burned out of control could quickly ignite the bleached stalks and spread swiftly in the lightest of breezes, consuming all combustibles in its path. As the first fires were lit the men tipped their rations of barley, salted meat and bread into the small cauldrons suspended from iron tripods and an aroma of woodsmoke and cooking wafted across the camp.

There was still one party of foragers cutting wood from the trees and the faint *tok . . . tok* of axes carried to Cato's ears as he sat on a folding stool to write a report of the meagre intelligence on the uprising he had gathered from those he had met on the road to Asturica. The angled light made it easy to keep track of the marks he carefully made in the wax of the tablets. He would hand the report over to the first merchant they came across the next day, with strict instructions that it be delivered to the legate as soon as possible. If the column did not encounter anyone on the road by noon, then Cato resolved to have one of his mounted men ride back towards Tarraco.

Metellus approached with a jug, a small basket and an iron pot, from which wisps of steam rose. Cato held up a finger.

'A moment.'

He finished the report and signed it before closing the tablet with a snap and setting it down beside him, just as Macro joined them, lifting the folds of his chain mail over his head. He let the armour drop to the ground.

'Bloody hell, that's a relief! I'm not sure which is better cooked, me or the dinner.' He leaned towards the pot that Metellus had set down between them and sniffed. 'Mmmmm! That's good. Not just the usual mash of meat and barley then.'

'I've added some herbs, sir. Bought 'em back in Tarraco. And a bit of saffron. Thought you could use a change.'

'Good lad.' Macro patted the optio's back, then eased himself down beside Cato. 'We're all set for the night, sir. Petillius and his men are on watch. Just waiting for the last of the foragers and the carts to return before the pickets are posted.'

'Very good,' Cato replied, reaching for the mess tin that Metellus had filled. Then he paused and turned to look towards the village. Cristus should be on his way back by now, but there was no sign of the carts, or indeed any movement at all from the direction of the village. Not even the faintest trail of smoke from the buildings as they too prepared their evening meal.

He felt an icy twinge in the small of his back and the weariness and hunger of an instant earlier had gone. Cato stood up and took a few paces towards the village before stopping to stare, straining his eyes and ears for any sound that might confirm his fears.

'What is it, lad?' asked Macro.

'Quiet!' Cato raised a hand as he scrutinised the lifeless village. Then he turned towards the trees where the foragers were still hard at work. As he stared he caught the faint glint of sun on metal in the patches of scrub on the slope behind the trees.

'There's the enemy. We need to recall the foragers at once.'

'The enemy?' Macro's forehead creased as he tried to see what Cato had spotted.

'Behind the trees. If I'm right they're in the village too. I don't want us caught in the open. Macro, give the order to stand to. When the cohort's ready, and the foragers are safe, make for the village.'

'Where will you be then?'

Cato pointed towards the village. 'Up there. Unless I miss my guess, Cristus is in trouble. Besides, we need the village. If we can take that, we'll have somewhere we can better defend. You've got your orders, so go!'

Macro snatched up his chain-mail vest and sword. Metellus was standing still, jug in one hand, ready to pour. He shook off his surprise and set the jug down.

'You!' Macro ordered the nearest of the Praetorians. 'Run over to the forage party. Tell 'em to drop everything and return to camp at the double.'

The stillness of a moment earlier was shattered as Macro jogged towards the heart of the camp, calling out, 'Centurions! On me.'

Cato snatched up his helmet and ordered Metellus to come with him and they ran towards the horse lines where the men were busy rubbing the animals down with tufts of dry grass before they saw to their own needs.

'Metellus, get them armed and into the saddle at once!'

Leaving the optio to carry out his orders Cato ran on, closer to the village, and stopped. His heart was beating hard against his ribs. He struggled to hear beyond the pounding in his ears, but then he heard it, the faintest tinny clash of blades. He turned back to the mounted contingent, pulling on his padded skullcap and then his helmet before he tied the straps securely, feeling the leather bite into the skin under his chin. Metellus and his men were hurriedly re-saddling their mounts and helping each other into their armour. Cato's horse was one of the first ready and he stiffly pulled himself up to the saddle and swung a leg over before settling in between the saddle horns. He spurred the beast clear of the other animals and the dust they were kicking up to get a better view of the gathering threat to the cohort.

Then he saw the first of the carts career out from between the buildings of the village, the driver cracking his whip furiously as the mules trotted down the track leading onto the plain. It was clear that the cart was in danger of running down the team. The driver realised at the last moment and dropped his whip to pull hard on the braking lever. The cart slewed to one side and began to tip, until the inertia was overcome and it dropped back heavily onto all four wheels, shedding several amphorae that shattered in its wake as the cart continued down the track.

Cato turned in his saddle and saw that the man sent to warn the foragers had reached them. They were just visible, shadowy figures almost lost against the trunks and boughs of the oaks beyond which the sky was a lurid orange, making it hard to see. But there were the enemy, outlined on the crest behind the trees, a line of men, mostly on foot, charging down the slope. Behind Cato, in the camp, came the shouts of the optios and centurions as they roused their men, cursing at those whose exhaustion made them slow to react. Macro's voice rose clearly above them all.

'On your fucking feet, you dogs! Call yourselves soldiers? I've seen raddled old whores get back on their feet quicker than you bastards!'

Another cart emerged from the village, then one of the Praetorians, limping. Most of the men had mounted and Cato cupped a hand to his mouth to make sure that he was heard above the shouts of the other officers. 'Mounted contingent! On me!'

Those in the saddle pulled on their reins and turned their horses to canter over to the prefect, as the last of their comrades finished putting on their armour, taking up their weapons and climbing onto

155

their mounts. Cato did not wait for the stragglers and spurred his horse into a gallop as he raced across the plain towards the village. The riders rapidly closed on the first of the carts, still being driven as fast as the mules would go, their short legs and hooves kicking up red dust. Cato raised a hand to halt the cart and the driver eased up on his team.

'What happened?'

'Ambushed, sir. In the heart of the village.' The man was struggling for breath.

'How many?'

'Dunno, sir. They're on the roofs, mostly. Using slingshot and rocks. Scores of them.'

'Right, get back to the camp. Don't lose any more of your load.'

The driver nodded, took up his whip and cracked it over his team as he urged them back into motion. Cato dug his heels in and charged on down the track towards the hillock on which the village sprawled. More of the carts had escaped the trap and as the riders reached the foot of the slope Cato saw the first of the enemy, moving over the roofs close to the edge of the village as they harried the Romans. He led his men up the rutted track and reined in at the edge of the village where there was a timber gatehouse.

'Dismount! First five men hold the horses. The rest of you, with me!'

Taking a shield from one of the horse holders, Cato drew his sword and waited as the Praetorians formed up behind him. Then, shield raised and presented to the front, he entered the village. The street was just wide enough to take the carts, and the buildings on either side were stone for the first storey and then wood-framed and plastered above, with flat roofs for the most part. Voices and cries, together with the thud of weapons on shields and the clatter of blades, came from a short distance ahead. Cato passed an open door and glanced into the darkened interior where the body of an old man lay on his front, dried blood pooled beneath him. Some of the villagers had resisted then, or at least refused to join the rebels.

Then a flicker of motion above and to the left alerted Cato to danger. He glanced up and saw a bearded man with long tangled locks standing on the parapet of the roof. The rebel gritted his teeth

156

and began to raise a rock above his head with both hands. Cato snatched a breath.

'Shields up!'

The Praetorians thrust their left arms out and swung their shields up to cover their heads. Just in time. There was a loud crack and the man next to Cato grunted as his shield was driven down onto his helmet by the impact.

'Keep going!' Cato ordered. 'On me!'

More of the enemy were alerted to their presence and soon there was a steady rain of missiles hurled down from the buildings on either side. But the Praetorians held their nerve and followed their prefect up the street and around a corner, and there ahead of them lay an open space, roughly square, in which the remaining wagons, five of them, were still trapped. Half of the mules were down, bloody rents in their coarse coats. Some struggled lamely in their traces while others bellowed in agony. Those still standing, unable to move, brayed with panic. Cato saw that six of the Praetorians were down, four of them lying still, while the others, including Cristus, were crawling for shelter beneath the carts. Three of the wagons were a short distance apart and the survivors of the baggage train were huddled between them as slingshot and rocks smashed off the wooden frames of the carts. The surrounding roofs were lined with the enemy, shouting savage threats and curses as they attempted to pick off the Roman soldiers and mules.

'Follow me!' Cato ordered above the cacophony.

Keeping closed up, and covered by their shields, Cato and fifteen Praetorians paced across the open ground towards the wagons. At once the rebels turned their aim on the new arrivals, pelting them furiously. The Romans had almost reached the wagons when the man next to Cato staggered to one side, with a pained grunt. 'My leg . . .'

Glancing down Cato saw the blood coursing from a slingshot wound. 'Help him, Metellus! Keep moving, lads!'

The casualty slowed them down but they reached the cover offered by the carts a moment later and squatted down with Cristus and the others as stones and slingshot rattled and crashed off the large wheels and high sides of the vehicles.

'Thank the Gods you're here, sir,' said the tribune. 'I thought we were done for.'

Cato glanced round the other survivors, seven Praetorians, including Centurion Pulcher. Some were badly shaken, but some regarded him with gritty determination as they waited for orders; veterans from the legions then, Cato decided. He turned back to Cristus.

'I wouldn't count any chickens yet, Tribune.'

'We can't stay here.' Cristus jerked his head down as a slingshot splintered the side of the wagon above him, showering him with fragments of wood.

'I'd already worked that out for myself, thank you,' Cato replied drily and some of the men around them managed a quick grin. 'At least some of the carts managed to get out. We'll have saved some of our supplies at least.'

'Supplies?' Cristus looked astonished. 'What in Hades does that matter?'

Cato gestured towards the smashed jars lying around the carts, wine and water puddled around them. Bags of barley lay in the square too, mostly burst, their contents spilled onto the beaten ground. 'That's what keeps the men going, Tribune. We'll save what we can, if we get the chance. Right now, we're corked up here. If we try and move they'll hit us with all they've got. If we stay put they'll eventually run out of ammunition and have to take us on hand to hand.'

'Let 'em,' Metellus growled, patting his scabbard. 'Then they'll see what Praetorians are made of.'

'That's the spirit,' Cato responded. Then he steeled himself and raised his head just enough to take a quick glimpse round the square. There had to be at least a hundred of the rebels out there. More than enough to overwhelm the small party of Praetorians caught between the carts. Regardless of what Praetorians were actually made of, Cato thought wryly. A dark shape came sailing through the gloomy dusk and he ducked back down just in time to avoid the rock that swept overhead and crashed into an amphora inside the cart behind him.

'Fuck me . . . That was close.' He laughed, trying to cover up his

158

nerves. 'What did we ever do to piss this lot off? Whatever it was, it'll be nothing compared to what they get for ruining my meal.'

It was bravado, but it was what the men needed to hear, if they were going to have any confidence in their prefect leading them out of the deadly ambush they had walked into.

# CHAPTER SIXTEEN

'Come on! Come on!' Macro yelled as the last of his men fell in and hefted their shields and spears, ready for orders. He looked round the area where the cohort had been settling down for the night just moments before. The six centuries had formed up in a rectangle and the enclosed space was littered with those personal effects they had brought with them and the rations they had been about to consume. Most of the campfires had been extinguished, but two still burned and Macro resolved to see to them as soon as there was an opportunity to put them out. The flames provided a lurid glow immediately around them as the last sliver of sunlight burnished the horizon and was gone. Half a mile away the men of the forage party were running for their lives. Behind them dark figures were bursting out from between the trees and racing after the Praetorians, desperate to run them down and butcher them before they could reach the safety of the cohort.

Macro gauged the distance between himself, the foragers and the enemy and was satisfied that his comrades had sufficient lead to save themselves. He spared a look towards the village where Cato and his men had dismounted and were just about to enter the gateway. Whatever trouble Cristus and his party had encountered in the village Cato was on hand to sort it out, Macro decided. And once the foragers had reached the rest of the cohort he would give the order for the formation to join the prefect in the village and shelter there for the night. Morning would bring a clear view of the plain, and the scale of the enemy force that had surprised them. Of course the men would have had little sleep and would be hungry, but such were the travails of army life.

A new sound reached his ears, above the war cries of the rebels chasing the foragers: the rumble of hoofs. Macro turned back to the trees just as a large party of mounted men cantered round the edge of the wood and spurred their horses into a charge. With a sick feeling of certainty Macro realised that the forage party would be cut down before they could make it back to the cohort.

'Bollocks to that,' he growled as he tightened his grip on his shield handle and ran out in front of his men. 'First five sections, column of fours! Follow me. Optio Drusus!'

'Sir?'

'Extend the rest of the men to cover the line.'

'Yes, sir.'

As the forty men took their position behind Macro, the centurion drew his sword. 'Keep it closed up, until I give the order to form a wedge. Do it smartly, lads. Our lives depend on it. Let's go!'

Macro broke into a trot and his boots pounded the dry soil and the stalks of grass rustled against his calves as he led his men directly towards the foragers and the horsemen beyond. Now the sun had set, the ruddy glow of the landscape and the long shadows had gone and the plain was bathed in the gloom of dusk. They had run over two hundred paces before the first group of foragers reached them. Without breaking his stride, Macro bellowed at them to keep going, and make for the cohort. Fifty paces further on were the rest of the forage party, running as hard as they could, with some flagging and falling behind. Well to the rear was the last of them, limping, as if he had sprained an ankle.

The Praetorian heard the drumming of hoofs directly behind him and turned at the last moment. A bare-chested rebel thrust his hunting spear home, catching the Roman squarely in his stomach. The impact made him fling his arms out as he folded over the broad blade of the spear tip, an instant before it burst out of the back of his tunic. The Praetorian fell out of sight into the grass as the rider reined in sharply and wrenched his spear back, stabbing down again to finish his victim off. Then he raised the bloodied tip of his spear and spurred his mount on to find fresh prey.

Tempted as he was to increase his pace, Macro knew the value of keeping in formation and not reaching his enemy too blown to fight well. Besides, he could see that they would win the desperate race to reach the foragers first. As the gap closed he called out to them.

'Form up to the rear! To the rear!'

The first men rushed past, either side of Macro's small force, and then he filled his lungs to give the order. 'Halt!'

The forty men at his back stopped, and stood breathing heavily.

'Form wedge!'

The men fanned out on either side behind Macro, angling their shields towards the enemy and lowering the heads of their spears towards the oncoming rebels. What he had in mind was going to be difficult to pull off, and was unorthodox, but at that moment it was all he could think of to save himself and his men. The last of the forage party stumbled by, some twenty paces ahead of the first of the horsemen, who bent low to the side of his horse's neck as he readied to make an underhand thrust with his spear. Macro felt a flash of professional disdain at the sight. Only amateurs used that grip. He raised his shield so that the rounded rim covered his throat and chin and drew his sword arm back ready to strike.

The transverse crest on Macro's helmet marked him out clearly, as did his position at the very point of the small Roman formation, and the rider pulled his reins and swerved his mount towards the centurion. Macro drew his right foot back and braced himself to absorb the impact. There was a flash of metal and the point of the spear struck high up on the shield, forcing the trim back against the brow guard of Macro's helmet with a sharp clatter. The blow was too weak to splinter the shield and deflected harmlessly to Macro's left, leaving plenty of space for him to step inside the man's spear arm. The sweaty tang of horseflesh filled his nostrils, and the flank of the horse pressed into his shoulder, nearly knocking him off balance. But Macro's fighting poise was second to none and he adjusted his stance easily, throwing his weight behind his sword arm as the blade angled up into the side of the rebel looming above him. He felt the jarring impact, then the give of muscle and bone as the point of his blade ripped into the rebel's vitals. Macro twisted his wrist, both ways, and tore the blade back. His enemy gave a pained grunt as he pulled hard on his reins to break free of his Roman opponent. The horse whinnied and shook its head in protest before succumbing to the pressure of the bit and swerving aside. The rider swayed in the saddle, caught himself and cantered away, his spear hanging limply at his side.

Macro recovered into the ready position and glanced to either side. More of the rebel horsemen were approaching the formation, drawn by the desire to close with the enemy, but the bristling lines of spears caused their nerve to fail for the most part. Some did try to charge the formation, flailing at the shafts of the spears, trying to parry them aside and press home their charge, but that only exposed them to the spear thrusts of the Praetorians on either side. One of the horsemen managed to force his protesting horse into the line, and the beast snorted with agony as a spear pierced its neck. It reared up and threw its rider who landed heavily on his back right at the feet of a Praetorian, who kicked him in the head before opening his throat with a savage jab.

A glance over his shoulder revealed that the foragers were safely within the formation and that the rear of the wedge was closed up.

'Stay in formation, lads! And on my order . . . Withdraw!'

The Praetorians edged back towards the rest of the cohort, keeping their shields and spears facing the enemy. The horsemen were all around them now, darting forward and thrusting their spears at the Romans, with little effect. Macro was confident that the closed ranks of his soldiers would fend off mounted men easily enough. The real threat was from the rebels on foot who were rapidly closing on the formation. They would be able to engage far more directly, while slowing the pace of the withdrawal.

The wedge was perhaps a hundred paces from the cohort when the first figures weaved through the horsemen and hurled themselves at the Roman shields. They were wild-looking men with long hair tied back. Many sported beards which added to their savage appearance as they snarled and roared with anger. They rushed forward, wielding spears and axes and some had crooked swords weighted towards the end of the blade that delivered terrible wounds if they connected with force.

A young man in a patterned tunic, not old enough to be a legionary recruit, burst out between two of the horses and came at Macro with a boar spear clenched in both hands. The leaf-shaped spearhead struck the rim of Macro's shield and glanced aside. He made to move inside the weapon and strike his attacker down, just like the horseman before him. But with a quick flick of his wrists, the youth lodged the short crosspiece behind the trim of the centurion's shield and wrenched the shaft of his spear, pulling the shield round and throwing Macro off balance so that he instinctively twisted to stay on his feet. At the same time he fought back with his left arm, wrestling to keep the shield from being ripped from his fingers. For a moment the two of them strained against each other, and then Macro summoned his greater strength and with a roar violently ripped his shield back, pulling the youth round in front of him, before punching the guard of his sword into the side of his opponent's head.

The blow would have knocked a normal man out, but the skull of the rebel was thicker than most and he staggered back with a dazed expression, shook his head and came at Macro again, thrusting the spear with his full weight behind it. This time Macro parried the spear down, using the crosspiece to give him purchase, and then slammed his shield into the youth's chest, knocking him back. He stumbled a few paces away and for an instant Macro's instinct was to charge home and finish off his enemy. But then he recalled he was in formation, and he was the officer in charge who set the example, and he backed into position as the wedge continued to retreat in the fading light.

The Praetorians were fighting every step of the way now, weapons hammering on their shields as the Romans traded blows with the rebels. Their armour, discipline and training gave them a distinct advantage over the lightly equipped tribesmen, but they were not invulnerable, and the first of the Praetorians fell to a spear thrust into his thigh. The soldier limped back, gushing blood. As his comrades closed up the gap he transferred his spear to his shield side and pressed a hand to the wound, but the gore coursed round and through his fingers as the blood pumped out of the severed artery. Two of the foragers held him up in the heart of the formation as the wedge crawled across the grassy plain. He had bled out before they had moved another ten paces and the foragers set him down. One took his shield and eased his way into the front line, before his abandoned body was set upon by the rebels who hacked and stabbed at the hated Roman even though he was dead.

More men were wounded and taken into the centre of the wedge as it closed up on the rest of the cohort, but Macro could see that he and his men would make it now. He stepped back and ordered the Praetorians on either side to close up. It was time to take stock of the situation around him, and be ready to manoeuvre once he was reunited with the rest of the cohort.

'Sir!' a voice cried out close at hand. 'Look there! Fire!'

Macro turned and saw that the nearest ranks of the cohort were darkly outlined by the glow of flames beyond, where the campfires had been lit. Some careless fool had dropped kindling too close to the flames when the alarm had been given, Macro guessed. Or some fluke of the breeze, or spark falling in the grass. It didn't matter. The blaze was spreading even as he watched and glittering tongues of yellow and red flitted up into the twilight.

'Oh, shit . . . Just what we needed.'

The wedge reached the cohort and the men, harried all the way by the rebels, dropped into line, as the wounded were taken to the rear, around the edge of the spreading fire. Macro saw Centurion Placinus directing two sections of men as they attempted to beat out the flames, while the rest of their comrades fought off their attackers. Macro trotted over to him.

'What, in Jupiter's name, is going on?'

Placinus saluted. 'One of the piles of cooking fuel went up, sir. When I find the twat responsible he'll wish he was never born.'

'Never mind that,' Macro responded curtly. He could see the fire spreading steadily through the dry grass and already thick curls of smoke were swirling over the Roman position. 'We can't make a stand here, or we'll burn. In any case, the prefect wanted us to fall back into the village. We'll try and keep the box formation as we move. Get these men back in the line and be ready to move.'

'Yes, sir.'

Macro stood alone, a short distance from the edge of the blaze, feeling its heat against his bare skin. Around him the fighting was spreading along the sides of the cohort as the rebels flowed like water around a rock. He took a breath and coughed as he inhaled acrid smoke. He coughed again and fought to clear his lungs and take in untainted air.

'Second Cohort! In box formation, on my order, retire towards the village!' He gave the men a moment to prepare, then, 'Move!'

It was at that moment that the folly of the order occurred to him. There was no way to manoeuvre over the fast-spreading flames. Not without breaking formation. Macro cursed himself and filled his lungs to issue a new order.

'Halt! By centuries . . . ! Retire on the village!'

The rectangle began to break up as each of the six centuries formed their own defensive formation around their standard. The surviving carts were surrounded by Petillius' men while the drivers struggled to control their mule teams who were frightened by the noise and the flames. Macro hurried over to the First Century at the side closest to the village. A blazing patch of grass separated them and he had to skirt round it, wincing at the heat stinging his skin. A figure cut in between him and his unit and Macro raised his shield and sword as a heavy-set rebel, his tunic stained with blood, swung a long-handled axe overhead and slashed it down at the Roman. Macro just had time to leap to the side as the axe head smashed into the grass and earth, sending divots flying. Before the man could recover, Macro powered forward and threw his full weight behind his shield, crashing into his enemy and driving him back towards the flames. He kept going, even as the flames licked up around his boots, and gave one last thrust as the rebel tumbled into the heart of the blaze with a panicked shriek. Macro back-pedalled swiftly, using his shield to protect himself from the heat until he was well clear. The other man had scrambled to his feet, in the heart of flames that rose twice his height, his hair and tunic already alight, his mouth open in a keening cry. He ran to the end of the flames and off into the mêlée, blazing like a torch.

Macro ran on, and joined his men, formed up in a square. He gave the command to march. They began to trudge away from the blaze, and all the while the enemy rushed up to make spear thrusts, or a wild exchange of blows, before dashing back beyond the range of the Praetorians' spears.

Meanwhile, the flames hungrily spread through the parched

grass, as the Romans and the enemy struggled on while trying to keep clear of the fire. Porcino's century had been forced to halt, their progress blocked by the blaze, while the rebels pressed them back on themselves. Slowly they were being forced towards the flames, harshly illuminated by the glare. Then, as Macro watched, the century broke, men spilling round the flames and fleeing individually or in small groups, doing their best to cover each other's backs. The largest group clustered around the centurion and the standard as they fought their way through the loose ranks of the enemy.

To the crackle and roar of the blaze was added the pleas for help and tormented cries of agony from the injured lying in the grass as the flames spread to them and began to cook them alive. But in the desperate struggle taking place in the garish hue of the fire and the choking swirls of smoke there was no chance to save them. Most of Porcino's men managed to join the other centuries and his expression was ferocious as he led his party inside the lines of Macro's century.

'Well done, Porcino!' Macro welcomed him. 'You saved the standard. Good effort.'

Porcino looked round at his standard bearer, and nodded dumbly. 'The rest of my men?'

'Most are saved. But we're not out of it yet.'

Sparks from the fire were spinning through the velvet darkness and dropping down to ignite other patches of grass in the surrounding plain so that it was beginning to take on the appearance of a sea of flames. To Macro's relief, the rebels, fully alert to the danger they shared with their enemy, were now breaking off to escape the conflagration. Meanwhile, the Praetorians kept to their formation as they steadily marched clear of the fire and made for the village rising up on the hill a short distance away. Some of the more stout-hearted of the rebels shadowed the Praetorians, and harassed the Romans with the odd slingshot or thrown rock, but most of them had melted away into the gathering darkness.

As the First Century began to climb the slope leading up to the village's gateway, Macro looked back at the vista of fires burning outwards from the cohort's campsite. The roar of the flames was muted at this distance but the shrill cries of the wounded, and those already caught in the blaze, cut through the night and chilled his heart. Even though they were mostly the voices of his enemy, Macro was moved to pity. No man should have to die like that. Then he turned back towards the village and wondered what had become of Cato. The horses were still being held just outside the village by some of the men, but there was no sign of the prefect or the other men who had followed him into the settlement and Macro felt his guts twist in anxiety over what new peril the fates had in store for the men of the Second Cohort of Praetorians.

# CHAPTER SEVENTEEN

'Where in Hades is the rest of the cohort?' Cristus demanded, hugging his knees and rocking backwards and forwards gently. 'How much longer are we going to be pinned down here before they get stuck into those bastards on the roofs?'

Cato sat with his back to a wheel and his knees drawn up. One hand loosely clasped the handle of his shield resting on the ground next to him. The other was over the top of the pommel of his sword as he twisted it slowly from side to side.

'You don't want to be doing that, sir.' Metellus nodded at the weapon. 'Blunts the point.'

'What?' Cato looked up, then nodded. 'Oh, right.'

He wiped the grit off the end of the sword and sheathed it. The centre of the village had been quiet for a while as the Romans stayed under cover and the enemy realised there was no point in wasting their efforts with slingshot and other missiles.

'Where are our men?' Cristus muttered.

'The cohort has other fish to fry,' Cato responded quietly. 'I'm sure Centurion Macro will come for us the moment he has recovered the foragers. It's only a matter of time. Until then, Tribune, I'd be grateful if you kept your concerns to yourself. Set an example for the men.'

Cristus turned to stare at him. 'I never wanted to be a soldier.'

'Nevertheless, you wear the uniform and take the Emperor's coin. You chose to do that. Like everything else in your life.'

There was a nervous flicker in the tribune's expression and he swallowed. 'What do you mean, sir?'

Cato said nothing for a moment. He was sorely tempted to stick the knife in and give it a twist. The man deserved it. But this was not the time or place for any confrontation over matters that had no bearing on their immediate plight. That could come later, when – if – they escaped from this trap.

'Just what I said. We all have to take responsibility for the consequences of our choices, Tribune. You chose to be a soldier. You chose to accept the rank of tribune. This is the price you pay for that. Understand?'

Cristus hesitated, then gave a nod.

'Good, then you keep your fears to yourself and make sure the men under your command have the leader they deserve.'

'Yes, sir.'

Cato looked round at the other men. Besides himself, Cristus and Metellus there was Centurion Pulcher, grim-faced and cross-armed, eight men of the baggage train and the mounted contingent, twenty-eight in all. Three of the drovers were wounded. All were packed closely together between two of the carts with shields covering the gaps at each end, and more held overhead to protect them from the rebels' slingshot and rocks. The light was fading quickly and the square was in shadow. Occasionally there were shouts from the rebels but otherwise there was a tense stillness that Cato found acutely unsettling. Particularly as he had no idea how things were going for Macro and the rest of the cohort. The strained braying of a handful of wounded mules continued unbroken, starting to fray Cato's nerves.

'You see that?' one of the men said. 'Over there. Smoke.'

Cato rose just enough to look over his shield and out of the gap between the two carts. Above the roofline he could make out a greasy smear against the pale sky to the west.

'It's a fire,' said one of the men.

Metellus snorted. 'Of course it's a fire, you daft cunt. Smoke and fire go together. Question is, what does it mean? Are the rebels still on the roofs? Can anyone see?'

The helmet of one of the injured men had been removed and Cato pointed to it. 'Give me that.'

The Praetorians passed the helmet along to Cato and he drew his sword again. Balancing the helmet on the point he used his spare

170

hand to draw down the chin ties to steady the helmet, and then took a breath.

'Here goes.'

Rising slowly, he held the helmet up, between two of the shields overhead, and then lifted it far enough that it would be clearly visible to any men on the roofs. There was no reaction. Cato waited a moment, and then began to turn the helmet from side to side, as if scanning the roofline. The next moment there was a loud clatter as a slingshot struck one of the shields close by and deflected off the crest of the helmet. Cato lowered his arms and squatted down.

'Someone's still out there. So we stay put for a bit longer.'

'Sir!' one of the men at the far end of the crowded space called out to him. 'I can see 'em. There's a group at the edge of the square.'

'What are they doing?'

The Praetorian watched closely between the shields before he reported again. 'Nothing . . . Wait, there's more of them coming out of another street.'

Metellus nudged Cato. 'They'll be making an attack, I'm thinking. While they've got a chance to wipe us out before Centurion Macro gets here.'

'Makes sense. And if they've nearly exhausted their slingshot then they'll have to go hand-to-hand.' Cato thought quickly. 'If they come at us then I want three men in each of the carts. You take charge in one, Metellus, and Pulcher, you get the other. The rest of us will cover each end. If we lose either of the carts, or they break through at either end, then we're all dead. We've no chance of escaping from the village, and nowhere to retreat to. We hold on here, or die. Hold on as long as possible, and if we fall, then we take as many of the bastards with us as we can. They'll not forget the Praetorians in a hurry.'

There was no time for any further encouragement as a voice shouted from the corner of the square. Cato hunched down, made his way to the far end of the cart and looked warily over the shields. One of the rebels was standing in front of a band of his comrades as they spilled out around the square, working them up, ready for the moment to attack the small pocket of Romans. He was dressed in a checked tunic of red and black and wore a legionary

171

helmet to which he had attached a flowing red crest. Punching his sword into the air, he exhorted his followers and they returned his final cry as they raised their weapons and brandished them at their enemy. Their voices echoed off the walls of the buildings, amplifying the din. Cato glanced round and saw Cristus grinding his teeth, his jaw muscles flickering. Some of the other men revealed their nerves as well through small tics, and Cato spared an instant to reflect on the peculiar intimacy and loneliness of soldiers the moment before battle was joined.

With a deep-throated roar, the leader turned towards the carts and he clashed the flat of his sword against the side of his shield. Those who carried shields took up the rhythm and the sound assaulting the ears of Cato and his party rose to a terrifying crescendo. And then the rebel leader stopped, raised his sword and swept it down towards the Romans as he broke into a run.

Cato cupped a hand to his mouth to ensure that he was heard. 'Here they come! Get to your positions!'

Metellus and Pulcher led the men assigned to the carts as they clambered over the splintered sides and readied their spears. Cato took his place at the end closest to the oncoming enemy, raised his shield and held his sword ready, the tip just protruding beyond the edge of the shield, his sword arm tensed and ready to punch forward with all his strength. He ordered Cristus to stand at his side and behind them the Praetorians raised their spears, ready to strike over the heads of the two officers.

Cato spat to clear his throat and called out as calmly as he could manage, 'Do your duty, lads! For Rome!'

Before him, in the gloom of the village square, was a surging horde of savage faces, wild eyes, and gaping mouths framed by shaggy dark hair that made them appear as barbaric as any enemy he had ever faced. Several of the men, more lightly armed and wearing no armour, had overtaken their leader and raced towards the carts, eager to strike the first blow. Cato braced himself for the impact of the charge, pressing his boots into the packed earth of the square, and leaning slightly forward on his left foot. He heard Cristus offering a prayer loudly at his right.

'O, Jupiter, Best and Greatest, preserve me.'

Then the first of the enemy slashed down at Cato with a long sword and he thrust his shield up to meet the jarring blow, followed an instant later by the torso of the rebel slamming, shoulder first, into the oval shield. Cato recoiled, but he had trained for this and had fought often enough to instinctively absorb the blow, retain his balance and then thrust back. A small gap opened between himself and his foe and he struck his sword into the man's guts as savagely as he could, twisting the blade to ensure it did not lodge in his enemy's body before he snatched it back. The blow only enraged the man and he grasped the edge of the shield with his left hand as he raised his sword to strike again, even as blood and the grey of intestines bulged through the tear in his stomach. Cato did not give him the chance to make another blow, but punched his shield out, battering the man and crushing his nose. This lesser injury had more effect than the mortal wound and the rebel fell back, clutching a hand to his nose as blood coursed from his nostrils and spattered onto his tunic.

Cristus tumbled against Cato as he stepped aside to avoid the blow of an axe.

'Keep your fucking shield up!' Cato yelled at him. 'Block him!'

Cato shoved the tribune away and readied himself for the next opponent just as a spear was thrust directly towards his eyes. Instinct caused him to turn his head and lean to the side and the weapon glanced off his cheek guard, the impact wrenching his neck painfully. Cato swung his sword up and more by luck than judgement the edge caught the rebel on the knuckles, cutting flesh and shattering bone, so that his grip was lost and the spear shaft angled to the ground. A powerful thrust of the shield knocked the man back and gave Cato a moment's respite.

The muscles in his neck burned with the slightest movement of his head and he struggled to concentrate. The rebels had surrounded the two carts and the thud and clatter of weapons, the grunts and cries of men, filled his ears. The man whose hand Cato had cut into was trying to back away from the end of the carts but his comrades paid him no heed and pressed forward, forcing him back towards Cato, and up against his shield. Looking over the rim, Cato saw the other man's face inches from his own; someone of his own age, with thick dark eyebrows and greasy locks of curly black hair. His eyes were wide with a mixture of terror and rage and his lips curled back to reveal snaggled teeth gritted in a snarl. The rebel managed to free his uninjured hand and the fingers closed over the rim of Cato's shield as he attempted to prise it away from the Roman. Cato rammed his helmet forward, clenching his teeth against the tearing pain in his neck as he did so. The forehead guard gouged the rebel's brow, tearing the skin. Cato struck again, enlarging the wound, and blood flowed over the man's eyelids, blinding him. Still he strained to pull the shield aside, and managed to expose Cato's face, enough to snap at him with his teeth. Hot breath, fouled by garlic, blasted over Cato and he lowered the brim of his helmet and struck again, while stabbing into the man's guts in short, vicious thrusts. Each blow caused the man to gasp, but there was no escape for him as he was pressed into Cato's shield and forced to endure each strike of the sword.

Steeling his muscles, Cato took a half step back and then threw his weight forward, battering his victim with the shield and forcing him into those behind. As Cato eased back, the rebel slumped onto his knees. A hand grasped the collar of his tunic and bodily hauled him aside to make space as a fresh opponent took his place. The pain in Cato's neck burned and his vision blurred briefly as he fought against the urge to throw up. In front of him reared a giant of a man, half a head taller than him, but powerfully built like Macro. He wore a legionary helmet and a chain-mail vest and advanced a round shield as he readied to make an overhead slash. The blade gleamed dully in the failing light and Cato just managed to thrust his shield up and out in time to block the cut. But the brutal power of the blow was enough to cut through the trim and split the cross-ply wood of the shield for several inches.

The blade lodged there, and as the rebel tried to rip it free, he almost tore the handle of the shield from Cato's numbed fingers. Cato just managed to hold on as his shield arm was wrenched away from him. The sword jostled wildly as his foe tried to tear it out. Then, with a roar of frustration, he charged at Cato instead, slamming the shield back against him with great force and Cato's fingers lost their grip on the handle as he fell amongst the Praetorians behind him and tumbled onto his back. The giant released his hold of the sword, still wedged into the shield, and let it fall to the side as he snatched out a long-bladed dagger and leaned forward to stab the stricken officer before his comrades could fill his place.

'No you don't, fucker!' Pulcher yelled from the cart. The giant glanced up just as the tip of the centurion's spear stabbed deep into the soft flesh above the rebel's collarbone. The giant let out a great roar of shock, rage and then agony. He staggered to the side, slamming Cristus into the side of the cart, then Pulcher worked the tip of the spear about, as if stirring a huge ladle in a barrel of pitch, before wrenching it free with a great gush and spout of gore. The rebel stumbled back, limbs trembling, before going down on his knees a short distance from the cart. His face screwed up in pain and his thick lips worked and he spat a bloody gobbet into the faces of his enemy before pitching forward on the ground. There was a brief pause in the fighting around the body before Pulcher shouted:

'What you waiting for? Fill the bloody gap!'

Two Praetorians stepped forward to replace Cato and Cristus, and locked shields as they readied their spears to strike. The loss of their comrade had disheartened the rebels in the front ranks, but those behind who had not witnessed his death pressed on, pushing the nearest rebels onto the waiting spears.

Cato propped himself up on his elbows. The impact of his fall had winded him and he struggled painfully for breath. One of the Praetorians laid his spear down and bent to help him up.

'Sir? Are you wounded?'

Cato shook his head, and was about to order the man to pick up his weapon and stand ready, when the Praetorian's jaw snapped wide open in surprise. He looked down to see a deep gash on the back of his heel. The tendon had been cut through, and the Praetorian dropped to his knees. Behind the stricken Roman, in the gloom beneath the cart, Cato saw one of the rebels on his stomach, wriggling towards him, readying his sword to strike again. Snatching at the shaft of the spear Cato raised it, took aim at the rebel and thrust it as hard as he could. His strike was one-handed and lacked weight, but the tip pierced the man's sword arm and he recoiled quickly, shuffling back a short distance, out of the range of the spear.

'Get out of my way,' Cato wheezed at the wounded Praetorian and the latter did his best to roll aside. Now Cato had a better view of his target and struggled onto his knees, bending low and using both hands to engage his opponent. They exchanged feints in the shadows beneath the bed of the cart, neither able to wound the other.

'Cristus! Here. Help me out!'

The tribune glanced down with a puzzled expression at his superior, seemingly writhing beneath the cart.

'Now, damn you!' Cato snapped at him.

Cristus crouched and squinted, then saw the enemy. Drawing his sword he dropped down and crawled towards the rebel. Caught between two threats, the man parried Cato's spear, then turned to strike at the tribune who recoiled smartly, but the rebel was too late to fend off Cato's next thrust, as he lurched forward. The point of the spear struck him in the side of the jaw, shattering bone and teeth and piercing through to the other side of his head. He dropped his sword and rolled away, crawling between the legs of the rebels fighting along the side of the cart. Cato nodded his thanks to Cristus and then waved him forward.

'Have a go at their legs!'

The tribune nodded and scurried under the cart while Cato edged forward beneath the other vehicle and stabbed at the nearest of the limbs, which belonged to a hairy-legged rebel with a long brown tunic cinched by a band of cloth about the waist. Cato stabbed into the thigh and gave the spear shaft a violent twist before snatching it back and striking again, this time into the man's calf. The rebel staggered back, bleeding heavily, and Cato turned to the side and stabbed up, this time into the groin of another enemy. It was a shallow wound, but enough to distract him, while the Roman in the cart above struck a mortal blow. He fell in front of Cato, blood gushing from a tear in his throat.

There was an angry shout and Cato looked round to see a man crouching to his left, axe handle already swinging back to strike. Cato frantically threw himself to the side as the axe head swung through the space where he had been an instant before. Now that he had been detected there was no more advantage to remaining far enough under the cart to strike at the enemy attacking from the side and Cato held back, ready to engage any who thought to emulate the man he had stabbed through the face. A quick glance round revealed that Cristus had just downed a man and was jabbing his blade into the rebel's guts as he writhed in the gloom.

'Look!' Metellus shouted. 'The bastards are running!'

Sure enough, as Cato watched, the legs of the men along the side of the cart backed away, then turned to flee, racing across the darkened village square. He shuffled back from beneath the cart and wearily rose to his feet, leaning on his spear for support. Around him the Praetorians were breathing hard, scarcely able to believe they had survived. Besides those who had been wounded in the initial ambush another two bodies lay at the other end of the cart Cato had been defending. One man's helmet was deeply cloven and blood and brains oozed from the rent in the metal. The other was propped up against a wheel, sitting in a pool of his blood as he pressed a hand against the inside of his thigh. Cato swallowed and took a breath so that he could speak calmly.

'Metellus, Pulcher, how are your men up there?'

'One wounded,' Metellus replied.

Pulcher loomed over Cato, spear in hand. 'One dead here, sir.'

'What can you see?'

Pulcher turned and scanned the square. 'They're on the run. No surprise because here come our lads now.'

The sound of boots echoed off the buildings and swelled as the first of the Praetorians from the camp charged into the square, close behind those they had chased through the streets. Cato pushed his way clear of the Praetorians at the end of the cart and strode out into the open. The ground around the two carts was scattered with dead and wounded rebels, perhaps as many as twenty of them, and Cato felt a professional pride in the performance of his soldiers. He paused, and looked up at Pulcher.

'Thanks for saving my skin back then.'

The centurion was silent for a moment and then shrugged. 'You're one of us, sir. That's all there is to it. I'd no more let you die than any other Roman.'

'But I thank you all the same.' Cato gave a slight bow of his head and turned away.

Petillius was the first of the centurions to reach the square and Cato beckoned to him.

'Keep after 'em. I want the village cleared of the enemy.'

'Yes, sir.' Petillius saluted, then smiled grimly. 'Glad you're still with us.'

'Not as glad as I am. Now go.'

The Praetorians of Petillius' century surged into the streets where the enemy had fled and shortly afterwards Macro emerged from a gap between the buildings at the head of his men. He paused as he looked round the carnage of the scene, just visible in the dying light.

'Quite a fucking mess you got yourself into here, sir.'

'Good to see you too, Centurion. What's the situation in the camp?'

'There is no camp, sir. I gave the order to move out shortly after the grass caught fire.'

'Fire? Bad?'

Macro indicated the red hue above the roofs to the south of the village. 'Quite a blaze. We'd have cooked if we'd stayed to fight it out.'

'What about the enemy?'

'Scarpered, soon as the flames spread. Last we saw of them was when we reached the village. They were heading back to the west. Just have to clear the village and we'll be safe enough for the night.'

'Good work,' Cato gestured towards the carts and the handful of mules still on their feet. 'But the damage is done. We've lost most of our baggage train and supplies. I dare say we'll have suffered quite a few casualties. And we've lost any element of surprise. The rebels know we're coming, and how many of us there are.' Cato sighed. 'Macro, my friend, I fear our troubles are just beginning.'

# CHAPTER EIGHTEEN

'As far as I see it, we have three options, which I will come to in a moment,' Cato announced as he addressed his officers and Cimber at the small tavern in the village square, some two hours after night had fallen, as close as he could estimate. The surviving carts had been driven back inside the gate and Porcino's century had been assigned the first watch as the rest of the cohort rested in the village. Most of the inhabitants had been massacred in their homes by the rebels when they had appeared two nights before. The handful of survivors that had emerged from hiding once the Praetorians had driven the rebels out related what had happened after the initial attack. The survivors had been herded into the square and offered a stark choice: join the revolt or die. And so the ranks of the rebels had increased, as some of them had been forced to fight Cato's men.

Cato looked round at his officers before he continued. He knew that he could depend on Macro to support him without question. The veterans could also be relied upon. Cato was within his rights to make a decision without having to justify his reasoning, but he had only been in command of the cohort a matter of days and he needed his officers to understand both the situation and his think-ing. It would also present a further opportunity to get to know them better by judging their reaction to his briefing. He ordered his thoughts and began.

'Today's encounter was proof of just how far the rebellion has spread. Far further than anticipated. And fast enough to catch me by surprise, otherwise I would have given the order to construct the marching camp at the end of each day. I took the view that the need

179

for speed justified the risk. I was wrong, and should have listened to the advice of Centurion Macro in that respect. We all know that Rome shows little pity towards those who fail to stick to procedures when advancing through hostile territory. The responsibility for being surprised by the enemy is mine, gentlemen. I give you my word that I alone will be subject to any reprimand or disciplinary action taken as a consequence of my failure to construct a marching camp in the face of the enemy. Assuming we live to see that day, of course.'

Most of the officers smiled wryly, except Macro, who just pursed his lips and shrugged.

'Culpability aside, we are in a difficult situation. Our orders are to secure the mine and wait for Legate Vitellius to catch up with us. Those orders were given on the assumption that the uprising was still confined to the territory around Asturica. Clearly that is no longer the case. They know we are here. They will also know that we are marching in the direction of Asturica. Therefore they will have ample opportunity to attack us again, possibly in far greater numbers on ground of their own choosing. Our difficulties are made worse by the loss of most of our baggage train. Thanks to the ambush we have enough mules left to draw only three carts. Four if there are men to assist the mules in difficult terrain. That means that we cannot count on much of a reserve with respect to the men's rations. Then there's another issue. This evening's action has cost us a number of casualties. Centurion Macro, you have the strength returns?'

'Yes, sir.' Macro took a waxed slate from his sidebag and held it up to the flame of an oil lamp to see the figures clearly. 'Eighteen dead, twenty-three wounded and twelve missing. Either captured or lost in the grass fire.'

'Quite.' Cato tried not to imagine their hideous fate, either way. 'The problem lies with the wounded. If we take them with us, then they can only slow us down. So, as I said, we are left with three choices. Firstly, we put the wounded into the carts and turn back and march towards Tarraco until we link up with the main column. We can draw supplies along the way from the towns and villages that are not affected by the rebellion. Secondly, we can hold out in the village until Vitellius reaches us. There must be adequate food here to satisfy our needs and we can fortify the village to withstand any attack by a much larger force than that which ambushed us this evening.' Cato paused briefly. 'Which brings us onto the third course of action. Namely that we proceed with our orders, and march to the mine and secure it until the main column reaches the area.'

He gestured towards the officers. 'Your thoughts, gentlemen?'

There was a short pause before Pulcher spoke. 'Orders are orders, sir. If we were told to hold the mine, then that's what we do, unless we receive new orders. I don't even know why we are discussing it.'

'Because I say so,' Cato replied sharply. 'Anyone else?'

Porcino glanced at the others, then leaned forward earnestly. 'Sir, whatever your orders may have been, the situation has changed. Like you said, the enemy knows we are coming. There's no question of being able to catch them by surprise anymore. There's every chance of falling into another trap. It's obvious what we have to do. We have to retreat. We don't have any choice about it.'

'You're right, *we* don't have any choice in the matter,' said Macro. 'The decision is down to the prefect. We only get to offer an opinion, and even then only when it's asked for.'

Porcino understood the point well enough, but persisted. 'Sir, if we continue, then we'll be marching to our deaths.'

Cato nodded. 'Very likely. The odds are against us, but then the stakes are high. If Iskerbeles takes the mine, the Emperor will be deprived of the coin he needs to pay his soldiers. We can prevent that.'

'But it's more than likely that the rebels have already captured the mine, sir.'

'We don't know that. We'll only find out when we get there.'

'If we reach the mine,' Tribune Cristus intervened.

Cato turned to him, stifling his annoyance. 'Yes, if we reach the mine. And it's my job to see that we do. And if anything happens to me, then the duty to carry out our orders will fall to you as the senior surviving officer. If you are killed then the job goes to the next man, all the way down the chain of command. That is our

181

duty. That is why we have been entrusted with the rank we hold. Let no man here fail to understand that.'

Cristus chewed his lip. 'It sounds like you have already made a decision.'

Cato arched an eyebrow and inclined his head meaningfully so that Cristus corrected his mistake.

'It sounds like you have already made a decision, *sir.*'

'I have, yes. But I need all of you to understand why we must go on, in case anything does happen to me. It is imperative that we accept any risks involved in reaching the mine. That goes for every one of us . . .' Cato let his words sink in before he continued. 'So, at dawn I want the wounded loaded onto the remaining carts which will return to Tarraco. Together with most of the horses and the cohort's strongbox. That's too heavy to take with us and, in any case, I'd rather not take the risk of letting it fall into enemy hands. The carts will need an escort. A half century will do. Centurion Placinus will be in command.'

Placinus nodded. 'Yes, sir.'

'I'll give you a report to hand to the legate before you leave. The rest of the cohort will take whatever supplies we can find from the village and continue the advance. Given that our presence here will be reported back to Iskerbeles, we dare not continue with a direct approach towards Asturica.' Cato paused, as he noticed Cimber had raised his hand, and taken a half step forward to ensure that his intention to speak could not be ignored.

Cato gave an impatient sigh. 'What is it?'

The guide could not hide his nervousness, nor meet anyone else's eyes as he spoke. 'Prefect, I request permission to return to Tarraco with the wounded.'

Macro turned towards him and made a show of looking him up and down. 'You don't look wounded to me. Did you twist an ankle or something while the rest of us were fighting earlier on?'

Cato saw Cimber grimace with shame as he said, 'You're coming with us.'

Cimber looked up then, and shook his head. 'No. You can't make me. I'm a civilian. A Roman citizen. I know my rights.'

'You can complain about me directly to the Emperor afterwards, if that is your wish. But you'll have to join the back of the queue.'

Cimber did not share the amusement of the others in the tavern. 'You can't order me to come with you. I've given you as much help as I can. I've done my bit and I am free to go if I wish. After all, I'm not a soldier. I'm not subject to your authority.'

'Then I'll have to do something about that. Centurion Macro.'

'Sir?'

'Enter Cimber here onto the strength of your century as a ranker. You can kit him out with the armour and weapons of one of the wounded. He'll be subject to the usual discipline. Clear?'

Macro grinned. 'Yes, sir.'

Cato turned back to the guide. 'Welcome to the Praetorian Guard, Cimber. I'm sure you'll do us proud.'

Cimber's jaw sagged, then he shook his head. 'You can't do this!'

Cato stepped up to him and looked down into his face. 'I just did. And as you are a new recruit I'll forgive you the breach of discipline, on this one occasion. In future you call me "sir" and you do not address a superior officer unless called on to do so.'

Cimber made to protest again but Cato raised a hand to silence him. 'Any further remark from you will constitute an act of insubordination. And what do we do with insubordinate soldiers, Centurion Macro?'

'We flog 'em, sir.'

'We flog them . . .' Cato repeated, staring directly at Cimber. 'Do you understand?'

Cimber's face screwed up into an expression of frustration and anxiety, before he nodded. 'Yes. Sir.'

'And don't think about trying to desert us. What does the army do to deserters, Macro?'

'They get executed, sir. Stoned to death by their comrades, or worse.'

'Exactly . . . Now then, Praetorian Cimber, it is clear that it would be dangerous to continue advancing along the present route to Asturica. What I need to know from you is if there is an alternative route. One that will allow us to escape the attention of the enemy and get us to the mine without too much delay. Do you know of such a route?' It occurred to Cato that the man might be tempted to deny the existence of such an alternative in the faint hope that it might dissuade Cato from continuing the advance. 'If there isn't then we'll have to stay on the same road, regardless of the danger of doing so . . . Speak up, man.'

The new recruit was still dazed by his change of fortune but had enough wits about him to respond before Cato threatened him with further punishments. 'There is another road, sir. A track, really. Through the hills to the north. It's not suitable for wheeled traffic, and there are only a handful of small settlements along the way. It passes quite close to the mine.'

Macro eyed him suspiciously. 'And how did you come to know about it?'

'I had an uncle in the mule trade, sir. I accompanied him on the annual drive a few times as a boy.'

'Can you remember it well enough to guide us along the way?' asked Cato.

'I think so, sir.'

'You're a soldier now, Cimber. Thinking so isn't good enough. Can you do it or not?'

'Yes, sir.'

'Then it sounds like it will suit us well,' Cato concluded, then turned his attention back to his officers. 'We'll march into the hills tomorrow, gentlemen. I want the village scoured for supplies to carry with us. We'll have to live off the land along the way while we follow Cimber's road. And this time, I will be sure to give orders to erect a marching camp every night.'

'What about the enemy, sir?' asked Petillius. 'Won't they be keeping watch on us? They'll be able to keep Iskerbeles informed of our progress, and they will be sure to harass us even more effectively in hilly terrain.'

'We'll send the mounted men out at first light, and drive off, or kill, their scouts before the cohort makes a move. At the same time, Placinus can attach brushwood drags to the back of the carts to stir up sufficient dust to make it appear as if it is the whole cohort retreating to Tarraco. Let's hope they buy the deception and we can continue our advance without further harassment.' Cato looked round the faces of the other men and was relieved to see that even Porcino and Cristus were making no further attempt to object. 'Good. Then once our mounted patrols report that we're in the clear, the wounded can go into the carts and Placinus can set off at once. The rest will march north. Any more questions . . . ? No? Then we're all clear about what lies ahead. Best get as much rest as you can tonight. It'll be a very hard road ahead of us. Dismissed.'

The officers and Cimber rose from their benches and stools and filed out of the inn into the darkened square. The sky was clear and scattered stars gleamed across the dark mantle of night. Macro paused on the threshold and waited until the others were out of earshot.

'Do you think we can trust Cimber? What if he misleads us once we're on this mule-track of his? To take us away from the danger?'

'If he even thinks about it then I'll have him flogged to within an inch of his life. I think he knows that.'

'I hope so. This mission ain't exactly working out as planned, lad.'

'When does it ever? You know how it is, Macro. The first casualty of war is always the plan.'

'Not just the plan.' Macro gestured to the line of bodies beside the cart. 'I'll have a pyre built for them here in the village. No sense in starting another blaze out there on the plain.'

'Good idea.' Cato nodded. Then, as Macro lingered, he asked, 'Anything else?'

'One thing. Why send Placinus back with the wounded? He's the kind of man we could use when the fighting starts. Why not send back someone we could afford to lose, like Pulcher, Porcino, or that waster, Cristus?'

'I don't trust Pulcher to deliver the report, or give an accurate account of things if Vitellius questions him. Same with Porcino and Cristus, though for different reasons. They'd be likely to say that Iskerbeles has a huge host behind him and that might make the legate pause and request reinforcements. Any such delay will give the rebels more time to grow in influence. The report has to be made by someone I can rely on. A professional soldier who can describe the situation accurately.'

'But why Placinus and not one of the others? Or me?'

'Because he is down the chain of command. Only senior to Porcino. And you?' Cato smiled and gave his friend a light punch on the chest. 'Do you really think I'd ever consider going into battle without you at my side, brother?'

# CHAPTER NINETEEN

The dawn air was filled with the acrid stench of burning. A large area of the plain was scorched black around the site where the Romans had intended to make camp the previous evening. Scores of charred bodies littered the area; those who had died before the fire consumed their bodies lay sprawled where they had fallen. Those who had been wounded and unable to escape lay curled up, having tried to protect themselves from the flames and the heat. The Praetorians were clearly identifiable from their armour and Cato could not help wincing as he imagined the horror of their final moments. He cleared his throat as he spoke to Macro.

'There's some we can cross off the list of the missing.'

Macro squatted down beside one of his former comrades and reached over to probe the taut, blackened flesh around the throat. Though the leather strap had burned away, the lead seal was intact. He prised it loose and rubbed the dark smears away from the impressed marks that identified the soldier. Some letters could still be made out but the heat had been intense enough to start melting the seal, making it impossible to be sure of the name. Not that it made much difference, Macro reflected. If the number of those missing matched the number of the bodies then they would all be listed as killed in action, and any family back in Rome would be able to benefit from their wills. He dropped the seal and stood up.

'I'll have some of the lads take the bodies up to the village.'

Cato glanced up at the oily smear of smoke rising above the tiled roofs of the village into the sky. The funeral pyre had been lit as the first rays of the sun heralded the new day. He shook his head. 'No time for that.'

'No time? We can't just leave the lads out here to rot. It ain't right.'

'They're past caring, Macro.'

'But I'm not, sir. Nor should you be. Can't be leaving fallen comrades like this.'

'We have to leave them.'

Macro grimaced. 'Look, sir. If you let me have a half century, we can get the job done quickly and double-time to catch up with you.'

'I'm not going to divide the column any more than necessary. In any case, the men are already tired enough. I can't waste any time waiting for stragglers when it can be avoided. We need to get moving as soon as the scouts report.'

The mounted patrols had set off before dawn to scour the immediate area for the enemy and drive off any rebels who might be keeping the village under observation. There had been no further trouble from the rebels during the night and Cato hoped that the fire and their heavy losses had encouraged them to move off in search of easier pickings. But it was important to make sure that the cohort threw them off the scent when the Praetorians continued their advance in the shelter of the hills. The detachment returning to Tarraco had already formed up below the village. Four carts loaded with wounded under the protection of Centurion Placinus and his men. They were busy tying bundles of brushwood to the rear of the carts.

Macro had been following the direction of his friend's gaze. 'They'll be ready to leave any moment. I'd hate to be in the rearmost carts when the drags stir up the dust. Poor bastards will choke to death if their wounds don't put an end to 'em first.'

'Can't be helped. Just as long as they are visible from miles off. If we're lucky, the rebels will think they have seen us off and will report their victory back to Iskerbeles. He'll think he's won himself some breathing space while we make for the mine.'

Macro picked some grit from his nose. 'Unless he's already there. Or been and gone, and taken the bullion with him.'

'We'll know soon enough.' Cato craned his neck at the distant sound of hoofs. 'Ah, here comes Metellus, at last.'

The optio came cantering across the scorched earth and reined in close to the two officers before he snapped a salute at Cato.

'No sure sign of the enemy, sir. Just a small party of riders off to the west. Got the impression they were watching out for us. In any case, they turned and rode off as soon as they clapped eyes on us.'

'And no sign of anyone else?'

'No, sir. Though there are a few deserted farms around. I dare say the locals have gone to ground until both the rebels and us have gone.' Metellus straightened up in his saddle and indicated a low ridge to the south. 'We've covered the ground from there all the way round to a few miles north of the village, sir. It's clear.'

'Good. Then we'll be on our way. Ride to Placinus and tell him to get moving. Then let Cristus know he can bring the rest of the cohort out of the village and form them up to the north. We'll be over directly. Go.'

'Sir!' Metellus saluted and wheeled his mount round and spurred it towards the carts. Cato and Macro strode in the same direction.

'A half century to escort the carts?' Macro mused aloud.

'It's enough, together with the drags, to give the impression of a cohort on the march to anyone watching from the distance. Besides, if this goes as badly as I fear it may, then at least I'll have saved a few lives.'

Macro shot him a quick glance. 'I'd have thought it would be best to take as many men with us as we can.'

'Another forty or so will make little difference.'

'Come now, lad!' Macro laughed. 'Surely you don't really think the outlook is as grim as that? The men did well yesterday. Stood up to 'em like veterans and kept in formation like they were on the parade ground. We saw off those rebels easily enough, and we'll do the same for the next lot foolish enough to try it on with us.'

Cato sighed. 'Macro, we are still several days from the mine, and you heard Cimber: the road's going to make tough going through the hills. If, by some fluke, we approach the mine undetected, then it is rather more than likely that Iskerbeles will have beaten us to it. If we are spotted, then he'll be sure to try and trap us and annihilate us before Vitellius comes up. I don't fancy a retreat like the one we experienced last winter in Britannia. Better to hold up and stand our ground until the last man. Better that than be harassed, and watch the stragglers picked off, while discipline goes to pieces and it becomes every man for himself. At least if we make a stand we can give a good account of ourselves. Enough to make them fearful about taking on the main column.'

Macro paced at his side in silence for a moment. 'So we're the sacrifice for the greater good?'

'Something like that. You know how it is – "Go tell the Spartans . . . "'

'Spartans?' Macro frowned. 'What have those toga–lifters got to do with it?'

'If we're lucky, not a lot.' Cato breathed deeply. 'That's enough words. Save your breath. You're going to need it.'

A short time later the cohort was stepping out along the dusty road leading towards the hills, with Cato and Cimber on horseback at the head of the column, while Macro marched at the head of the infantry. Pulcher, no longer required to command the baggage train, led the remaining men of Placinus' century while Cristus marched with the small headquarters party. Ahead, and to each side, rode the mounted patrols, watching for any sign of the enemy as the Praetorians tramped over the rolling plain. As they crested a low ridge Macro turned to look briefly at the smaller formation marching east. A large cloud of dust rose from the carts, almost shrouding Placinus' soldiers at the rear. It certainly gave the appearance of a much larger force and Macro offered a prayer to the gods that any rebel sympathisers who happened to catch sight of Placinus were as easily fooled as Cato hoped they would be.

By noon they had reached the foothills and the road climbed through forests of pine which richly scented the summer air and provided shade for the soldiers as the afternoon wore on. They passed through a small town where the road joined the route stretching east and west that Cimber had told them of. The inhabitants, more used to occasional patrols of auxiliary troops, were curious to see a larger formation, and were keen to sell them food and wine when they halted in the small forum. The senior magistrate of the town council came from his home to greet Cato and Macro in person, at the head of a small procession of local dignitaries and town clerks. He was an avuncular figure in a plain ochre tunic with a heavy purse hanging from a belt that encompassed a large belly, the whole being supported by two stocky legs.

'Gaius Hettius Gordo.' He spoke good Latin as he bowed with difficulty. 'At your service. As are all the people of Antium Barca.'

'Prefect Quintus Licinius Cato, commanding the Second Praetorian Cohort. I need supplies for my men,' Cato added curtly. 'I will give you a warrant to recover the costs from the governor at Tarraco.'

'Ah, of course we would be happy to provide for your needs, but we would prefer it if you paid in coin.'

'I'm sure you would, but I am not able to pay you at present. Now you can either accept the warrant and bring the supplies to me here, or I will order my men to enter your storehouses and requisition whatever we need, and leave you to take the matter up with the governor.' He met the magistrate's anxious gaze with a steely, unbending expression. 'Your choice.'

Gordo waddled off to confer with his companions before he gave his response. 'We are happy to accept a warrant. We are sure it will be honoured when it is presented in Tarraco.'

'Good. Then I shall need two hundred and forty modii of wheat, two thousand pounds of cured meats, and five hundred waterskins.'

Gordo's mouth opened in shock. 'This is an outrage. We have given Rome no trouble. We always pay our taxes on time and offer regular sacrifices at the temple of the imperial cult. It is an affront to our loyalty to the Emperor for you soldiers to treat us this way and make such unreasonable demands of us. Surely you cannot expect us to find such quantities at such short notice without considerable difficulty?'

'No. But that's your problem. I want everything here by nightfall. Or I will order my troops to enter your homes and storerooms to take what we need. Now see to it.'

Gordo hurriedly issued instructions to his party and the clerks went off to give the orders. When the magistrate turned back Cato tackled him on a separate issue.

'I take it you are aware of the uprising in Asturica.'

Gordo rolled his eyes. 'A troublesome region! Barbaric people . . . Never content to live under the Roman peace. But Rome will be dealing with them most harshly, I'll wager. And rightly so.'

'All in good time. Have you heard of any rebel activity in this region?'

'Here?' Gordo looked amused. 'No. Events in Asturica are too far away to present any danger to Antium Barca. Thank the Gods.'

'I think you might not be so grateful to the Gods when you hear the news,' said Macro.

'What news?'

Macro looked questioningly at his superior and Cato gave a light nod of approval.

'The rebels sacked a village a day's march to the south. Took what they wanted, killed most of the villagers and forced the rest to join their cause.'

The blood drained from Gordo's face. 'As close as that? But we've heard nothing. No word that they were anywhere so near to us. How many of them? What happened?'

'We drove them off,' said Cato. 'Iskerbeles might have sent them to raid deep into the heart of the province to cause panic, or they may simply be brigands who claim allegiance to Iskerbeles. Either way, they constitute a danger. I'd advise you, and your council, to take every precaution to ensure the safety of your town and its people.'

'But . . . But, you must protect us. We pay our taxes. We are entitled to protection. You must stay here until the danger has passed. We'll feed your men. Even pay them to defend us, if necessary.'

'Impossible. I have my orders. We'll be leaving Antium Barca at first light. With our supplies,' Cato emphasised.

'And leave us defenceless, with rebels marauding through the region? I demand that you leave us some of your men at least.'

'You have sturdy walls, a good gatehouse and you must have some town militia.'

'A handful of old men and boys, yes.'

'Then draw on the able-bodied to bolster the ranks. You must fend for yourselves until the rebellion is crushed.'

'And if the rebellion isn't crushed?'

'Then I dare say you'd be well advised to make your peace with Iskerbeles when he and his host arrive before your walls. In the meantime, do what you can to defend yourselves. Seal the town gates at night, and make sure they are well guarded when they are open during the day. Stock up on provisions and keep a close eye on your slaves and anyone else who might be tempted to sympathise with the rebels.'

'That's all?'

'You and the other tax-payers could write a stiffly worded letter of complaint to the governor, if you think it would help,' Macro suggested wryly.

'That'll do, Centurion,' Cato said curtly before turning back to the magistrate. 'Just make sure that we have what we need. My cohort will be quartered in the forum for the night. I'll need billets for the officers close by. Please see to it directly.'

Gordo nodded and beckoned to his colleagues as he led them back to the council chambers at the far end of the forum. Macro sucked in a breath as he watched them.

'Not exactly winning over hearts and minds here, sir.'

'We're the least of their problems if the uprising spreads. Besides, I'm too tired to court their good opinion. I want us back on the road before dawn.' Cato saw Cimber standing a short distance away, close to the entrance of an alley. 'And keep an eye on our friend there. In case he is tempted to desert.'

Macro glanced at the guide and rubbed his hands together. 'There's plenty of ways to keep a new recruit on his toes, trust me.'

The centurion looked round at the buildings lining the forum. 'Nice place this. Prosperous even. Funny how they resent us when we ask for something, and then in the next breath beg us to save their skins . . . I've had my fill of bloody two-faced civilians.'

Cato gave a dry laugh. 'Don't be too hard on them, Macro. After all, it's their taxes that provide for our pay.'

'Maybe,' Macro admitted, grudgingly. 'But perhaps it would be easier if we just took what we needed from them directly.'

'And then what would distinguish us from mere brigands? Or the likes of Iskerbeles? We're an army, Macro. Not a bunch of bandits.

We're fighting to defend something bigger than ourselves. And that's why the Gods are on the side of Rome.'

Macro sniffed. 'You might want to remind them about that sometime. Rather too often I get the feeling the bastards are sleeping on the job.'

'Even Jove nods.'

'I'd rather Jove evens up the odds.'

Cato looked at him in surprise. 'Why, Centurion Macro, it appears you have developed a sense of humour.'

Macro scowled and answered in a manner that only professional soldiers of longstanding friendship, regardless of rank, feel able to. 'Fuck off, why don't you?'

The road from Antium Barca led west, running through the hills that stretched across the north of the province towards Asturica. As Cimber had said, it was only suitable for those on foot, horses and mules. Only the stretches between the larger settlements were usable by wheeled traffic. Away from the baking plains the men marched in more comfort through the heavily wooded slopes where the air was cooler, there was more shade and plenty of streams to slake their thirst and refill their canteens and waterskins. There was even some game, the odd boar and deer that fell victim to the remaining scouts who brought their catch into camp at the end of each day's march. If there was a town or village close by at dusk then Cato was content to rest his men there. Otherwise the day finished with the back-breaking toil of digging out a ditch and heaping the spoil into a rampart into which sharpened stakes were driven. Only then could the men make fires and cook their evening meals. Each morning the stakes were taken down, the rampart shovelled into the ditch and the cohort moved on.

The absence of campaign tents was not felt until the rain fell one night. A storm broke across the hills, with blinding flashes and bolts of lightning scarring the night as thunder echoed off the cliffs and bare slopes higher up. And all the time the rain poured down in a constant drumming hiss, drenching the men and horses and soaking their kit. The cohort rose, sleepless and wet, but a few hours of marching under a clear sky soon dried them off and restored their spirits. There were plenty of opportunities to obtain supplies from the settlements along the way, cheese, meat and bread made from nuts replacing the grain they had eaten before moving into the hills. Each time Cato left another warrant to cover the eventual payment for what they had taken, and he felt a guilty pleasure at the prospect of the governor having to pay off the trail of debts that marked the course of the Praetorian cohort.

Cimber proved to be a fine, albeit reluctant, guide and led them on a more or less direct route towards the mining region. Cato's main concern remained the fear of being detected by the enemy in sufficient time for them to obstruct his advance, or spring another ambush. Especially given the close terrain, where the forested slopes on either side of the road could conceal an army with ease. However, Metellus and his handful of mounted scouts reported no sign of the rebels as they marched ever closer to Asturica and the heart of the rebellion.

Then, twenty days after leaving Tarraco, Metellus and Cimber came galloping back down the road towards Cato and Macro marching at the head of the column, as the noon sun beat down from a clear sky. The cohort had reached the peaked hills and mountains of the mining region the day before and all of the men, and especially their prefect, had been watching the surrounding landscape warily.

'We've sighted the mine, sir!' Metellus reported as he reined in and saluted. 'No more than five miles beyond the next ridge.'

Cato glanced past the optio and saw that the road ahead inclined sharply towards a saddle between two rocky peaks, spotted with stunted trees.

'Any sign of the enemy?'

'Only a handful of men as far as I could see.'

'What about the mine? Is it still in our hands?'

Cimber cocked his head to one side. 'I can't tell, sir. There's little sign of life. No sign of slaves. We got as close as we could without giving ourselves away but couldn't see more than a handful of men around the gate of the main compound. Could be the mine garrison, or rebels. No way of telling without getting closer.'

Metellus spoke up. 'That was my decision, sir. Given your orders I didn't want to risk being spotted.'

'Quite right,' Cato agreed. 'You've done well, Cimber.'

The guide bowed his head in acknowledgement, then braced himself to speak. 'Then I have served my purpose, sir. I take it that I am free to return to Tarraco now.'

'You're speaking out of turn, soldier,' Macro growled as he hefted his vine cane. 'That's bordering on insubordination. Shall I put him in his place, sir?'

Cato could well understand Cimber's desire to remove himself from the danger to come. He was not a soldier and had no heart for fighting. That said, this was his homeland. It was his family and friends who were threatened by the rebels. He should be prepared to fight for that cause at least, and not abandon his moral duty and wait for the army to act on his behalf. Besides, Cato still had need of his knowledge of the region and its people.

'Not yet. Guardsman Cimber has proved his usefulness.' The words were spoken to Macro but the comment was directed at Cimber, who looked pained but had the good sense not to utter another word. 'I have every confidence that he will continue to do so while his services are required.'

Cato looked towards the ridge again and came to a decision. He turned round. 'Tribune Cristus! On me.'

Cristus trotted forward. 'Sir?'

'We'll halt the cohort on the reverse slope, up there. Metellus, pull in your patrols. I want the horses back with the column, then send two men to the top of the peak on the left. They're to report any sign of the enemy at once to the tribune. Cristus, the men are to be kept out of sight. If any rebels stumble upon us, or any locals for that matter, I want them taken prisoner.'

'Yes, sir. I understand.' He struggled to hide his concern. 'But where are you going?'

Cato unfastened the clasp-pin at his shoulder and removed his cloak and handed it to Metellus. 'Guardsman Cimber, Centurion Macro and I are going to have a closer look at the mine.'

# CHAPTER TWENTY

'Hmmm.' Macro scratched the bristles on his chin. Cato and Cimber lay in the dry grass to his side, in the shadow of the large grove of olive trees that had been planted on terraces around a gently sloping hill overlooking the small settlement that had grown up outside the mine, separated by the ditch and wall that guarded the mine workings themselves.

'I had no idea that the imperial mines were on such a scale,' Macro continued. 'The place looks big enough to house a full legion, and the hangers-on.'

Cato nodded as he surveyed the scene. Macro's comment was apt in some respects. The settlement was similar to those that grew up outside nearly every established legionary base. An unplanned accretion of inns, trading posts, whore-houses and other dwellings. Temporary structures at first, but gradually giving way to timber, stone and tile. Here though the settlement was small, catering for the garrison of the mine and the overseers and clerks that worked there, as well as the passing trade made up of slave dealers, grain merchants, suppliers of mining equipment and those soldiers assigned to guard the bullion convoys that periodically departed from the mine. The thousands of slaves who worked in the mine had no life outside it, and only eventual death inside, and were never given the chance to enjoy the limited pleasures on offer in the settlement.

Beyond the wall was a spectacle that looked almost as if Jupiter himself had reached down to scar a great sweep of the landscape and leave it a barren wreck as a sign of his omnipotence. To the left there were high cliffs of red and orange soil and rock, above which

197

a green fringe of stunted bushes spread for a distance. There was a ledge at the top of the cliff, giving way to mountainside that looked impassable. At the foot of the cliff the ground was bare of growth, and heaped with spoil, stretching down to the edge of a shallow ravine through which a river flowed over and around boulders in a rush of silvery spray. There were several timber-framed entrances to tunnels along the foot of the cliff with stacks of shoring posts close by. The area being worked extended for perhaps quarter of a mile before the cliff gave way to more solid rock and there was a wide track at the far end that bent back on itself to lead up to a large ledge protected by the precipitous slope of the mountainous ridge that stretched along the length of the mine. Cato could see an expanse of tiled roofs on the ledge and pointed them out.

'What's up there?'

Cimber followed the direction his superior indicated. 'That's the quarters of the procurator and his staff, sir, as well as the slave compound. Those are the barrack blocks you can see.'

'How many slaves work the mine?'

Cimber thought a moment. 'At its height, perhaps as many as five thousand. But most of the silver has been mined out so it's nearer three thousand these days. Those cliffs used to extend as far as the ravine.'

Macro let out a low whistle of astonishment as he appreciated for the first time just how much the landscape had been altered. 'They've pulled down most of a bloody mountain.'

'How did they do it?' asked Cato.

'You see the tunnels, sir? Those are driven deep into the cliff, with others branching off on either side. That's to weaken the base of the cliff. Once they're ready, they set fire to the supports and the tunnels collapse, bringing a section of the cliff down with them. And that exposes a fresh stretch of the silver seams.'

'Really? I'd have thought that bringing that lot down would create something of a mess?'

'It does, sir. That's why they have sluice tanks on the top of the cliff. They release enough water to wash off the loose soil to expose the seams.'

Macro nodded thoughtfully. 'Very clever. But where do they get the water from? I don't suppose they haul it all the way up from the river.'

'They did, once. Many years ago, sir. But that was before the aqueduct was built that supplies Asturica and some of the other towns in the region. It passes by a few miles beyond that ridge, and there's a spur that feeds the mine's reservoirs. Most of the excavation of the cliff has happened since the construction of the aqueduct.'

Macro sucked his teeth. 'Isn't progress a wondrous thing?'

Cato was looking at the small dark openings of the tunnels, trying to imagine the thousands of slaves who had been driven to cut their way through the base of the cliff. Working in cramped conditions, by the light of torches or the weak glow of oil lamps. The air would be foul, and made worse by the stink of the piss and shit of the chain gangs. And it would be dangerous too, with the constant threat of a tunnel collapse, burying the slaves alive.

'There must be a high rate of attrition,' he said quietly.

'Attrition, sir?'

'Loss of life amongst the slaves?'

'Oh, yes. Of course, sir. More than a hundred a week, I'd say. That's why there's such a demand for slaves in the region. If the work doesn't kill them, then hunger or sickness will. Being condemned to the mines is a death sentence. Everyone knows that.'

'And now Iskerbeles is setting those slaves free,' Cato mused.

'Great,' Macro growled. 'And every one of them will no doubt fight to the death rather than face the prospect of returning to the mines.'

'Quite.' Cato thought a moment. 'While places like this exist, and there are men like Iskerbeles around, then we're making a rod for our own backs.'

He turned his attention to the settlement. Only a handful of figures were visible in the market place, sitting on benches around what was clearly an inn, if the discarded amphorae that littered the ground about them were anything to go by. Aside from them the only rebels visible were the men guarding the gate to the workings.

'One thing's clear enough. We're too late, sir,' said Cimber, gesturing towards the mine. 'Iskerbeles has beaten us to it. He has the bullion . . . There's no point in continuing. Better to fall back and wait for the legate, sir.'

Cato cocked his head to one side. 'It looks that way. But we need to know for certain.'

Cimber shot him an anxious look, keen to withdraw to the safety of the cohort waiting out of sight beyond the ridge at their backs. 'Sir, you can see the situation for yourself. We should go.'

'We go when I say and not before. Right now I need information.' He turned to Macro. 'We need a little chat with someone.'

An hour later they had worked themselves into the settlement, staying out of sight of those on the gate to the mine. They entered a narrow street on the opposite side and stealthily followed it towards the small open area at the heart of the settlement that Cato had observed earlier. There was no sign of life in any of the buildings they passed, apart from a lean-looking dog that was startled by their appearance and trotted off as it cast anxious glances over its shoulder. They heard the carousing rebels before they saw them, drunken conversation and laughter echoing off the walls of the street as it opened out on the market.

Cato signalled for his comrades to stop and crouch down, before he continued, taking care to make as little noise as possible with his boots on the cobbled street. He felt his pulse quicken as he approached the corner, and paused. From the lurid graffiti and illustrations above a door that opened onto the alley it was clear he was standing outside a brothel. Reasoning that such an establishment would be likely also to have an entrance opening onto the market, Cato stepped cautiously inside. It took a moment for his eyes to adjust to the gloom, then he saw that he was in a low-ceilinged room divided by a dingy-looking bar. One wall opened onto a series of small cubicles furnished with rolls of soiled bedding. Grimy curtains provided limited privacy for the women and their clients. Clay cups and empty and broken jugs lay strewn about, together with discarded strips of cloth and the short tunics favoured by prostitutes. The air reeked of wine, cheap scent and the cloying odour of blood spilled days before. There was also the stink of decaying flesh and Cato saw the body of a young girl lying under a table. She was naked and her groin and thighs were smeared with dried blood. A short distance beyond, in the shade of the corner of the room, was a heap of dirty clothes. On the far side of the bar was another entrance, covered by a yellow curtain, and Cato picked his way towards it, wincing as a shard of a beaker crunched loudly beneath the sole of his boot. He froze, ears straining as his fingers closed round his sword handle, not daring to breathe.

Then, certain from the tone of the voices outside that there was no hint of alarm, he continued towards the curtained entrance and eased the edge of the cloth aside, squinting into the bright afternoon sunlight. Thirty paces away from him eight men were sitting at a table, sharing a large jug of wine. Two were slumped forward, heads resting on folded arms, asleep. The rest were still going strong, swilling from their cups. Despite the good quality of their clothing, their hair was long and tangled and they were unshaven, their exposed skin streaked with grime. None of them looked well nourished and Cato guessed that they must be slaves from the mine, intoxicated as much by their freedom as the drink they were consuming. Drunk or not, they carried swords and daggers hanging in scabbards from their belts. Cato thought quickly. With two out cold, that left six to take on. Odds of two to one. Not promising. Worse, given that he had little confidence in Cimber's willingness and ability to fight. Without helmets or shields, he and Macro would still have the advantage of their training and experience, but as Macro had pointed out, they would be facing men made dangerous by their brief experience of freedom and utter determination never to be returned to the living death of slavery.

A sudden throaty snort and grumbling smack of the lips from behind caused Cato to jolt as his heart leaped inside his chest. He dropped the edge of the curtain and whirled round, drawing his sword in a smooth sweep as he lowered into a crouch, ready to strike while his left arm rose to the side to balance him. What he had taken as a bundle of rags was stirring into life and a loose arm flopped out onto the floor. The man groaned and began to prop himself up on his elbows, face wrinkled into a pained expression, before he blinked his eyes open. He looked round blearily and then fixed his gaze on the Roman poised ten feet away.

As the man's jaw sagged and his eyes widened in surprise, Cato sprang across the gloomy interior and made to strike with his sword. At the last moment he grasped the opportunity to take the man alive and raised his sword arm to strike him on the head with the pommel instead. The hesitation gave the rebel just enough time to throw up a hand and clench his fingers round Cato's wrist. Thin though he appeared, the former slave possessed a fanatic's strength and he held off the blow. Muscles straining, the two men stared into each other's eyes, their jaws clenched. Then the rebel made to call out, but only a wheezy grunt came from his dry throat. Bunching his spare hand into a fist, Cato arced it in a vicious hook straight into the rebel's jaw, snapping it shut and knocking his head back against the plaster wall with a soft crack. At once his fingers loosened their grip and slipped from Cato's wrist as he slumped back onto the floor of the brothel.

Cato knelt over his victim, breathing hard. When he was certain that the man was out cold he scooped up a discarded tunic and cut it into strips using his sword. Then he sheathed the blade and bound the rebel's hands and ankles before gagging him. Satisfied with his efforts he bent down, slipped his hands under the unconscious man's armpits and raised him into a sitting position. Bracing his shoulder into the man's midriff Cato straightened up with a grunt, and the rebel flopped over his shoulder. A moment later Cato emerged back into the street with his captive and Macro looked up in surprise.

'Fuck, you don't hang about when you want a prisoner. How'd you get hold of him?'

'Nearly tripped over the bastard. Come on, let's get out of here.'

'What are we going to do with him? You planning on carrying him all the way back to the cohort?'

'Hardly. Let's find a quiet place on the edge of the settlement to ask him a few questions. You lead on. Cimber, you cover my back.'

The small procession moved away from the market, back down the street from which they had come. When they were far enough away from the raucous voices of the drinkers, Macro went ahead to search for a place to conduct the interrogation. Cato struggled on beneath his burden, glancing back a few times to make sure that Cimber was doing his job. The guide had drawn his sword and made no effort to hide his fear as if he expected the rebels to come charging after them at any moment.

'Cimber, for Jupiter's sake, control your nerves, man,' Cato whispered fiercely. 'You're more likely to do yourself, or me, an injury with that blade. Put it away unless you absolutely need to defend yourself.'

'Yes, sir.' Cimber glanced round before reluctantly sheathing his sword.

Around the next corner, Cato saw Macro standing on the threshold of a house close to the edge of the settlement.

'This'll do us,' he said quietly to Cato as the prefect approached. 'A nice quiet room out the back.'

He stood aside to let Cato and his prisoner pass inside, followed by Cimber. With a quick look up and down the street to make sure that they would not be disturbed Macro ducked inside the building and gently closed the door behind him before bolting it. Cato saw that they were standing in a cloth merchant's shop. Rolls of wool and linen were stacked on shelves. Some had been pulled down and lay in heaps on the floor.

'This way.' Macro led them through a door at the rear of the shop into a small courtyard with an opening to the sky. It was barely bigger than the previous room, and affected a design that betrayed the owner's taste for Roman styles, but lack of sufficient wealth to carry it through comfortably. A plain wooden table with stools on each side stood beneath the opening which provided enough natural light to see clearly. Cato deposited the rebel onto the table and the impact made the man wince and blink his eyes. He squinted into the light from above; then, as his senses returned, he glanced round anxiously, saw the Romans and briefly struggled with his bonds before curling up on his side, breathing deeply around the gag in his mouth.

Cato gestured to Macro. 'Keep an eye on the street while I deal with this.'

His friend nodded and left the room. Cato looked down at the prisoner. 'You speak Latin?'

The man showed no reaction, so Cato tried again. 'Latin . . . ? Or Greek?'

At the word 'Greek' the prisoner nodded.

Cato turned to Cimber. 'You'll translate, then. Tell him I have some questions for him. I want honest answers. If he tries to trick me, I'll know, and he'll suffer.' Cato took out his dagger and let the light from above play on the polished steel of the well-honed blade. 'I'll cut a bit off him, every time I think he's lying. If he tries to raise the alarm or cries out, I'll put the gag back in, and cut him again.'

Cimber repeated the threat and the man shrank away from Cato, as far as his bonds would allow. Then Cato untied the gag and loomed over him on one side of the table while Cimber stood opposite.

'Let's get started. I want to know precisely what happened here. How long ago did the rebels take the place? How many of them were there? How many did they leave behind?'

Cimber translated and there was a brief exchange before the guide looked up at Cato.

'He says they came five days ago. In the night. They overwhelmed the settlement before the garrison of the mine surrendered. Then they set the slaves free. Those who wished could join the rebellion, the rest could go where they wished. He does not know how many. He says it was a host.'

Cato nodded. It was often the case that peasants were innumerate as well as illiterate. Any number bigger than the small scale of their experience blurred into general terms. A host could be anything from hundreds to several thousand.

'They were led by Iskerbeles himself,' Cimber continued. 'He had the slaves watch as most of the garrison had their throats cut. Them and the people living in the settlement. He saved only the procurator and a few others. They are being held as hostages so that Iskerbeles can demand a ransom for them from the governor in Tarraco.'

'Where are the prisoners being held?' Cato demanded.

'Up in the camp. In the procurator's quarters, he says.'

'Where precisely?'

Cimber questioned the prisoner. 'In the slave quarters at the rear of the villa.'

204

'You know the building?'

Cimber nodded. 'I remember.'

'Good.' Cato returned to his earlier line of questioning. 'Where did Iskerbeles go?'

The prisoner gabbled his response. 'He says that once Iskerbeles and his men had taken what they needed, they set off to liberate the slaves in other mines. He does not know where they went. He was drunk and they left him behind.'

'He's been drunk ever since, I'll warrant.' Cato leaned forward, watching the man closely. 'Ask him what his name is.'

'Basicus, sir.'

'All right, you ask Basicus if the rebels took the bullion with them when they left the mine.'

The prisoner looked genuinely confused when the question was put to him. He mumbled something and shook his head.

'He says he doesn't know anything about the bullion.'

Cato narrowed his eyes and stared hard at the man. The prisoner met his eyes for a moment and then glanced away. 'I don't believe him . . .'

The prefect set his dagger down on the table. Reaching for the strip of cloth that had served as a gag, Cato thrust the thick wad into the captive's mouth and tied the ends tightly behind Basicus' head. Then he took up his dagger and held it to the prisoner's face. Basicus flinched as Cato snarled, 'I told you what happens when you lie to me. Watch.'

He took Basicus' bound hands and pinned them to the table with his left hand. Then he lowered the edge of his dagger onto the flesh of the little finger, just below the knuckle, and cut. At once Basicus writhed and a deep agonised cry tried to escape his throat but was muffled by the gag into a keening whine. The edge of the blade hit the bone and Cato pressed harder and began a sawing motion. The bone snapped with a dull crunch and the finger came free. Blood pumped out onto the table as the prisoner's eyes rolled up into his head. His chest heaved and vomit squirted out around the gag.

'Shit,' Cato muttered, setting the dagger down and hurriedly untying the gag. Chunky spew sprayed from the prisoner's lips as his body was racked with coughing and attempts to breathe. Cato pushed him onto his side and waited until the vomiting stopped and Basicus was gasping for air through gritted teeth. An image of the dead girl in the brothel filled Cato's head and he felt no pity for the man.

'Tell him it'll be his thumb next time. Then I'll work my way through his fingers and end by cutting off his cock.'

The man's face was screwed up in agony but even so he managed to look Cato in the eye and draw a deep breath before he responded.

'He swears he is telling the truth. He doesn't know anything about any bullion. He just worked in the mine and never had any dealings with the smelter crew. He never knew anything about what happened to the silver after that. Iskerbeles did not take anything from the mine when he and his men left. He swears it's true on the lives of his entire family. He begs you not to hurt him again.'

Cato glared down at the man for a moment, scrutinising his expression, his eyes, for any sign of deception.

'Very well. I believe him . . .'

Basicus grasped the Roman's meaning and slumped back on the table in relief.

'How many men did Iskerbeles leave behind to guard the hostages?'

'Twenty men, in addition to a similar number of slaves who remained here to loot the settlement.'

'Men like him, eh? Looter, rapist and murderer.' Cato spat on the prisoner and related what he had seen to Cimber. 'You can be sure that what they did here is the same as they did to all those friends and family you knew in Asturica. You might want to think about that, before you insist on running back to Tarraco with your tail between your legs. If I were you, Cimber, I could not rest until I had avenged those who had butchered my kin. I would hold my manhood cheap if I had fled from the chance to take my revenge.'

He let his words sink in and then used Basicus' tunic to wipe the blood from his dagger before he snapped it back into its sheath. 'I'm done here. He's all yours.' Cato picked up the gag and forced it into the prisoner's mouth before he left the room.

Macro was holding the door slightly ajar as he kept watch on the street. He turned as he heard the crunch of Cato's boots on the stone floor.

'Did you get anything out of him?'

Cato nodded. 'It looks like the bullion is still here. Hidden some-place.'

'Well that's not much help. How in Hades are we supposed to find it?'

'By asking the procurator. He's still alive and being held hostage with some others up in the mining camp. He must have concealed the bullion before the rebels turned up. We have to find him.'

'Right now? The three of us?'

Cato shook his head. 'It's time to get out of here. We'll return with the cohort when it's getting dark. The trouble is going to be getting to the procurator before the rebels guarding him realise what's happening and kill him.'

They were interrupted by a stifled cry of terror from the next room. It came again, this time broken up by the sound of sword blows striking flesh and bone. Macro took a pace away from the door towards the adjoining room but Cato stopped him.

'We've got what we need from the prisoner. We can't take him with us, and we can't risk him raising the alarm. Cimber's dealing with it.'

'Dealing with it?' Macro regarded his friend and saw the flicker of a smile on Cato's lips. Macro tilted his head to look past Cato. The only sound from the other room now was the last few blows being struck. Then there was a silence before Cimber appeared. His face, body and arms were sprayed with blood, and he was wiping the last of the blood from his sword with a strip of cloth, which he tossed aside before sliding the weapon back into its scabbard. Macro was long inured to the sight of gore, but something about the scene caused a faint shudder to course down his spine. He had been aware of a growing coldness in the heart of his friend that had not been there before. It was more than mere indifference to suffering, thought Macro. It was worse than that. That smile on Cato's face. He recognised the expression well enough. It was the face of a man who had become cruel, and took pleasure from the fact.

'Let's get out of here,' said Cato.

207

# CHAPTER TWENTY-ONE

It had been a long hot day and the guards on the gatehouse of the mine workings were looking forward to being relieved when dusk came. A reed-thatched shelter covered half of the tower and provided shade from the harsh glare of the sun, but the air was still and heavy and the tedium of keeping watch over the approaches to the mine was broken only by occasional conversation or rounds of dice while they took it in turns to keep watch. The jubilation with which they had greeted their liberation when the rebels had stormed the mining camp and set the slaves free had been short-lived. Iskerbeles had indulged them, and given the slaves free rein over the camp, the procurator's house, and the settlement outside the mine. There had followed a veritable orgy of looting, violence, rape, murder and drinking as the slaves took their revenge on their former masters and those who catered to them. It had lasted for two days, and then the rebel leader had taken control, assigning a handful of men to remain at the camp and guard the prisoners while the host moved on to continue spreading the rebellion across the region.

It felt good to be free of the chains that had been a part of their lives for many months, years in the case of the more hardy. No longer did they have to face the daily terror of being forced down into the dark tunnels running beneath the cliff. No more labouring in cramped conditions, in stinking airless passages where every fall of loose soil, or creak from the posts propping up the roof of the mine might herald the collapse of a tunnel, burying alive those trapped underground. From time to time the slaves had dug into the rotting corpses and bones of those who had died in earlier tunnel collapses and their remains were discarded along with the rest of the spoil dug out of the cliff. Freedom also brought an end to a miserable diet of thin gruel, and the cramped barracks blocks wherein they were locked every night. The thick walls were made of unworked stone without mortar, and the icy winds of winter contrived to find easy access to chill the bones of those within, while the hot air of summer stifled them, making the fetid stench of sweat, piss and shit overwhelming.

Gone was the need to keep your head bowed and avoid meeting the eyes of the overseers who needed no excuse to mete out a beating or a flogging. They were cruel men whose only duty was to exact the maximum amount of work out of each slave before they died and their bodies were thrown into the grave pit that lay at the bottom of the track leading up to the work camp. Those that dared to defy the overseers with word or gesture were savagely beaten, and the few who were driven by sufficient desperation to strike back were crucified and left to die, their mournful cries and groans serving as ample warning to those who forgot their place in this merciless world. It was even worse for the small number of women condemned to the mines. Those deemed more attractive by the overseers and guards, or simply available as the mood arose, could be dragged aside and raped, degraded in any way that took the men's fancy, before being sent back to work, or returned to the barrack blocks. Even there, they were not safe from the depredations of fellow slaves.

Under such conditions, it was no surprise that there were those who could endure no more and took their own lives. It was possible to hang oneself by fixing chains to the stout beams that supported the barrack block roofs. Or to dash your brains out against a wall, or cut your throat or wrists on a jagged piece of rock or splintered piece of wood. Some even managed to swallow their tongues, choking themselves to death in an agonising fit before they succumbed. Whatever method was chosen, their bodies would be dragged out of the barracks block and thrown on top of the other dead rotting in the grave pit, the flesh and organs of their corpses torn at by the beaks and claws of birds and other wild animals.

All of this endured for the sake of mining the seams of rare metal to slake the appetites of the rich and powerful living in far-off Rome. Blood money, paid for by the crushing misery and cruelty inflicted on the wretched living dead who shuffled to and from the dark mouths of the tunnels.

Until the day that Iskerbeles came and set them free.

Now life was good and the boredom of their guard duties a luxury that free men never appreciated. It felt good to hold the weapons of their oppressors in their hands. Although all knew that one day soon the Romans would come back determined to crush the rebellion and punish the perpetrators of the uprising harshly. When that day came they would grimly commit themselves to fight to the death to preserve the freedom they had come to know as the most precious of all gifts. Sooner that than face a return to the dark and dangerous mere existence of life as a slave, where death was no more than a relief from suffering.

The man watching the approaches to the mine was leaning on the wooden rail of the tower. He was wearing a finely spun green tunic that he had found in the procurator's house. The fingers of his spare hand gently rubbed a soft fold of the cloth. His boots had been taken from the body of an auxiliary; they were the first boots he had ever owned. In addition to the spear in his hand, a sword hung from his belt where an ornately inlaid handle protruded from its sheath. His stomach was comfortably full and though the last of the wine had been drunk the previous day he was looking forward to searching some of the houses in the settlement to see if there was any more that had escaped the attention of earlier looters, the last of whom had returned from the settlement an hour or so ago. Behind him three of his comrades were sitting with their backs to the rear parapet dozing contentedly. The Asturian warrior left in command of the camp would not be making his rounds until the change of watch so they would not be troubled for a while yet.

A movement caught the eye of the watchman. A small cloud of dust puffed over the crest of a hill a short distance from the settlement. A figure appeared, leading a mule. Then some more mules and a handful of other men, drovers. They were making straight for the camp. The watchman straightened up, tightening his grip on his spear. His first thought was to raise the alarm. After all, the men and mules approaching the mine were the first to come here since Iskerbeles had marched away. But when he saw that there were only four men in all, he hesitated. What danger could they possibly pose to those protecting the mine? If he sounded the bell then the Asturian would come running down from the camp demanding to know the cause. When he saw the strangers and their mules he was sure to be angry and cuff the watchman for wasting his time, just as he had beaten any of the former slaves who he had determined had fallen short in their duties. So the watchmen watched the small mule train approach and as it continued towards the settlement he turned to his comrades.

'Up you get, boys. We've got company.'

One of them cracked open an eye and coughed. 'What's up, Repha?'

'Some men and mules approaching the camp.'

'How many?'

'Four of 'em. Who do you think they might be?'

'I don't know. Don't care much either. If they come any closer tell them the mine's under new management and they can bugger off.'

The other two men beside him had stirred during the exchange and smiled blearily at the comment.

Repha stepped towards them and prodded the nearest man with the toe of his boot. 'Looks like those mules are carrying amphorae. Wine maybe.'

'Wine?' His companion climbed to his feet and stretched his shoulders. 'Well, why didn't you say? If they come up to the gate then let's see if they can be persuaded to part with a few jars. Eh, boys?'

'O'right,' one of the others grinned as they joined Repha at the front of the tower and looked down towards the settlement just in time to see the last of the mules enter the main street. The new arrivals were lost from sight for a while but then emerged from between the nearest buildings making straight for the entrance to the mine works. The leader was mounted on a mule, his legs dangling either side of the beast. He wore an off-white cloak with a hood which had been swept back to reveal the dark hair and features of a man of the region. He raised a hand in greeting as he led his small mule train up to the bridge that stretched across the outer ditch.

'You can stop there!' Repha called down.

The man pulled on the mule's bridle and the beast halted. The others slowed their beasts to a standstill and Repha saw that they wore simple tunics and boots and carried no visible weapons.

'What's your business?'

'Manlius Oscorfus, wine merchant of Palastino, at your service,' came the reply in the local dialect. 'I have heard that there is a change of regime here at the mine. Men of newfound fortune who might have some coin to spend on the finest wines available in all of Asturia.' He gestured towards the amphorae nestling in wicker baskets either side of the mules. 'Enough to slake the thirst of a hundred men. If the price is right. Would you care to try a sample, friend?'

'Why not?' muttered one of Repha's comrades as he turned to descend the ladder leading to the bottom of the gatehouse. The others made to follow him but Repha blocked their path.

'We have our orders. No one enters or leaves without permission.'

'You going to let that Asturian be your new master, then?' one of his companions mocked. 'Where's the harm in having a look? Besides there's only four of 'em and they're unarmed. Come on, Repha. Just a little look.'

The man did not wait for a reply, but brushed past him and was already clambering down the ladder before Repha could respond.

'What about the orders?'

'Orders? Fuck 'em, I say. I ain't taking no orders from  no one ever again.'

A moment later, Repha was alone. He hesitated briefly and then hissed in frustration before he descended to join his comrades behind the gate. The bar had already been removed from its brackets and one of the men on guard duty was heaving the gate open. Repha clasped his spear tightly and led them through the gap in a final effort to take charge. 'Watch 'em closely, boys. First sign of trouble then we stick them with our spears first and ask questions later. Got it?'

He led them slowly out of the gateway and across the bridge, his hands tightly gripping his spear shaft. Repha stopped short of the merchant and scrutinised him. Well fed and with flesh to spare on his cheeks.

He greeted the rebels with a smile as he slipped off his mule and bowed. 'Honoured customers, I swear by all that's holy that you shall not be disappointed by my wares. Here, let me show you what we have.' He gestured towards the jars slung over the back of a beast halfway down the small column. 'Start with my most popular wine.' He leaned towards Repha and tapped his nose as he spoke in a conspiratorial tone. 'And leave the best to last, eh?'

Repha glanced at the merchant's men but there seemed to be no expression on their faces aside from a certain anxiety and watchfulness as the four heavily armed guards advanced on them. That was only natural given the risk they were taking in selling wine to the rebels. But then some merchants would always be prepared to take risks where the potential profits were highest.

'Here!' The merchant hurried forward a few steps and slapped one of the amphorae carried by the mule in the charge of the nearest of the drovers, a short man with a sturdy build. 'Honeyed wine from Barcino. Sweet and refreshing.' He pulled the stopper from the neck of the amphora and leaned down to take a sniff.

'Ah! Heady stuff. Try some?'

'Why not?' said one of the guards. 'And who knows, we might even buy some, rather than take all of it and send you on your way.'

'Come now!' Oscorfus chuckled lightly. 'There's no need for threats, my friends. Not with a good, honest man like myself.' He beckoned to the other drovers. 'Bring our friends some cups!'

Obedient to their orders the tall, thin drover at the rear of the small mule train hitched his reins to the animal in front and then rummaged for a basket slung over the back of a mule. He lifted it up and approached the merchant and his customers. As he passed behind the first drover he seemed to trip and drop the basket. His comrade turned to help the man up and an instant later both straightened up, swords and daggers to hand, and charged on the startled guards. The merchant plucked out a sap from his sidebag and swung it savagely at the head of the nearest rebel. The man dropped like a rock.

'Get 'em!' snarled the short drover as he rushed towards the nearest of Repha's comrades and drove the point of his sword up into the man's midriff as violently as possible, before tearing the blade from side to side as his victim groaned. His companion swung his sword in a sharp cut to the head and the edge of the blade cracked the skull and plunged into the grey matter beneath.

It had happened so swiftly that the merchant was swinging his long sap again at Repha's skull before he thought to react. He ducked aside at the last moment and the packed leather pouch swished by his ear. Repha went into a crouch to steady his balance and lowered the point of his spear, summoning up all his strength to drive the weapon clean through the treacherous merchant. Out of the corner of his eye he saw the last of his comrades felled by a punch to the jaw. It had all happened so fast. These men were no drovers, but professional killers who had beguiled the men tasked with protecting the mining camp. Then they would pay dearly for their treachery, Repha resolved as he bunched his muscles and prepared to impale the merchant. The man stumbled back, his cheerful salesman's face transformed into a mask of fear.

A blur of gleaming metal slashed through the air and Repha felt pain shooting through his fingers and up his arms as the edge of a sword bit deep into the shaft of his spear. The blow drove the tip of the spear into the ground and before Repha was even aware that it had happened, a dagger sliced through his throat and hot blood gushed onto his tunic. Instinctively he dropped his spear and staggered away, clutching his hands to his throat in a vain effort to try and stem the flow. He was already feeling light-headed as he looked about him and saw that his comrades were all down. One motionless, the other two writhing on the ground from mortal wounds. Repha tried to speak, to cry out, to raise the alarm but the only sound was a gurgling splutter. Darkness crowded the periphery of his vision and he began to feel dizzy. Almost his last thought was for the guilt over failing in his duty to protect the rest of his comrades in the mining camp. Then, one hand clamped to his throat, he snatched out the dagger from his belt and stumbled towards the stocky drover. The man dodged the attack easily enough and tripped Repha so that he fell headlong onto his face. He made to rise, but he had no strength left and lay gasping as his lifeblood drained from his body.

'You stay put, you rebel bastard,' said Macro as he stamped his boot down hard on the man's wrist, grinding it until the fingers opened and the dagger dropped to the ground. Macro kicked it away and retreated a step before he looked round. Metellus was wrestling his sword free from the back of his man, while Cimber swung his cosh against the head of a man struggling to sit up. Instead he went out like a candle and crashed to the ground unconscious. Cato was already striding away from the scene of the brief skirmish. He raised his sword as high as he could and waved it slowly from side to side, the signal for the rest of the cohort to come up. From the top of the hill overlooking the settlement there came a response, and a quick flash as the sun reflected off polished metal. Cato prayed that it had not been seen by any of the rebels still in the camp, as he sheathed his blade and turned back to the others.

'We'll take their spears. Put the bodies under the bridge, and, Metellus, get the mules back to the buildings and leave them somewhere out of sight.'

While his orders were carried out Cato looked back towards the cohort and was pleased to see that there was little evidence of any movement as the Praetorians followed a dry riverbed that meandered close to the settlement before joining the river that flowed past the mine. Only a faint dust haze marked their progress. Hopefully not enough to draw the attention of anyone keeping watch from the mine camp higher up. He turned his attention to Cimber who was leaning against the gatepost breathing heavily.

'Good job.'

Cimber shook his head. 'I never thought we'd get away with it.'

Macro laughed. 'Oh, you were very good, mate. Very good indeed. Remind me never to buy a used chariot from you.'

Cimber smiled weakly and eased himself away from the gatepost as he took a deep breath to try and calm his nerves.

'That's better.' Cato patted him on the shoulder. 'But we've done the easy bit. So keep your wits about you, eh?'

'I'll do my best, sir.'

'I can ask for no more.'

As soon as Metellus returned from concealing the mules Cato led his small party through the gates and into the mine workings. To their left was a row of toolsheds, open-fronted with picks and shovels in long racks. And then the long stretch of the red earth and rock cliff that looked like a vast wound cut into the side of the mountainous ridge along which it ran. The base of the cliff was pierced by regularly spaced tunnel openings that looked out onto the bare ground running down to the edge of the ravine where the river flowed. Here and there lay heaps of spoil from the mineshafts.

'Stick close to the cliff,' Cato ordered, trotting into its shadow before continuing towards the track that led up to the mine camp four hundred paces away. There was no sign of life from the workings, except for the lazy circling of dark birds at the far end of the mine, but Cato was not surprised. It was a desolate place and those who had been forced to labour here no doubt wished to avoid it, scarred by the memory of what they had endured. He increased his pace to a run and glanced back to make sure the others were keeping up. It was vital that they found the procurator before the enemy became wise to the presence of the cohort. As they approached the start of the track leading up to the ledge on which the camp had been constructed, Cato saw a line of stout posts in the ground from which chains hung from iron fittings. Behind them, in a small cutting into the cliff that became visible only as they neared the track, were several taller posts with cross beams. A man had been nailed onto each one. All but one were dead, and the last slowly rolled his head from side to side as his dried and cracked lips moved soundlessly.

They slowed as they came up to the crucified men and the blood drained from Cimber's face as he stopped and stared in horror at the bloated and mutilated bodies.

'Who are they? Slaves?'

'Overseers, or soldiers from the garrison, more like,' Macro replied. 'Poor bastards.'

At the sound of their boots crunching on the gravel the surviving man opened his eyes and stared at them, his mouth working as he tried to speak, but all he could manage was a rasping guttural moan.

'We have to help him,' Cimber decided, taking a reluctant step towards the line of crucified men.

'No,' Cato snapped. 'There's no time. We keep moving.'

'Sir,' Metellus protested. 'We have to—'

Cato rounded on him, glaring. 'He's already dead. It's too late to save him. Now keep your mouth shut and obey orders.'

'Wait,' said Macro. 'There is something we can do for him.'

He stepped up to the foot of the post and raised his spear. He lodged the tip in the soft flesh under the man's ribcage and looked up to see awareness gleam in the man's eyes, before he clenched his jaw and nodded. Without hesitation Macro thrust powerfully, driving the point up into the man's heart. His head flung back and his jaw gaped in a silent cry as his body stiffened, then writhed within the constraints of his nailed hands and feet, before he slumped and hung like meat in a butcher's shop. Macro wrenched the spear back and stepped aside to avoid the spatter of blood from the wound.

'All right,' Cato said grimly. 'Show's over. Let's keep moving. Cimber. Move!'

They hurried on, climbing up the steep track. Overhead the birds called out with shrill, coarse cries as they wheeled through the hot air. A hundred paces ahead the path bent back on itself for the run up to the camp and they kept to the shadows as they ran on, breathing hard from the exertion. Closer to the bend Cato caught a foul, cloying stench, sour and sickly and he knew at once what it was. The odour of decaying bodies.

'Fuck me,' Macro grumbled, his nose wrinkling with disgust. 'I thought this place couldn't get any worse.'

Cimber clasped a hand to his face, pinching his nose and covering his mouth as he struggled on. They reached the bend and then saw the cause of the noisome odour. Below, a deep pit had been dug into the ground and it was almost filled with heaped corpses. Most were naked but some wore rags. The older corpses that were visible were mottled and bloated. Some had burst, leaving gaping holes where the birds and wild animals had gone for the organs and entrails. The most recent bodies lay sprawled on top, many carrying wounds from edged weapons. Cato was sickened to see that there were many women and children amongst them. Doubtless, the inhabitants of the settlement and the families of those who had worked at the camp. Brought here, butchered and thrown into the pit with the bodies of the slaves off whose backs they had once lived. The bloody cycle of revenge turning, forever turning.

'The bastards,' Cimber choked.

'Which ones? Theirs or ours?' Cato replied pointedly. 'Come, we haven't much time. You know the way, so you lead from here on.'

Cimber was still ashen-faced and Cato grabbed his shoulder and shook it hard. 'Pull yourself together, man. Otherwise, we'll end up down there with the rest of them.'

Cimber nodded, swallowed nervously and turned his back on the grim spectacle. He began the ascent of the last stretch of the track to the ledge where the camp had been constructed. As they came within sight of the first of the buildings Cato quietly called a halt and crept forward with Cimber, keeping to the rocks along the side of the track as it opened out onto the wide ledge in the shadow of the mountain ridge. Crouching down, Cato took stock of the layout of the mining camp. To his right was the procurator's house. Plain whitewashed walls built on dressed stone foundations. The roof was tiled and at the rear of the house leafy boughs indicated a garden within. The house was separated from the rest of the camp by fifty paces, where a number of smaller buildings lay. The accommodation for the garrison, overseers and others employed at the mine, Cato decided. Just beyond them was a wall with a fortified gateway. There was a walkway running along the wall that overlooked the slave quarters on the other side. The gate was wide open, and where vigilant sentries had kept watch over the slave quarters the rampart and gate was now abandoned.

Most of the rebels left behind to guard the camp had occupied the garrison blocks and sat outside on benches as they played at dice, laughing and talking, relishing their new-won freedom. A man had been posted outside the entrance to the procurator's house, but he sat on a stool, back against the wall and head slumped onto his breast as he dozed.

'Can't say I'm impressed by the way the rebels are guarding this place,' said Cato. 'They might be brave, but their discipline is piss poor. Is there another way into the procurator's quarters?'

Cimber nodded and pointed to the side of the house built up to the edge of the cliff next to the track. 'There's an area at the back of the house the previous procurator had cleared for a training ground. There's a doorway next to the slaves' quarters.'

Cato looked along the wall and although there was only a narrow gap between the wall and the cliff, it appeared to be easy enough to negotiate, provided they were not spotted. If that happened it would be easy enough to block each end and trap them. He beckoned to Macro and Metellus and explained his plan.

'That's the way we go in. Then we find the procurator and keep him safe until the cohort takes the camp. On my signal.'

There was a stretch of open ground between them and the corner of the building. No one was looking their way and the sentry outside the house still appeared to be asleep. If they ran across together there was a risk they might be spotted. So Cato went down on his stomach as he emerged from behind a rock and crawled across the gravel and tufts of grass until he reached the corner then rose up into a crouch as he waved to the next of his party. Macro was followed by Metellus and then it was Cimber's turn. The guide glanced to his left, lowered himself onto his stomach and began to cross on his hands and knees, scuffling along and leaving a small swirl of dust in his wake.

Cato looked towards the rebels and saw one man rise from his bench and take a few steps in their direction, staring towards the procurator's house.

'Cimber!' he hissed. 'Get down! Now!'

The guide paused and looked at Cato questioningly and for a moment it seemed as if he would simply continue. Cato made a violent slamming motion with his hand and Cimber dropped onto his stomach and pressed himself into the ground. A faint haze of dust stirred around him and then dispersed as Cato peered cautiously around the corner to observe the rebel. The man continued staring in their direction for a moment longer before he stretched his arms out to the sides, rolled his shoulders and returned to his comrades. Cato let out a long sigh of relief and gestured to Cimber to continue.

As he reached the corner Macro stabbed a finger at him. 'What were you doing, you fuckwit? Trying to get us all killed?'

Cimber was trembling. 'Sorry, sir. I–I . . .'

'It doesn't matter,' Cato intervened. 'Stay with me.'

He led them along the wall, picking his way carefully over the places where the cliff edge dropped down to the road. As they neared the far end there was a distant shout, and then another. Then the ringing of a bell sounded across the camp. Cato and the others stopped and looked back.

Cimber flinched as if he had been struck. 'Oh, sweet Jupiter, they're onto us!'

'It's the cohort they've spotted, you fool. Not us. Keep going.'

They scrambled over the rocks until they came to the end of the wall and Cato paused, heart pounding; then he looked round the corner. It was as Cimber had described. A patch of ground had been cleared and a training post had been set up, together with a large butt for archery and javelin practice. The previous procurator had clearly fancied himself as something of a warrior. No one else was in sight, although now they could hear shouting from within the house. Cato waved his men on and moved along the rear wall towards the arched door halfway along. There was a heavy iron latch and Cato put his ear to the door but there was no sound from the other side. Grasping his spear in his right hand he steeled himself and tested the latch. It rose with a grating noise and the door opened on its hinges with a light groan, revealing a small yard. On either side were cells. Opposite Cato was the opening to a short passage giving out onto a garden courtyard.

Leading the others inside, he glanced warily into the small rooms on either side. They were mainly empty, aside from the odd scrap of clothing or a blanket. One contained baskets of spare roof slates and bricks. Close to the passageway were two larger cells with heavy studded doors. Both were bolted shut and had small barred openings to admit light. Macro peered through the first and in the dim interior picked out three men in chains sitting on the stone floor. One squinted up at him and spat.

'Those cunts are back to give us another hiding, lads.'

'Charming,' said Macro. 'But if that's what you're after . . .'

The prisoner started. 'You're Roman? Romans!' He shoved the man next to him. 'They're our boys. At fucking last.'

'Quiet,' Cato ordered as Macro slid back the bolt and opened the cell. 'Pipe down, damn you!'

The light flooded the cell and Cato could see that the men's faces and arms were cut and bruised and they were sitting in their own filth. The first of them raised his chains and shook them. 'Get these off!'

'Keep it down!' Cato growled. 'Is one of you the procurator?'

'Gaius Nepo? He's in the other cell.'

Cato drew back out of the entrance. 'Metellus, get these men out of here.'

He moved to the next door, slid back the bolt and entered. A man was lying curled up by the door. He was naked and his skin, marked with burns and cuts, was purple from the savage beating he had endured. Cato knelt beside him and shook his shoulder gently. The man let out a groan as he recoiled from the prefect's touch.

'Cimber, get the procurator something to wear and then guard him with your life.'

Outside the cell Macro met him with a concerned expression. 'They're in pretty poor shape, sir. We can't move far with them.'

'Then we'll have to stay in here until the cohort takes the building. If we—'

They were interrupted by a cry of alarm and turned towards the passage to see one of the rebels cup a hand to his mouth as he shouted towards the front of the procurator's house.

'Shit!' Cato lowered his spear and sprinted towards the passage, Macro running behind him. At the sound of their boots the rebel glanced round, mouth agape, then turned and ran, leaping over an ornamental bush as he raced across the garden towards the main house. Already another man had appeared, sword drawn, and he grasped the situation at once and shouted for help. Cato and Macro had run on a short distance into the garden. In stark contrast to the harsh landscape of the rest of the mining camp, the courtyard was lined with cypress and fruit trees of various kinds. Neatly tended shrubs ran around the edge of the gravelled area and also divided it into quadrants. At the centre was a square pool in which a small

221

fountain splashed across a sculpted dolphin. Sturdy wooden benches were arranged at intervals around the garden. It was a picture of cultured serenity against the harsh backdrop of the imperial mine, but the thought was fleeting as Cato drew up and stared across to the passage on the far side of the garden. More men were emerging from the house, led by a large figure in a polished cuirass. He glared back at Cato and snapped an order to his men before breaking into a dead run.

Cato shoved Macro towards the slave courtyard. 'Back!'

They rushed into the passage and slammed the studded door shut.

'Metellus! Cimber! On me!' Cato shouted as he dropped his spear and braced his shoulder against the door and set his feet to absorb the impact from the other side. Macro did the same as the others rushed to join them.

'There's too many of 'em,' said Cato. 'Use your spears on anyone who tries to get through the door.'

They nodded, raising their weapons in an overhand grip, ready to strike. The sound of voices and the crunch of boots on gravel came from the far side of the door and an instant later bodies thudded against it. Cato and Macro recoiled and then pressed forward with all their strength. Cato was closest to the edge of the door and as it opened an inch in his direction he snatched out his dagger and clenched the handle tightly. The door moved again, and despite the two officers' best efforts, they began to give ground inch by inch. Fingertips appeared, close to Cato's face, and at once he slashed at them with his dagger, cutting through to the bone. A howl of pain and rage came from the other side as the hand was snatched back and for an instant the door ceased moving inwards.

'Heave!' Cato snarled, throwing himself against the woodwork.

Suddenly, the door leaped back against him with a crash, opening a gap large enough for Metellus to see the enemy.

'They've got a bench!' he warned as he thrust his spear past Cato and snatched it back.

The makeshift ram struck again, jarring Cato's shoulder, and the rebels on either side of the bench pressed home their advantage as they forced the two Romans to give ground.

'It's no good, lad!' Macro growled as he began to be pressed in the angle between the door and the wall of the passage. 'Can't hold them.'

Cato saw that the struggle for the door was pointless now. 'On the word, step back. Hold the passage.'

Macro nodded. They stood their ground as best they could until the bench struck again.

'Now!'

The two officers scrambled back as the undefended door crashed inwards, depositing a startled rebel onto the floor of the passage. Metellus struck quickly, stabbing down between the man's shoulder blades and snapping his spine. He slumped to the floor and spasmed as his startled comrades dropped the bench and made ready with their weapons. There were several of them, armed with spears and swords, bunched around the large warrior who had drawn a gladius and hacked at the shaft of Metellus' spear, slamming it against the side of the passage where it clattered against the wall and snapped. The optio raised his eyebrows at the broken shaft before thrusting the splintered end into the warrior's forearm and ducking down to snatch up Cato's spear. The wound only served to enrage the rebel leader who plucked the broken spear shaft out and hurled it into Cato's face. It struck him lengthways on the forehead. It was a sharp blow, but only enough to force him back a step. The warrior barged forward, knocking Cato aside to expose Cimber.

The guide's hand trembled but he stood his ground and made a desperate thrust with his spear. There was insufficient weight behind the blow to fell the man, but the point caught the Asturian warrior high on the cheek, tore through the flesh, glancing off the bone before piercing his eye. He let out a roar of anger and staggered back clutching a hand to the ruined socket as blood and fluid burst from the wound. His men, shaken by his retreat, momentarily lost their resolve and paused on the threshold. Macro seized his chance and charged forward, slashing his sword side to side. The rebel slaves fell back and some turned to run, fleeing across the garden. The Asturian warrior backed off then, hand to face. He watched Macro with his good eye as he held his sword up, ready to deal with any attack. But Cato was conscious of the imbalance in numbers and called out,

'Leave him! Hold the passage. Metellus, get that bench in here and close the door. Before the bastards recover their nerve.'

Cato spared Cimber a grin. 'Well done! We'll make a soldier of you yet. Now come with me.'

They ran back to the cell where the building materials were stored and hurried back with the baskets of tiles and bricks, packing them against the door, then wedging the bench solidly under the latch before stepping back, weapons ready, waiting for the enemy to try and force their way through again. There was shouting from the garden, but now the notes of the cohort's handful of trumpets carried across the walls of the yard. Cato had ordered Cristus to make as much noise as possible once he had entered the camp to distract the rebels away from the attempt to rescue the hostages.

'Won't be long now,' Cato said calmly, to encourage Cimber and the prisoners. 'We just have to keep those bastards back for a moment.'

On the far side of the door a loud voice intoned a rhythm and then with a loud crash the door shivered and loose plaster trickled down from the ceiling of the passage as the enemy renewed their assault with a second bench.

Cato readied his sword and took a deep breath to try and calm his leaping heart. 'Steady . . .'

The next blow came and this time one of the door panels cracked and Cato felt small splinters patter off his body. He pressed his weight against the bench to keep it in place, just before the door lurched again and this time a section of plaster collapsed onto the floor of the passage. The wooden panel burst inwards and when the new ram was drawn back Cato could see the men beyond, urged on by the Asturian warrior. Outside the house the sound of the trumpets was growing in volume and now Cato and his comrades felt their hopes rise as shouts and the faint clash of weapons could be heard. There were another three blows and a second panel cracked, before the attack stopped.

Cato and his men heard cries of anguish on the other side of the door and above them rose the angry shouts of the Asturian warrior, but to no avail. Through the splintered gap Cato could see the rebels fleeing across the garden. Then his view was blocked as the warrior picked up the bench and rammed it into the opening in one last act of frustration and defiance before he turned away. As the sound of boots on the gravel of the garden diminished, Cato exchanged a look with Macro.

'Gone, I think.'

'Let's hope so, sir. A few more blows and that door would have flown apart like a whore's legs.'

Cato winced at the simile. 'Not quite how I would have put it, but true.'

They lowered their weapons, but kept them to hand, ears straining for the sound of the enemy returning.

Cimber licked his lips nervously. 'Do you think they've gone for good, sir?'

'No idea. But be ready, just in case.'

They did not have to wait long. The sound of movement came from the garden and Cato gave the order to stand ready. His comrades readied their weapons and fixed their gaze on the door. A moment later the end of the bench shifted in the breached panel, then it was dragged aside and a shadow fell across the opening. Finally, they saw the face of Tribune Cristus, warily peering through the gap.

'Prefect Cato, is that you, sir?'

'Of course it bloody is.'

Macro nudged him gently. 'You're bleeding, lad. From when that bastard hit you with the spear shaft.'

Cato sheathed his sword and sensed for the first time the pain across his forehead. He touched it tenderly and his fingers came away warm and sticky. A flesh wound only, he realised with relief. Then he looked back at Cristus.

'Never thought I'd ever say it, but I'm glad to see you. Now get that bloody thing open and send for the surgeon. The procurator's in a bad way.'

# CHAPTER TWENTY-TWO

'He's got a broken arm, broken ribs, several teeth have been knocked out and his knees have been smashed. There are burns to his buttocks and genitals, aside from several wounds and many small nicks from a sharp blade . . .' The cohort's surgeon ticked off the injuries on his fingers and then paused and shook his head. 'Those rebel bastards gave him a proper working over, and then some.'

'Will he recover?' asked Cato.

The surgeon arched an eyebrow. 'Of course not, sir. He'll be lucky if he lives at all. Even if he does, he'll never regain anything like full use of his legs, and there'll be scars he'll carry for the rest of his life.'

'All right,' Cato said impatiently. 'But will he be able to talk soon?'

'Talk? The man needs rest, sir. I've done what I can for him, and given him a sleeping draught so that his body can relax and start to recover.'

'Sleeping draught?' Cato frowned. 'Damn you. I need him awake. I need to talk to him as soon as possible. How long will he be out?'

The surgeon stroked his jaw contemplatively. 'Until the morning, if I'm any judge. Maybe longer.'

Cato ground his teeth and then nodded. 'Very well. But you send word for me the moment he opens his eyes. Understand?'

'Yes, sir.'

'And what about the butcher's bill? How many men did we lose?'

The surgeon smiled. 'There we have the good news. Not one

death. Six wounded in the skirmish once we reached the camp. Three of those were nothing more than cuts, two with broken bones and one lost his hand. Some big bastard with one eye took it off with a sword before the lads cut him down. All in all, we got off very lightly, sir.'

'Good. Where are you treating them?'

'Procurator's dining room, sir.'

Cato glanced down at the sleeping official. Nepo had been treated in the cell, and then laid on a mattress brought from his house. It was frustrating that he would be unable to question the procurator for now, but one of the other hostages would have to do. And after that, he must turn his attention to the camp and make it ready to defend. Word of its capture was bound to reach the ears of Iskerbeles soon and it was a certainty that he would take the chance to crush the isolated cohort if he could. The destruction of an elite unit of the Roman army would inspire his followers and prove that the imperial overlords of the province were not invincible.

The three other hostages were standing outside in the yard. Macro had removed their chains and though they had open sores around their ankles, wrists and necks, they were grateful to be able to stretch their limbs in the open air once again. They did their best to stand to attention as Cato emerged from Nepo's cell. They were still covered with filth and stank so badly that Cato could not help wrinkling his nose.

'First order of the day when I'm done here is to get yourselves cleaned up.'

'Yes, sir. Sorry about that.'

'At ease. Who is the senior rank here?'

The shortest of the three, a light-haired man with blue eyes and fair skin – a Celt, Cato guessed – nodded. 'Optio Pastericus, sir. In command of the garrison. From the Third Gallic Cohort.'

'Tell me what happened here. I didn't see any sign of any action on the way up to the camp, so I'm assuming Iskerbeles didn't have to fight hard for it.'

'No, sir.' Pastericus shifted uneasily. 'We didn't get to put up a fight. Thousands of them, there were. We could have held them on the wall, for a day or two maybe, but the procurator wouldn't let us.

227

Iskerbeles sent him a messenger to tell him to surrender the mine by the following dawn, or every person taken in the camp was to be put to death, and Nepo himself flayed and crucified. To prove that he was serious, Iskerbeles had ten men, Romans, brought up from the settlement and beheaded in front of the gate, with the heads thrown over the wall to the procurator.' He hesitated before continuing. 'To be honest, sir, Nepo ain't the fearless warrior type. But he managed the mine well enough, I suppose. Anyhow, at dawn the next day he said he would give up the mine if the rebels granted a free passage to Tarraco for the garrison, and those who worked at the mine and their families. Iskerbeles gave his word. Then, the moment we had given up our weapons, his men turned on us. Marched us over to the death pit and then started cutting throats and throwing the bodies in. Me and these lads were only spared because we're the procurator's bodyguards, and Iskerbeles said he might need a few fresh heads to bargain with when he ransomed Nepo.'

'Thank fuck for us then, eh?' Macro commented.

'What happened afterwards?' said Cato.

Pastericus scratched his armpits. 'We weren't around to see it, sir. But the rebels guarding us told us later on. Seems that Iskerbeles set the slaves loose and allowed them to do whatever they liked to the camp and the settlement. When the slaves were finished with the locals, the Romans were killed and joined the others in the death pit.'

Cato was silent briefly, as he vowed to make the rebel leader and his followers pay dearly for the atrocity they had carried out. Provided that he actually got a chance to avenge the victims. That was far from likely in the present circumstances. He put the thought aside and turned to a more vital matter.

'What happened to the mine's stock of silver?'

The optio shook his head. 'I don't know, sir. I guess the rebels took it with them. I never heard anything about it when they put us in the cell.'

'You're sure? No mention of it at all?'

Pastericus thought a moment. 'None, sir. Sure of it.'

Cato thought it odd, if that was truly the case. Such a treasure was bound to occasion some comment. But maybe word of its fate had not reached the ears of the hostages. Hopefully the procurator would provide more details when he regained consciousness. In the meantime, there was much to do to safeguard the camp. He scrutinised the optio. 'How are you feeling, Pastericus?'

The man stretched his back and winced. 'I've felt better, sir. A lot better.'

'I need you to show me and Centurion Macro over the mine. Can you do that?'

'Yes, sir.'

'Good man, then come, let's be about it.'

They passed through the passage and across the gardens into the house. The garden demonstrated refined taste and had been well tended, and the interior revealed a similar degree of opulence, with fine furnishings, intricately painted scenes of hunting and mythology on the walls and a muted hollow echo to their footsteps as they passed through the procurator's living quarters. Cato turned to the optio and pointed at the floor. 'Hypocaust?'

'Yes, sir.'

Cato pursed his lips and glanced at Macro. 'Seems that Nepo was very fond of his creature comforts.'

Macro gave a sly smile. 'I never knew that imperial procurators were so well paid. I guess not all the silver dug out of these hills made it back to Rome after all.'

'So it would seem.'

They left the house, crossed the front courtyard and emerged into the open space that separated the procurator's quarters from the rest of the men who had worked at the mine. Hundreds of Praetorians were sitting and standing around and those closest hurriedly stood and saluted as Cato and his two companions passed by. He made for the area where the standards rose above the helmets of the soldiers, and found Cristus and the other centurions with the colour party. They exchanged a salute before Cato spoke.

'Finished sweeping the place for rebels?'

'Just now, sir. The last of 'em were hiding in the slave sheds. Unless we missed a few. Anyway, there are no prisoners.'

'None?'

'They refused to surrender, sir. I gave them the chance, but they

229

fought to the end, like cornered animals.' He nodded to a heap of bloodied bodies near the top of the track leading down to the workings.

Cato stared at the corpses. 'Have them thrown into the pit.'

'Yes, sir.'

'I want two centuries on the wall to the mine workings at all times, taking turns to stand to. I also want them to search the settlement for any supplies before they close the gate. Centurion Pulcher?'

The heavy-set officer stepped forward. 'Sir?'

'Take forty men. Search the camp for the same. Anything you find is to be taken and stored in the procurator's house. See to it now.'

Pulcher saluted and trotted away to his century. Cato turned back to Pastericus and Macro. 'Right, let's have a look over this hell-hole. We'll start at the far end of the camp. Lead on.'

They passed through the wall into the slave quarters where the stink of human waste clung to the long barrack blocks that had been built close enough together that a man might stretch out his arms and touch the buildings on either side. There were small holes at intervals along the wall to allow the sewage to trickle out into the drains that ran between the blocks and led over to the cliff before running down to the mine workings. Mercifully the channels had dried out since the slaves had been freed by Iskerbeles. On the far side of the slave quarters there was another ditch, wall and gate, giving out onto a large expanse of low stone structures packed round with rock and soil.

'What's that lot?' Macro asked.

'Water tanks, sir,' Pastericus replied, then pointed out a natural gully that ran down the steep slope behind the structures. 'They're fed from a spur of the aqueduct that taps a spring up in the mountains and runs down to Asturica. There's a sluice gate up there. But you can only access it from the other side of the ridge, due to the cliff.'

Cato climbed onto the lip of the nearest tank to gain an overview. It was an impressive sight. The tank was some forty paces long and twenty wide and sealed with concrete. The water level stood at perhaps two thirds, he calculated, and looked to be as much as ten feet deep. A considerable volume of water then. A large sluice gate was built into the side facing the mine workings and it fed a deep, concrete-lined drain that ended at the edge of the cliff. There were six more tanks stretching out along the base of the hill, each gleaming with water. It was an impressive feat of engineering by any standards, and proof once again of the scale of the tasks that Romans routinely set themselves. Cato could not resist a thrill of pride in the civilisation to which he belonged. This was an achievement that barbarians could not even dream of. Then he recalled the darker side of this place, and cast a sombre look back towards the slave quarters. There was always a price paid by the many for the achievements claimed by the few.

'We're not going to be without anything to drink,' said Macro. 'But water will have to do now those rebel bastards have drunk the place dry of any wine.'

Cato walked down the slope to the cliff where the end of the drain crumbled away. Two hundred feet below lay the barren expanse of the mine workings, dotted with foreshortened Praetorians as they picked over the unfamiliar surroundings. It was a good vantage point to see the mine, the settlement and the landscape beyond, stretching out over rolling countryside between the hills until distant haze obscured the view.

'I'll want a watch kept from this position from now on.'

Macro nodded. 'Yes, sir.'

Cato focused his attention on the settlement. 'The buildings are too close to the outer ditch. We'll have to remove them. We'll burn as far back as the forum and pull down what we can of any remains. That'll give us a decent expanse of open ground in front of the defences.'

'Destroy the settlement?' Pastericus sucked in a deep breath through his teeth. 'That ain't going to be a popular decision, sir.'

'I dare say most of the owners of the property down there are past caring,' Cato responded drily. 'If anyone else takes issue with my decision then they can refer the matter to the governor.'

He switched his gaze to the ditch and wall. Both had been built more for policing purposes than to withstand a determined attack. The ditch was too shallow, the wall not high enough, nor thick enough.

'We'll have to do what we can to strengthen the first line of defence. Then we'll need another line . . . there, where the ravine bends in towards the cliff. Nothing elaborate, just enough to buy us time to fall back in good order. Our last line of defence will be at the top of the track. The enemy will have a hard climb and have to attack on a narrow front, which suits us.'

'And if the rebels get through that?' Macro prompted.

'Then we can fortify the procurator's house, or we defend the wall in front of the slave quarters.'

'And make our last stand.'

'Yes,' Cato concluded. 'But let's assume it doesn't come to that.'

'Feel free to assume away.' Macro smiled fleetingly before his expression became grim. 'I ain't too keen on the alternative, given what we saw earlier.'

Cato nodded with feeling as he shifted his gaze to the steep hillside behind the camp. There were crags along the top and the slope was sheer in many places.

'It appears that there is no access to the camp from that direction. Do you know of any paths or tracks that lead up there, Pastericus?'

'There's nothing, sir. Even the goats are wary of venturing too far up.'

'Then that's one less thing to worry about, unless the enemy occupy the heights and use it to roll boulders down onto the camp. But that's more likely to be a nuisance than a danger most of the time.' Cato considered the rocky ridge looming above them. 'They might try to use ropes to get men down the crags. So we'll have to post some pickets beneath just in case . . . Is there anything else I should know, Optio? Any other possible ways into the mine workings or the camp? Any potential danger spots? What about the ravine below the mine?'

Pastericus shook his head. 'That's a sheer drop, sir. Not more than fifty feet, but the river is mostly rapids. No way to get across it. It'd be a foolhardy man that tried to get a boat down there with a view to scaling the ravine.'

'I'll have a closer look as soon as I get the chance.' Cato took a last glance round to make sure he had considered all the obvious dangers and then slapped a hand on his thigh. 'Very well. There's still an hour of light left. Let's get started.'

The piles of spoil from the tunnels provided ample material to strengthen the first wall. While two centuries stood ready to fight, the rest of the cohort laid down their weapons and took off their armour before using tools and handcarts from the mine's stores to move the rocks and soil to the rear of the wall where they were packed down hard, layer by layer. It was exhausting work following the day's march and the capture of the mine, but Cato drove them on until the last of the light had faded. Only then were the men dismissed to eat their rations and find a billet in the blocks that had been used by the mine's garrison, the overseers and other staff. There was not enough space for all and Macro's century shared the procurator's house with the officers.

There was one final task to perform and Cato led one of the centuries on the wall out into the settlement. They worked from the nearest buildings outwards, piling up furniture, baskets, cloth and anything else that could burn before liberally sprinkling oil over each pile. When they reached the edge of the forum Cato gave the order to stop preparing the incendiary materials and ordered all but one section to return to the mine. Then, together with the remaining men, he used a tinder box to light torches, which were used to set the fires going in the buildings closest to the wall. The flames were already rising into the night as Cato joined Macro in the tower above the gatehouse to watch the spectacle. Several of the nearest houses were ablaze, orange and red tongues darting from doorways and windows. Wavering light gleamed along the edges of roof tiles before the timbers beneath burned through and collapsed, opening gaps in the tiles through which more flames eagerly licked into the darkness as the fire spread from building to building. There was very little breeze to fan the flames and the progress of the blaze was slow as it consumed more of the settlement. Even so, the rising heat stung the faces of the men along the wall and on the gatehouse and they had to step back and shelter behind the hoardings as they continued to watch.

'That is going to be seen for miles,' said Macro.

'Can't be helped. If we fired the settlement by day then the enemy would see the smoke in any case. It had to be done now in order to give us time to demolish what remains once the heat has died down. We don't want to leave much cover for the enemy when they arrive.'

Macro stared at the flames, his face lit with the wavering ruddy glow. 'Do you think Iskerbeles will come for us?'

'Yes, with every man he can scrape together.'

'You seem very sure, lad.'

'I would in his place. For two reasons. Firstly, the prestige to be had in wiping out a Praetorian cohort. That will add lustre to his reputation in the same proportion that it shames the Emperor. Secondly, he'll be wondering why Vitellius has despatched a single cohort in advance of the main column, and more to the point, why it was sent to take control of this particular mine. From what Pastericus told us, it seems that he didn't get his hands on the bullion. But now that we're here it won't take him long to work out that we think there's something of value at the mine.'

Macro looked at him. 'If the silver's still here, then where in Hades is it?'

Cato thought briefly. 'I'm hoping the procurator will be able to tell us that tomorrow.'

'What if the bastard ups and dies on us?'

Cato smiled. 'The phrase "finding a needle in a haystack" comes to mind. One more challenge set by the Gods to vex us, brother.'

'Fuck that,' Macro responded. 'I'm more concerned about finding a bloody great spear in my guts when Iskerbeles comes calling . . . What if the rebels already have the bullion?'

'They might have it,' Cato conceded doubtfully. 'But that won't make any difference to Iskerbeles' determination to annihilate us. That, I think, we can take as a given. A further thought occurs to me. What if Iskerbeles has already got wind of the fact that there is a silver hoard in one of the mines? In that case, our presence here is going to show him exactly where to come looking.'

Macro puffed his cheeks. 'At times like this, you're such a comfort to have around, Cato.'

# CHAPTER TWENTY-THREE

The fire blazed throughout the night, spreading steadily towards the forum, and then continuing to consume every building in its path, so that the entire settlement was a sea of flames just after midnight, the glare lighting up the nearby hills and surely visible to eyes far in the distance. The roar of the flames was punctuated by the sharp report of bursting timbers and the rumble and crash of masonry and roofs as buildings collapsed. Gradually the flames began to die down, like wild animals slumping to rest after the hunt. Red glows filled the shells of buildings and every so often the fire would discover a fresh morsel to devour and flare up briefly. By the first light of dawn the fire had reduced to small pockets across the charred, smoking ruins of the settlement. Only the shrine to the imperial cult remained intact, still standing above the surrounding desolation, thanks to the stone used in its construction.

Cato and Macro surveyed the ruins from the far end of the camp. Even though they were some distance from and above the scene, the air was still thick with the acrid tang of burning. Many buildings had burned to the ground. Those with blocks of stone for lower courses, or which had somehow escaped the full attention of the flames, still rose up from the charred timbers around them.

'When you do a job, you don't do it by half,' Macro commented with an amused click of his tongue. 'If we survive Iskerbeles' attempt to wipe us out, then you're going to have some angry property owners to answer to. We seem to be leaving a trail of ashes behind us in this province.'

'Litigious landlords and landowners are the last thing on my mind right now. We need to complete our defences before the rebels turn up. I want that second wall built as high as the first, and with a deeper ditch in front in it.'

'You think we'll lose the first wall, then?'

'Maybe. But we'll make them pay for it. Then, if they break through that, I want them to see that the second line is an even tougher proposition. That'll give their morale a kick in the guts.'

Macro chuckled. 'You've a devious mind, lad. You should have been a politician.'

Cato sniffed. 'That's a low insult, even from you, brother. I'm just trying to think like the rebels. They're a mix of hill farmers and slaves. I don't doubt the strength of their desire to punish Rome for what they have been forced to endure. I don't doubt their courage, determination or even their desperation. But they're not trained soldiers. They're not used to discipline and seeing orders through to the bitter end. They'll be spirited, but brittle. Our best chance of defeating them will be to wear their spirits down. There's a lot at stake here, Macro. If they win, it'll inspire defiance against Rome right across Hispania. If we demonstrate to them that they can't win, we'll cut through the very roots of this rebellion and it'll wither and die. Then we'll have peace and order again. Even if they still hate Rome with every fibre in their bodies.'

'Well, you can't have it all,' Macro concluded flatly. 'Let 'em hate, as long as they fear, eh?'

Cato looked at him silently for a moment. 'As you say. That's the price of empire.'

A trumpet sounded the morning assembly and Cato and Macro strode back through the slave quarters and passed through the guard wall as the last of the Praetorians were emerging from the accommodation blocks to form up in the open ground in front of the procurator's house. Porcino and his men were still on duty on the wall overlooking the settlement and were due to be relieved after the assembly. Cato waited in front of the colour party while the centurions supplied their strength returns to Macro. Then he in turn presented them to Cato. He signed off on the wax tablet that Macro presented to him and walked steadily out into the open to address his men.

Despite the long march and the fighting they had endured, the

Praetorians were neatly turned out, having made every effort to clean their kit the previous night. Cato felt a grudging admiration for the fussy professionalism of the guardsmen. Despite what the men of the legions may have said about the Praetorian units, they were not just for show and obsessed with bullshine. They had fighting spirit and a reputation to uphold. They were good men, he conceded. As good as any in the army, even the veterans of Macro's beloved Second Legion.

Cato cleared his throat and drew a deep breath. 'Gentlemen, we have reached the objective assigned to us by Legate Vitellius. It was a hard march, and we lost some good comrades along the way. But we have carried out the first part of our orders successfully, in the best tradition of the Praetorian Guard.' He let his praise sink in before he continued. 'Now comes the real challenge. The mine is in our hands, and the enemy is sure to want to destroy us and take it back. But we will not let him . . . You may ask why we have to defend this place. Why here? The answer is, as it always is, because we're here. It has fallen to us to show these rebels that Rome cannot be defied. That Rome cannot be humiliated. That Rome cannot be defeated. That the Praetorian Guard has no equal in all the empire and it will prove, before all the Gods, that the Praetorians can master many times their number on the field of battle. No more so than the men of the Second Cohort.' Cato punched his fist into the air. 'Long live Emperor Claudius! Victory to Rome!'

The Praetorians brandished their spears and repeated the cry and it echoed off the side of the ridge above, swelling the noise so that it seemed the voices of thousands of men rather than hundreds. Cato allowed them to continue for a while before giving a nod to the trumpeter who sounded several shrill notes to call them to silence before their commander continued.

'There is much work to do before the enemy reaches us. Hard work, but vital work. Let every man bend to the task he is set and do his utmost to perform it well. When the rebel host left this place it was but a mine. When they return, let them find it transformed into a fortress against which they will throw their might in vain.' He thrust his arm towards the cohort's standard, already ringed with a silver wreath in addition to the disc bearing the portrait of the

Emperor and below it the scorpion symbol of the Praetorian Guard. 'And when we return to Rome in triumph, the Emperor himself will be sure to add a new decoration to our standard. He will reward us with gold, and we will be the heroes of all Rome, and the envy of every Praetorian who was not here to share our glory!' He paused to draw a breath and then raised his fist again as he shouted, 'All glory to the Second Cohort!'

Again the men joined in, cheering themselves and their commander, until the cries began to fade and Cato judged that the moment was right to call for order again, and send the men to their work.

As the centuries trudged off down the track leading to the mine workings Macro folded his arms.

'Best soldiers in the army? Better even than our old legion? Bit over the top, don't you think?'

'Maybe, but it's the tradition to work their spirits up before a unit goes into action. I see no reason to part with that tradition at least.'

'You sounded like you believed it.'

'It doesn't matter what I believe. It's what they believe that matters. And if they think that they are the sons of Mars himself, that suits me. Then it'll be a case of what they can make the enemy believe about Roman soldiers. If we win, then the rebels will think we're invincible. If we lose, then they'll see that we fight to the very last breath and are indomitable. Either way, they'll think twice about tangling with Rome again.'

'I hope you're right, lad.'

'We'll find out soon enough, or then again, we won't.' Cato gave a genuine smile. 'Come, it's time to pay the procurator a visit. Nepo's got some answering to do.'

The cohort's surgeon had moved the procurator back into his private suite and Nepo was sitting propped up on a bolster when Cato and Macro entered the room. His face was heavily bruised and the surgeon had placed his legs in splints. One of the medical orderlies was sitting on a stool beside him, feeding him gruel. As he turned and saw the prefect, the orderly instantly put the mess tin down and stood to attention.

'Wait outside,' Cato ordered.

Once the door had closed Cato made his introductions. 'Prefect Quintus Licinius Cato, commander of the Second Praetorian Cohort. This is Centurion Macro, my second in command.'

Nepo tried to shift himself more upright, but his face twisted in agony and he gave up. He swallowed and nodded. 'Then I owe you my thanks, Prefect. I hear that you and your men saved my life. And my bodyguards as well.'

'I'd save your thanks. From what I've learnt, the rebels were permitted to take over the camp without a blow being struck. On your say-so. If we get out of this mess, then I may well have to give evidence against you when the Emperor enquires into why a vital silver mine was allowed to fall into rebel hands.'

Nepo winced. 'What else could I do?'

'You could have done your duty, sir,' Macro said harshly.

'I did what I thought was best. There was no way we could have withstood an attack. I decided that any attempt to fight would lead to a pointless loss of life. Better to take the offer of safe conduct and have my men live to fight another day.'

Macro snorted. 'Except the offer was a lie. You placed your trust in a common criminal and as a result nearly every man under your command was butchered. And their families with them.'

Nepo glared back at him. 'I don't have to damn well justify myself to a mere centurion.'

'Might as well get used to it,' said Cato. 'No one is going to accept your feeble excuses when you are called to account for this disaster. You'll be lucky if you get away with being banished from Rome for the rest of your days. The Emperor will have your property confiscated and your family name will be ruined. Unless, of course, you have powerful friends. After news of this gets out in the capital, I doubt there will be many who will claim to know you.'

Nepo smiled slowly. 'As it happens, I do have some powerful political friends. You might want to bear that in mind before you consider speaking out against me, Prefect Cato.'

There was a time when Cato might have felt more anxiety over such a threat. But he no longer had a family to protect. His wife was dead and his son was being raised by his father-in-law. Cato leaned forward and prodded Nepo in the chest as he responded in a cold, quiet tone. 'Fuck you. Fuck your friends. No one betrays the trust of the men placed under his command in the way that you did and gets away with it. If the Emperor doesn't hang you up by your balls, then I'll see to it myself. And I dare say there'll be friends and family of those lying in the death pit just down the track from here who will be lining up to help me. I swear this, by Jupiter, Best and Greatest, and Centurion Macro is my witness.'

'Yes, sir.' Macro smiled. 'Just give the order.'

Nepo pressed himself back into the bolster, trying to gain even the smallest measure of distance between himself and the scarred face of the prefect whose lips had curled into a contemptuous sneer.

Cato allowed the man to squirm a little and then straightened up and looked down the angle of his nose at the procurator. 'Do you know why my men and I were sent here?'

'I can guess. You were sent to get hold of the silver bullion. Though I'm surprised that you have only been given one cohort for the job.'

'It was all that was available. Legate Vitellius had to wait for the rest of his force to arrive before marching on Asturica.'

'Vitellius? Here in the province?' Nepo's surprise betrayed him.

'Is there any reason why he shouldn't be here?' asked Cato, the first quiver of suspicion tingling at the back of his neck.

Nepo glanced towards the window and blustered, 'No reason. It's just that he's a playboy. I'm surprised to hear that he's been chosen to command the forces sent to deal with the uprising. That's all.'

Cato glanced at Macro and the latter spat on the floor. 'Bollocks.'

Nepo's eyes darted towards the centurion. 'I'd advise your man to watch his tongue, Prefect Cato. I'm not a forgiving man, nor a forgetful one.'

'Small world,' Macro responded. 'Neither am I. You might bear that in mind when you answer the prefect's questions. It'd be an easy thing for us to go back to Rome and claim you'd succumbed to your wounds and we had you buried in among the poor sods in the grave pit. Who would know any different?'

Cato pursed his lips, keeping his gaze fixed on the procurator. 'He's got a point.'

Nepo's eyes widened anxiously for an instant before he sneered, 'You're bluffing.'

Cato reached down and gently pressed the procurator's leg. At once Nepo's mouth opened wide and he let out a cry of pain. Then he snapped his jaw tightly and gritted his teeth as he fought off a wave of agony. Cato removed his hand and for a moment Nepo sat, eyes shut, sweat glistening on his brow. There was a knock on the door, and without waiting for an answer the surgeon entered and stood on the threshold, uncertain of what he was observing.

'What's, er, troubling the patient? Procurator, is there anything I can do for you?'

Nepo glanced at each of the officers, one either side of his bed, and shook his head. 'No. Nothing. I'm fine.'

'There you go,' said Macro. 'He's fine. Off you trot.'

The surgeon looked to Cato for confirmation.

'I'm sure you have other patients you could be attending to.'

'Yes, sir.' The surgeon backed out of the room and closed the door behind him.

Cato folded his hands together and cracked his knuckles. 'Can I take it you are now in a more co-operative frame of mind?'

'I'll tell you what I can, yes, you bastard.'

Macro gave him a warning look, and gestured towards his legs. 'Careful . . .'

Glancing round Cato saw a stool and fetched it and sat beside the procurator. He collected his thoughts briefly then began. 'Let's start with the silver. It was being stockpiled here ready to be taken by convoy to Tarraco just as the uprising started. Correct?'

'Yes. There's no mystery to that. It happens regularly throughout the year. Just bad timing on this occasion. I decided that it was not safe for the convoy to set out while the rebels were abroad. I thought that Iskerbeles and his followers would be dealt with soon enough and the silver could go on its way. But you know the rest. The rebellion grew quicker than anyone could have anticipated and by then it was too late to try and get the bullion safely out of the region. When that cur Iskerbeles and his rabble turned up, I knew I had to keep the silver from him. We were lucky he gave me time to consider his surrender terms. So I waited until the middle of the night, then called on a handful of men I could trust, took the chests down into one of the tunnels and then set fire to the pit props. When they burned through the tunnel collapsed and the silver was safe from Iskerbeles. Those who helped me were put to death by the rebels before they even had a chance to try and trade their knowledge for their lives. Even if they had attempted it, I dare say Iskerbeles would have had them killed in any case. Only I know where the silver is, and now you two do as well. So what do you intend to do about it?'

He watched the two officers for a response.

'How much is there?' asked Macro.

'Equivalent to about ten million sestertii, give or take a few thousand. Securely locked in paychests, twenty of them in all.'

Macro's jaw sagged. 'Ten million . . . Fuck.'

'Doesn't matter how much it is,' said Cato. 'It has to stay out of the rebels' hands. So we leave it where it is. The fewer that know about it, the better. If we keep Iskerbeles out of the camp until Vitellius arrives, then it can be dug up then. If the rebels take the camp, they won't be able to find the silver. Not on purpose that is. When the uprising is put down, then the mine will be reoccupied and the silver will come to light at some point, I trust. So it stays where it is and none of us mentions it again. Is that understood?'

Nepo nodded and Macro followed suit with a sad sigh. 'Would have been nice to see such a sum all in one place.'

'You will, if we get through this.'

'I hope so.' Macro thought briefly. 'Something occurs to me, sir. You and I will take this to our grave, but what's to stop matey boy here spilling his guts if Iskerbeles takes the camp? He's got form.'

'That's true. But if his past treatment is anything to go by then I dare say that the procurator would rather not take the risk of falling into the enemy's hands alive. Next time around Iskerbeles will have a pretty shrewd idea about what's being hidden from him. There'll be no limits to the torture he'll inflict on Nepo. In his place I would rather take my own life.'

'But you're not in his place,' Macro replied. 'You've got the guts to do what's necessary. He's already proved that he hasn't.'

Nepo coughed. 'I am in the bloody room, you know. I can speak for myself, gentlemen. I give you my word that I will make sure that the rebels get nothing from me if the camp is taken.'

Macro gave him a doubtful look. 'Right . . .'

Cato stood up. 'We'll make it easy on you, Nepo. If the camp is taken then the centurion or I will save you the job. Don't worry, we'll make it quick and painless.'

Macro shrugged. 'Quick at any rate. I'm not so good on the painless front.'

The procurator blanched and Cato had to turn before the man saw his smile. He gestured to Macro to follow him and made for the door. Before they reached it, the door opened quickly and a breathless Praetorian offered a salute.

'Centurion Petillius sends his respects, sir. He says you should come to the watch post at once. It's the enemy, sir.'

A section of men was starting to erect a small watchtower beyond the water tanks as Cato and Macro came trotting up. Petillius greeted them with a nod of the head and then pointed out a party of horsemen approaching the burned settlement from the south-west. Cato estimated there were at least fifty riders. Sunlight occasionally glinted off polished helmets and spear tips as they surveyed the smouldering ruins and the Praetorians labouring at deepening the ditch in front of the mine workings.

'Theirs or ours, I wonder?' Petillius said quietly.

There was a moment's pause as Cato strained his eyes to better see the distant figures. 'If they were ours, I'd expect a more ordered column. It's safe to assume that's the enemy.'

'What are your orders, sir? Think we should send a contingent out to drive them off?'

The riders halted on a low ridge overlooking the approaches to the settlement and the mine beyond. Cato shook his head. 'No. Besides, they won't get close enough to learn anything useful. Let 'em watch for a bit and go and report back to Iskerbeles. Unless he's down there with them.'

'You think? He's taking a bit of a risk.'

'He's travelled far down that road, Petillius. He was taking the biggest risk of his life when he started the uprising. And he's been pushing his luck ever since, to very good effect. He's not afraid of us.'

'Still,' said Macro. 'If he is there and we send the lads out, we might get lucky and knock him on the head and put an end to this.'

'We might. It's not worth risking our men on the off chance. We'll bide our time for now.' Cato looked down at the blackened ruins of the settlement. 'I guess they saw the glow of the fire last night. We've announced our presence to the enemy. Now we had better make sure we are ready when they come calling in force.'

# CHAPTER TWENTY-FOUR

The news that the enemy had been sighted spread through the ranks swiftly and lent urgency to the men's efforts to prepare the mine's defences for the anticipated attack. Porcino and Secundus took their men out to pull down as much of the charred remains of the settlement as possible, raising a swirl of choking dust and ash that forced the men to pull their neckscarves over their mouths and noses as they laboured in the stifling heat. Petillius' century planted stakes and other obstacles in the ditch beyond the wall before packing rock and earth against the back of the rampart. Then they piled more rocks close to the gatehouse, ready to reinforce the gate when the last of the men were withdrawn from the settlement. The men who had done their best to demolish the settlement were then set straight to work aiding Pulcher, charged with the construction of the second wall across the narrowest part of the mine workings.

It was most fortunate that they had been given the task of defending a mine, Cato reflected. Every tool that was needed was on hand and the men were able to excavate a ditch in front of the second wall in good time. There was a small stock of dressed stone in the camp, left over from the construction of the barrack blocks, and this provided enough material to build solid foundations for the gatehouse and much of the rampart stretching out on either side. The gatehouse was completed with a timber frame and rocks covered with earth were used for the rampart upon which a palisade was constructed from the mine's pit props.

'Nice job.' Macro patted the palisade approvingly as he and Cato inspected the nearly completed wall late in the afternoon. 'I wouldn't fancy making a frontal assault on this.'

'Nor me,' said Cato. 'But it will only serve our purpose as long as we have enough men to line the wall. If our losses are high enough, then we'll have no choice but to call back to the last line of defence up at the camp.'

Macro had been used to his friend's pessimistic frame of mind for years now and made no comment as he looked over the defences Pulcher's men had constructed. The ditch was ten feet deep and the steep slope closest to the wall was lined with sharpened stakes. The rampart was as tall as the ditch was deep even without the walkway and palisade on top and short stakes projected from the wall to restrict access to the palisade. Without proper siege weapons the rebels were no more likely to break through this second line than the Gauls had been at Alesia over a hundred years earlier. Truly, Macro thought, the most effective weapons in Rome's arsenal were the picks and shovels wielded by her soldiers.

Centurion Pulcher approached from the gatehouse, his tunic stained with red dust and soil and his face dripping with perspiration. He exchanged a salute with his prefect.

'Just about done, sir. Only the gates to fit in place now.'

Despite his earlier mistrust of the centurion, and the previous history of enmity, Cato had to concede that Pulcher was a first-rate soldier who deserved recognition. 'You and your men have done a fine job.'

There was a brief glimpse of surprise in the hardened veteran's expression before he replied, 'Thank you, sir. I imagine the lads will fight like hell to make sure that they hang onto the wall after all the sweat that's gone into making the bastard.'

Cato could not help smiling. 'Glad to hear it. Once we're done here, I want your men to start work on the wall across the top of the track.'

Pulcher ground his teeth. 'I think the lads deserve a short breather first, sir. Or they'll start dropping like flies.'

Cato considered briefly and nodded. 'All right. Get them some food from the camp, and wine. There's still a few jars of wine from the stock we brought with us on the march. Watered down, though. I want them content, not drunk.'

'Yes, sir. I'll let 'em know you'll flog any man who can't hold his drink.'

'And I will. That'll be all, Pulcher.'

They exchanged a salute and the centurion turned and strode off smartly. Macro watched him and shook his head. 'I don't trust him.'

'He's done his duty well enough so far.'

'So far . . .'

Cato leaned against the parapet. 'Look, what happened between us took place ten years ago. Pulcher was obeying orders. We've not seen him since, and now we meet up again. He's proved his worth. I think he deserves to be given a chance to put past differences behind us.'

'Past differences? That bastard would have killed us given half a chance. And as for orders, well let's put it this way, there's soldiers who carry out ruthless orders and soldiers who enjoy carrying out ruthless orders. Our man, Pulcher, likes to harm people. He likes to torture. You forget what happened in the past if you like, but I ain't going to. I'll not give Pulcher the chance to stick a knife in my back when I'm not looking. And I advise you to take the same approach, lad. Trust me on this one.'

'I always trust you, Macro. I've never had reason not to. But—'

'Don't "but" me, Cato. Just don't be a fool.'

Cato stood up and stared hard at Macro. Despite the closeness of their longstanding friendship they were soldiers and the difference in rank that divided them was ever present. 'You forget yourself, Centurion.'

Macro stiffened and stared back as he replied flatly, 'I never forget myself. I never forget those who pose a threat to myself, and my mates. You'd be wise not to either, sir.'

'I'll take your advice when I need it.' Cato intensely disliked the sudden tension that divided them and decided to divert their attention away from it as swiftly as possible. 'We . . . I need to decide where to place that final wall. Come.'

He clambered down the steep slope behind the rampart and set off for the track leading up to the camp, furious with himself for that 'we' when it should so obviously have been 'I'. His friend had been right to warn him about being too trusting of Pulcher. Yet the situation demanded that Cato concentrate on conducting the defence of the mine. Every man was needed, and in such a perilous position a veteran with Pulcher's qualities was needed more than most. Macro's suspicions could not be allowed to undermine the professional relationship between the officers of the cohort, nor indeed the authority of its commander. It had pained Cato to slap down his friend, but it had been necessary, he told himself. Once again, he could not help wondering about the motives behind Vitellius' selection of the officers to accompany him to Hispania Terraconensis. The legate was aware of the conflict between Cato and Pulcher all those years before. Had that been why they had been chosen? In which case, there must be some scheme that Pulcher was in on, and Vitellius was pulling the strings, but what it was eluded Cato for the present. His mind was already taxed to the limit. Besides, he had far more pressing concerns.

Macro followed him dutifully, deeply troubled by his friend's unwillingness to be wary of Pulcher. Although the man had played his part well enough, Macro could not bring himself to believe that Pulcher had changed in the years since their last encounter. Some men were like that, of fixed character, immutable, for good or for evil. Pulcher was such a man, Macro was sure of it. And therefore a danger to himself and Cato as long as he was allowed to live.

Cato paced across the width of the track where it emerged onto the ledge where the mine camp had been constructed, hands on hips.

'Twenty feet, I'd say. That's good. A very narrow front indeed.' He half turned to indicate the stretch of ground leading up to the corner of the procurator's house. 'If we continue the wall along there then we can hit the rebels with javelins and rocks, in their right flank.'

Macro nodded. It was an ideal set-up. The enemy would have to climb the track and endure the barrage on their unprotected side, and then only be able to bring no more than eight men into action at once. While those waiting to join the fight would be whittled down by a rain of missiles from above. It was the kind of position that could be held by a very small number of committed men against an army. For a while at least. As the Spartans had discovered at Thermopylae.

'The trick of it will be making sure we have time to withdraw from one wall to the next in good order,' Cato continued. 'Good timing will be vital.'

'If anyone can handle that then the Guards can, sir. They're good soldiers.'

Cato shot him a sidelong glance. 'Good as the men of the Second Legion?'

'The men of the Second Legion aren't just anyone, sir.'

Cato laughed. 'Well said. And it might even be true.'

Long shadows stretched across the mining camp as the sun dipped towards the hills. It would be dark within the hour, Cato calculated. 'I'd better sort out the watch roster and passwords for the night. Your century will be on first watch, so get them off the work detail and get 'em fed. I'll see you later.'

'Yes, sir.' Macro saluted and marched off down the track while Cato made his way to the hall of the procurator's house that now served as the cohort's headquarters. In the normal run of things there would be a daily round of paperwork to deal with concerning strength returns, disciplinary issues, inventory reports, leave applications, promotional recommendations and the plethora of other matters requiring the attention of a cohort commander. Being on active service had the virtue of dispensing with some of those burdens at least. As he sat at his desk Cato sent for some food and watered wine, then bent to the task of setting out the watches for the coming night, as well as the password. He paused a moment, searching his mind for inspiration, and then inscribed a phrase on the waxed tablet, 'they shall not pass'. It seemed apposite, and would remind the men of their duty in the days to come. Then, as Metellus brought him a light meal of cured pork and bread, together with a goblet of wine, Cato set aside the tablet and stylus and ate hungrily. Replete, he made his way to one of the sleeping chambers that opened onto the garden. Night had fallen and the sky was cloudless and Cato paused on the threshold, looking up at the cold serenity of the stars.

There had been nights like this he had shared with Julia in Palmyra, a city under siege. Soon he would be under siege again, but this time there was no Julia to share the keen poignancy of being alive and in love in the face of imminent death. Instead his heart felt cold and his mind was preoccupied by the responsibilities and loneliness of command. He had made all the necessary preparations for the defence of the mine. He shared Macro's grudging confidence in the quality of the Praetorians and knew that they would acquit themselves well in the coming battle.

Cato entered the sleeping chamber, sat on the corner of his bed and untied and took off his boots, before flopping back onto the horsehair-stuffed bedroll. The aches in his muscles began to ebb away, replaced with a warm, weary glow that soon lulled him to sleep before he was aware of it. A moment later he was snoring. And that's how Macro found him after the signal for the first watch sounded over the mine. At first Macro was tempted to wake his friend, but there was nothing to report. All was quiet along the wall overlooking the ruined settlement. It was better to let the younger man rest, Macro reasoned. In the days to come, the cohort would need its commander on good form, sharp and responsive. The lives of the men would depend on Cato's unclouded judgement. So he left Cato to sleep and went to his own bed in the room shared by the other centurions. Those off duty were already asleep and their snores rumbled fitfully as they slept. Macro undressed in the darkness and eased himself down onto his bed. He folded his arms behind his head and for a while mused about the darkness of spirit that seemed to have overtaken his friend, caused by the loss of his wife. Thoughts began to slip and slide and blur into each other and then Macro too was asleep, adding his deep snores to the unrhythmic cacophony of the others.

'Sir! Wake up!'

Cato felt a hand shake his shoulder, gently at first, then more rigorously as he refused to stir. He blinked his eyes open and then wished he had not, as bright light pierced the room through the window overlooking the garden. Squinting, he made out the face of the surgeon, ashen and worried.

'What . . . What is it?'

'It's the patient, sir. Procurator Nepo.'

'What about him?'

'He's dead, sir. Stone-cold dead when I went to him just now.'

'Dead?' Cato sat up at once and swung his legs out of the bed. He was furious with himself for letting himself fall asleep without leaving instructions to be woken before dawn. He feared it would make him look weak and self-indulgent, and give the lie to the impression he always strove to create of being the kind of tough, cool-headed, ascetic officer that set the best example to the men that followed him. He rubbed his eyes.

'What happened?'

The surgeon shook his head. 'He was fine when I looked in on him last night. Sleeping peacefully. No reason to think there was any problem. And now . . .'

'Let's go.' Cato paced to the door barefoot and out into the corridor as he led the way to the procurator's sleeping chamber. The door was open and Cato saw one of the orderlies standing helplessly beside the bed. Nepo was lying on his back, one arm outstretched at his side while the other lay across his stomach. His eyes were open wide, staring up at the ceiling, as his mouth gaped open around a protruding tongue. Cato took this in, then leaned his ear to the procurator's mouth for a moment, but there was no breath on his lips. He pressed his ear to the chest, but there was no heartbeat. The skin was cool, the cold of a man several hours dead.

Cato stepped back. 'When did you last check on him?'

'An hour before midnight. Last thing on my rounds before I turned in, sir.'

'I see.' Cato looked to the orderly. 'Find Centurion Macro and bring him here at once.'

The man saluted and hurried from the room.

'What was the cause of death, in your opinion?' asked Cato. 'Did he die of his wounds?'

The surgeon rubbed his cheek. 'I don't see how, sir. He was much improved since we rescued him. I had set the limbs, dressed the cuts. There's no sign of bleeding. Not enough to kill him at least. He was not feverish. I did everything I could for him and I'd say he had every chance of a good recovery. Aside from the damage to his legs, that is. I can't see how anything I did contributed to his death, sir.'

'Easy there, I'm not blaming you. I just need to know your opinion on what might have caused his death.'

'Sometimes people die, despite my best efforts, sir. For no apparent reason at all. Their hearts just give out. After all, given what Nepo has been through, that wouldn't be beyond the bounds of possibility.'

Cato thought a moment and shook his head. 'I don't believe that. He was well enough when I spoke to him before. And I have every confidence in your care of your patients. So . . .'

The surgeon looked at him, chewed his lip for an instant. 'So, what are you suggesting, sir? That he was killed? Who would do such a thing?'

'Who indeed?' Cato sighed. The most obvious candidates would be those he had betrayed when he surrendered the mine to Iskerbeles. But they were all dead, save the procurator's three bodyguards. Pastericus had made no secret of his contempt for the procurator's action, but had given no sign of murderous intent.

'Sir? You sent for me.'

Cato looked round as Macro entered the chamber, already fully dressed and wearing his mail vest. Cato gestured towards the body and said simply, 'Nepo's dead.'

Macro strode over and looked over the corpse and then glanced at the surgeon. 'Nice work, friend.'

'Me?' The surgeon clutched a hand to his chest. 'No. But I had nothing to do with it, I swear.'

Macro rolled his eyes. 'Just a soldier's joke. Poor old Nepo,' he continued without feeling and then paused a moment to contemplate the body. 'Trusting the word of Iskerbeles did for him in the end after all, just like all the other poor bastards. Won't be many tears shed for him, I'll warrant.'

'Maybe not,' Cato agreed. 'But you're not addressing the obvious question.'

'All right, then. How did he die?'

'The surgeon can't explain it. Not yet.'

'Glad to see that the army is continuing its policy of recruiting the brightest and the best in the field of medicine.' Macro hunkered down beside the bed and examined the body. There were many bruises on Nepo's chest, arms and face, some quite livid in hues of yellow and purple. The procurator's head was pressed into the soft silk bolster and Macro eased it up so that his ears and neck were fully exposed. He took the man's chin, turned it firmly to the side and clicked his tongue. 'See there?'

He pointed to a cluster of red marks just visible beneath the bristles on Nepo's neck. Forcing the stiffening muscles of the neck the other way he revealed similar marks on the other side.

'What do you think?' asked Cato.

'Looks like someone throttled him.' Macro turned to the surgeon. 'I'm surprised you didn't see that.'

'But why would I?' asked the surgeon. 'Why would anyone want to kill one of my patients?'

'It doesn't matter,' Cato responded. 'There's nothing for you to do here now. Go and see to the wounded. Close the door behind you.'

The surgeon bowed his head and left the room. Once they were alone Cato went to the opposite side of the bed and crouched down for a better look at the marks. They were distinguishable enough and distributed as you would expect from Macro's conclusion. 'Strangled then.'

'Best way,' Macro mused. 'You might get away with it, given all the other bruises. A slit throat would give the game away. Strangling the man would be quick enough and quiet enough. It's what I'd have done.'

'And did you?' Cato raised a slight smile.

'Got better things to do than waste any effort on a spineless tosser like Nepo. And thank you very much for the slur on my good character.'

'Well, someone strangled him.'

Macro snorted. 'Ah, come on, Cato. Let's not beat about the bush. It's obvious. This is Pulcher's work.'

'Why Pulcher?'

'Because this is what he does. He's the one the bigger fish go to when they want someone dead. That's how it was back in Gaul, and I'll bet it's how it has been ever since. The Gods know how many people have died at his hand.'

'Macro, that's all supposition. We have no proof.'

'Trust me, Pulcher did this. If not him then who? Tell me that.'

Cato considered the notion. It did sound feasible. Pulcher may have been acting under the orders of someone else. Someone who wanted the procurator killed. Then again, it was possible that one of the men had stolen into the room in the hope of looting something valuable, and disturbed the procurator. But if so, it would have been dark and they would have fled without any chance of being identified. No, whoever had killed Nepo had done it very deliberately. For a reason. And maybe Macro was right that Pulcher had been put up to the job by someone. If so, who would want the procurator dead? And why?

Macro had been watching him, and pursuing his own line of thought. 'Pulcher was sent to kill him. That's why Pulcher has been with us all along. It's why he was chosen for this expedition. And who chose him? That snake Vitellius, that's who. Are you seriously suggesting there is no connection? So the question is, why would Vitellius want Nepo silenced?'

Cato thought a moment. 'What did he know that could be so important that he would be killed to prevent him speaking of it? He's been stuck in this mine, in the arse end of the province. Far from the seat of power in Rome . . . So it's likely to be something to do with the mine. But what?'

Macro gazed down at Nepo for a moment and shrugged. 'Beats me. But it has to be something to do with the silver. After all, what else is there in this Gods-forsaken hole?'

They were interrupted by a shout and the sound of boots running down the corridor outside the sleeping chamber. There was one knock before the door flew open and a breathless Praetorian entered and saluted quickly.

'What is the meaning of this?' Cato demanded, angered by the intrusion on their line of inquiry.

'Enemy in sight, sir . . . Just come from the observation post . . . The optio says to tell you that it's the rebel army.'

'Fuck, they're quick off the mark,' Macro muttered.

Cato was already making for the door. 'My respects to the optio. Tell him we're coming directly.'

'Yes, sir!' The Praetorian saluted, turned and dashed off along the corridor.

Cato ran back to his quarters and hurriedly put on his boots. He left word for Metellus to follow on with his armour and weapons and then left the procurator's house, running ahead of Macro as they made their way through to the slave quarters and the water tanks and observation tower beyond. The duty optio was standing on the small platform and squeezed to one side as the two officers climbed up the ladder to join him. There was no need for the optio to point out the enemy's location. A large cloud of dust marked their passage across the plain as they made for the mine. Tiny bands of men were visible on the edge of the cloud and sunlight glittered off weapons and armour so that it looked like the ripples of a distant river. Ahead of the enemy host rode a screen of horsemen, scouting ahead. Cato calculated that the nearest of them was no more than four miles away. The scouts would reach the mine within the hour, the rest of the army following up shortly after noon. Time was short.

'Optio, go back to headquarters. Tell the officers that the enemy will being investing the mine before the end of the day. I want our defences finished before then. Centurion Musa is to have his men start work on the final wall at once. Go.'

As the optio clambered down the ladder and ran back past the water tanks, Macro scrutinised the approaching enemy, trying to estimate their numbers. 'What do you think? Five, no . . . ten thousand?'

'Hard to say with all that dust. Could be more.' Cato watched them a moment longer before he turned to look to the east. 'I don't think we can pin our hopes on Vitellius reaching us any time soon. It's up to us, Macro. The Second Cohort is going to have to handle this by itself.'

Macro nodded and spat. 'Or die in the attempt.'

# CHAPTER TWENTY-FIVE

'What do you reckon they'll do first?' asked Macro.

Beside him, Cato was surveying the rebel army as it set up camp a quarter of a mile beyond the blackened remains of the settlement. Macro's earlier estimate of their strength was about right, he calculated. Over ten thousand, many of whom were women and children camp followers on closer inspection. Still, they considerably outnumbered the Praetorians and they would be inspired by the success of their rebellion. Morale would be high, and the fear of the consequences of defeat was sufficient to motivate their desire to fight even more fanatically. There was no urgency in their actions as they set about making camp. They divided into clusters of wagons, carts and shelters and Cato guessed that these represented different tribal groupings. The heart of the camp was dominated by a collection of Roman military tents, no doubt looted from the stores of an outpost overrun by the rebels. The tents were set up in a square around an open patch of ground at the centre of which was the largest of them, the headquarters of Iskerbeles.

Cato cleared his throat. 'I dare say he will try to make the same offer to us that he made to Nepo. Only this time I'm afraid we will have to disappoint him.'

Macro laughed. 'Too fucking right we will. The lads are spoiling for a fight.'

Cato looked both ways along the wall. To the right, the men of Macro's century stood shoulder to shoulder, shields and spears grounded. There was no sign of nerves in their expressions. The Second Century stood ready to the left, while Petillius' and Musa's men stood in reserve a short distance behind the wall, either side of the colour party where the cohort's standard rose into the still air. Behind them Porcino's century defended the wall, with Pulcher in command of Placinus's half century acting as their reserve. Cato felt confident about his preparations and turned back to continue his inspection of the enemy.

'There's no sign of siege weapons of any kind,' said Macro.

'No surprises there. There hasn't been much call for them in Hispania for nigh on a hundred years. They'll have to start from scratch. Anything that takes up time is to our advantage. We've got food for twenty days and plenty of water. More than enough to last out until the legate arrives.'

'Never thought I'd witness the day when I looked forward to seeing Vitellius again.'

Both men were silent for a moment before Macro continued. 'I wonder if he has anything to do with Nepo's death?'

'If he does, then he's got a pretty long reach.'

'That's not so unlikely, sir. Remember, even at the arse end of Britannia we were still touched by the political infighting back in Rome. I'm telling you, that spat between Narcissus and Pallas may see the end of us yet.' Macro picked at his teeth for a moment. 'Which is why we have to be wary of Pulcher.'

'We've been over that,' Cato responded testily. 'He's given no cause for us to suspect him of anything sinister while we've been with the cohort.'

'Except now that Nepo's dead. Someone murdered the procurator. And I'd bet my life on it being Pulcher.'

'I will look into Nepo's death the moment I get the chance. Right now we both have more pressing concerns. Look there.' Cato raised his hand and pointed out a horseman picking his way through the ruins towards the gate. The rider stopped as he reached the edge of the settlement and raised a horn to blow three loud notes, then continued towards the wall.

'So Iskerbeles wants to talk,' said Macro. 'If he thinks he can pull the same trick twice then he must think we're as thick as cold porridge. Give the word, sir, and I'll have one of our men take him down as soon as he gets within easy range.'

'No. We'll hear what he says. Anything to buy time, Macro.

That's the nature of the game we need to play with the rebels.'

'As you wish, sir.'

The herald emerged from the settlement, stopped fifty paces from the gate and sounded his horn again, then flicked his reins. He had advanced no more than a few steps before Cato cupped his hands to his mouth and shouted, 'Stop there!'

The herald slowed and then came on again.

'Stop there, I said! Or I will have you cut down!'

This time the herald reined in and came no closer. He looked haughtily at the faces lining the rampart of the wall and then pointed to the officers on the gatehouse.

'You, Romans! Iskerbeles sends word that he wishes to speak with the officer in command at the mine.'

The man's Latin was fluent. He was tall and well built with a leather cuirass. His dark locks were tied back from his forehead with a broad leather thong.

'I am the commander,' Cato called back. 'Tell your leader to come forward in person if he wishes to parley with me.'

'He says that you should come to him. He offers you safe passage through his lines.'

'I think not. I have learned what happens to those who trust Iskerbeles' word. You tell him that if he wishes to speak then he comes to the gatehouse. I will speak to him down there.' Cato pointed at the dead ground between the outer ditch and the edge of the settlement.

'And why should Iskerbeles trust your word, Roman?'

'Because I am a Roman,' Cato responded simply. 'A Roman soldier, and officer. And my word is good enough for any man, even your Iskerbeles.'

The rebel herald laughed. 'Very well, I shall take your message to my leader.'

He tugged on his reins and wheeled his mount back before trotting off through the ruins. Macro nodded with satisfaction. 'Well said, sir. Those rebel bastards need to be taught the meaning of honour.'

Cato watched the rebel ride back to the edge of the enemy camp and confer with a small group of riders waiting there. Presently a handful galloped off into the heart of the camp. A while later, in the heat of the mid-afternoon sun, a column of fifty or so men set out from the camp, followed by the group of riders. As they approached, Macro exchanged a questioning glance with Cato.

'I wonder what he's up to. Unless he likes to conduct all his conversations mob-handed.'

'That's his personal bodyguard, perhaps,' Cato suggested. 'If he's that concerned for his own safety then maybe there's division amongst his followers. That's something we might play on if we get the chance.'

The column wound its way through the ruins and as it drew closer Cato and Macro could see that only the men at the front and the rear were armed. Those in between, thirty of them, wore rags and were in chains.

'What's his game?' asked Macro.

Cato shook his head. At the same time he felt a chill in his spine as he considered the fate of the prisoners being forced along by their escorts. Did Iskerbeles intend to use them to prove his ruthlessness somehow? An object lesson to demonstrate that the enemies of the rebels could expect no mercy?

As the armed men at the head of the column reached the edge of the ruins they steered the prisoners to the front in an extended line and forced them towards the gatehouse at spear point, stopping no more than ten paces from the drawbridge over the outer ditch. The herald and another man reined in and dismounted. The herald's companion was even larger in physique and wore a scale armour vest and a centurion's helmet, with long red feathers in place of the original owner's horsehair crest. They strode towards the line of prisoners serving as a human shield and stopped just behind them as the herald called up to Cato.

'Iskerbeles has done as you requested. Now he requests that you come down from your tower and discuss terms.'

'Terms?' Macro said quietly. 'Surrender, he means.'

'I imagine so. But let's hear him out. Come, Macro.'

They descended the ladder and Cato beckoned to Musa. The centurion came over. 'Sir?'

'I want four sections from your century in close formation behind the gate, in case the enemy tries to rush it. And send Cimber to me. As you heard, Macro and I are going out to negotiate with the rebels. If there's any trouble, I don't want any heroics. You get the gate shut as swiftly as possible.'

'Yes, sir.'

'Right, let's go and see what the bastards want.' Cato led the way under the tower to the gates and Macro helped him slide the locking bar far enough to permit the right gate to open. They waited until Musa and his men were formed up just behind them and Cimber had joined them.

'I need you to listen, Cimber. Say nothing and show no reaction to anything you hear. Is that clear?'

'Yes, sir.'

'Good.' Cato took a deep breath. 'Here we go.'

He pulled the gate inward, just wide enough to let a man pass through the gap, then stepped out of the shade beneath the gatehouse and into the bright afternoon sunlight. With Macro at his side, and Cimber two paces behind, he slowly approached the line of prisoners and they shuffled aside with a dull clink of chains. Some gut feeling caused Cato to stop a half stride outside the gap as the rebel leader and his herald stood waiting for them.

'That's as far as we come,' Cato announced. 'Just in case you were thinking of trying to trap us.'

The herald affected a hurt expression as he grasped the accusation. 'Roman, these men are prisoners. They merely serve as a living shield, in case your men on the wall attempt to use javelin, sling or arrow against us. I see you suspect them of not being what they seem. Here, let me prove my good faith.' The herald drew a dagger from his belt and took a few steps forward to close on one of the haggard men in chains.

'Careful, lad,' Macro hissed as the fingers of his right hand curled round the handle of his short sword. 'Be ready to run for it.'

Cato nodded discreetly. 'On my word – if we need to.'

The herald drew his arm back and savagely drove the blade in between the shoulder blades of the prisoner. The man's head snapped back and his jaw sagged open as the air was driven from his lungs by the impact. He coughed violently and flecks of blood sprayed into the air, before he slipped onto his knees, gasping. He fought for breath and steadily sagged forward, gasping as blood filled his mouth and he tried to clear his throat.

The herald looked down, expressionless. 'See? If this man meant anything to me I would not have done that. But he is an enemy, a Roman, and therefore he means nothing. I would kill him as easily as I would kill any other vermin. So, as you can see, this is no trap. But if you attempt to harm me or my comrades before we have retired beyond bowshot then your countrymen will be the first to die. Do you understand, Roman?'

'Yes.' Cato refused to look at the dying man. His voice was cold and calm as he replied. 'I understand that you are pitiless barbarian criminals. You cannot defy Rome. In the end you will be subjected to our justice.'

'We are fighting *for* justice. We are not criminals,' the herald corrected him. 'Fighting for freedom from the Romans who enslaved us and treated us like dogs.'

'What is your purpose here?' asked Cato. 'Ask your master to speak his mind.'

The herald wiped the blood from his dagger with the hair of the man he had just stabbed and then kicked him in the back, sending him sprawling on the ground. The prisoner lay on his side, groaning softly as blood pumped from his wound and frothed his lips and beard.

'My master?' He cocked his head to one side with an amused look. 'How typical of a Roman. I choose to serve my cause. No man is my master.'

Cato gestured towards the figure with the feathered helmet who had been standing in silence, watching the exchange imperiously. 'I would discuss matters with Iskerbeles, not his mouthpiece.'

The herald smiled. 'You are discussing matters with Iskerbeles . . .'

Cato pressed his lips into a thin line, contemptuous of himself for making assumptions too easily. A man who could be taken in by so simple a ploy was a danger to himself, and worse, to those he led. The rebel leader was watching him closely, trying to follow his thoughts.

'A small deceit, just in case you were considering having your

261

men try to do me some mischief as we approached. But since you have shown the backbone to come out from the shelter of the wall I can dispense with the deception. I am Iskerbeles, leader of the rebellion. And you are?'

'My name is not yours to demand, rebel. I am the prefect in command of the Second Praetorian Cohort. And I have enough backbone for both of us. What is that you have to say to me?'

'Ah, the usual Roman combination of directness, and arrogance. Very well, to the point. I demand that you give up the mine and that your cohort surrenders. If you do as I say, then I will spare the lives of you and your men.'

'Spare us? Like you spared the mine's garrison? Like you treated Nepo?'

'That was different. Nepo was procurator in charge of the mine. I take it you have seen the conditions within the mine. It is a place no man should have to endure. How many thousands of my people have been enslaved and taken there to die? At the hands of the procurator and his men. They forfeited their right to mercy long ago. You and your men are soldiers. Doing your duty. I understand that. Which is why I am prepared to let you leave the mine in peace, and return to Tarraco.'

'With our weapons?'

Iskerbeles shook his head. 'I need your weapons and armour for my followers. You have my word that you and your men will have free passage, under my protection, as far as Clunia.'

'I see.'

'Your word?' Macro laughed harshly. 'Your word is shit.'

'Macro . . .' Cato growled as he turned to glare at him.

'I see your centurion lacks trust. A pity. Then let him trust me when I say this. The choice is that you surrender, or be annihilated, and those who are foolish enough to be taken alive will die slowly, in great pain.'

'*Pffffit* . . .' Macro sniffed.

Cato paused, as if in thought, and then responded. 'Even if I did decide to surrender, I could not accept those terms. My men and I will retain our arms. I would not hand those over to you under any circumstances.'

'You are in no position to make such demands, Prefect.'

'I think I have a rather stronger bargaining position than you realise. I have an entire cohort of the best troops to be found anywhere in the empire. Our defences are formidable, whereas you have a rabble and no siege engines. I have food and water to last me months. Why would I even contemplate surrendering?' Cato hardened his tone as he continued. 'So here are my terms, Iskerbeles. You and your followers will surrender to me. Except for you and your lieutenants, I will permit the rest to return to their villages. To them I give my word that there will be no repercussions. All those who were slaves will be returned to their masters. I give you until dawn tomorrow to give me your answer. After that, I cannot guarantee that any of those who are foolish enough to follow you will be spared.'

The rebel leader looked at Cato as if he were mad. 'Your bravado is misplaced, Prefect. However, I am a chief of the Astures. Our tribe is a proud tribe, and our men are the finest warriors in all Hispania. We admire bravery, so I am prepared to let you leave with your arms. You may take nothing else from the mine. Including the procurator, assuming he still lives.'

Cato did his best to keep his expression neutral. 'Why would you want me to leave Nepo behind?'

'Because the man has blood on his hands,' Iskerbeles replied quickly. 'Thousands of slaves have perished since he was appointed to run the mine. Many of those who fight with me now were freed from Argentium. They want his head.'

'Then why did you not give them what they wanted when you took the mine in the first place, I wonder?'

The rebel leader's eyes narrowed a fraction. 'He would have been worth something if we could ransom him. Now I have sufficient loot that I no longer need such a ransom. So I will present him to his former slaves, and let them take their revenge.'

'First, you will have to fight your way past me and my men,' Cato responded firmly.

They stared at each other for a moment before Iskerbeles spoke. 'I said I admire bravery, Prefect. However, I despise stupidity. You know you cannot hold this mine. So, out of my regard for your courage, I will give you until dawn to consider *my* terms. Choose wisely.'

He turned abruptly and his huge lieutenant fell into step at his side. They talked in low voices as they strode to their horses, mounted and trotted back towards the rebel camp. The armed men drove the prisoners back into a column and withdrew from the gatehouse. Cato waited until he was sure they were out of earshot before he spoke softly to Macro.

'He must know about the bullion. He's been told, or worked it out for himself. That's why he wants Nepo. To finish beating the truth out of him.'

'Then he's left it too late.'

'Yes, but he doesn't know that. And he'll do all that he can to take the mine, and get Nepo to tell him where the bullion is hidden. Which serves our purpose nicely.'

Macro raised his eyebrows. 'It does?'

'Of course. While the rebels are busy trying to recapture the mine, they aren't spreading their rebellion. And they're giving Vitellius time to reach us. We've got him where we want him.'

'Funny. It feels like it's the other way round.'

Cato grinned. 'I thought I was supposed to be the "amphora half-empty" one? Come on, I'll be happier once we have the gates between us and the rebels.'

As they made to cross the bridge over the ditch Cimber cleared his throat. 'Sir . . .'

'What is it?'

'Something I overheard when Iskerbeles and his friend were walking back to their horses.'

'Well?'

'I only caught a few words, sir. The larger one asked something and Iskerbeles said, "They'll find out soon enough tonight."'

Cato took a deep breath and nodded as he glanced back towards the rebel leader riding away. 'Very well then, tonight it is, my friend. Do your worst. We'll be waiting.'

# CHAPTER TWENTY-SIX

'Can't say I'm very impressed by our friend's sense of honour,' Macro grumbled as he and Cato stood on the tower over the gatehouse. 'Says he's going to give us until morning to consider the offer, only to go and try and shaft us while we're thinking it over . . . Any Greek blood in him, d'you think?'

Cato smiled. 'Maybe. And if the Gods will it then we'll find out what his blood is made of soon enough.'

'Or he'll find out what's in our blood.'

'Hmmm,' Cato responded rather than replied.

As a result of Cimber's warning Cato had given orders for the entire cohort to be ready to repulse any attack that night. Ten men stood on the wall, in clear view of their enemy, while their comrades sat out of sight behind the parapet. Two centuries were on the wall, while the remaining men formed the reserve at the foot of the ramp. The prefect had given strict orders not to make a noise and the men sat or lay on the ground. The veterans took the chance to rest, or even sleep, while their less experienced comrades stared into the mid distance, or fiddled with straps or parts of their kit, trying to find some form of comfort or distraction while they awaited the attack. Stocks of kindling had been bound in old rags soaked in oil and these makeshift faggots were arranged in piles along the wall. Braziers were placed at a safe distance between the faggots and the flames kept as low as possible so as not to provide any illumination that might betray the presence of the men behind the wall and rampart. The sharp tang of heated pitch hung over the gatehouse from the pot simmering away above another small brazier at the rear of the tower.

'Shame there're no caltrops to be had,' Macro mused. 'Nothing like caltrops for delivering a nasty surprise for anyone making a night attack.'

'We're as ready as we could be.' Cato stood with a straight back, trying to exude a reassuring calmness in front of the other men in the tower. At the same time his hand was rhythmically closing and opening around his sword handle and he frowned as soon as he was aware of the movement, forcing his hand to drop to his side. Despite the quality of the men he commanded, there were some aspects of the Praetorians' equipment that disadvantaged them in such a situation. Whereas the legions carried javelins and fought with short swords, the Praetorians were armed with spears in addition to their swords. Heavier than javelins and not so well designed for piercing shields and skewering the men behind, the spears were only useful for when the enemy closed in. What stocks of javelins, bows and other weapons the garrison of the mine might have possessed had been cleaned out by the rebels. A few men had slings of their own, used for hunting, and the only other missiles that could be deployed were the small heaps of stones and rocks along the rampart. There was going to be little to prevent the enemy from getting close to the wall before they suffered any casualties.

'Must be the sixth hour of the night by now,' said Macro. 'If those bastards leave it much longer it'll be dawn before they get anywhere near the walls.'

Cato looked at him by the very faint light of the stars and a sliver of the moon that looked like an incision in the firmament. 'If I didn't know any better I'd say you were a little nervous.'

'Fuck that,' Macro whispered irritably. 'I'm just impatient. Sooner they try to rush us the better as far as I'm concerned. I need to get stuck in.'

From almost any other man Cato would have regarded the remark as an overconfident boast. But Macro meant it, and his eyes and ears strained for the first indication of the enemy's approach. The rebels seemed to be in no hurry. As night had fallen their camp had resounded with snatches of song and cheers as some of the men wrestled or boxed, surrounded by dense circles of their peers. It was only as the fires began to die out that the sounds began to diminish and the hiss of cicadas took over.

'There!' Cato risked leaning a little over the parapet, his head turned towards the sound his keen ears had detected: the faint susurration of bare feet through the ashes of the town. Sure enough, a moment later he fancied he could see dark shapes flitting from cover to cover amid the ruins. He waited a moment longer to be certain, rather than risk the humiliation of jumping at shadows in front of his men. Then he turned to one of the soldiers at the rear of the tower, his face just visible in the wan flame of a small oil lamp burning in an iron bracket nailed to the corner post.

'Make the signal.'

The Praetorian snatched up the torch lying at his feet and offered it up to the small flame. The oil-soaked rags wrapped round the head of the torch caught fire readily. As soon as the flame flared the Praetorian leaned over the rail at the rear of the tower and held the torch out as he moved it from side to side. At once the centurions and optios moved down the lines of their centuries, shaking, kicking and prodding the men into life. Others began to stoke up the fires in the braziers and add more fuel, sending small swirls of sparks into the dark air. The men concealed behind the parapet took up their weapons and prepared to defend the rampart.

Cato and Macro were still listening hard when a voice cried out in the night and the sound of feet became a rush, and running figures abruptly emerged from the darkness, as if rising up from the ground. All along the wall they surged forward, clasping their weapons tightly.

'Here they come!' Cato called out. 'Cornicen, sound the alarm!'

He exchanged a brief nod with Macro before the latter hurried down the ladder to join his men.

The trumpeter pursed his lips, puffed his cheeks and blew hard into the mouthpiece. A flat note blasted from the horn and echoed off the cliff above. At once, the men concealed behind the parapet leaned their spears on the walkway as they stood up, raising their shields and holding rocks ready to hurl at the oncoming rebels. Those armed with slings were given space on either side and whirled their weapons before throwing their arms forward and releasing their shot into the massed ranks surging out of the night. It was impossible to see the fall of shot, or indeed whether they struck an enemy, but it was hard for Cato to believe it was possible to miss a target amid the seething horde rushing towards him.

'Get the faggots over!' Cato called down to the Praetorians behind the wall. Men impaled the bundles on the tips of their spears and ignited them over the braziers before carrying them up to the top of the wall. Then, swinging them back, they bunched their muscles and flung the blazing faggots up and over the wall. Inscribing a brief fiery arc across the ditch they plunged down, bursting on the ground, and across the heads and shoulders of the nearest attackers as they illuminated the scene along the front of the wall. The red glare highlighted the rebels, their mix of weapons and armour, their wild expressions of battle rage and the bewildered terror of those swept up in their first action.

Cato cupped his hands to his mouth. 'Rocks!'

An instant later the defenders were hurling them down at the rebels. Some fell harmlessly, while others cracked off shields and deflected off helmets, but the rest struck home, tearing flesh, cracking bones or simply delivering numbing or stunning blows to the enemy. Those that fell simply disappeared in the flow of bodies rushing towards the wall. Now Cato could see the ladders carried with them.

The arrows and slingshot of the rebels were upon the defenders before they realised it. Splinters flew off the rail close to Cato's hand and he felt the impact of the lead shot as it glanced off his shoulder over his head. Others were not so lucky and the first Praetorian casualties tumbled back from the wall, some with arrow shafts protruding from and through their arms and necks. The air was filled with the crack of impacts and the whirr of missiles whipping past the heads of the defenders to fall some distance behind the wall.

'Shields!' Cato called out. 'Shields up!'

He hefted his own, covering his chest and as much of his face as he could without obscuring his overview of the fight. Around him and along the wall the Praetorians held their oval shields higher as they continued to bombard the enemy with rocks. As the furious exchange of shot continued the rebels swarmed over the lip of the outer ditch and scrambled down the slope towards the obstacles planted at the bottom of the incline. Stretches of the ditch were illuminated by faggots that had fallen short and now provided enough light for attackers to pick their way through the sharpened stakes. Others were not so fortunate and blundered onto them, or were impaled as they were pushed forward from behind. The rebels pressed on, wrestling the obstacles free and throwing them down before they reached the steeper slope at the foot of the rampart. There were more obstacles in their way now. Sharpened stakes driven into the rampart with the points angled down so as to make them impossible to use for climbing the wall. The ladder carriers reached the ditch and began to raise their burdens up before letting the tops fall against the wall. At once men scurried up, working their way round the sharpened stakes protruding between the rungs, then readying their shields as they neared the top of the wall where the Romans were waiting.

The rattle of slingshot and arrows ceased as the rebels could no longer continue for fear of hitting their own men. Despite the cessation of the missile barrage Cato kept his shield raised as he watched the progress of the assault from the top of the gatehouse. Now was the time for the Praetorians to take advantage of the reach their spears afforded them. Leaning between the battlements the men on the wall thrust down at their enemies climbing to the top of the ladders.

Macro took his shield and spear from his optio and edged in between two of his men just in front of the century's standard bearer. The wall had been built primarily to keep brigands out of the mine, and prevent slaves attempting to escape, and the battlements were lower and more widely spaced than they would have been on an army fort. No doubt the contractor had built it this way to save on costs and bump up his profit margin. As a result Macro and the other soldiers would be exposed to more risk. Three of his men had already been downed, two struck in the face by slingshot, one of whom was dead, while the third had taken an arrow just below his throat. All three were already laid out at the foot of the rampart where the surgeon and his orderlies were attending to their wounds of the living as best they could.

'You know the score, boys!' Macro yelled as loudly as he could. 'Don't let any of the bastards set foot on our wall!'

Some of the men had time to answer with a cheer before the first of the ladders rose up and clattered against the battlements. The Praetorians raised their spears and angled the tips down as the rebels scrambled up towards them. There was a sharp rap of wood on masonry close by and Macro's head snapped to the right. The stiles of a ladder projected a short distance above the battlement and were already trembling as the first rebels scaled the rungs. Macro leaned his shield against the wall and thrust his spear at the man to his left. 'Hold this!'

Then he grasped the stiles and pushed at them, but the angle and weight were too great to send it back. Instead Macro wrenched the top of the ladder to the side as he looked down to see the panicked expression of a rebel six feet below. The momentum was just sufficient to carry the ladder over and it crashed to the side, taking two men down with it as they tumbled onto their comrades and swept them into the bottom of the ditch.

'Ha!' Macro snarled with satisfaction as he took up his shield and spear again. A glance to either side revealed that his men were managing to throw back some of the ladders and dealing with those rebels who were scaling the remaining ladders. A few feet away one of the Praetorians stabbed down into the bare shoulder of a young warrior and the man flung out his arm and arced his back, lost his grip and fell back into the ditch. The next man on the ladder did not hesitate to climb the rungs to replace his downed comrade. Closer to the battlement he raised a shield over his head and the Praetorian stabbed at it without effect.

Macro pushed along the wall and taking a firm grip on the shaft of the spear he thrust at an angle beneath the shield into the rebel's armpit, feeling the momentary jarring as a rib gave way and the point tore into the man's lung. Macro pulled the spear free with a gush of blood and, by the light of a faggot blazing just below, saw his foe's face twisted in agony. But he forced himself up the last few rungs and thrust himself over the battlement, tumbling onto the walkway, knocking down the Praetorian who had stood in his path. The soldiers on either side stabbed him several times as he tried to regain his feet, then tossed him down the rampart behind the wall where one of the reserves finished him off. A quick glance revealed shadowy figures, highlighted in red by the glare of the faggots, fighting along the wall, but none of the enemy had yet crossed it. Romans and rebels traded blows in an unequal struggle as the former had all the advantages of the high ground and cover to fight from. Bodies dropped regularly from the ladders, flattening their comrades or hitting the ground directly and rolling down into the ditch. There were a handful of Roman casualties, caught by a weapon or hit by rocks thrown from below. But Macro was content that the fight was going their way. The wall would be held and the spirit of the enemy would waver, and then they would fall back. More than likely that would be the only action of the night.

'Keep those bastards back, lads!'

Then he noticed a group of men moving in unison emerge from the dark mass of the ruins, working their way through their comrades as they approached the gatehouse. A moment later he made out the long dark length of the reinforced post that they were carrying. Forcing his way along the rear of the walkway, Macro leaned his spear against his shoulder and cupped a hand to his mouth.

'Prefect Cato!'

He called out twice before one of the men in the tower heard him and drew Cato's attention. As soon as Cato appeared Macro thrust his hand in the direction of the rapidly approaching danger.

'They've got a ram!'

Cato dashed back across to the front of the tower and quickly picked the group of men out, still some fifty feet from the gates.

'Sir!' Metellus shouted at him. 'Keep your bloody head down!'

It took a brief instant before Cato reacted to the warning, and the rim of his shield was rising as an arrow struck the trim and shattered in front of his face. He felt a sharp, burning sensation in his left eye and tried to blink as he instinctively recoiled and stumbled back from the battlements. His eyelid caught on something protruding from the socket. Cato reached up a hand and lightly traced his fingers up his cheek until they touched blood and grazed a splinter, two inches or so in length. At once his eyeball exploded in intense pain and he clenched his teeth and groaned deep in his throat. Then he recalled the ram and dropped his hand as he spun round.

'Get the pitch over to the front of the tower! You two. Now.'

The Praetorians set down their shields and spears and picked up the wooden handles on the iron bars either side of the gently bubbling cauldron. When both were ready they heaved it off the brazier and carefully paced across the tower as Cato and the others kept out of the way in case they stumbled and the heated pitch was spilled, causing terrible injuries to those nearby. Almost blinded by pain, Cato took shelter behind his shield as he returned to the front of the tower. Since there was no attempt to scale the gate-house it was the only target the rebels could aim for without hitting their comrades, and they now turned their attention on it with a vengeance as the men carrying the ram reached the bridge across the ditch and made for the gate.

Cato thrust his hand towards the men carrying the pitch. 'Get some cover over them! Now!'

With shields angled high the soldiers held them sideways to make the most of the shelter as the group took up position by the front of the tower. Cato risked a glance over the battlement as a slingshot crashed off the rounded iron hand guard. Twenty feet below, the men holding the ram were foreshortened and now he could see that all of them were wearing Roman helmets and armour. At the side of the ram was a large warrior urging his comrades on. He looked up just then and met Cato's gaze and gave a harsh shout in his own tongue. Cato recognised him as the man who had stood with Iskerbeles earlier. Then the pain from the splinter struck again, like a red-hot pin thrust into his eye. Each blink only seemed to make the pain worse and he felt light-headed.

'No!' he hissed to himself, fighting the urge to faint. Not now. Not when his men needed him. Growling with anger and agony, Cato snatched a spear from the nearest Praetorian and raised it swiftly, taking aim at the warrior. He hurled it down with all his strength and it flew true. But the warrior's reactions were just as swift and he threw himself against the side of the gate and the point of the spear bit deep into the thick planks of the bridge and quivered there. Cato stepped smartly back into the shelter of the battlements as two arrows flashed through the gap.

'Get ready to pour the pitch, on my order!'

The two Praetorians hunkered down next to the wall as their comrades continued to provide cover with their shields. Then the tower trembled under Cato's boots. There was a short pause and again the impact and this time Cato heard the thud of the ram against the gates. It was time to act. He bit back on the torment from his wound and forced his mind to think clearly. Drawing a deep breath he pointed to the men carrying the pitch.

'Make ready.'

They bunched their muscles and braced their boots as they prepared to take the strain.

'The rest of you, listen. As soon as the pitch is over, you rise up and you use your spears, rocks, whatever you can on the rest of the men on the ram. Kill 'em all. You hear?'

There were some nods. Some faces were in darkness but Cato sensed their readiness to act. He braced his shield, looked over and saw the Asturian warrior slowly swinging his arm and calling off the rhythm. Then the ram swung forward again, crashing against the gate timbers.

'Now!'

The Praetorians rose swiftly to their feet, continuing the upward and outward movement of the small cauldron with their arms and then at full stretch they dropped the handle nearest the battlement and the thick smoking liquid gushed down towards the men on the bridge. Cato did not see it hit them but every man for fifty paces on either side heard the shrieks that pierced even the din of the battle. The front of the ram dropped and those at the back kept hold as their burned comrades staggered back screaming in agony. There was no respite for the injured as the Praetorians hurled their spears down and followed up with rocks. Two men went down, pierced by spears, another was struck on the head with a rock and fell senseless onto the bridge. More were injured by further rocks and those at the rear of the ram released their grip and turned to flee.

Their leader had been untouched by the boiling pitch and roared at them in frustration, running back across the bridge to try and drag more men forward. But the missiles from the tower undermined their courage. Even so, such was their fear of him that he soon gathered a group about him and began to force his way back to the ram. Below the tower the front of the ram and the bridge were splashed with the steaming fluid.

Casting his shield aside, Cato ran to the brazier used to heat the pitch and tore off his neck scarf. He wrapped the material around the base of the brazier and lifted it off the boards. Taking care not to let it tilt he paced steadily towards the front of the tower and tipped it over the battlement. The coals flared bright orange and white as they fell and landed across the front of the ram. Flames licked up from the pitch, spreading rapidly over the ram and across the bridge. One of the wounded, writhing on the boards, caught fire, the fibres of his clothing, drenched in the scalding pitch, going up in flames. He struggled to his feet and with an inhuman wailing howl ran from the gates, across the bridge, like some figure from a terrible nightmare, arms flailing as he blazed a path through his comrades and into the ruins.

The impetus of the assault died away as all eyes were drawn to the fire on the bridge and no fresh rebels were prepared to climb the ladders. Fear flowed through their ranks and almost as one, they began to fall back, climbing out of the ditch and retreating past the still-blazing faggots, and then on into the shadows and darkness, leaving the bodies of the dead and wounded strewn along the ditch in front of the wall. One of the Praetorians jeered and his comrades joined in and hurled contemptuous insults at the rebels. Until a stream of arrows and slingshot resumed, sending the Praetorians ducking behind the cover of the battlements.

Once Cato was certain that the attack was over, he staggered back to the rear of the tower and gestured to Metellus. 'Keep a good watch. They might try again later. Though I doubt it.'

'Yes, sir.' There was no mistaking the concern in the optio's expression. 'Shall I fetch the surgeon, sir?'

'No. I can manage.'

Cato steeled himself for the climb down the ladder and then

walked as steadily as he could to the field dressing station the surgeon had set up a short distance behind the gate.

'Sir!'

He turned to see Macro striding from the bottom of the rampart, a wide grin on his face.

'Did you see 'em run? Like bloody sheep with a wolf at their backs, they were!' Then, as he caught sight of Cato's face in the light of the nearest brazier, Macro's step faltered. 'Oh . . . fuck.'

'That good, eh?' Cato forced a smile. 'Seems like I ain't going to be famed for my good looks when we get back to Rome. Walk with me, Macro.'

As they made their way towards the surgeon Cato did his best to hide his pain. 'I have to get this seen to. Take command for now. Keep the enemy back from the walls, and get the fire out, before it spreads to the gatehouse. Then report the casualty list to me. Clear?'

'Yes, sir.'

Macro hesitated, and Cato clapped him on the back. 'I'll be fine. Not the first time I've had something annoying in my eye. You've got your orders, Centurion.'

Macro nodded and turned away towards the gatehouse, calling for Petillius and his men to form up to fight the fire.

Cato continued towards the dressing station and waited until the surgeon had finished extracting an arrow from a Praetorian's arm. He handed over to one of his orderlies, wiped the blood from his hands on a strip of linen and turned towards Cato.

'And what have we . . . Oh, it's you, sir.' He expertly looked over Cato's limbs before his gaze returned to the prefect's face. 'What? Ah, I see now. Over here, where the light is better.'

He led Cato to a brazier and sat him down on a stool before he leaned forward and inspected the injury closely.

'Nasty . . . very nasty. Does it hurt?'

Cato sighed. 'What do you think? Just get it out and patch me up.'

The surgeon tilted his head to the side. 'It's going to hurt, sir. I'll do my best not to do any more damage.' He turned to the instruments spread out across a trestle table and selected a pair of brass pincers and a scalpel. He used his fingers to gently position Cato's head so as much light fell on the wound as possible, then reached forward with the pincers.

'Keep still and look straight ahead. You ready, sir?'

'As ready as I'll ever be.'

'Then let's start . . .'

# CHAPTER TWENTY-SEVEN

'How's the eye, sir?' asked Macro as he entered the procurator's office. The late Nepo's flamboyant taste was as evident here as elsewhere in the house. The desk was constructed from polished walnut and the chair behind it was comfortably upholstered. A scroll case lined most of one wall and the others were painted to give the impression of looking out over luxuriant Campanian countryside with Vesuvius towering in the background. Given the actual surroundings of the house, this was a much-needed relief from the harsh spectacle of the mine workings and the camp that loomed above.

After the splinter had been extracted and the wound dressed Cato had ignored the surgeon's advice to rest until he had assessed the damage done by the burning pitch to the front of the gatehouse and the bridge. Some of the timbers had suffered superficial charring but there was no visible structural damage. The ram was dragged inside the wall and sawn into four lengths that were used to brace the interior of the gates. Cato returned to the tower and kept the men on the wall until dawn when there was enough light to see that the enemy was not lurking amid the ruins, ready to spring another assault on the wall. Only then had Cato handed command over to Macro in order to lie down for a few hours and rest his eye. He had left orders that he should be woken at the fourth hour, but the pain in his eye socket had made sleep impossible and he had given up after lying restlessly for a while and made his way to the office and sent for food and wine, the latter in the hope that it might dull the edge of the searing pain in his eye.

'It's fine, thank you,' Cato replied. 'Any movement from the enemy?'

'Not much. Just some small parties retrieving the wounded. I let 'em get on with it. Didn't seem worth the risk to send any men out to harass them.'

'Quite right.' Cato nodded. 'Nothing else?'

Macro thought a moment. 'Not that I saw. They've sent forage parties out, and a few patrols. There's one scouting along the far side of the ravine, but I've got a section of our lads shadowing them. If they discover anything useful, then so will we and block any chances they might have to try and take us unawares.' Macro paused, a concerned expression on his face as he looked at the dressing that was tied around Cato's head and covered the linen wad the surgeon had applied after the splinter had been removed and the wound cleaned. 'What did the surgeon say about the eye? Any permanent damage?'

Cato recalled looking at the bloody sliver of wood in the surgeon's fingers some hours before. The extraction had been more agonising than anything he had previously experienced in his entire life. He had nearly passed out as he felt the slight pop as the end came out of the eyeball, and then again as it was drawn out of the bruised and swollen fold of skin below the eye. Almost as painful was the sharp burn of the vinegar the surgeon had used to clean the wound, and douse the dressing. The swelling had all but closed the eye, and through the small slit that remained everything was grey and blurry. After that it had been covered up by the dressing and bandage.

'The surgeon said it should heal. Once the swelling goes down, he'll have a better idea. In the meantime, I'm supposed to rest it as much as possible. Somehow, I suspect that Iskerbeles will not be so indulging as the surgeon might wish.'

'Not much hope of that.' Macro grinned briefly. 'Typical . . . Bloody surgeon must think we're still back in Rome and his patients can just take a few days off to recover.'

'I suspect he has been disabused of that prospect by the events of last night. Have you got the butcher's bill?'

Macro nodded and fished a waxed tablet out of his sidebag and flipped it open. 'Eight dead, twenty wounded, eight of whom are ready for duty. Most of the casualties were hit by slingshot and arrows. The rebels did not get much of a chance to go hand-to-hand with us.'

'Not this time,' Cato said. 'I think we got off lightly. Iskerbeles must have thought we were going to be easy game after his encounters with the province's garrison troops. Otherwise he'd never have risked a frontal attack like that. He'll be wiser next time.'

'Let him come. We'll be ready for him. And he and his friends will get the same treatment.'

'Any estimate on the enemy losses?'

'Yes. Had a rough count as soon as there was enough light. Nearly a hundred dead, and as many wounded. Most of them were recovered by the rebels, but a fair few of those are out of the fight for good.'

Cato considered the relative casualties. 'The men did well. You can pass that on from me. And let the first two centuries have an extra wine ration. That should give everyone a little incentive to want to be on the wall when the next attack comes. Assuming the Praetorians love their drink as much as any other soldiers.'

'I should think so,' Macro responded wryly. He looked round at the painted walls for a moment before his gaze returned to Cato. 'Any further thought about Nepo?'

'The subject has been on my mind, yes. Especially after Iskerbeles was so adamant that we hand him over. He must prize the procurator rather highly to be prepared to let us march out of here and promise us safe passage.'

'Not that he would have kept his promise. More than likely we'd have ended up in the grave pit like the rest of them.'

'Maybe, but I got the sense that he might have kept his word. It's Nepo he's really after. Or rather, he's after what the procurator knows.'

'About the silver bullion, you mean?'

'Of course. Iskerbeles must have realised that Nepo has hidden it. That's why he wanted to keep his hands on the procurator when he offered us surrender terms.'

'Then he is going to be heartily pissed off when he discovers that Nepo is dead. And there'll be no question of letting us proceed on our merry way once he knows. He'll assume that we know where the silver is, and then we're going to get the same treatment as Nepo. Starting with you.'

'Exactly.' Cato folded his hands. 'I don't particularly want to have to go through that. So there's no question of surrender. We have nothing to bargain with, except that we know the bullion is buried in a collapsed tunnel. We could tell Iskerbeles that, but he's hardly likely to let us go until he's checked to see that it's where we say. In any case, our orders are to ensure that the rebels don't get their hands on the silver, at any cost.'

They stared at each other for a moment before Macro shrugged. 'We're fucked either way, then.'

'That's one way of putting it. I prefer the more felicitous "Death or Victory".'

Macro slapped his hand on his thigh and roared with laughter. 'Always said you knew how to use your tongue better than the best whore in the Subura.'

'Not the most elevating of comparisons, but I thank you all the same, brother.' Cato smiled, then gave in and laughed with his friend. As the laughter died down Cato drew a deep breath. 'I needed that.'

'It's been a while since I've seen you enjoy something. Not since we got back to Rome.' Macro gestured towards one of the chairs opposite Cato. 'May I?'

'Be my guest. But spare me any lectures on grieving.'

Macro hesitated before he sat. 'I don't mean to lecture. Just want you to know that I understand how great a loss Julia was. Damned fine girl. Beautiful and smart as a whip. A fine mother she would have been, and as good a wife as a man could—'

'Stop!' Cato spoke harshly. 'You have it all wrong . . .'

He could not say any more. How much could he bear to tell Macro? The truth? Surely not all of it. Not while Cristus served alongside them. That would be too much of a burden for Macro, as it already was for himself.

'What do you mean?' Macro was confused. 'Cato, lad, what is it?'

Something within Cato revolted at the idea of sharing his pain. It was not just pride, it had to do with his rank and responsibility.

He was in command of a cohort. Five hundred men looked to him as their leader. He had no right to reveal any weakness to them. To unburden himself. Not even to Macro, who he had known and befriended when Cato had first turned up at the fortress of the Second Augusta, a thin, shivering boy who had loved books and never brandished a sword before in his entire life. They had been fast friends across many years, first when Cato was a lowly optio, and then as centurions together, before Cato had been promoted to a higher rank. He was conscious of how much he owed to the closest friend he had ever had. And yet he felt reluctant to admit to any weakness in front of Macro.

'I am not grieving for Julia. Not any more. Not since I found out she was seeing another man while I, while we, were campaigning in Britannia.'

Macro's jaw sagged slightly and he shook his head. 'I knew something was up. But that? I don't believe it, lad. Not Julia.'

'Yes, Julia,' Cato responded very deliberately. 'There is no doubt. I saw the evidence with my own eyes. She loved someone else and would have told me so if she had lived long enough to be there for my return. I was betrayed by Julia, Macro. Now you know it all. Well, you know enough at least.'

'I'm so sorry. I had no idea. You should have said.'

'What could I say?' Cato responded wearily. 'I was shocked. I felt like someone had ripped a hole in my chest and torn out my heart and guts. And I felt ashamed. Humiliated. Can you understand why I could not tell you at the time? It was far too painful to speak of. Even to you, my friend.'

'I suppose so.' Macro thought a moment. 'But I'd have known exactly what to do. You needed to be taken out for a night of drinking that would have drowned all thought of Julia. I'd have made sure of it. That would've sorted you out.'

'What doesn't kill you makes you horribly hungover . . .'

Macro laughed. 'Damn right! The Gods only know but you've been an utterly miserable sod ever since we got back, and now I know why. Poor fucking bastard. And it only gets worse from here.'

'How so?'

'You already had that scar across your face. Now you might end up with a patch over that eye. I'm telling you, Cato, you'd better set your sights on a blind woman next time, pardon the pun. No one else will have you, not without paying for it.'

'Thanks for the comforting words.'

'Oh, come on. We're trapped here, with a mob of bloodthirsty rebels beyond that wall, itching to take our heads off and stick 'em on the top of a spear for all to see. We might be saved. Probably not. So, get things in perspective. Julia has gone. She was going to abandon you anyway. Best to put what you can't change well behind you and deal with what is ahead, I say.'

Cato stared at him. 'And that's supposed to cheer me up?'

'No, just stop you behaving like a stock cuckold in one of those cheap stage comedies they put on in Rome. Pull your shit together, lad. The men need you.' Macro rose from the chair. 'We should check on the rebels and see what they're up to. If you can manage it, sir.'

Cato pushed his chair back and stood. He crossed to the pegs by the door and swung the sword belt over his shoulder. 'Let's go, Centurion.'

As Macro followed him out of the office he allowed himself a small smile of satisfaction. Hard words. It had not been easy to speak them but they were what the situation demanded, and more important still, what his friend most needed. His smile faded as he reflected on the torment that Cato must have endured since he had discovered the truth. No man should have to bear that. There was also disappointment with Julia. Macro had thought he knew her better than that. It just went to show, you could never be sure about what anyone else was really like. He glanced up at Cato's back as the prefect strode ahead of him through the courtyard of the procurator's house. Well, he concluded, nearly anyone.

It was late in the morning by the time they had concluded an inspection of the defences, which included a walk along the edge of the ravine that ran along the workings. The depth and force of the river rushing over and around the boulders fifty feet below precluded any easy crossing there. As did the steep cliffs on either side. Nevertheless they spotted an enemy patrol picking its way along the course of the river from the end of the ravine, searching for a crossing place.

'Good luck with that,' said Macro.

Cato nodded in agreement, and watched the rebels for a while longer. Then one looked up and saw the Romans above them. He called his comrades' attention to their observers and they shouted something that was lost against the rush and roar of the current. But the accompanying gestures were unmistakably hostile.

Despite the formidable appearance of the torrent rushing through the ravine Cato did not want to leave anything to chance. 'I want a watch kept over the ravine at all times.'

Macro shot him a questioning look before he responded. 'As you like, sir. Two men should cover it. Won't take them too long to walk the line.'

'No. A section, posted at regular intervals.'

'Yes, sir.'

Cato took a last look down at the gesticulating rebels and turned away towards the wall where Pulcher's reserves were on watch while the other centuries rested. The three officers exchanged a salute as Cato and Macro joined Pulcher in the tower.

'Any sign of trouble?' asked Cato.

'No, sir. Quiet as lambs. I think after last night's set-to they've lost the stomach for a fight. They'll not be trying that again in a hurry.'

'Let's hope not.' Cato crossed to the front of the tower and looked out over the open ground before the settlement. Although the enemy had retrieved the wounded, the dead were still lying out there in the ditch and already the hot air was humming with the sound of flies. Several buzzards were wheeling overhead and more were stalking over the corpses, plucking at them with their sharp beaks.

'Want me to have the men remove the bodies, sir?' asked Macro.

'No. Leave 'em out. It'll let the enemy know what to expect if they make another attempt.'

'Yes, sir. But they are going to get a little high in this heat. A few days from now, this place is going to stink worse than a tannery.'

'Then let's hope the breeze blows away from the mine. The odour will help undermine their spirit.'

Beyond the ruins, the enemy camp sprawled across the landscape and a fresh column was marching to join them from the south, stirring up a dusty haze in its wake.

'What do you think they'll do next, sir?' asked Pulcher.

Cato considered for a moment. 'They might try to starve us out. But that suits us. Time is on our side. Not theirs. The longer they remain sat there, the more they hand the initiative over to Vitellius and the other forces we have in Hispania. Iskerbeles must know that. I doubt we'll have to wait long before he attempts something else. In his place, I'd try another ram, only covered this time. If he does then we'll destroy the bridge. He'll then have to fill in the ditch before he can move the ram up . . . Measures and counter-measures, Centurion. That's how sieges play out. I've seen enough of them to know.'

Macro glanced at the other centurion. 'But you wouldn't know much about that, would you? Being as you've served in the Guard, except for that brief spell when you were acting as a spy and assassin in Gaul.'

Pulcher stared straight ahead, unflinching. 'I was doing my duty and obeying my orders, just like any other soldier.'

'Except your duties were not quite like most other soldiers', were they?' Macro half turned towards him. 'I'm curious, what exactly are your orders right now?'

Pulcher pursed his lips and sniffed. 'Meaning what?'

'Meaning, I wonder what you know about the death of Gaius Nepo?'

Pulcher faced Macro directly. 'Are you accusing me of being involved in that?'

Macro did not flinch. 'Not so much being involved as being responsible, actually.'

'I see. And you have proof to back up such an accusation? No you don't. So kindly keep your wild speculations to yourself . . . sir.'

'I know you, Pulcher. I know what kind of man you are and what you're capable of. And we're a long way from any place where due process counts.'

Pulcher's lips lifted in a sneer. 'Sir, if you really believe what you say, and I am capable of the kinds of things you think I am, then wouldn't the wisest course of action be to leave me alone, eh?'

Cato drew a sharp breath. 'That's enough of that, gentlemen. We'll have plenty of time to investigate the procurator's death once we have seen off the enemy. Which, while you have been enjoying your little chat, has been on the move.'

All three turned to stare over the battlements towards the enemy camp. A column of men was making its way towards the ruins, accompanied by several carts. There was no sense of haste about them, nor any sign of siege ladders or another ram.

'What are they up to?' asked Macro.

'We'll know soon enough.'

The column passed through the settlement and halted, safely beyond the range of slingshot. While a handful of men marked out a square some forty paces on each side with posts, the rest downed most of the tools they had been carrying and returned to the burned settlement. Soon the first of them returned with cut stone and began to build up the sides of the square, with the foundations of towers on the wall closest to the gatehouse. The sound of sawing and the occasional crash of falling debris came from the settlement as more men emerged between the buildings to stockpile timbers.

'They'll be erecting some protective earthworks,' Cato decided. 'The question is, what will they be protecting? A siege tower, maybe?'

'Or a catapult,' said Pulcher. 'Or a mantlet for another ram.'

As they continued watching, more men from the cohort climbed onto the wall to observe the enemy at work. Slowly an earthwork rose around the square, with stones at the bottom, then earth piled over that and packed down. Another party of rebels began to dig out a ditch to surround the small field fortification, while others constructed a large timber shelter in the heart of the site.

The three officers continued to watch the work progress throughout the afternoon until dusk approached. It was then that Pastericus climbed into the tower and approached Cato and saluted.

'Sir, if I may?'

'What is it?'

'I know what the enemy are up to. I've seen it before. Plenty of times. Right here.'

Cato cocked any eyebrow. 'So?'

'They're digging a mineshaft. That shelter in the middle, that's the entrance to the tunnel, sir.'

Cato and the two centurions turned to scrutinise the work. Sure enough, there were men emerging from behind the shelter carrying wicker baskets to add to the steadily rising ramparts. Cato was furious with himself for not seeing the obvious earlier. He had assumed the soil was being dug out solely for the fortifications.

'He's right,' said Macro. 'So that's what they're up to. And why not when they've got themselves a few thousand slaves with mining experience? Shit, we should have seen that coming.'

Cato nodded. He was already imagining what the enemy had planned for them. The tunnel would steer a course directly towards the gatehouse, and then undermine it. Once they were ready, the pit props under the foundations would be set on fire and the whole structure would collapse, creating a massive breach through which the rebels would pour in their thousands.

# CHAPTER TWENTY-EIGHT

It was a moonless night three days after the rebels had started digging their tunnel and Cato took one last look at the enemy fortification less than a hundred paces away. The turrets on the wall facing the gatehouse were clearly discernible against the backdrop of the campfires of the rebel army half a mile beyond. There was a sentry in each turret, and two more on the wall, as well as regular patrols in front of the mine. The soft hue of braziers around the entrance to the tunnel illuminated the workings for those labouring through the night as the tunnel crept underground towards the gatehouse. The sound of voices drifted across the open ground as the slaves worked, as well as the sounds of sawing and more voices amid the ruins away to the left where the rebels seemed to be gathering most of their timbers for the pit props. The sickening sweet stench of mortification that came from the bloated bodies in the ditch was mercifully less egregious during the cooler hours of the night. Even so, Cato's nose wrinkled as a fluke of the breeze wafted the air up from the foot of the gatehouse. He turned his mind away from the reminder of the dead lying outside the wall.

According to Pastericus the rebel mine workers were able to dig out as much as fifty feet of tunnel a day. In which case they were already halfway to their target. Given that it was likely that it would take perhaps ten more days for Vitellius to arrive, it was time to put a stop to it, Cato decided. He had resisted the temptation to attack earlier. It was better to let the enemy toil for a few days before destroying their work and forcing them to start again.

He winced as there was a sharp stab of pain in his eye. The

287

surgeon had been inspecting the wound each evening and pronounced that he was satisfied with his progress. The pus discharge was quite normal, he claimed, and the absence of any foul smell from the dressing was a good sign that the wound had not gone bad.

'A nice clean injury,' the surgeon had smiled earlier that night as he peered closely at Cato's eye. 'And, if I may say so, a textbook extraction of the splinter with minimal trauma as a consequence.'

'Easy for you to say.' Cato sniffed. 'It was somewhat traumatic from my end of the splinter, I can assure you.'

The surgeon affected a hurt look. 'I defy you to find anyone who could have done a better extraction by the light of a brazier, sir.'

'Give me time.' Cato could not see clearly out of his left eye once the dressing was removed. A thick grey veil seemed to obscure most details of the world about him, and when he blinked it was as if a small rough stone was caught under his eyelid. 'Will I recover enough to have full sight?'

The surgeon straightened his back and scratched his cheek. 'It's possible. Hard to say. Most eye injuries like yours lead to blindness. But the fact that you can see anything out of it is a good sign. There may be some lasting damage. I think you were very lucky, sir.'

'Lucky?'

'Of course. If the splinter had struck you in the pupil, or even the iris, then as likely as not you would have lost sight in that eye for good. As it was, it entered through the flesh beneath the socket before piercing the muscle at the bottom of the eye.'

'I feel so fortunate.'

The surgeon ignored the sarcasm as he prepared a fresh dressing and carefully placed it over the eye before tying a new bandage around Cato's head. 'Of course, I would advise plenty of rest, sir. But I know that's not possible under the circumstances. So just try not to irritate the eye with rubbing or over-exerting yourself.'

Cato stared at him with his good eye. 'We are under siege, you know.'

'Yes, sir. But I am bound to give you the benefit of my opinion, as your surgeon. If you ignore my advice then that's up to you, but there my responsibility ends.'

'I wish I had your job.'

The surgeon stepped back a pace and revealed the bloodstained apron tied over his tunic. 'Really, sir?'

Now, it was close to midnight as far as Cato could tell, and it was time to put his plan into action. He climbed down from the tower and approached the dark mass of men waiting silently a short distance behind the gatehouse. Behind them loomed the curve of the inner wall that the Praetorians had been toiling to construct in an arc around the rear of the gates. It was the standard countermeasure when a breach was expected. If the enemy succeeded then they would climb over the ruins only to encounter the inner wall. When it was completed, it would contain them for a while at least, Cato hoped, but it would not be as strong as the existing wall. And time was short. The stock of dressed stone had already been used up in constructing the second wall and this new effort had required using the irregular rocks and boulders littering the base of the cliff above the mining camp. Hauling them down to the workings had taken much effort and, so far, the wall was barely more than a breastwork. If nothing was done to upset the progress of the enemy's tunnel then the inner wall would only serve to delay them a short while before it was overwhelmed.

Macro was waiting a few paces in front of the workers. He had stripped off his armour and wore a tunic, boots and sword belt. His face and limbs were blackened with a mixture of ash and fat so that his features were all but invisible.

'Centurion Macro,' Cato whispered. 'If I didn't know you were there, then I would never notice you.'

'That's the idea, sir.' Macro grinned and his teeth loomed dully in the blackened oval of his face.

'Are you and your men ready?'

Macro nodded towards a group of twenty men standing slightly apart from the others. They too wore only tunics and carried only their swords. 'They're ready, sir.'

'Centurion Secundus?'

'Sir?' Another figure stepped forward and saluted.

'You understand what you have to do the moment the signal is given?'

'Yes, sir.'

There was a figure standing at the centurion's shoulder. Leaning closer, Cato recognised Tribune Cristus.

'What is the meaning of this, Tribune?'

'I thought I would volunteer, sir. Now that my services are no longer required for keeping stock of our supplies.'

Cato could not help a thin smile at the man's umbrage. 'Never underestimate the importance of that role, Tribune. That said, I dare say you can be spared such duties for the present.'

'Yes, sir.'

'You can fight with the Second Century until the siege is over. Just do your duty, and do as Centurion Secundus tells you.'

'Yes, sir.'

Cato looked round at the shadow figures facing him. Much depended on the success of the night's enterprise. All the officers had been over every detail, and the men had all the equipment they needed: axes, ropes, jars of oil and tinderboxes. Unlike Macro's team, the men of the Second Century were in full armour and their extra equipment was packed into several of the mine's small handcarts. There was a tense stillness about the men and Cato knew that they could do with some encouragement. He cleared his throat gently before he began in a quiet tone.

'Not a sound, lads. Not until you go into action. When the fighting starts, you can make it as loud as you like. Louder. Anything you can do to shake them up and make 'em panic. Go in like the Furies themselves and make the rebels regret the day they ever dreamed of defying Rome and our emperor . . . But don't fail me. Or the rest of the cohort. That tunnel is days away from the wall. If you don't succeed tonight then we're going to lose our first and best line of defence.' He paused to let them reflect on the importance of their task. 'So go in hard. Destroy everything you can, and then get back here as fast as possible the moment you hear the recall. You're already heroes. You don't have to go and prove it by dying for

Rome pointlessly. Any man who disobeys the order to withdraw will be on a charge, and have to endure fatigues until the siege is over. Do I make myself clear?'

He detected some faint smiles in the dark faces of the nearest men.

'Don't worry, sir,' Secundus said quietly. 'We'll play our part.'

'Good.' Cato clasped his forearm. 'May the Gods go with you.'

'Thank you, sir.'

Cato turned to Macro, not quite certain what to say as he was concerned for his friend's safety. Macro saved him any embarrassment by giving him a quick farewell nod and turning to his men.

'Come on, boys, on me, and keep it bloody quiet.'

They padded off along the wall and were quickly swallowed up by the darkness. Cato stared after them a moment longer before he returned to the gatehouse and climbed back into the tower, his good eye straining to pick out any possible sign of danger that might further imperil Macro or the other men. But there was no sign that the enemy was alert to any threat. Over in the camp he could see tiny figures huddled about the hundreds of small fires and a large group about a big blaze near the tents of Iskerbeles and his closest followers. Cato smiled to himself. If all went well the rebel leader would soon be cursing his misfortune and his followers would start to question his ability to serve as their leader.

Macro tested the rope one last time. The end was tied securely around a stake driven deep into the rampart behind the wall. There was no give in the rope and he held the coiled loops in his hand as he cautiously peered between the battlements at the very end of the wall next to the cliff. The rocks loomed to his right and towered up into the night, ready to echo any noise. Which was why Macro was moving with deliberate slowness and care. He glanced across the open ground that ran down to the edge of the ruins but the only sign of movement was far off, close to the entrance to the rebels' tunnel. Several men were picking their way along the line of the wall, just beyond the range of any missiles hurled at them by the Romans.

'Here we go,' Macro muttered to his men. He lowered the rope down the front of the wall, paying it out until it was taut. Easing his legs over the parapet Macro grasped the rope in both hands and slowly descended into the ditch. The attack on the mine a few days earlier had concentrated on the gatehouse and the walls immediately either side. Macro was grateful that there were no bodies at the end that bordered the ravine, or here under the cliff. The last thing he wanted was to step in someone's rancid guts, and then have the stink of it stick to him and risk giving away their position when they made for the enemy's fortifications around the entrance to the siege tunnel. He felt the soles of his boots touch the ground and eased himself down gently. His heart was beating quickly as he looked round to make sure that he was quite alone in the ditch. Then, satisfied that it was safe for the others to follow him down, he gave two sharp tugs on the rope and stood to one side as it snaked around in the darkness and the first of his squad shimmied down beside him. Macro sent him directly to the top of the ditch to keep watch and signalled the next man to descend.

When all of them had come down Macro gave a final tug and the sentry on the wall drew the rope up over the battlement.

'Stay close, lads,' Macro whispered. 'Don't want any of you to lose your way in the dark. Keep a close eye on the man in front of you and never lose sight of him. Wait here for now. When you get the word, you follow single file.'

He climbed up the outer slope of the ditch and crouched down beside the man on watch.

'See anything?'

'No, sir. No movement. At least not between us and the tunnel.'

Macro strained his eyes and swept the open ground in front of them. He waited for a moment longer before he was prepared to accept that there was no sign of the enemy to their front, then turned to call softly to the men in the ditch. 'Let's go.'

He rose up into a crouch and crept forward a few paces before glancing back to make sure the others were following closely. Even as they moved as quietly as possible Macro was still agonisingly conscious of the light rumble of their boots and the faint rustle of the dry grass as they crossed the open ground towards the nearest of the burned-out buildings. At any instant he feared that they would be spotted, the alarm would be raised, and they would have no choice but to turn and race back to the wall and climb to safety. It would be the end of any attempt to deal with the tunnel that night. And more than likely that the enemy would take every precaution to keep the defenders bottled up behind their defences.

When he reached the crumbling wall of the first building Macro flattened himself against it and waved the men to take positions to his left. Once they were ready he moved on, pausing at the gaps between buildings to peer round the corner, only moving on when he was certain that the street was clear. They covered most of the distance without any trouble. Then, no more than fifty paces from the rear of the fortification, Macro heard voices close by and instantly halted his men and waved them down. Obediently they crouched down and were silent and still, all but invisible against the dark buildings in the night. Two rebels armed with spears emerged from the ruins six feet from Macro. They talked casually and Macro almost dared not breathe as he eased his sword from its scabbard and gestured to the man behind him to do the same, then pointed out one of the rebels as his target. Muscles tensed, Macro was about to spring forward, but the rebels strolled off in the opposite direction, quite unsuspecting of the Roman soldiers at their backs. Macro let them go, watching as they moved past the rear of the earthwork and turned away into the ruins.

The small column moved forward again, inching towards the rear wall where a gate was open and guarded by two men. There was no ditch at the rear of the earthwork. No doubt because it was closest to the rebels who had only anticipated a frontal assault by the Romans. The glow of a fire highlighted the corners of two ruins nearby and Macro glanced round the corner to see a large party of men, perhaps as many as fifty, he estimated. They were sitting around a fire, some fifty paces down the street. Their weapons were close to hand and there were the glows from other fires in other parts of the settlement. One at a time, the Romans crossed the gap and continued their approach. Macro moved as close as he dared and stopped as a small party of men dressed only in loincloths emerged through the gate pulling a handcart piled with soil. They dragged the cart to one side, where there was already a large mound of earth, and began to shovel the spoil from the cart. Their backs were to Macro as they worked and he realised that there would be a brief opportunity to act before they had emptied the cart and returned to the tunnel.

Turning to the next man, Macro whispered, 'Spiro, with me, and wait until I strike before you do. Understand?'

'Sir.'

Macro eased himself away from the side of the building and gestured to the Praetorian to fall in alongside him. They approached the men at the gate at a casual pace. They were almost upon the sentries before they were spotted and one of the rebels readied his spear in both hands to challenge them. Macro raised his canteen in his left hand and pretended to take a swig before offering it to the nearest of the rebels as he laughed. The sentry grounded his spear with a nervous chuckle and reached out for the proffered drink. Macro made to stagger and trip and as he stumbled towards the man he thrust his sword into his guts, angling up under the ribcage. At the same time he let his canteen drop and pressed his spare hand over the man's mouth as they both fell against the earth rampart. The shocking violence of the attack surprised the other sentry who hesitated a fatal instant, and then Spiro was on him, close up, thrusting his sword under the rebel's chin and punching the blade up into his skull. There was a soft gasp and then a light, keening whine, before he too was silenced.

A quick glance reassured Macro that the men working around the cart had not been alerted to the presence of the raiders, and he waved the rest of his party over to the gate.

'Get the bodies inside,' he detailed two of the men; then he led the rest through the gate and into the fortification. Directly ahead lay the timber-framed entrance to the tunnel, with an oil lamp hanging from a bracket fixed to the crossbeam. There were piles of rocks to one side and a large mound of soil. The dying embers of a fire glowed in a far corner, illuminating several men sleeping nearby. On the side facing the wall of the mining camp, four figures were visible, and another two in the towers. Macro turned to his men.

'You four, stay here. If those miners with the cart return shut and bar the gate. Spiro, take ten men and deal with the men sleeping by the fire, and the sentry in the far tower. The rest of you come with me.'

Macro kept to the shadows along the side of the rampart as he stealthily made his way towards the watch tower in the left corner facing the mine. Spiro and his party crept along the opposite side. As they reached the earthen slope leading up to the parapet Macro detailed four of his men to deal with the sentries along the wall, and then he began to climb the ladder into the watch tower, testing his weight carefully on each rung in turn. His head was just level with the floor of the tower when there was a cry from the wall, swiftly silenced. The tower creaked lightly as the sentry moved to the side in response to the noise and called down. Steeling himself, Macro exploded up the final few steps and threw himself at the rebel as the latter turned back. The cry of alarm died in his throat as Macro slammed into his midriff and carried him back against the corner post. Badly winded, he gasped for breath and tried to draw a dagger from his belt. But Macro had already braced his legs as he grabbed the man's thigh and wrenched him off his feet, tipping him over the rail. At the last moment he snatched at Macro's arms, but he was too late and his fingers merely brushed Macro before he tumbled headlong into the ditch facing the mine's gatehouse, landing with a heavy thud and rolling to the bottom of the ditch in silence. A quick glance along the wall showed that the other sentries had been taken down. Then Macro saw that Spiro and his men had not yet completed their task and were only just coming up on those sleeping by the fire. The sentry in the other tower was still in place, and yet he had not moved at all in reaction to the slight commotion along the wall. Macro could guess why, and smiled grimly to himself.

'The bastard's asleep . . .'

That was a capital offence in the Roman army, and necessarily so. A man on sentry duty carried the responsibility for the safety of his comrades' lives. But clearly there was not the same disciplinary code amongst the followers of Iskerbeles. Spiro detailed one of his men to the tower and a moment later the sleeping sentry paid for the dereliction of his duty with his life as his body tumbled down to join his comrade in the ditch. At the same time, Spiro and the rest of his men sprang upon the slumbering rebels, cutting their throats and stabbing them in a frenzied effort to kill them before they could make a sound that might alert their comrades outside the earthwork.

From his vantage point in the watch tower Macro could see that the miners had emptied their cart and had turned it round to return to the gate. Now was the time to bring the rest of the prefect's plan into action. Cupping a hand to his mouth, Macro called across the enclosed area.

'Bar the gate!'

At once the four men rushed from the shadows on either side and closed the gate and dropped the locking bar into its brackets to secure the entrance. Outside, the rebels with the cart paused and stared towards the earthwork. Turning towards the gatehouse Macro bellowed:

'Secundus! Now's your time!'

A moment later he heard the groan of the mine gates being opened and the harsh shout of the order to advance. A dark mass of men surged over the bridge above the ditch and came across the open ground at the double. It was then that the rebel miners with the cart guessed that something was badly amiss and several ran towards the gate, shouting as they came. The others ran into the ruins, crying for help.

'Get onto the rampart!' Macro ordered his party. 'We have to hold this place until the job is done!'

Secundus and his men reached the ditch and began to lay their ladders across and onto the top of the palisade while half of his century fanned out to either side to cover the flanks. The first of the men, carrying their tools and incendiaries, scurried up the ladders and climbed into the earthwork. Macro came down to meet them and led the way to the entrance to the tunnel. The rebels had set up small oil lamps in brackets attached to the pit props and by their light Macro and the others hurried down a steep slope before the tunnel levelled off and headed towards the gatehouse. The tunnel was barely higher than Macro, and the taller men had to bow their heads. They did not go far before they came to a dead end and Macro stared at the wall of earth and rock in surprise.

'They should have made twice as much progress as this, according to Pastericus.'

Secundus stood aside as his men began to work their picks into the gaps behind the props. 'It seems that freedom ain't much good for productivity. Iskerbeles might be wondering if it might not have been a better idea not to liberate all the miners.'

Macro inspected the tunnel quickly. 'You take charge here. Pull down whatever you can, and then burn the stock of pit props outside. As soon as you're done, take your men back to the gatehouse. We'll be right behind you.'

'Yes, sir.'

As Macro trotted back down the tunnel he heard the first thud of falling pit props and then the low rumble of the roof and sides of the tunnel caving in. Emerging into the night he raced over to the rear rampart and scrambled up to the palisade. The miners had rushed to the gate and were attempting to force it open by brute strength. It was a pointless effort and it cost them two men as they were struck down by rocks hurled from the parapet. As the third casualty stumbled back clasping a hand to his head the others fell back and carried their wounded to the shelter of the street between the nearest buildings.

Further into the ruins the alarm had been raised. The notes of a horn brayed into the night and were answered shortly afterwards by a horn in the rebel camp. Men spilled out of the tents in the heart of the camp where Iskerbeles had made his headquarters and were soon streaming past the fires towards the settlement and the earthwork. It would not take them long to arrive on the scene in sufficient numbers to overwhelm the raiders. But there was a more immediate danger as a party of men carrying spears appeared at the end of the street onto which the gate opened. They charged towards Macro with angry shouts, and then more men came after them.

A quick glance to either side showed that there was no threat yet to the flank walls and Macro snatched a breath and bellowed, 'On me! And bring rocks!'

The others and Spiro's men came racing over to the piled rocks and then onto the palisade to line the defences as Macro jabbed his sword towards the oncoming rebels. 'Let 'em have it, lads!'

His men needed no further encouragement as they unleashed a hail of missiles into the faces of the spearmen, downing one and injuring others as they struck home against their bodies. The charge stalled as the rebels stopped and crouched, arms raised to protect their heads, and then moved aside to take shelter in between the buildings. A few stooped to pick up some of the rocks and throw them back at Macro and his men. Most of these clattered off the wooden posts of the palisade, but one of the raiders was unfortunate to be caught square on the forehead and he lurched away from the palisade and fell back down the rampart, out cold.

'That's enough for now!' Macro ordered.

Sounds of chopping and splintering came from the mouth of the tunnel, interspersed with the protesting groan of timbers and the rush of soil and rock. Then Centurion Secundus appeared in the light of one of the lamps. He reached up and took it down as he and Cristus led some of their men over to the stockpile of wood stacked in the corner of the earthworks. There were also a few jars of oil for the lamps which were smashed over the logs.

'Douse that lot with pitch and get the kindling over by the braziers!'

As Secundus' men prepared the fire, Macro's attention was drawn back to the street beyond the gate. More men had emerged at the far end and there were men with shields at the front this time, raised and ready to deflect any further missiles hurled by the Praetorians defending the rear of the earthworks. A movement at the edge of his vision drew Macro's gaze to the cart the miners had been hauling shortly before. A number of men had returned to it and dragged it back to the pile of soil. They were hurriedly heaping earth into it by the light of the fire that still glowed close by. Macro divined their purpose a moment later when a rebel shouted an order and pointed back at the gate. There was not much time left to complete their work now, Macro realised. He turned to where Secundus and his men were piling small lengths of firewood against the pitch-saturated timbers.

'Get the fire going. Quick as you can!' Macro shouted.

Secundus nodded and crouched down with his oil lamp and carefully applied the small flame at the end of the wick to a heap of

298

wood shavings. The delicate flicker lapped at the thin combustible curls and then hungrily worked its way into the pile, as the flames spread to the pitch with a smooth, almost cold blue flow of ghostly tongues of fire. As the flames drew in air it fanned them all the more and the timbers began to char on the outside as the fire took hold, casting a bright pool of illumination across the interior of the earthwork. Very soon the roar and crackle of flames rose to a loud din.

The rebels with the cart dragged it to the gate as fast as they could, until they came under a barrage of rocks and had to stop and wait for some of their comrades equipped with shields to cover them for the last final rush to the gate. There they reversed the cart and, taking a run up, rushed it forward against the gate where it crashed against the timbers and caused the locking bar to almost leap from its bracket. Macro saw the danger at once and dived down to hold it in place just before the cart struck again, jarring his arms.

'Secundus! Get the men out of the tunnel. Collapse the entrance and get your men out of here!'

The centurion raced over to the mouth of the tunnel and called down, and a moment later his men came out, breathing hard and soiled by dust and dirt. They worked at the timbers at the entrance and collapsed one, then the other, bringing down the sides and leaving a small crater in the middle of the earthwork.

'Good, let's go!' Secundus waved them towards the far side where the ladders waited. 'Leave the kit. Just run!'

The Praetorians threw their tools aside and left the spare buckets of pitch where they lay as they fled. One by one they descended the ladders stretched across the ditch and made for the gatehouse where the gates yawned open and Cato beckoned to them.

Inside the earthwork Macro held the bar down as the cart smashed against the gate again, this time opening a gap between two of the timbers. It would not hold for much longer now and Macro could hear the sound of more men arriving all the time, urging their comrades on and clashing their weapons against the edge of their shields in a rising cacophony. He turned to look for Spiro and saw him on the rampart in the ruddy glow of the flames as he hurled another rock.

'Spiro! Spiro! Down here, with two men, now.'

Once they joined him Macro pointed to the bar. 'Keep that down. Hold the gate for a little longer.'

'Yes, sir.'

Macro ran over to the nearest bucket of pitch, but it was empty, and so was the next, but the third and last was still half full. He snatched it up and ran on to the edge of the blaze consuming the stock of pit props. The heat stung his exposed skin as if he had been struck an almighty blow. Gritting his teeth, Macro grasped the end of a thin length of wood and darted back, the hair of his arms singed. He ran back to the gate and dowsed the rear of the gate with the pitch and then rammed his sword down between the bar and the gate to wedge the bar in place. The gate shuddered under the impact of the cart once more and the gap between two of the boards split open wide enough for him to see the faces of the men on the far side. As they saw Macro they let out a roar of triumph and dragged the cart back for the next charge. Macro thrust the burning end of the length of wood against the pitch-smeared gate until the flames spread and licked hungrily up the timbers.

'Right, that's it! Fall back.' He cupped his hands to his mouth and shouted across to the rest of the men. 'Fall back!'

The men on the rampart hurled their last rocks and turned to pick up their unconscious comrade before rushing after Secundus and his party. Macro halted one of Spiro's companions and relieved him of his sword before sending him on his way. He let the rest of his men get a head start and looked round the earthwork, noting the fire, the ruined entrance to the tunnel and the rebel bodies lying by the blaze in the far corner. Macro nodded with satisfaction. They had achieved all they had set out to do.

The cart crashed into the gate again, widening the gap enough for a man to reach through. Sure enough, an arm snaked through and made to shift the sword that jammed the locking beam. But it got caught in the flames instead and was hurriedly snatched back with a loud curse.

Macro turned and made his way back towards the rear wall where the last of his party was clambering down the ladders to follow the others back to the mine. Secundus had joined the half century guarding the flanks and was forming them up into a box, closing the ranks to present shields on all sides. It was a timely precaution as the first of the rebels were moving round the earthwork to cut off the raiders' escape. As Macro reached the ladder, the gate gave way as the cart burst through the flames and ran on a short distance and men poured through the gap, racing to get past the flames consuming the timber posts and shattered panels of the gate. Macro drew a deep breath to make his farewell.

'That's what you get when you fuck with Rome!'

Then he sheathed the sword and swung himself onto the ladder, climbing down as quickly as he could. Already, loose groups of rebels were cutting across the route of Secundus and his men and the centurion gave the order to move the instant Macro was inside the box and his men had closed ranks again. As Secundus called the time they tramped steadily towards the gatehouse. The nearest of the rebels turned on them, charging in and hacking and slashing at the shields in a futile display of frustration. Those who got too close invited a counter-attack from the Praetorians, who stabbed their spears into whatever flesh came within their reach.

Macro could hear Cato's voice in the darkness, ordering those men who had reached the mine to form up just beyond the bridge over the ditch so that the gate could be kept open for the last men to return from the raid. All the while more of the rebels were streaming out of the darkness to attack Secundus and his half century. They were forced to slow down, but kept moving all the way, until at length they merged with Cato and his men and fell back across the bridge and under the gatehouse. The rebels made a last desperate effort to keep the gates open and Macro pressed himself into the fighting line and laid about them with vicious cuts from his sword. The example of the ferocious centurion caused the nearest men to hesitate and Macro bellowed an incoherent war cry at them and then leaped back as the Praetorians heaved the gates into place and slammed down the locking bar. At once the timbers shook as the rebels surged forward again, beating the gates with their weapons and bare fists. Pulcher gave the order for the men on the wall to hurl rocks at the attackers and within moments they had turned away to retreat into the darkness.

Cato sought out his friend and smiled as he caught sight of his blackened face, singed hair and seared tunic by the light of the torch flickering in a bracket beside the gate.

'How did it go?'

Macro licked his lips and swallowed as he caught his breath. 'As good as we could hope. The tunnel is destroyed and we've burned their pit props.'

'Then we've won several more days. Good job, Macro.' Cato laughed with relief. As much because his friend had returned unharmed as for the damage he had caused to the enemy. 'Now tell me that you didn't have fun out there.'

'Fun?' Macro shook his head. 'You have a peculiar sense of fun, my friend.'

'If you say so. Here, something for you.' Cato pressed a wineskin into Macro's hands. The centurion eagerly pulled out the stopper and raised the wineskin, squirting a jet into his open mouth. Because of the dark, he missed at first and the liquid splashed over his face. Then he adjusted it and drank deeply and wondered if wine had ever tasted so good, or been so hard-earned.

# CHAPTER TWENTY-NINE

Over the next few days the Romans were afforded a measure of satisfaction and feeling of security as the rebels went about repairing the damage. The sounds of sawing from the remains of the settlement resumed as they gathered more timber and materials to replace those lost during the raid. Macro made a detailed report the morning after and Cato was surprised at the slow progress the rebels had made with the original tunnel, given Pastericus' estimate. But it was all to the good, he concluded. The slower they advanced, the more time that gave Legate Vitellius to arrive with the main column. But he was not content to wait and be idle and take the arrival of Vitellius for granted. Work on the inner wall a short distance behind the gatehouse continued, as they gradually built it up to the height of the outer wall. This way there would be a contingency plan ready if the rebel tunnel managed to reach the defences.

Cato also decided to take another, more aggressive approach to foiling the enemy. Two days after the raid he marked out a square in between the gatehouse and the inner wall as he explained to Macro, 'We're going to dig a countermine. Start here and go twenty feet straight down before making for the enemy's earthwork. If we begin now we should break into their tunnel before they reach the outer ditch, and then we can destroy their latest effort. That should help discourage them from continuing to dig under us.'

Macro pouted and raised his eyebrows. 'It's going to be tough work, sir. The Praetorians have got bugger-all experience of digging mines; it's exhausting work, and dangerous with it.'

'The danger we can mitigate as far as possible by making sure the shaft and tunnel are thoroughly supported by as many pit props as we care to use. There's plenty of timber in the stores cut for the purpose, and we can take more from the existing mineshafts if we need to.'

'True,' Macro conceded. 'But is it really necessary? If Iskerbeles' lads dig as slowly as before then Vitellius should be on the scene long before they could bring down the gatehouse. In that case our men will be wasting their time, and putting themselves in some danger.'

'We'll take as few risks as possible,' said Cato. 'Iskerbeles will drive his men hard to tunnel under us. I'd be willing to bet that they will ensure they make progress in line with Pastericus' estimate from now on. In any case it will give the Praetorians something to do while they're waiting for the cohort to be relieved.'

'Hmmm.'

'You say it yourself. Idleness is not good for soldiers. And if they haven't done this kind of work before then it will be a useful experience. Consider it on-the-job training. It'll be good for them, and who knows? It will also be a necessary precaution in case Vitellius is delayed, for good reasons or bad.'

'You think he means to do us harm, sir?'

'Don't you? He comes out of this well, whatever the result. If he reaches us in time to save us before Iskerbeles can retake the mine then he will be able to report that he saved the cohort. If the cohort is wiped out then he will avenge us and gain renown for that. I'd rather not hand the initiative to either him, or Iskerbeles. We will keep it for ourselves, and a countermine is the best way of doing that. I'll need a rota of mining teams. Say five to dig and fifteen men to remove the spoil on each shift. We can use the spoil to reinforce the inner wall. Of course, we'll have to do it carefully. No point in alerting the enemy that we're playing them at their own game. Besides, we have all the tools we need for the job right here in the mine.'

'Yes, sir. I'll see to the necessary arrangements.'

Cato nodded, pleased with his plan. It was sensible to cover as many contingencies as possible, he reflected. Vitellius should be able to reach them before the tunnel was completed. Even if the enemy succeeded in bring down the gatehouse, they would then have to contend with the inner wall. And if that fell there was the second wall and then the final defence at the top of the track leading up to the mining camp. In the meantime, there was a good chance of the countermine foiling the rebels' fresh attempt. Yes, Cato mused, there was every reason to be pleased with the way he was conducting the defence of the mine.

As Macro had anticipated, the prefect's orders were greeted with disdain and irritation by the Praetorians, but discipline soon reasserted itself and they bent to their new task effectively, if not enthusiastically. Stripped down to their loincloths, the men wielded picks and shovels for two hours at a time before being relieved. As they went deeper than sunlight could penetrate they worked by the weak glow of oil lamps. Those relieved climbed the ladder up to the surface, covered in grime and sweat and desperate for water to slake their thirst. Digging down was straightforward enough and timbers were used to reinforce the sides of the shaft. Once they hit the required depth they charted a course directly towards the original tunnel constructed by the rebels. It was painstaking work carried out in poor light and stale air. Cato made sure that the Praetorians' tunnel was propped up far more thoroughly than those that penetrated the cliff of the mine workings. The spoil was carted away at night to ensure that any rebels watching from one of the nearby hills would not realise what the defenders were up to.

Both sides continued to regard each other warily as the days passed and they dug their tunnels. The rampart of the rebels' earth-work was raised to a greater height and outworks were added to ensure that there was no repeat of the raid that had rendered their previous attempt a wasted effort. By day and night the rebel patrols were strengthened and made more numerous and soon they extended along the entire length of the wall protecting the mine. All the while the putrefaction of the corpses in the ditch continued and some of the Praetorians resorted to wearing strips of cloth over their noses while on sentry duty, dousing the cloth with oils and scents looted from the procurator's house. It made little difference and the Romans had no choice but to endure the stench and the sight of buzzards and other animals gorging themselves on the soft tissue of the corpses rotting below the wall.

Each morning and at dusk, Cato submitted to the ministrations of the cohort's surgeon who changed the dressing, cleaned away any discharges of pus, and then examined the wound. He pronounced himself very happy with the recovery of the gouged flesh, and the small puncture to the bottom of the eyeball. He was more sanguine than Cato about his inability to see much better with the eye. After five days the bandage came off and Cato used an eyepatch to hold the dressing in place. This amused Macro mightily, who suggested that Cato might want to consider a change of career and seek a transfer to the imperial navy, or even set himself up in business as a pirate.

Then, at dusk on the fifth day since the raid, Cato and Macro were carrying out their routine evening inspection of the defences and crossing the mine workings when a shout from one of the Praetorians drew their attention to the cliff. A stream of silvery water was gushing over the ledge above and running down the cliff face, washing away soil and rock as it did so.

'What in Hades is going on there?' Macro demanded as the flow splashed down at the foot of the cliff and began to follow the easiest course across the workings to the ravine.

'Only one way to find out,' Cato replied, turning and starting to jog back to the track and up to the ledge. By the time they had passed through the slave camp to the water tanks the rush of water had dwindled to a slow flow, cutting across the ledge to the cliff. Centurion Porcino was standing by the tank nearest the drenched ground, together with Pastericus, as the others squelched over the mud. They were in conversation but the optio stopped to salute.

'What's happened?' Cato demanded.

'Tank sprang a leak, sir.'

'I think we might have guessed that,' said Macro, kicking some of the mud at Pastericus to emphasise his point.

'Show me,' Cato ordered and Porcino led him to the corner of the tank where some of the earth buttress had been washed away. The masonry beyond had collapsed and a steady trickle of water was still flowing. Porcino pointed towards the breach. 'Pastericus says it's the concrete lining, sir. Sometimes the heat causes it to crack. Normally it's not a problem as the tanks are inspected daily and repairs made on the spot. But that hasn't been happening for a while, and . . .' He nodded at the wide expanse of mud and rivulets covering the ledge all the way to the cliff.

Cato surveyed the damage, not unduly worried by the escape of water as the tank was still half full and in any case there was plenty of water in the tanks that were still intact. All the same, it would be wise to know more. 'Pastericus, how often do the tanks need repairing? Is this likely to happen again within the next month or so?'

The optio shook his head. 'It's not really my field, sir. But I've only seen this happen once before. Creates a bit of a mess, which is why they use those lined channels when they start the hushing process. Of course, they only ever use one tank at a time.'

'Hushing?' Macro frowned. 'Care to explain?'

'It's when they release the water to expose the silver veins in the side of the hill, sir.'

Macro nodded. 'Hushing? Bloody stupid name for it.'

'Not my fault, sir. I just work here.'

Cato climbed onto the rim of the tank and looked down at the damage. 'Right, well let's try and avoid a repeat of this. Porcino, you get the job of tank inspector from now on. I want them checked for leaks at dawn and dusk. If you spot anything then there'll be some materials to repair leaks in the mine's stores. Get a team on it straight away.'

'Yes, sir. Though wouldn't Pastericus here be a better man for this? He knows the place better than I do.'

'I've given you the job, Centurion. That's the end of the matter.'

'Yes, sir.'

'Then get some men, find what you need, and get on with it.'

'Yes, sir.'

They exchanged a salute before Cato and Macro picked their way back across the mud. The latter could not help an amused grin. 'That'll help keep Porcino on his toes, and burn off some of that fat.'

'I imagine so,' Cato replied absently and then stopped and looked at the tanks. There was no sign of any leak from the others and once again he marvelled at the expertise of the engineers who had constructed the mine. There was a huge volume of water stored

307

here. Ample for the needs of the garrison and all those slaves who had once toiled under the cliffs below, as well as providing the means to wash away swathes of the cliff face to get at the valuable minerals hidden beneath the earth.

'Hushing,' he sniffed. 'You're right, it is a stupid word for it. You can be sure no soldier came up with that.'

Macro looked up at the deepening velvet of the evening sky. 'We'd better get on with the inspection, sir. It'll be dark soon. And still no sign of Vitellius . . .'

Cato was woken by Metellus an hour after midnight. The optio was holding a lamp above the bed as he firmly shook his superior's shoulder. Cato's face creased into a grimace as he stirred. He had been deep in a bad dream where he had returned to his house and Julia had been alive. At first he had been overjoyed to see her, but then she had told him about Cristus, and packed a chest with her clothes to abandon Cato and their child and go to live with her lover. Cato had been begging her to stay at the point the optio had awakened him and it took a moment to adjust from the fading agony of the dream to reality.

'What? What's happened?'

'Centurion Musa's compliments, sir. He says you should join him in the atrium. Right now, sir.'

'Why?'

'He didn't say, sir. Just that it was urgent.'

Cato's mind cleared. 'What time is it?'

'Not long to the fifth hour of the night, sir.'

The watch would be changing soon, but Musa should still be with his men on the wall. Cato sat up abruptly and swung his legs over the side of the bed and into his boots. He laced them up quickly and pulled a tunic over his body before accompanying Metellus out of the chamber and down the corridor to the main hall just inside the entrance of the procurator's house. A number of lamps were providing illumination for the men waiting for him. Centurion Pulcher and his optio were about to go on duty and were helping each other put on their mail vests. There was also Musa and four of his men, and with them another man, dressed like one of the rebels

308

but with the unmistakable cropped hair of a Roman soldier. He was in a filthy condition with scratches and cuts on his exposed flesh. Cato had been about to demand the reason for being disturbed, and castigate Musa for leaving his post before being relieved by Pulcher, but his attention was drawn to the man with them.

'Who is this?'

Musa saluted. 'Claims to be Optio Collenus of the Fourth Cohort of the Guard, sir. He says he has been sent by Legate Vitellius to give you this.' The centurion held out a slim leather tube, sealed at both ends with the crest that Cato recognised as belonging to Vitellius. Cato took it and stared hard at the man with his good eye.

'What are you doing here? More to the point, how did you get here? And where is Vitellius?'

The man who called himself Collenus was at the point of exhaustion, but drew himself up stiffly in order to answer his superior. 'The legate is in the hills, no more than twenty miles from here, sir. He aims to attack the rebel camp at dawn the day after tomorrow and sends you his orders. He chose me to bring them to you. I left camp a day ago and worked my way through the rebel lines to get to the mine. It took some persuading for the centurion to let me in, sir.'

'Quite right,' said Cato. 'Get this man something to eat and drink.'

Musa nodded and sent one of his men to the kitchen as Cato broke the seal and took out the slender scroll. Moving close to the light of one of the lamps he unrolled it and began to read. The legate's instructions were brief enough. He would make his attack at the time Collenus had said. Cato and his cohort were ordered to sally out of the mine and attack the rebel camp first. Once the enemy was preoccupied and certain that they were about to crush the cohort, Vitellius would strike in full force and the rebels would be crushed between the two forces. It was a bold enough plan, Cato conceded as he returned the scroll to the leather case, but its very boldness caused him to feel uneasy at once. What if Vitellius' attack arrived too late to save the Second Cohort? A darker possibility occurred to him. What if that was the real plan? The destruction of Cato and Macro by the rebels before they were destroyed by Vitellius and his forces in turn. That would tie things up rather neatly for the legate. But at the cost of the cohort. It was hard to believe even Vitellius was that ruthless. Then again, Cato thought. What if this message was not from Vitellius at all? What if it was a ruse by Iskerbeles to entice the cohort out from behind the safety of their defences. Collenus, if that was his name, spoke Latin, but that might be for any number of reasons. He might be a criminal, a former soldier possibly, condemned to the mines. Cropping the hair was a neat touch if the enemy was trying to pass him off as a soldier.

Cato turned to Musa. 'Do you recognise this man?'

'No, sir. Never seen him before. But then there're thousands of men in the Guard.'

'I know him,' said Pulcher. He crossed over for a closer inspection. 'That's definitely Collenus. I had to discipline him for fighting in barracks when I was on duty a few months ago. He's one of us.'

Cato thought a moment and nodded. 'Fair enough. So, Collenus, tell me, how did the legate manage to get here so quickly? I wasn't expecting him for a few more days at least.'

'We force-marched, sir. Then left the siege train behind to make its own way while the cavalry and infantry went ahead. Can't say it wasn't tough, sir.'

The other men in the room shared a knowing smile and Pulcher growled. 'You don't know the half of it, sunshine.'

The soldier sent in search of food returned with half a loaf of dry bread, a hunk of salted pork and a wineskin and set them down on a table for Collenus. He looked at the food and licked his lips and Cato nodded. 'Tuck in. You've earned it.'

Collenus needed no further prompting and gulped several mouthfuls of water before tearing at the bread.

'Centurion Musa.'

'Sir?'

'I'd be obliged if you did not quit your post for any reason in future before your watch duty is complete. Send a man in your place. But never leave your post again.'

'Yes, sir.' The centurion looked chastened.

'I will be in the procurator's office if I am needed.'

As Cato turned and strode towards the corridor, Pulcher went over to the new arrival and patted him on the back to offer him a few quiet words of congratulation for his efforts, before heading to lead his men down to the wall and take over from Musa and his century.

# CHAPTER THIRTY

'Well I don't like it,' said Macro the next morning as they conducted their morning walk around the mine and inspected the defences. 'We've no reason to trust Vitellius. Not given our past experience of him. The man's a scheming bastard. Whatever he does or says the only thing we can be sure of is that it serves his own interests, usually at great cost to someone else. Speaking for myself, I am sick of being that someone else. If we form the cohort up and march out of here to do battle, what guarantee have we got that he will play his part? None. None at all. Chances are we will march out to our deaths, and then when our heads are decorating the top of some cunt's spear, only then will he put in an appearance.'

'Quite so,' Cato agreed. 'You paraphrase my thoughts precisely.'

'So what are you going to do? Stay inside the fort and wait for him to move against the rebels first? That's what I'd do.'

Cato sucked in a breath. 'That's exactly what I should do. But his orders are quite explicit. I am to attack first, in order to lure Iskerbeles out of his camp and distract him long enough for Vitellius to close the trap. If they see Vitellius first then the rebels will have enough time to reach the plain and escape. And for that, I will be held to account.'

'So, once again, we're fucked if we do, and fucked if we don't.'

'More or less.'

'Shit . . .' Macro ground his teeth. 'Why can't this ever just be about soldiering? Why is there always some bastard scheming away in the background?'

'That's how it always is, Macro. We just get a better view of it the further up the chain of command we go.'

312

'Then I wish I had stayed a ranker. Just did my duty and tried to be a good soldier. Life was simpler back then.'

'No. It just seemed that way. Besides, you were born to be a centurion and Rome is better served for having you raised to the centurionate. Rome, the army, and the men you command. They all need you. As do I. To go into battle without you at my side would be unthinkable.'

Macro shook his head and laughed self-consciously. 'Bollocks to that. You do fine with or without me.'

'With is better. Trust me,' Cato concluded as they reached the top of the shaft leading down to the countermine. Two men worked a large bellows connected to a leather hose to pump fresh air down into the tunnel to allow the men working there to breathe, and to prevent the lamps from being suffocated. A makeshift crane had been erected over the opening and a basket of spoil rose out of the gloom. It was swung out to the side and emptied into a handcart before the earth and rocks were wheeled away to add thickness to the rampart at the rear of the wall. Centurion Petillius had just climbed the ladder and stood mopping his brow with his neckscarf. Even covered in soil and sweat he still managed to look handsome and flashed a winning smile at the prefect as Cato and Macro approached.

'How is the tunnel progressing?'

Petillius tied the neckscarf back in place as he replied. 'As far as I can calculate it we've dug past the gatehouse and outer ditch by twenty feet or so. We're not going to win any prizes for the speed of our work, but we're on course to intercept their mine before it reaches our defences. That could be any day now.'

'Then we need to be ready for that. Macro, make a note. Have a half century posted close by. They'll go into the tunnel the moment we detect the enemy.'

'Yes, sir.' Macro took out a waxed slate and stylus from his sidebag and wrote it down.

'Now for the fun part,' Cato muttered humourlessly as he swung himself onto the ladder and began to descend into the shaft. Already he could feel the anxiety weighing on him as he thought about the cramped tunnel below. There was no need to put himself through this, but it was important to show the men that he endured what they endured. Being in the cramped space filled his heart with mortal terror of the roof collapsing and burying him alive. Despite the care with which the countermine had been constructed and the use of more pit props than was necessary, on the occasions that Cato had inspected the work at first hand, he had been expecting the tunnel to cave in at any moment. It was irrational, he told himself. And therefore he must conquer the terror, in the name of reason and to prove to himself that he could overcome such fear.

He had to pause halfway down as the empty basket swept past him ready for the next load of spoil to be raised to the surface. Peering down he saw the gloomily lit space at the bottom of the shaft. Two Praetorians stood waiting for the basket, a bucket of spoil in each hand. They made space for their commander as Cato stepped off the ladder into the cramped space. Above him Macro began to descend, muttering bitterly that he had not joined the army to become a bloody mole. The air felt clammy and close and Cato peered through the stout timbers that framed the tunnel inclining down in the direction of the wall. Oil lamps fixed to pit props lined the route and provided barely enough illumination to light their immediate surroundings. The tunnel was wide enough to permit two handcarts to pass each other, but hardly more than five feet in height so that everyone had to bow their heads and walk stooped.

Macro reached the bottom and they shuffled round the men with the buckets as Cato led the way down the incline. It levelled out after a short distance and the air was hot and dank and smelled musty.

'Can't say I will miss this place when it's all over,' said Macro. 'It ain't natural for a man to be underground.'

Cato did not reply, and kept his jaws clenched as he struggled to control his fear. He was determined not to let it show. There was movement ahead and two more men carrying buckets approached, strips of cloth tied round their brows to keep the sweat from their eyes. They offered a quick nod by way of salute and bustled by the two officers. There was a little waft of better air and the chinking of picks increased in volume as they approached the end of the tunnel. Spare pit props lay along the side, waiting to be fed forward and

314

driven into position around the workface before the next two feet of earth and rock was dug out and the process repeated as the tunnel slowly advanced. Then, up ahead, Cato could discern the small team at work, bodies glistening with sweat as they wielded their tools as best they could in the confined space. Three relays of two men toiled away, swapping over as they tired. At the sound of the officers' approach one of the men glanced back and then called out to the others.

'Prefect is present!'

The Praetorians tried to stand to attention in what Cato thought was a quite ridiculous attempt to preserve the formality of a visit from the commanding officer.

'At ease,' Cato called back. 'Rest your men for a moment, Sentiacus.'

Petillius' optio nodded. 'Thank you, sir. You heard him, lads, tools down and take a breather.'

The Praetorians leaned their picks against the sides of the tunnel and hunkered down as Cato spoke with the optio.

'How is it progressing?'

'Very well, sir. I reckon on . . . over ten feet on our shift. Well over what Porcino's lot did before us.'

'That's good.' Cato was pleased that the men were working competitively, as soldiers often will even under the most trying of circumstances. Every challenge was a chance to prove themselves. 'Fine effort, lads. If you manage another two feet before your century is relieved, there's an extra ration of wine in it for you.'

The exhausted Praetorians nodded with appreciation and Cato stepped up to the workface to examine it closely. There was more rock mixed in with the earth than had been the case during the previous day and that would make the going somewhat harder, he realised. Sentiacus and his men had done very well indeed.

'Quiet!' Macro interrupted the muted conversation of the resting Praetorians. 'Listen.'

Cato turned back to his friend quickly. 'What is—'

'Shhh. Keep still and listen.'

Cato froze, as did the others, ears straining and trying to ignore the dry rasp of their own breathing and the light rhythmic wheeze of the leather airhose. Cato was about to give up and demand an explanation from Macro when he heard it, the faint sound of tools working the earth and rock, then snatches of muffled voices. The Praetorians grabbed their own tools and Cato and Macro eased their swords from their scabbards.

'That's the enemy but where are the sounds coming from?' Cato whispered.

His men listened some more and Sentiacus pointed towards the workface. 'Should be coming from there.'

Cato listened again and shook his head. 'More to this side, I think.'

He touched the left side of the tunnel as if to feel vibrations through his fingertips but there was nothing. The noises were louder now and the sound of picks working the earth more pronounced.

'Shit . . .' one of the Praetorians said softly.

'Shut your mouth,' Macro snapped. 'All of you.'

A short distance back down the tunnel there was a trickle of soil and then the thud of metal biting into wood.

'Get back,' Cato ordered. 'Quickly!'

Sentiacus roused his men and thrust them ahead of him, in the direction of the shaft. Cato and Macro followed. They had just passed a pit prop when a clod of earth exploded from the side of the tunnel and struck Cato in the side of the head. The metal end of a pick appeared briefly from the earth, then it was wrenched back leaving a hole through which a dull orange light glowed. More earth tumbled into the tunnel as the gap increased in size, and soon was large enough to reach an arm through. A few more blows from the other side and the wall collapsed between two of the pit props, revealing a large group of wiry-looking men, lit by candles guttering in small saucers in iron brackets fixed to pit props. Cato could see that they were working on a wider, larger tunnel than the Roman effort, running across the latter at right angles at a slightly higher depth. Now all looked on in shock as the soil between the two tunnels crumbled.

There was a moment of stillness on both sides and Cato could see at once that they were outnumbered. He pointed to the nearest of the Praetorians. 'Go for help! Run!'

As the man scrambled back down the tunnel towards the shaft the rebel miners hurriedly set to work clearing away the remaining obstacles between the two tunnels, so there was space to get at the Romans. Then the first of them attempted to thrust himself through the gap between two of the pit props. Sentiacus took a step forward swinging his pick and the long, blunt point caught the rebel under the sternum, tearing into his soft tissue and organs. Sentiacus braced his boot against the man's groin and ripped his tool free before slamming the head into his opponent's face, battering him into unconsciousness so that he slumped down, blocking the gap between the two props. The rebels grasped what needed to be done at once, and began to dig away the soil at the base of the props, driving bodily into the timber posts in an effort to dislodge them. Loose soil cascaded down on the Romans as the overhead beam shifted.

'Stay clear of that!' Sentiacus warned them, and the officers and men drew aside as they held their weapons ready. Cato could hear the urgent shouts of the man he had sent back up the tunnel.

'We have to hold 'em off as long as we can, lads.'

One of the props fell into the Roman tunnel and the roof beam sagged down with it, releasing a fall of soil and rock through the gap between the neighbouring beams. The Romans shook the debris from their heads as the rebels forced their way through the enlarged gap between the two tunnels. Hunched over, breathing foul air and by the thin light of oil lamps and candles, the two sides brutally contested the tightly enclosed space. For an instant Cato felt his bones chill at the nightmare he was caught within. Then the spell broke as he saw the semi-naked Praetorians and rebels hurl them-selves on each other. There was no room to wield weapons with any force and they had to use the picks like clubs, punching the iron heads and wooden shafts into limbs, torsos and heads as they gasped for breath and the sweat glistened on their soiled skin. Some cast aside their weapons and used their bare hands, throttling and gouging.

Even though the slaves had the greater number they could not get more than a few men through the breach where the Romans fell on them in a vicious fight for survival. There was no time to reflect on the savage horror of it all as Cato pressed himself forward, striking out with his sword at the thigh of a man emerging through the gap. The point cut into muscle and glanced off bone and Cato twisted the blade left and right as he pulled it free. The rebel turned to him, staggering between Cato and the nearest lamp so that his features were invisible. However, Cato could hear the wild growl as the rebel thrust his pick out and sprang forward behind it. The shaft struck Cato on the chest and knocked him back, catching his heel on one of the spare props. He fell onto the floor of the tunnel with the rebel on top of him. He felt the man's breath on his cheek, then the hard pressure of the shaft sliding up his chest towards his throat as the rebel attempted to crush his windpipe. There was no room to wield his sword effectively and Cato slammed the pommel into the rebel's bare ribs to little avail. In desperation Cato thrust his head up but there was not enough impetus to the blow to make any impact. None the less he had a clear sense of where the man's features were in relation to his own in the darkness. Cato opened his mouth, curled back his lips and sank his teeth into his enemy's nose, biting down hard on flesh and cartilage and feeling hot blood drip into his mouth and roll down his tongue into his throat. He shook his head violently, and there was a soft crunch and his head fell back with a large lump of warm gristle in his teeth which he spat out. The rebel let out a howl of agony and released one of his hands from the pick shaft to grope towards his ruined face. Cato drew up his knee and rolled the man off, and struck with his sword, stabbing a series of short, shallow blows that crippled his opponent.

Struggling back onto his feet Cato could just see three more bodies writhing on the floor of the tunnel, the nearest under Macro as he knelt on the man's stomach pressing his sword down into his foe's chest with both hands and all his weight. As the rebel's movements became feeble, Macro rose up, braced his boot next to the wound and wrenched his sword free, before turning at once back towards the breach. It was clear to Cato that they could not hold out for much longer. Something had to be done.

'Sentiacus! Hold them off. When I give the order, you and the men fall back.'

The optio nodded quickly before striking out with his pick once

318

again. Cato retreated ten feet further up the tunnel and slapped his spare hand against one of the thinner pit props.

'This will do. Help me, Macro.'

The centurion came up to him. 'Do what?'

'Shift this. We have to collapse our tunnel, here. Before we lose it all.'

'But the lads?'

'Will get out in time. Help me.'

Cato worked furiously at the soil around the top of the post while Macro dug around the bottom. All the time the grunts and cries of the fight a short distance away added urgency to their efforts. Cato leaned against the post and felt it give.

'Enough digging. Push!'

Macro stood and braced his shoulder to the timber as Cato pushed higher up. 'Heave.'

The post gave ground and the top came to the edge of the beam.

'Stop there!' Cato ordered. 'Next prop!'

They repeated the process and then returned to the first as Cato called down the tunnel, 'Fall back! Now!'

The first of the Praetorians scrambled by, then another, clutching a hand over a wound to his side, as a third man covered his back. Only the optio remained, with one more Praetorian. In the weak light Cato saw that both had been wounded. Sentiacus' left arm had been smashed and shattered bones protruded from his forearm as he swung his pick in his remaining good hand, wildly sweeping it at the faces of the rebels facing him across the tunnel. The other Praetorian turned to escape, limping up the tunnel a few paces before a rebel caught up with him, shoved him face forward onto the ground and swung a pick into his spine with brutal force.

'Sentiacus! Run!'

Even as he called out, Cato could see it was too late. Two of the rebels had already got past the optio and were moving up the tunnel as more made to follow them. Sentiacus looked up, saw the two officers standing ready to collapse the tunnel and shouted, 'Do it, sir!'

There was no time to deliberate, just act, and Cato thrust his weight against the prop. It lurched free of the beam which promptly collapsed in front of Cato and Macro, bringing down an avalanche of soil and rock that buried the two rebels rushing towards them, and cut off their view of Sentiacus just as the optio hurled himself forward amongst the enemy.

'Get back!' Cato ordered and they retreated to the next prop as the nearest of the rebels rose up from the falling soil and struggled on a step, shaking his head. The second collapse had a much greater effect, bringing down a wider stretch of the tunnel completely as earth and rock crushed the rebel and buried him alive. Cato dragged Macro back several paces until they were clear of the debris. The air filled with choking dust and all sound of the struggle on the far side of the collapsed section was cut off. The only noise was the coughing of the Romans as they stumbled back up the tunnel towards the sunlight shining down the shaft.

As they approached, Petillius and a handful of his men had started down the tunnel.

'Too late,' Cato gasped. 'Had to collapse the tunnel . . . before we lost it . . . Get your men down there. Make sure they don't dig through.'

'Yes, sir.'

Cato, Macro and the survivors of the working party pressed themselves into the side of the tunnel as the heavily armed Praetorians made their way past. When the way was clear they moved into the bottom of the shaft. Cato allowed another ten men to follow Petillius before he ordered Sentiacus' men to climb out, followed by himself and Macro. The air back at the surface was warm, dry and sweet to breathe and the filth-covered men sat or stood bent over, chests heaving as they struggled to catch their breath.

As soon as he could breathe easily Cato forced himself to stand straight. Macro turned his head to look up at him.

'Seems like we found their mine, right enough.'

'No, they found ours.' Cato said bitterly. 'I should have thought they'd anticipate a countermine. I'll not underestimate Iskerbeles again.'

'What are you talking about, sir?' Macro stood up and arched his back, rubbing the base of his spine. 'It was just bad luck. Damn, but they worked fast this time round.'

'No . . . No, I think not.' Cato frowned as he recalled the details of the action shortly before. 'They came at us from the wrong direction. From the left, over there.' He gestured to the wall beside the tower. 'Like they fully intended to cut across our countermine. Or cut over or underneath it to get at the gatehouse.'

Macro considered this briefly. 'It's possible. But we've blocked them for now. Long enough to stall them until Vitellius begins his attack at least.'

Cato went to run his hand through his hair but found it still covered in dirt and endeavoured to brush it off instead as he continued his line of thought. As the enemy had broken through he had seen their tunnel, lit by small lamps and candles, stretching out behind them for a long distance parallel to the wall. It made no sense to start a new tunnel angling towards the wall only to cut back along it towards the gatehouse. If Iskerbeles had intended to intercept the countermine from the side he could have chosen a far more direct line of approach. In any case, the enemy would have had to work like demons in order to dig this new tunnel . . . Unless . . . He felt a cold veil settle over his mind as he realised that he had been fooled by the enemy. Comprehensively misdirected and humiliated.

'Sir!'

Cato looked up in the direction of the call and saw a Praetorian on the tower waving to attract his attention.

'What is it?'

'The enemy, sir. They're moving up from the camp.'

'How many of them?'

There was a pause before the sentry shook his head. 'I don't know, sir. Looks like all of them.'

Cato raced across to the ladder and climbed the tower, Macro close behind him. Rushing across to the battlement Cato looked out over the ruins and saw a broad sweep of the landscape beyond the settlement covered by figures moving down from the camp towards the mine. Many thousands of them.

Macro appeared at his side, breathing hard. 'Looks like they ain't going to wait until Vitellius arrives. At least that saves us making any decision about whether we trust the bastard or not. I just hope we're still around when the rest of the Praetorians join the fight.'

Cato nodded and turned to the sentry who had raised the alarm. 'Sound the call to arms.'

The man nodded and picked up the brass horn resting in the corner of the tower. Raising it to his lips he took in a deep breath, pursed his lips to the mouthpiece and blew three sharp notes, paused and repeated the call several times. The men from the duty century resting behind the wall snatched up their kit and raced into place on the walkway as the first men from the remaining centuries came running down the track from the mining camp, some already in full kit, others struggling to put it on as they hurried along.

'I can't believe Iskerbeles is going to attempt another frontal assault,' said Macro. 'Not in broad daylight. Not without bringing the gatehouse down first.'

Cato said nothing but kept watching the steadily approaching rebel horde. It made no sense to attack now, as Macro said. How could they possibly hope to succeed when they were so easily repulsed before?

The men of the cohort were in position long before the first of the rebels emerged from the ruins and formed up in front of the wall, just beyond the range of slingshot. The cohort adopted the same arrangement as before, with the first two centuries manning the wall, the Third behind the gatehouse and the Fourth and Sixth in reserve behind the wall, with Pulcher, and the remaining men of the Fifth, stood to the rear as a reserve of the last resort. Petillius and his men had been pulled out of the tunnel and the ladder taken out of the shaft in case the enemy dug through the collapsed tunnel.

As the rebels formed up Cato noted that there were few assault ladders, and that many of the men were carrying fascines, tightly bound bundles of wood and brush to fill in crossing points over the outer ditch. The main weight of the enemy line seemed to be to the Roman left, opposite the wall manned by Secundus and his men.

Metellus climbed up into the tower to hand Cato his felt skull-cap, helmet and shield.

'Thank you.'

As Cato fastened the strap Metellus muttered, 'What are they waiting for?'

Cato ignored the question. There could be any number of explanations. Then a horn sounded from the enemy host and two riders came forward. Cato instantly recognised Iskerbeles and his huge lieutenant. The latter raised a horn and blew again as they walked their horses slowly forward. Both men carried shields, held ready to protect themselves in case the Romans attempted a long-range shot from bow or sling.

Cato allowed them to come closer before he cupped his hands and shouted, 'Stop there!'

The riders reined in obediently.

'What do you want?' Cato demanded.

Iskerbeles drew himself up in the saddle and replied clearly in Latin. 'Romans. This is your last chance to surrender. Do it now and I will be merciful. You shall be spared and sent back to Tarraco. The choice is yours. Surrender now, or die . . . What is your reply?'

Macro snorted with derision. 'Is he joking? Or drunk? Or just mad?'

Cato shook his head. 'I don't know . . .'

There was a long pause before Iskerbeles called out again. 'Well, Romans?'

Cato cupped his hands to his mouth again to make his reply. 'I need time to consider. I shall give you my reply at noon tomorrow.'

Iskerbeles shook his head. 'You have already given me your reply, Prefect. You have chosen death. So be it.'

Iskerbeles gestured to his companion and they quickly turned their horses about and cantered back into their lines. The defenders stood in tense silence and waited for the attack to begin. There was no movement from the rebel side. Their men stood still, under the sun, also waiting . . . And waiting.

'What the fuck are they up to now?' Macro demanded at length. 'They trying to bore us all to death?'

It was the faint rumble that first revealed the enemy's hand. A dull sound like a heavily muffled drum roll, away to the left, and Cato and Macro moved to the side of the tower to investigate. Half-way along the wall the Praetorians were stirring anxiously and looking down at the ground beneath them. Suddenly a section of the walkway and rampart seemed to tremble and started dropping into the earth, taking the men with it. A breach was opening up, and widening. Then the same thing began to happen further along the wall, and again closer to the tower. The men on the unaffected stretches began to fall back from the wall in panic.

'What in Hades is happening?' Macro asked in astonishment.

Cato had already guessed. 'Dear Gods . . . There was another tunnel all along! The first was just a diversion. That's why it never got very far. That bastard played me for a complete fool. All the time they were digging to undermine the wall, not the gatehouse.'

Before he finished speaking the horn sounded again from within the massed ranks of the enemy, a long, clear, defiant note. This time the rebels let out a terrifying, deafening roar of triumph and broke into a charge over the ground in front of the stricken wall and the dazed men who had survived the sections that had collapsed, leaving wide breaches for the enemy to pour through in their thousands.

# CHAPTER THIRTY-ONE

Cato rushed to the back of the tower and called down, 'Porcino! Petillius! Get your centuries forward to hold the breaches! At the double!'

He turned to Macro. 'Looks like they are going to give your section of the wall a miss, so take half your men and back up the others.'

'Yes, sir.' Macro swung himself onto the ladder and clambered down to the walkway as quickly as he could.

Cato thought quickly. Iskerbeles had handled the siege brilliantly, wrong-footing the Romans and destroying the best line of defence at a stroke. The inner wall, around the gatehouse, had been all but complete and now stood as a mute, useless tribute to the guile of the rebels. The three breaches accounted for over a hundred feet in the wall, and the stretches in between were cracked and subsiding. Half of the men defending that sector of the wall had gone down with it and the survivors were struggling to extricate themselves from the rubble while their unaffected comrades scrabbled over the heaps of masonry, earth and rocks to come to their aid. It was obvious to Cato that any attempt to defend the first wall would surely fail. The cohort had to fall back to the second wall, and the withdrawal had to be handled carefully if there was not to be a rout, resulting in the complete annihilation of the Praetorians.

Already the first of the rebels had reached the ditch in front of the breaches and were hurling their fascines on top of the rubble in the ditch. The enemy massed beyond the breaches, cheering loudly as they scented victory. They would have usable causeways across the ditch very soon and be ready to storm into the breaches. Then, no matter how well the Praetorians fought, the overwhelming weight in numbers would decide the issue. Cato turned to call down to the commander of the last reserve.

'Centurion Pulcher! Pulcher!'

The stocky officer looked up. 'Sir?'

'Take your men and get back to the second wall and hold the gate open for the rest of us.'

The din created by the jeers and cheering of the enemy rose and fell like a wave and Pulcher cupped a hand to his ear and shook his head helplessly.

'Fuck,' Cato muttered to himself, and filled his lungs and cupped his hands to his mouth and tried again. 'I said, take your men and fall back to the second wall!'

Pulcher heard the order this time and nodded before turning to convey the order to his men.

'Fall back!' another voice cried out and Cato's head spun towards the breached wall as Centurion Musa raised his sword and jabbed it to the rear and repeated the call. 'Fall back!'

'No!' Cato shouted, but there was already too much noise. Too many voices shouting for help, shouting orders, shouting encouragement to each other, and he was drowned out. Already the Praetorians of the Third Century were turning away from the enemy to pick their way back over the rubble, and blundering into the first of Macro's men as they hurried round to reinforce the men who should be defending the breaches.

The defence of the mine was falling apart before Cato's eyes and he had to do something at once before the rebels started to surge across the causeways and fall upon the disorganised soldiers of the Praetorian cohort. He turned to the other men in the tower. 'Get out! Get back to the second wall.' A glance over the parapet revealed that the enemy was making no attempt to attack the wall to the right of the tower. Cato turned to one of the men still with him. 'You go to Petillius and Porcino and say I want their men to form up halfway between here and the second wall. Go!'

Cato ordered the trumpeter to follow him. Then he was on the ladder, dropping two rungs at a time before leaping off a few feet from the bottom. He ran towards the nearest breach as Musa's men began to retreat across the open ground towards the second wall. It was already too late to stop those who had a good head start, and Cato realised that it was as well to have as many men behind the second line of defence as possible, ready to receive those who survived the first enemy onslaught into the breaches. Centurion Musa was still bellowing at his men to fall back when Cato grabbed his shoulder and spun him round.

'What the fuck are you doing, you fool?'

'Sir?' Musa looked stunned. 'You gave the order to fall back . . .'

'The order was for Pulcher.' Cato waved his hand at the men still coming off the rubble 'Get them back into the breach.'

Musa pointed to the men already heading back to the second wall. 'What about the rest?'

'Too late for them. Get the others forward before you get us all killed!' Cato shoved him towards the nearest section of collapsed wall. 'Hold that breach.'

Musa took charge of his senses and nodded before striding up to the breach, bellowing for his men to follow him. Cato ran on, and found Macro forming up his half century.

'You take the centre. Hold on as long as you can. We have to buy time to restore some order. When you hear the trumpet, fall back on Petillius, with the rest of the men. Once the cohort is together, we'll withdraw to the second wall. Clear?'

'Yes, sir. May the Gods preserve us.'

Cato nodded and with the trumpeter close behind sprinted towards the last breach where most of the survivors of the Second Century had gathered around the standard, some fifty men in all. Cristus was with them, covered in dust and barely recognisable.

'Where's Centurion Secundus?'

Cristus gestured towards the ruined wall. 'Gone, sir. Buried in that lot.'

'Where's the optio?'

'He's missing as well, sir.'

'Shit . . .' Cato muttered under his breath. The century needed to be taken under control. Cristus was obviously too shaken for the role. Cato reached for the century's standard. 'Give me that and find yourself a weapon.'

Cato took a firm hold of the standard and raised it high as he moved to the front of the men of the Second Century. 'Follow me!'

They set off up the slope, stepping carefully on the loose rocks and soft earth. Ahead lay the uneven line of the remains of the wall, and beyond, Cato could see the tips of the enemy's spears and swords, then, as he continued to climb over the rubble, the crests of the helmets that had been looted from the Roman troops they had killed. Finally he could see the rebels themselves, a seething mass of shouting men, brandishing their weapons as they waited for the last of the fascines to be hurled into the ditch. Their cries and shouting reached a crescendo as they saw the Praetorians clambering over the rubble and forming a double line across the width of the breach. Cato took his place at the centre of the line, on the highest point, and planted the spike at the bottom of the standard as firmly as he could before he drew his sword and gave the order.

'Shields, to the front!'

The Praetorians advanced their left arms and closed ranks enough to present an unbroken wall of shields to the enemy while they held their spears at eye level, ready to strike. A stone arced from near the front of the enemy horde and rattled off the shield of the man directly in front of Cato, and then more followed and he realised that the standard made him the most obvious target for the enemy. He crouched slightly. Not enough to forsake his dignity but sufficient to keep most of his face sheltered behind the shields of the Praetorians. They did not have to endure the barrage long before a horn sounded and the rebels surged forward with a great roar. They funnelled towards the makeshift causeway and so were packed into a dense mass as they crossed the ditch and charged the Roman defenders. Fortunately the uneven surface of the slope broke the impetus of the charge as they reached the shields in a ragged series of man-on-man duels.

'Steady, lads!' Cato called out as calmly as he could manage. 'For Rome and the Emperor!'

The air around him filled with the clash of weapons and the thud and clatter of blows landing on shields. The Praetorians held the high ground, had the longer reach and were far better equipped as most of their foes wore no armour and had been farmers or slaves before the rebellion had made them into any kind of warrior. Yet the rebels fought with the fanatical courage of their forefathers who had defied Rome for nearly two hundred years. But courage does not render a man immune to injury and they fell to the spear thrusts of the better trained and disciplined Praetorians. Bodies piled across the front of the Roman line, still living, but then crushed underfoot as their comrades pressed forward to close with their enemy. The rebels hacked at the spearheads or snatched them and attempted to wrestle them from the grasp of the Romans, all the time being pressed forward by those following on behind so that the two sides were crushed together in a tight mêlée.

'Front rank, down spears!' Cato bellowed. 'Draw swords!'

The first line of Praetorians hurriedly passed their spears back to their comrades while keeping their shields to the enemy. Then they snatched out their short swords, a weapon more suited to close combat, and thrust and stabbed with their blades into the tightly packed mass of rebels before them. It was all but impossible to evade the swords and scores more of the enemy went down in front of the Roman shields, even as the momentum of the rebel charge began to force the Praetorians back, inch by inch.

Cato looked to the right and saw that Macro and Musa were holding firm for now. Just over a hundred paces behind the first wall Petillius and Porcino's men were still forming a line across the open ground between the cliff and the ravine. Beyond them, Pulcher was doubling his men back to the second wall. Cato knew that the men around him must hold firm in the breach a little longer. If they gave way then the enemy would flood through into the mine and take Macro and Musa from the rear. The men of the Second Century must not give any more ground. They needed something to stiffen their resolve. There was one thing that could be depended on, Cato realised. One way of encouraging the men to dig in. He readied his sword and, leaning the shaft of the standard against his shoulder, pulled it free of the rubble and forced his way forward between the soldiers immediately in front of him so that he stood in the middle of the front rank. At once the nearest of the enemy pressed towards him with eager expressions, determined to win glory by taking the

Praetorians' sacred standard, entrusted to them by the Emperor himself.

Cato raised his sword and hacked at the head of the nearest rebel, slicing off his ear and cutting deep into his jaw. He snatched the blade back just in time to thrust the point into the throat of another enemy coming at him with an axe. He called out desperately, his voice almost cracking with the strain.

'Praetorians! Defend the standard! On me!'

The men of the Second Century braced their feet in the rubble and leaned into their battered and blood-spattered shields as they continued to cut the enemy down. Both sides fought with a savagery born of desperation and a thirst for glory as they contested the ground immediately around the Roman standard. Cato, encumbered by the dressing and patch over his eye, kept looking right and left so as not to be caught on a blind side. His sword was in constant motion, darting at any foe who came within reach, sometimes failing to connect, sometimes inflicting a flesh wound, as well as striking disabling blows that dropped a rebel in his tracks, or sent him staggering back amongst his comrades. Then, a large warrior with a long cavalry sword thrust his way through the packed ranks. The man raised the blade overhead as he approached Cato and swung it in a vicious diagonal arc. Cato instinctively raised his own sword to parry the blow, but the weight of the other man's weapon drove Cato's sword arm down and he had just enough presence of mind to twist his wrist and deflect the blow. The rebel's sword scraped loudly down the length of Cato's blade, striking the hilt and knocking the weapon from the prefect's hand.

The man let out a triumphant roar and snatched at the wooden shaft of the standard with his spare hand. No longer armed, Cato desperately held on with both hands. The two men strained for possession of the standard for a moment before Cato dropped his right hand to rip out the dagger from his belt and slash at the rebel's fingers, lacerating flesh and chipping into bone. Raising the small blade, Cato slammed it deep into his opponent's forearm. With a howl of pained rage his opponent jerked his arm back, releasing the standard but snatching the dagger from Cato's grasp. As he recovered his balance the rebel raised his sword to strike again, a cruel glint in his eye at the prospect of striking down the defenceless Roman officer.

At once Cato took the standard firmly in both hands and swung the bottom up hard into the rebel's groin. The man's jaw gaped in a groan and the sword wavered in his grasp. Cato drew the staff back and punched the bottom into the man's collarbone, knocking him off balance and sending him tumbling back against a handful of his comrades who fell beneath him. Before Cato could do anything more, Cristus and one of the Praetorians thrust their way past him and closed ranks to protect their unit's standard. Cato hoisted it up and waved it from side to side as the Romans stood their ground, defying the enemy. At that moment, by some unspoken consent, there was a slight pause in the fighting as the rebels began to pull back. The combatants on both sides were breathing hard as they caught their breath and watched the enemy warily, waiting for the struggle to continue.

Cato glanced over his shoulder and saw that Pulcher had reached the second wall and his men were lined up in front of the gate. Closer to, the centuries of Petillius and Porcino were also in position. On the remains of the wall, Macro's guardsmen were standing firm, but further along Musa had been forced back, with the enemy threatening to spill round his flanks at any moment. It was time to withdraw, Cato decided. Before the men on the wall were overwhelmed and cut to pieces.

He called over his shoulder to the trumpeter, 'Sound withdrawal.'

The soldier raised the gleaming instrument to his lips and blew a feeble note. He tried again with a similar result.

'For Gods' sake, spit man!' Cato snapped. 'Spit!'

The Praetorian nodded, cleared his throat, spat to one side and tried again. This time the notes blared out clear and true. The trumpeter repeated the signal three times and lowered his instrument. Cato drew a breath and called out above the din of battle, 'Second Century! Disengage! Fall back on the standard!'

Along the battle line the Praetorians edged away from the enemy, leaving the heaped bodies of the dead and dying between the two sides. The Romans had withdrawn halfway down the slope before a shout rose from the rebel ranks. The cry was taken up, echoed and swelled into a roar as they climbed over the bodies to continue the struggle, pausing only to finish off several of the Romans who had been too badly wounded to make their way to the rear. There was nothing that could have been done for them, Cato accepted bitterly, as he watched his men die. Nothing, except swear to avenge them if the chance came. What was left of the century, no more than forty men now, reached the bottom of the debris slope and the flanks folded in quickly to form a tight box around the standard, shields facing out on all sides. Further along the line of the wall, Macro and Musa had done the same and merged centuries, along with the other half of Macro's century who had abandoned the wall to the right of the gatehouse and run to join their comrades. With the officers calling the time the two boxes paced steadily towards the second wall as the rebels swarmed on to the remains of the first, jubilant at their success, cheering themselves, and jeering the Romans, as if they had won a great victory.

Cato gauged the distance between his men and the larger formation no more than forty paces away. They would have a better chance together than divided, he calculated.

'On my order, break formation and make for the other box.' Cato looked at the rebels again and there was no sign of any urge to chase down the Romans. No doubt they had been chastened by their losses in winning control of the breaches.

'Break ranks!'

The Praetorians abruptly turned and ran across the open ground, Cato leaning the standard across his shoulder so that it would not encumber him as he sprinted.

The enemy reacted at once and greeted the Romans' sudden movement with a deafening, contemptuous jeering. A handful moved out ahead of their comrades and urged them on. More followed, and then, as if swept forward by some giant invisible hand, the horde lurched forward into a wild charge.

Ahead, Cato could see that the other box had halted and parted ranks on the nearest side to admit the men racing towards them. Weighed down by heavy armour and their shields, the Praetorians could not move nearly as fast as the rebels sprinting after them, but they had a head start, and the fleetest of the Romans stumbled into the opening left for them as Cato slowed slightly to look over his shoulder. There were a handful of men behind him and the first of the enemy not twenty paces away.

'Run, you fools! Run for your lives!'

Then he was passing through the gap, almost knocking over a man who had stopped too abruptly just ahead of him. Cato regained his balance, raised the standard again and turned to see the last of his men desperately sprinting as fast as he could, teeth gritted. Then his foot landed on a small rock, just large enough to turn his ankle, and the man tumbled to the side in a small shower of grit and dust. Cato instinctively took a pace towards the man, but before he could go any further the Praetorians closed the gap again, barring his way. It was too late to save the man in any case. Three rebels were on him before he could roll onto his knees. The first kicked him back onto his side and then his companions bent over the Roman, hacking at him, one with a short sword, the other with an axe, as blood sprayed over them.

'Sir, are you all right?' Macro held his shoulder as Cato gasped for breath, and nodded.

'Get the formation moving.'

'Yes, sir.' Macro tilted his head back and shouted, 'Advance!'

The men closed up, shield to shield, marching at a slow step with Cato and the survivors of the Second Century keeping pace in the middle of the box. The swiftest of the rebels charged into the rear of the formation, slashing at the shields and trying to cut their way through the ranks of the Praetorians. But the guardsmen held their positions firmly, coolly cutting down the more impetuous of their opponents. More of them flowed along the sides of the box as they caught up and soon the box was surrounded by a shimmering sea of waving blades and edged weapons as the stifling air filled with the clash of weapons and the war cries of the rebels. The Romans were silent. Faces stern and teeth gritted, they kept moving, under the orders and occasional words of encouragement of their officers. Cato, together with the standard bearers of the other centuries, kept the standards raised high. Macro took his place in the centre of the front face of the box, shifting his shield slightly up to keep it in line with the taller men on either side, and sparing a moment to silently curse those who recruited the guardsmen on the basis of their height.

As before, in the breaches, the equipment and training of the Romans gave them an immediate advantage and they were able to inflict many wounds while taking few in return. Their path was marked by the trail of enemy bodies left in their wake. But, as the numbers surrounding them rapidly increased, so their pace slowed as they were obliged to cut through the men ahead of them. And as the rebels became emboldened, scenting victory if they could break the formation up, or at least pin it down until the weariness of the defenders and the impetus of the rebels ultimately crushed the Romans, so the ranks of the Praetorians were whittled down. Cato saw one of Musa's men lurch out of formation as two rebels wrenched his shield arm towards them. Before the guardsman could react and rip his shield from their grip an axe swung down and all but severed his arm, leaving it mangled and hanging uselessly. One of the enemy grabbed his harness and hauled him out of line and he disappeared from view as his comrades closed ranks and moved on.

Just over a hundred paces away Petillius and Porcino's centuries were also forming a box, the sides of which bristled with spears. Keeping a steady pace, they began to fall back towards Pulcher's men. Cato was relieved that they had taken the initiative to change to a more defensive formation before the enemy reached them. Every man that survived the disaster of the collapse of the first wall would be desperately needed to hold the second.

There was no time for further reflection as a surge of enemy troops smashed into the rear of Macro's formation. Cato heard the shouts of alarm and turned quickly to see the huge warrior who served as Iskerbeles' lieutenant smash his sword down on the shoulder of Centurion Musa, cleaving through chain mail, and down, deep into his chest as he was driven onto his knees. Kicking the centurion flat, the warrior tore his sword free and slashed at the Roman to his right, hacking into his sword arm, before thrusting him against the next man in line. A gap opened in the box and more rebels were pressing forward, widening it as the first of them rushed through, making directly for Cato.

'Second Century! On me!' Cato ordered as he braced his boots and lowered the standard to present the point to the enemy. His men fell in on either side. 'Forward!'

A rebel charged at Cato. He carried a round shield and was armed with a long-handled axe, which he raised above his head. He drew back his arm to strike as he shouted his war cry. Cato stepped up to meet him, then at the last moment dropped the point of the standard and drove it into the man's right thigh. Even though the point was decorative rather than functional it proved to be as effective as any spear as the impact twisted the running man round and he fell heavily to the ground. Cato pulled the point out and then stabbed again, this time into the rebel's ribs. He worked the shaft round viciously as the point tore through his opponent's lungs and heart, then pulled it out and raised the bloodied standard high once more as he led the Praetorians forward to drive the enemy back and close the gap.

Their leader saw the danger and called on those closest to him to form on either side. The Romans threw their weight behind their shields as they smashed into the rebels. Only the giant Asturian stood his ground, and then snarled as he shoved the Roman who had the temerity to face him, sending the man sprawling on his back. Cato had no time to avoid the soldier. He caught his boot on the Praetorian's shoulder and tripped. He thrust out the bottom of the standard and managed to go down on one knee, directly in front of the enemy warrior. With a roar of glee the Asturian tore the standard from Cato's grasp with his spare hand and held it up and shook it for his followers to see.

His triumphalism was his downfall as the outraged Praetorians turned on him almost as one, desperate to prevent the dishonour of seeing their standard captured. Four of them set about the Asturian, hacking and stabbing in such a frenzy that he had no chance to defend himself as he retreated two paces towards his followers and sank down, blood spurting from his lips. Even then his killers were merciless, sinking their swords deep into his flesh and driving him onto his knees. Cato stood over him, prised his fingers from the shaft and retrieved the standard. With the loss of their leader the rebels hesitated and before they could react they were swept back and the gap was sealed.

The box fought its way towards the second wall, where the rest of the cohort stood ready behind a phalanx of spear points. Pulcher's men had moved onto the rampart and some were already hurling slingshot into the mass of the rebels surrounding Cato and his men. Before they could reach the wall, however, horns sounded from the main gatehouse, now occupied by the enemy. At once the rebels began to pull back and the depleted formation increased its pace as it closed with the unscathed units of the cohort. Porcino's men were the first to retreat behind the wall, followed by Petillius and his century. The bloodied Praetorians who had defended the breached wall and fought their way back through the enemy horde came last and then the gate was closed and secured behind them. Cato handed the standard to one of the men from the Second Century and, along with Macro and the other officers, made his way up onto the wall.

The rebels were making no attempt to continue the assault and were quietly resting on their weapons while their wounded were carried away.

'What are they up to now?' wondered Petillius. 'Why did they stop?'

'Perhaps they lost their nerve,' Porcino suggested.

'Fat chance of that,' Macro responded. 'Iskerbeles has another surprise for us, I'll warrant.'

Cato felt his limbs begin to tremble slightly from exhaustion and the strain of battle. He grasped the wooden rail of the parapet tightly to hide the tremor in his arms as he tried to fathom the intentions of his enemy. As he stared at the enemy lines a rider approached from the gatehouse and the rebels parted before him. Cato recognised Iskerbeles. The enemy leader dismounted and walked a few paces through the bodies of his men, and those of the Romans. He stopped and knelt down, lifting a man up under the arms and bracing him against his knees. Although they were at least a hundred paces away, Cato was sure that the stricken man was the Asturian giant. A friend of Iskerbeles then, and one for whom he now grieved. Despite the predicament of himself and his men, Cato was moved to a quiet moment of pity for his enemy.

'What's that coming through the gate?' Macro shaded his eyes.

Cato shifted his gaze and saw a train of mules drawing a long, low structure with an angled top. As it drew clear of the gatehouse Cato could see the wheels on each side more clearly and sighed wearily before he responded.

'It's a mantlet. And there'll be a ram following along shortly, I imagine.'

Sure enough a short column of men came in sight, using rope handles to carry the ram suspended between them. There was more. Carts filled with fascines and then at the rear more carts carrying wooden frames.

'They've been very busy,' said Macro. 'Far busier than we've given them credit for.'

Cato gave a brief, flat laugh. 'Just when I'd sworn that I'd not underestimate Iskerbeles again. It's a damn shame that man is our enemy. We could do with a few more like him in the legions.'

'Or a few less like him amongst those we find ourselves up against,' Macro countered.

'Well yes, quite.' Cato tilted his neck to crack the tension there. 'Centurion Petillius.'

'Sir?'

'Your men haven't been committed yet. I want them on the wall. The rest can stand down, for the moment at least. Porcino, have your century get some rocks behind the gate. Pack 'em down nice and firm.'

'Yes, sir.'

Once the two officers had climbed down from the wall Macro spoke in a muted tone. 'Think that's going to help much?'

'Some. Anything that buys us time is welcome. If we can only hold out until Vitellius arrives . . .'

The enemy wasted no time in preparing for the next phase of their attack, and it was clear to Cato that Iskerbeles was the complete master of the situation. He knew exactly what he was doing and had planned his final assault on the mine down to the last detail. The mantlet, a wooden-framed shelter covered in cattle hides and soaked in water, was positioned directly in line with the gate, a hundred paces away. As soon as it was in place the ram was carried in through the back of the mantlet and hung from the roof beam. The end projected six feet from the front of the mantlet and Cato could see that it was capped with iron plates. The gate on the second wall would not resist being battered by such a device for long. Once the gate was breached, the enemy would attack, assaulting the walls on either side as well as soon as the ditch had been filled with fascines. The final piece in the rebel leader's plan became clear once the wooden frames were assembled. Iskerbeles had made the most of the skills of those he commanded. Some of whom must have learned engineering skills in the mines he had liberated.

'Catapults . . .' Macro observed. 'That's not good.'

Shortly after midday the rebel preparations were complete. The crew assigned to the ram stood waiting outside the mantlet. Behind the six catapults trails of smoke rose into the air from small fires lit by the catapult crews. Iskerbeles himself came forward to give the signal to begin. At once the crews threw their weight against the levers and the ratchets clacked steadily as the weapons' throwing arms were drawn back against the tension of the tightly coiled bundles of sinew that provided the torsion required to hurl heavy rocks and other missiles over long distances on the battlefield. When all the siege engines were ready the crews loaded jars into the slings. The neck of each jar was stuffed with cloth. Rebels took torches from the fires and lit the cloths. Iskerbeles drew his sword and raised it so that all the men on the catapults could see him.

'Thank the Gods for what we are about to receive,' Macro commented before he shouted a warning to the defenders. 'Beware incendiaries!'

Iskerbeles swept his sword down, the crews threw the levers that released the throwing arms and they slammed up and against the leather restrainers in a ragged chorus of loud cracks. The slings released their missiles and the jars sailed through the air in lazy arcs, marked by thin trails of smoke, reaching the apex before plunging down on the second wall, and the desperate Praetorians defending it.

# CHAPTER THIRTY-TWO

The first jar struck the wall just below the parapet. The contents burst on the uncut stone and the fire swept across the spilled pitch. Three more overshot by some distance in two flaming ellipses, while the last two struck home. One smashed the top of the parapet, splintering the timbers as it sprayed burning pitch over Cimber, who had not been watching the fall of shot and had not followed his comrades as they had leaped aside. As he was engulfed in a blazing torrent of flame the man screamed and staggered back a step, rolling down the rampart and then writhing in a frenzy before his comrades surrounded him and beat the flames out with their bare hands and neckcloths.

But it was the last shot that did the most damage, bursting in the heart of the dressing station and setting light to the surgeon, two of his orderlies and the injured men whose wounds they had been dressing. All were burned horribly before they were dragged out of the flames and doused with buckets of water from one of the troughs once used to slake the thirst of the slaves. The rest of the Praetorians looked on in horror before they turned back to the enemy and heard the steady clank of ratchets as the catapult crews made ready to loose the next volley. Greasy smoke curled into the air from the impact points and a hush hung over the cohort as the men mouthed prayers to the Gods to be spared the fate of the surgeon and the others.

'Get the other wounded out of range!' Cato shouted the order to the surviving medical orderlies. 'Quickly, damn you!'

As they hurriedly picked up the wounded and dragged them to the rear Macro shook his head. 'Unless we do something about those catapults, then we're cooked.'

Cato nodded, without replying, then steeled himself not to flinch as the first of the catapults to reload released its missile with a loud thwack. It appeared that Iskerbeles had eschewed volley fire in favour of allowing his crews to shoot at will. The bombardment would be intermittent and so wear down the Praetorians' nerves more steadily than would be the case through regular volleys. More men were immolated and more fires were started along the wall, engulfing the parapet. Elsewhere, men dived out of the path of the incendiary jars and many had to be driven back into position under the blows of the canes wielded by their officers.

'We can't endure this for ever,' Cato decided.

'What choice have we got, sir? If we stay, we face fire, and there isn't enough ready water to put the blazes out. If we charge out and try to wreck the catapults, we'll be annihilated before we even get halfway to them. If we fall back to the mine camp, then we only put things off for a few hours.'

Cato knew that his friend was right. 'Getting those fires out is the priority. We have plenty of water in the tanks. We can send men up to bring it down if need be . . .' Cato paused, and then he slapped a hand against his thigh in frustration. 'What a fool I am!'

He turned to Macro. 'Take command here. Be ready to attack when the moment is right.'

Cato began to stride away from the wall and Macro called after him, 'What? What do you mean, sir?'

Cato shot him a weary smile. 'You'll see.'

Then he ran off, calling to Cristus and the survivors of the Second Century to follow him at the double. Macro watched him go, angry with his friend for leaving him without an adequate explanation. Then, as another catapult launched its fiery missile, Macro's attention instantly returned to the imminent danger and followed the arc of the shot, feeling a wave of relief when he saw that it was not going to land on his section of the wall. Instead it smashed down beside the water trough and surrounded it with flames, driving back the men on fire-fighting duty.

'That's all we need,' Macro growled.

★ ★ ★

340

The steep incline of the track leading up to the mining camp took its toll on Cato who was already exhausted, and Cristus and his men had caught up with the prefect by the time he reached the gap in the half-completed wall across the top of the track.

'What are your orders, sir?' asked Cristus.

Cato was too short of breath to explain and simply gestured them to follow him as he set off past the garrison blocks and through the slave quarters to the series of water tanks beyond. He climbed to the edge of the first, the same one that had leaked a few days earlier, and coughed the dust from his lungs before he explained his plan to Cristus and the others.

'I want four men on the sluices of all the tanks. When I give the word I want the sluices opened smartly. All of them, except this one. Or we'll give Macro and the others a shower along with the rebels and we wouldn't want Centurion Macro coming up here taking out his wrath on us, eh, lads?'

Some chuckled, others nodded with feeling, having grown familiar with the centurion's liberal use of insults and threats.

'As soon as the tanks are drained, close up the sluices and return to the second wall. Stop for nothing. With luck the tide of battle should have tipped in our favour by then. Questions? No? Then to your places. Quick as you can.'

Cristus ran along the line of tanks, assigning men to each in turn. The sluice mechanism was simple enough. A spoked wheel stood on top of each tank, beside the sluice gate. As they made ready, Cato ran to the edge of the cliff. The spectacle of the attack on the second wall lay spread out before him, two hundred feet below. Smoke billowed up from several fires along the wall and the tiny, foreshortened figure of a blazing soldier stumbling out of a pool of flames caught Cato's attention for an instant before he turned his gaze to the enemy. Seen from above he truly grasped the scale of the horde that dwarfed the Praetorian cohort. At least ten thousand men were massed behind the catapults, a sea of embittered and fanatical humanity impatient to wipe out every last Roman defending the mine. To Cato's right lay the breached wall and further off a trail of slow-moving figures making for the rebel camp; the wounded from the earlier action. In the camp itself there were perhaps another two or three thousand of Iskerbeles' followers, mainly women and children and those too old and infirm to fight.

A series of cracks drew Cato's attention back to the attack on the second wall as three more incendiary jars reached the top of their path through the air perhaps fifty feet beneath him so that he could clearly pick out the flare of the flames at the neck of each jar. They hung there briefly and then swept down onto the wall, two falling behind and scattering the men who saw it coming. The third struck the gate and engulfed it in flames, wreathing the tower above in smoke as the rebels let out a great cheer and brandished their weapons.

Cato ran back to climb up onto the rim of the second tank and turned to Cristus and the others.

'On my word . . .'

The men took firm hold of the spoked wheels and braced themselves.

'NOW!'

The wheels turned with a creaking that was quickly drowned out by the rush of the water spraying out from under the rising gates. It flowed down the channels, racing towards the cliff edge; then, as the gates continued to rise above the customary operating height, the flow turned into a raging torrent that swirled up and over the sides of the channels and churned over the ground on either side, carrying away loose soil and rocks as the wild, foaming tide roared towards the edge of the cliff and down onto the enemy below.

The front of the tower was scourged by the flames and choking smoke from the blaze consuming the gates below. Macro and the other men in the tower had been forced back and he had to use his arm to shield his face from the stinging heat.

'Get out of here!' he shouted to the others. 'Abandon the tower. Go!'

The Praetorians needed little encouragement and scampered down the ladder as quickly as they could and backed away from the swelling inferno. Macro was the last to quit the structure, his eyes almost closed as the heat seared his head and exposed flesh. As soon as he had dropped below the floor of the tower the structure sheltered him from the flames and a moment later he had withdrawn to a safe distance and watched the flames engulfing the gatehouse with some of the other Praetorians.

'Now we're truly fucked,' said Pulcher. 'When that dies down, there'll be precious little for their ram to knock to pieces.'

'That's the spirit,' Macro responded drily.

Pulcher chewed his lip. 'Perhaps it's time to think about surrender.'

'Surrender?' Macro raised an eyebrow. 'To that rabble out there? I think not. I doubt if they'd be interested in the notion . . . Anyway, I was under the impression that the Guard dies, it never surrenders.'

Pulcher spat to one side. 'That's just shit, that is.'

At that moment Macro became aware of a change in the noise of battle. The flames still roared but there was a new sound. A collective groan and a rushing rumble from beyond the wall. Frowning, he climbed the rampart to join the men behind the palisade, all of whom were staring fixedly up at the cliff to the right.

At first Macro could not quite take in what he was seeing. Water was cascading down from several points along the ledge above, gushing down the cliff. Then the flow abruptly spread along almost the entire length of the cliff as if the sea itself had risen up to drown the mine. Huge chunks of soil and rock peeled away from the ledge and tumbled along with the raging torrent. Fountains of muddy water burst into spray as they struck the foot of the cliff and then swept on towards the ravine, rising up the legs of the rebels standing transfixed with shock, jaws agape at the spectacle of the catastrophe about to engulf them. The full force of the flood hit them before they could turn and attempt to flee, knocking many off their feet and sweeping them into others and carrying them away as well. Bodies tumbled end over end. Those at the fringes of the horde threw down their weapons and ran. Some made for the second wall, others for the wall they had taken earlier, while more tried to run ahead of the rising water, heading directly for the ravine, only to realise too late that that direction promised only certain death.

Macro watched as the desperate rebels tried to stop at the ravine but were driven over the edge by those trying to escape the flood.

Hundreds fell, their cries and screams audible even above the loud roar of water and the crackle of the flames still hungrily feeding on the gatehouse. Great chunks of the cliff were collapsing all the time, sloughing off the side of the mountain and rolling boulders along as if they were corks in a stream. The water reached the catapults, surrounded them, rising over the wooden frames, and then they too were caught in the flow, spinning lazily, crashing up against each other and crushing a handful of their crews caught up with them. Steam exploded briefly from the fires that had been used to light the wicks and then they too were gone.

From the vantage point of his horse, Iskerbeles saw it all, and knew that his rebellion was doomed, crushed at a stroke, when he had been on the very cusp of a great victory. Macro saw it in the posture of his body, before he kicked his heels in and spurred his horse towards the second wall. He was halfway there when the wave reached his mount and suddenly the hoofs were kicking up sprays of water, until it rose up to the hocks and slowed the animal down. The rebel leader had almost reached the ditch when the water surged up the horse's barrel and it lost its purchase on the ground and began to slip and move with the remorseless current with a terrified whinny. Throwing himself from the saddle, Iskerbeles struck out towards the ditch and got caught in the flow as it swept down the far side, tumbling him over. He was carried a short distance up the other side and grabbed at one of the stakes driven into the stone foundations of the wall. He held on grimly as his body was buffeted by the deluge. His horse careered above the water, mane flying and hoofs thrashing, and then it reached the ravine and was snatched from sight.

All this Macro saw with a sense of awe and grim satisfaction and even pity. Pity for all those he had moments before regarded as an enemy he must destroy and die fighting against. Now they were humans, caught up in a terrible disaster on a scale that none of them could ever have imagined. Nor would be able to tell of, save the few who might survive. The main force of the flood was roaring towards the ravine, in a muddy tide of men, rocks and stunted vegetation. Nothing could stand in its path and Macro watched as those close to the edge of the ravine turned and stood helplessly until they were swallowed by the wave and were swept into the ravine to be dashed to pieces on the rocks below.

Gradually the torrent pouring over the ruined cliff began to ease and the flow slowed to a thin curtain of reddish-brown water, then a series of small streams, running down cuttings in the slope. So much of the ledge had collapsed that Macro could see the edges of one of the tanks. Several figures were standing surveying the devastation they had wrought, and one wore the crested helmet of a prefect, Macro was relieved to see.

Pulcher was standing close to Macro and shook his head in awe. 'Sweet Jupiter . . .'

Macro nodded and then gestured towards the tower. 'And it put the fire out. Nice work, Cato.'

Then he looked over the wall and saw that Iskerbeles was still there, clutching the stake. 'First things first. Let's get that bastard in chains.'

Cato hurriedly assembled the men of the Second Century and led them back down from the camp to rejoin the rest of the cohort. As they marched, he glanced sidelong at Cristus. The tribune was still smothered in dust, and bleeding from a dozen scratches and minor cuts. The stunned look on his face after the collapse of the first wall had gone, replaced by a grim expression of steely determination. He was no longer the playboy of the capital, but finally a soldier, tested in battle. While Cato was sure he would never find it in his heart to forgive the man for his affair with Julia, he had, surprisingly, discovered a measure of respect for Cristus. In time, he might make a decent officer after all. If he didn't get himself killed in a brawl with a jealous husband first, Cato concluded.

As soon as he returned to the second wall Cato gave orders for the remaining men of the cohort to form up and be ready to advance across the mine works to mop up the rebel survivors. Iskerbeles, soaked through, all his hopes shattered, sat in numbed silence, his hands clasped over his face. Four men were left behind to guard him as the cohort marched out of the charred gatehouse and crossed the ditch into a landscape wholly transformed since the sun had risen over it scant hours before. The cliff had gone, burying some of the tunnels and laying a few others bare. The ground in front of the mine was now a drenched landscape of shallow pools linked by small rivulets. Much of the edge of the ravine had been washed away as well and everywhere lay half-buried shields and weapons. There were bodies too, some still living, dragging themselves free of the mud and staggering around in a daze. Two, maybe three hundred had escaped the flood and reached the safety of the first wall. Leaderless and stunned, they stared at the Roman column issuing from the far gate, then turned and stumbled through the breaches and disappeared.

For Cato the overwhelming feature of this nightmare scene was its quiet. The deafening din of the rebels' cheering was no more. As was the roar of flames, and the crack of the catapults. Behind him the Praetorians' boots splashed through the puddles and mud, but no man spoke above a murmur. Cato halted the column a hundred yards beyond the wall and issued orders to Petillius and Porcino to take their men and pursue the enemy back to their camp before retiring to the ruined wall and holding their position there. Pulcher and the rest of the men were to sweep the open ground for enemy survivors and march them up to the slave barracks. The Praetorians spread out in ones and twos as they carefully picked their way over the sea of mud and debris. Macro stood with Cato a moment before the prefect crossed over to the crumbling edge of the ravine.

Once it was barely fifty paces across in some places. Now the gap to the far side was twice what it had been and the two officers stared down on a scene of appalling destruction. Thousands of twisted bodies lay amid rocks and boulders strewn along the course of the river. A few, a very few, still lived and some were able to make their way uncertainly over the piled limbs and torsos of their dead comrades downriver towards the exit from the gorge.

'I almost wish I hadn't done it,' Cato muttered.

Macro sniffed dismissively. 'Well, I'm glad you did and I imagine I speak for the rest of the lads as well. Them or us, Cato. As it always is. And I prefer it to be them, come what may.'

'Even this?' Cato gestured towards the view below them.

Macro nodded. 'Of course.'

Cato was not so certain. A victory on the battlefield was one thing. The annihilation of an enemy on this scale was quite another. 'Macro, you take charge of any prisoners. See that they aren't treated badly. Make sure they are fed before they are locked in.'

'Yes, sir. As you wish.'

Cato turned away, took off his helmet and walked slowly towards the cliffs, unable to shake his morose mood. Then, as he looked up at the muddy slopes that remained, he stopped mid-stride. Although the landscape was completely altered it was still possible to estimate where some of the tunnels had once been. He set off again, striding fast this time as he made for the mounds of earth and rock where the line of the cliff base had once stretched. He picked his way over slippery heaps of soil and between boulders washed down from the cliff. Here and there he came across pit props and roof beams in line with the tunnels that had been exposed by the flood.

And then he stumbled on what he was looking for. The corner of a sturdy chest was poking up out of the mud, and was itself streaked with dirt. A short distance away was the top of another. Cato bent over it, quickly scraping off loose soil until he saw a handle. He set his helmet down and pulled on the handle, then again with all his strength, but it refused to budge. He swore softly, then took out his sword and began to dig around the chest until he had exposed most it. He pulled again and this time it came free with a glutinous sucking sound and he fell back on his buttocks with a slight splash.

His heart was beating faster with the excitement of his discovery and he laughed self-consciously at his minor misfortune before rising to his feet and examining the chest. It was locked but one corner had been splintered by the impact of a rock. Cato drew his sword, worked the tip into the cracked lid and worried loose a section of wood. As it came free he tore it away and levered up another length, and continued until there was a large enough gap through which to insert his hand. Sheathing the weapon, he felt inside and his fingers closed over uneven lumps of what felt like stones. He withdrew his hand and opened it to reveal just that, stones. Not silver.

A shadow moved on the glistening mud beside him, but before Cato could react he was struck hard about the head. White light flashed and he felt the air driven from his lungs as he hit the ground.

Cato groaned and blinked and rolled onto his back and saw a figure between him and the bright blue sky. He closed his eye again and turned his face to one side to avoid the glare.

'Who?'

A hand reached down to pluck his sword from the scabbard and then his assailant squatted down just out of arm's reach. Pulcher.

'Who else did you think it would be?' The centurion smiled coldly.

'Why?'

'Because now you know something you really shouldn't.'

'About the silver Nepo had hidden from the rebels?'

'Except that he didn't. Just stones. He took the silver out before he had the men put the chests in the mine and collapse the tunnel.'

'Where is it?'

'The silver?' Pulcher scratched his jaw casually. 'By now, it should have reached Tarraco and be on its way to Rome.'

Cato frowned uncomprehendingly and Pulcher chuckled. 'But you've seen it already, Prefect. Remember the slave trader we met on the road. Those wagons he had? That's where the bullion was hidden. I got that from Nepo, before I killed him. Before he could spill his guts to you.'

'I don't understand,' said Cato. 'What was Nepo up to?'

'He was working for Pallas, but why worry about that, sir? In a moment you'll be dead. I'll hide your body and by the time it turns up things will have moved on and no one will care that you are missing.'

'Kill me? Why?'

'Legate's orders, sir.'

'Vitellius? But you saved my life earlier.'

'I had no orders to kill you then. You were a comrade, and I would do the same for any man I was fighting with. But orders are orders. Soon as Collenus tipped me the word, you were a dead man. Goodbye, sir.'

Pulcher hefted Cato's sword and rose to his feet.

'No!' Cato called out weakly, his head still throbbing from the blow. 'Wait!'

'Sorry. This has been a long time coming. You were a snotty

348

optio when we first met all those years ago. I'd have killed you back then, if I'd been given the chance. I guess all good things come to he who waits after all.'

Cato rolled onto his back and raised his arms to try and protect himself. Pulcher loomed above him, drew back his sword arm and made to strike the point deep into Cato's throat. Instead, he lurched suddenly, gasped and his sword arm flopped to his side. A long, low moan escaped his lips as he sank down on his knees to reveal Macro standing behind him. Macro placed his left hand firmly on Pulcher's shoulder and then wrenched his blade free from the man's neck where it had been driven down diagonally towards his heart. Blood surged from the wound.

'If you are going to kill a man, my lad, then kill him. Don't talk.'

Pulcher collapsed into the mud beside Cato, his eyes wide and staring, his mouth slowly opening and closing like that of a fish expiring out of water. Macro helped his friend up into a sitting position and sucked in a breath.

'Nasty bump you'll have there. To add to the scar and the dressing over the eye. You look like a wreck, Cato. You really do.'

Cato smiled back weakly. 'You should see the other man . . .'

At first light the next morning, a cavalry column approached the remains of the wall and rode through the gates into the ruined mine workings. Cato had been alerted by the sentries and was there to meet the legate and his staff officers. The last of the rebels had deserted the camp during the night and abandoned the shelters, and anything else of value that they could not carry away with them.

Vitellius looked around, failing to disguise his shock at the scale of the devastation, before he addressed Cato. The prefect stood before him, still soiled by the fall of earth when the countermine had collapsed. Streaked with sweat and blood, a filthy dressing and patch over his wounded eye and a fresh dressing over the cut in his scalp received from Pulcher.

'Ye Gods, Prefect Cato! I did not recognise you. I hardly expected to see you still alive.'

'Really, sir?'

Vitellius' expression was rigid for an instant. 'Yes, what with seeing the destruction of the settlement and the breaches in the wall when we crossed the ridge at dawn. And what in Hades happened to the mine? There's nothing of it left.'

'Sometimes you have to destroy a thing in order to save it, sir.'

'Is that supposed to be amusing?'

'No, sir. It seems rather apt to me.' For Cato the prospect of this mine being closed for ever, and no longer being a place of unremitting suffering, was for the best. To be sure, there were other mines, as bad or possibly worse than this place had been. But now there was one less of them.

'How many of your men did you lose, Prefect?'

'At least a third of the cohort, sir. As well as Cimber, centurions Secundus, Musa and Pulcher.'

'Pulcher? How?'

Cato went to answer but Macro got in first. 'Killed in action, sir.'

'I see.' Vitellius nodded and there was a brief silence, as if he was waiting for more detail. Then he glanced round the mine workings again. 'Well, you have carried out your orders successfully, it would appear. The bullion?'

'It's not here, sir,' Cato replied. 'It appears that it was removed before my cohort arrived.'

'Removed?'

'Yes.'

'By Nepo?'

'That's how it would appear, sir.'

'Do you know what happened to it?'

Cato looked at him steadily. 'I believe that your guess is as good as mine.'

Vitellius' lips twitched knowingly, then he changed the subject. 'What about the rebels? Where are they?'

Cato pointed towards the ravine. 'Most of them are over there, sir. Dead.'

'Dead? How many?'

'Several thousand, at least.'

The staff officers murmured amongst themselves incredulously. Vitellius shook his head and laughed. 'You jest. Surely?'

'See for yourself. Those that are not dead have fled back to their villages.'

'You chose not to pursue them?'

'Not with so few men left, sir. Besides, we were too exhausted to conduct a pursuit. The uprising has been crushed. It is over. Better to concentrate on rebuilding the region and let the people put the past behind them. What is left of the rebels have scattered in the hills. It would be pointless for you to try and pursue them, sir.'

'That is for me to decide.'

'There is one more thing. We have taken the leader of the uprising prisoner.'

'Iskerbeles? Excellent!' Vitellius beamed. 'I will take great pride in presenting him to the Roman people when we return to the capital to celebrate our victory.'

'*Our* victory?' Macro muttered under his breath.

Vitellius shot him a dark look. 'Did you say something, Centurion Macro?'

'I said, "Ah, victory!" sir.' Macro cocked his head and gave a languid pump of his fist. 'Nothing the Roman public like more than a victory. I'd be surprised if the Emperor didn't award you a triumph, sir.'

Vitellius looked at him and smiled. 'And so would I, Centurion Macro. So would I. It has all worked out rather better than anyone could have hoped . . . '

# EPILOGUE

### The Port of Ostia AD 54, early autumn

The troop convoy and warships from Tarraco sailed past the mole into the calm waters of the harbour shortly after midday on the back of the cool wind blowing from the west. It was late in the season for a direct voyage from Hispania and the captains and crews were relieved that they had been fortunate to avoid any storms, or squalls, during the ten days they had been at sea. The wind had been dead foul a day after leaving Tarraco and they had made almost no progress for the first three days before the wind had changed. Nor had they sighted any other sails since leaving the province. Food and water had started to run short and the crews and Praetorians aboard the small fleet were eagerly looking forward to making landfall and going ashore in order to get drunk and get laid in the fleshpots of Ostia.

Macro was leaning on the bow rail of the bireme carrying the surviving officers and some of the men of the Second Praetorian Cohort. He had had quite enough of the salty sea air and was trying to pick out the more familiar, and comforting, scents of land. In this case, the acrid tang of woodsmoke and the musty odour of cities from afar that seemed to be a mix of sweat and boiled vegetables.

Cato approached from the stern to join him. The injury to his eye was healing well according to the surgeon from one of the other cohorts who had tended to his wound after the mine had been relieved. There was a pronounced scar under the eye and a slight blur at the bottom edge of his field of vision. Otherwise the surgeon had pronounced that he had made a good recovery and that he had been most fortunate not to have entirely lost sight in the eye. It was strange how fortunate army surgeons seemed to think those they treated were, Cato mused. He would prefer to have a more conventional experience of good fortune.

'Here we are again in Ostia. Looking forward to getting a decent drink,' said Macro, rubbing his hands together. 'And settling down in front of a nice warm fire with a hearty meal in front of me and a nice plump woman on my lap.'

'I seem to remember you were anxious not to risk getting the clap last time we were here.'

'After all the risks I've taken over the last few months? I think I'm owed a lucky break or two.'

'Maybe. Anyway, the simple pleasures are always the best,' Cato replied.

'Nothing simple about what I have in mind once the meal is tucked away.' Macro winked. 'What will you be doing?'

'Me?' Cato shrugged. 'Heading back to Rome. I'd like to see Lucius. And then have a long think about what comes next.'

'Next?' Macro frowned. 'Why, it'll be another posting for the two of us. Another campaign. That or some cushy garrison somewhere hot and exotic. That's what's next, brother. If there's any justice. We've done our bit and could use a bit of peace and quiet.'

'I could use a rest indeed. But I think I'd like to watch Lucius grow up for a bit. Put some roots down perhaps. If Sempronius can find me an administrative post, or lend me money to get a small business going.'

Macro shook his head. 'What do you know about running a business? You can run a cohort well enough, but a business? That, my friend, requires a degree of ruthless cunning that is a rare commodity in this world. In Rome especially. It's a den of thieves and crooks who would stab you in the back as soon as shake your hand from the front. They'd eat you alive.'

'Maybe . . .'

'No maybe about it. You're much safer being a soldier. Certainly better off being one, on your pay.'

'That is something, at least.'

They were interrupted by the cries of the trierarch as he ordered his crew to take in the sail and prepare to unship the oars. Sailors scurried up the rigging and spread out along the spar as the sheets were freed and the tough linen sail flapped in the breeze. As the sail was furled the oars sprouted from the sides of the hull and a drum set the pace as the blades swept forward, dropped down into the sea, then thrust the ship forward.

The main quay of the new harbour was a short distance across the open water and the warship steered towards a space between two biremes that had already berthed. Close to, the order was given to ship oars and the steering paddle was put over so that the vessel gently turned beam-on to the quay as it lost way and came to rest. Mooring ropes snaked over to waiting hands on the other biremes and the ship was hauled in and made fast.

Shortly afterwards Macro led the way ashore. As soon as he stepped onto the quay he felt the peculiar continuation of the feeling of being at sea and paced unsteadily across to the open door of Neptune's Bounty. Cato's sea legs were no better and both men were relieved to sit down at a bench and wave one of the serving girls over.

'Jug of wine, my love,' Macro said cheerily. 'Two cups, and serve it with a smile, if there's no extra charge for that.'

She shot him a wary look and went off to fetch their drink. Macro looked round the inn and noticed that the mood of the other customers was more subdued than he would have expected of so well positioned a drinking hole.

'Dear Gods, what's happened to this place? Everyone looks like they've gone and lost a denarius and found an as.'

Cato nodded. 'Peculiar ambience, to be sure.'

The girl returned with a jug and two samian beakers and set them down. Macro nodded his thanks and smiled pleasantly at her. 'Cheer up, it may never happen.'

She frowned. 'You trying to be funny, mister?'

'Funny? No. Happy, yes. So why all the gloom here? What's wrong with everyone?'

'Where you been the last month?'

'At sea as it happens. Just got off the ship.'

'Oh . . .' She raised her eyebrows. 'Then you won't have heard the news.'

'What news?' Cato demanded.

She filled their cups. 'We've got ourselves a new emperor. Claudius is dead.'

'Dead?' Cato froze. 'How?'

'Old age . . . Food poisoning. Who knows? Anyway, that son of his is emperor now.'

'Britannicus?'

'No, the one he adopted. Ahenobarbus. Or Nero. Whatever he calls himself these days. He's the one. Says he will look after his younger step-brother, but I doubt it. Poor lad's days are numbered. He'll go the way of all them others. Been quite a clear-out at the palace, so I've heard. More than a few of 'em met a sticky end. Including that freedman of the old Emperor, Narcissus. He was in the grave even before his master. There's more joining them all the time. Which is why . . .' She gestured to the other customers. 'No one wants to draw the attention of the Vigiles here in Ostia. Same in Rome, where the Urban cohorts and the Praetorians are picking off troublemakers.'

Cato stroked a hand through his hair as he took in the change of regime. 'Was there much opposition to Nero taking the purple, then?'

The girl shook her head. 'Hardly. Most of those who might have supported Britannicus were out of Rome when his father died. And when the Guard declared for Nero it was over and done with. Mind you, given the size of the donative Nero handed over to the Praetorians there was never any doubt whom they would choose to serve. A cool ten million denarii.'

'Ten million?' Macro started. 'Isn't that—'

Cato caught his arm swiftly and hurriedly spoke over the top of his friend. 'Ten million? You're sure?'

She nodded. 'No great secret, that. It's all over Rome.'

She set the jug down. 'Anything else I can get you gents?'

'No. That'll be all for now. Thanks.' Cato tipped her a sestertius and she smiled gratefully and weaved back through the tables towards the counter.

Cato leaned back against the wall and folded his arms as he thought through the implications of what had occurred in Rome during their absence. The more he thought, the more he saw the depth of the plans that Pallas had made to secure the throne for his young protégé.

355

Macro took a large sip of wine and swilled it round his mouth before he swallowed. 'You thinking what I'm thinking, lad?'

'I can't think of anything else. We were played. All of us. From Emperor Claudius and Narcissus right down to you and me at the arse end of the empire . . . Fuck. That's why we were picked for the campaign. Us, and all the others. The officers they wanted off the scene when they made their move. Including those that Narcissus might call upon if he tried to push Britannicus' candidacy for the throne.'

Macro sniffed. 'And why Vitellius chose us to go to the mine. That should have been a one-way journey for the pair of us . . . Either Iskerbeles or Pulcher would have seen to it that we never saw Rome again. And then there's the silver. Nepo must have been in on the plot. That's why he sent it on and just pretended to have been gathering it ready for the next bullion convoy. And that's why he had to be silenced.'

Cato rubbed his chin anxiously. 'Exactly. It all makes sense now.' He was quiet for a moment before he spoke again, this time in a hushed tone that only Macro would hear. 'We're in deep trouble. Narcissus is dead, and Pallas knows that we worked for him from time to time. We're marked men.'

'But we had no choice,' Macro protested. 'Narcissus forced us into it.'

'I doubt that's going to make much difference to Pallas . . . Fuck.'

Macro took another sip and sighed. 'Like you say, fuck. What are we going to do, lad?'

Cato thought for a moment and shook his head. 'What can we do? We have to return to Rome and we'll just have to see what happens. Better make an offering to the Gods, brother. Something valuable enough that they really can't ignore it.' Cato took his cup and drained it in one go before he set it down on the table with a sharp rap. 'Life is about to get very interesting. Very interesting indeed.'

'Bloody dangerous, you mean?'

'Surely. That's how the dice seem to roll for us . . . Always.'

THE END

# AUTHOR'S NOTE ON THE PRAETORIAN GUARD

Despite the notorious reputation of the Praetorian Guard across the years, the origins of what became the elite formation of the Roman military were far more humble and practical. In the Republic age the term for a consul acting as a military commander on campaign was 'Praetor'. Those who accompanied him, his friends, staff and personal bodyguards, were collectively known as his 'Praetorian Guard'.

It is probable that such formations were fairly small scale and temporary in the earlier days of the Roman Republic. However, with the rapid expansion of Roman influence before, during and after the wars with Carthage, the Roman army took on an increasingly permanent and professional identity. This included the bodyguards of the ambitious generals of the late Republic. By the time of the final contest between Octavian and Antony, both leaders had bodyguards organised into several cohorts which accompanied them on campaign and fought in battles with some distinction.

Following the defeat of Antony, Octavian took on the title of Augustus and became the first emperor, although he did as much as he could to preserve the illusion that Rome still operated as a republic. In an effort to unite the forces that had been fighting each other for many years, one of the measures undertaken by Augustus was the amalgamation of his Praetorian units with those of Antony to create what became known as the Praetorian Guard.

The duties of the Guard were to protect the person of the emperor both in Rome, and on the various imperial peregrinations and while on campaign. They could also be deployed in Rome to control the mob if necessary, and to discourage plotters and stamp down on dissent. In addition they acted as imperial death squads when required. In the early days, Augustus did his best to conceal the true scale of his power. Hence, his reference to himself as 'first citizen' rather than any more ambitious title. The same approach applied to the Guard. Only three cohorts were based in Rome, billeted across the city, rather than in ostentatious central barracks. The other cohorts were garrisoned in nearby towns, ready to be summoned to Rome if the need arose.

This low-key approach may have suited Augustus, but on his death it became clear to all that the Republic was dead and that Rome would be ruled by emperors. Augustus was succeeded by his step-son, Tiberius, who favoured, and then came to rely on, the prefect of the Guard, Sejanus. It was Sejanus who was responsible for the rather unsavoury role the Guard was to play thenceforth. One of his early 'achievements' was to persuade the new emperor to concentrate the Guard cohorts at Rome, and build a camp for them on the Viminal Hill, much of which still remains. There was no limit to the ambition of Sejanus who carefully schemed his way towards his eventual goal of becoming the heir of Tiberius. Rivals and those who posed a threat were ruthlessly disposed of. It was only in AD 31 that Tiberius finally recognised the threat and had Sejanus executed.

By now it was acknowledged that the Guard had considerable power and had to be handled carefully by the emperors. Sadly Tiberius' successor – the unhinged Caligula – failed to learn the lesson and made the mistake of ridiculing a senior officer of the Guard so much that the individual in question, Chaerea, conspired to murder Caligula and his immediate family. Like so many conspirators, Chaerea failed to plan much further ahead than the death of the Emperor and there was a great deal of confusion in Rome during the immediate aftermath. The Senate was busily debating the need to return to the days of the Republic while the Guard looted the palace in anticipation of being made redundant in the event that their services might no longer be required. As it happened, some guardsmen came across a cowering survivor of the imperial family, Claudius, and carted him off to the Praetorian Camp. Claudius (or more likely one of his advisers – take a bow, Narcissus) had sufficient wit to suggest that if the Praetorians supported his claim to succeed Caligula then he would ensure that they were handsomely rewarded. And rewarded they were. To the tune of a bribe representing five years' pay for every man in the Guard. This was not the first time that their loyalty had been bought. Tiberius had gifted each man a thousand denarii after the execution of Sejanus to sweeten the pill of the execution of their commander. But the bribe paid by Claudius firmed up the precedent and from now on the Praetorian Guard were the most loyal of men . . . that money could buy.

Life in the Praetorian Guard was as comfortable as it got in the Roman army. The guardsmen were paid three times as much as legionaries, served for fewer years and received a larger discharge bonus when they retired. They enjoyed good accommodation and privileged seating at chariot races and gladiator fights. While the higher ranks were tempted to wield their political influence the rankers were content to remain neutral, as long as their direct interests were not compromised. Which was why emperors treated them to frequent rewards.

To join the Guard a man needed to be fit and of good character. Some men were transferred to the Guard from the legions as a reward for good service. Like the legions, the Guard trained hard and could fight well if called on to do so. They played a brief part in the campaign in Britannia in AD 43 for example.

There is some dispute over the size of the Praetorian cohorts, but it is reasonable to assume that they were on the same scale as those of the rest of the army. Each of the cohorts was commanded by a tribune, rather than the senior centurion of the formation. The main difference in detail was that they wore off-white tunics as opposed to the red or brown of the legions. There is plenty of evidence to suggest that their shields were oval, rather than rectangular, like those of the legions. For the purpose of this book I have gone with representations of the guardsmen holding spears as opposed to javelins since spears would be more useful for intimidating the mob in Rome, which was one of the Guard's key functions.

Although this novel is set in the early period of the empire, by that time the central position of the Praetorian Guard in the political world of Rome was firmly established and woe betide any emperor who failed to keep the men of the Guard onside.